應用英文寫作系列之五

Effectively Communicating Online
有效撰寫專業英文電子郵件

By Ted Kncy

柯泰德

Illustrated by Chen-Yin Wang

插圖：王貞穎

Ted Knoy is also the author of the following books in the Chinese Technical Writers' Series （科技英文寫作系列叢書） *and the Chinese Professional Writers' Series* （應用英文寫作系列叢書）：

An English Style Approach for Chinese Technical Writers
精通科技論文（報告）寫作之捷徑

English Oral Presentations for Chinese Technical Writers
做好英文會議簡報

A Correspondence Manual for Chinese Technical Writers
英文信函參考手冊

An Editing Workbook for Chinese Technical Writers
科技英文編修訓練手冊

Advanced Copyediting Practice for Chinese Technical Writers
科技英文編修訓練手冊〔進階篇〕

Writing Effective Study Plans
有效撰寫英文讀書計畫

Writing Effective Work Proposals
有效撰寫英文工作提案

Writing Effective Employment Application Statements
有效撰寫求職英文自傳

Writing Effective Career Statements
有效撰寫英文職涯經歷

This book is dedicated to my wife, Hwang Li Wen.

　　隨著時代快速變遷，人們生活步調及習性也十倍速的演變。舉郵件為例，由早期傳統的郵局寄送方式改為現今的電子郵件（e-mail）系統。速度不但快且也節省費用。對有時效性的訊息傳送更可達事半功倍的效果。不僅如此，電子郵件不受地域性的限制，可以隨地進行溝通，也是生活及職場上一項利器。

　　柯先生所著《有效撰寫專業英文電子郵件》，乃針對目前對電子郵件寫作需求，配合六種不同情境展示近二百個範例寫作。藉此觀摩他人電子郵件寫作來加強讀者本身的寫作技巧，同時配合書中網路練習訓練英文聽力及閱讀技巧。是一本非常實用且符合網路時代需求的工具書。

元培科學技術學院
經營管理研究所　所長

許碧芳

Table of Contents

Foreword

Professional writing is essential to the international recognition of Taiwan's commercial and technological achievements. "The Chinese Professional Writers' Series" seeks to provide a sound English writing curriculum and, on a more practical level, to provide Chinese speaking professionals with valuable reference guides. The series supports professional writers in the following areas:

Writing style

The books seek to transform old ways of writing into a more active and direct writing style that better conveys an author's main ideas.

Structure

The series addresses the organization and content of reports and other common forms of writing.

Quality

Inevitably, writers prepare reports to meet the expectations of editors and referees/reviewers, as well as to satisfy the requirements of journals. The books in this series are prepared with these specific needs in mind.

Effectively Communicating Online is the fifth book in The Chinese Professional Writers' Series.

Effectively Communicating Online（《有效撰寫專業英文電子郵件》）為「應用英文寫作系列（The Chinese Professional Writers' Series）」之第五本書，本書中練習題部分主要是幫助國人糾正常犯寫作格式上錯誤，由反覆練習中，進而熟能生巧，提升有關個人職涯描述的英文寫作能力。

　　「應用英文寫作系列」將針對以下內容逐步協助國人解決在英文寫作上所遭遇之各項問題：

A.寫作型式：把往昔通常習於抄襲的寫作方法轉換成更積極主動的寫作方式，俾使讀者所欲表達的主題意念更加清楚。更進一步糾正國人寫作口語習慣。

B.方法型式：指出國內寫作者從事英文寫作或英文翻譯時常遇到的文法問題。

C.內容結構：將寫作的內容以下面的方式結構化：目標、一般動機、個人動機。並了解不同的目的和動機可以影響報告的結構，由此，獲得最適當的報告內容。

D.內容品質：以編輯、審查委員的要求來寫作此一系列之書籍，以滿足讀者的英文要求。

Introduction

This writing workbook aims to instruct students on how to communicate online effectively in the workplace. First, how to write a letter seeking technical training is introduced, including how to summarize one's academic or professional experiences, request technical training, commend the organization to receive technical training from, explain the details of the technical training and express optimism in the possibility of technical training. How to write a letter to exchange information with another organization is then described, including how to propose an information exchange relationship, introduce one's professional experience or that of one's organization in relation to the proposed information exchange relation, commend the organization or individual to exchange information with, outline details of the information exchange relation, express optimism in the anticipated information exchange relation and initiate the information exchange relation. Next, how to write a letter to make a technical visit overseas is outlined, including how to request permission to make a technical visit, state the purpose of the technical visit, introduce one's qualifications or one's organizational experiences, commend the organization to be visited, outline details of the technical visit and request confirmation for approval of the technical visit. Additionally, how to write a letter to inviting speakers and consultants is described, including how to invite a speaker, describe the purpose of the lecture, explaining details of the lecture, describe transportation and accommodation details, instruct the speaker what to prepare before the visit and emphasize the importance of the upcoming visit. Moreover, how to write a letter to arrange travel itineraries is introduced, including how to list details of the travel itinerary and welcome suggestions about the proposed itinerary. Finally, how to write a letter to requesting information is outlined, including how to explaining why contact was made to request information and summarize one's academic or professional experiences.

Each unit begins and ends with three visually represented situations that provide essential information to help students to write a specific part of a career statement. Additional oral practice, listening comprehension, reading comprehension and writing activities, relating to those three situations, help students to understand how the visual representation relates to the ultimate goal of writing an effective career statement. An Answer Key makes this book ideal for classroom use. For instance, to test a student's listening comprehension, a teacher can first read the text that describes the situations for a particular unit. Either individually or in small groups, students can work through the exercises to produce a well-structured career statement.

簡 介

　　本書主要教導讀者如何建構良好的專業英文電子郵件。書中內容包括：1.
科技訓練請求信函：某人學歷及工作經驗概述；科技訓練申請；讚揚提供科技
訓練的機構；科技訓練細節解釋；表達對科技訓練機會的樂觀態度；2.資訊交
流信函：資訊流通關係的提呈；為資訊流通而提供個人或機構經驗；為資訊流
通而讚揚某機構或某人；資訊流通關係的細節詳述；表達對資訊流通關係的樂
觀態度；開始資訊流通關係；3.科技訪問信函：科技訪問許可申請；闡述科技
訪問的目的；介紹某人的能力或機構經驗；對訪問機構的讚揚；詳述科技訪問
的細節；科技訪問核准的確認申請；4.演講者邀請信函：邀請演講者；描述演
講目的；詳述演講的細節；詳述交通及住宿的細節；演講者行前必知指導；對
演講者強調訪問的重要性；5.旅行安排信函：行程細節列表；對行程細節列表
的建議；6.資訊請求信函：解釋請求資訊的目的；說明學術專業經驗。

　　書中的每個單元呈現三個視覺化的情境，經由以全民英語檢定為標準而設
計的口說訓練、聽力、閱讀及寫作四種不同功能來強化英文能力。此外，本書
也非常適合在課堂上使用，教師可以先描述單元情境而讓學生藉由書中練習循
序在短期內完成。

Seeking Technical Training

科技訓練請求信函

Vocabulary and related expressions 相關字詞

civil service examination 公職人員考試
administrative position 行政職位
generating income 增加收入
remitted funds 收到的款項
radiological technologist 放射技師
self-supported 自我支持的
supplemental literature 補充的文獻
global perspective 世界觀
remain abreast of 跟上時代
integrate 整合
familiarize me with 使自己熟悉
diagnose 診斷
incorporates 合併
patient histories 病歷
relevant data 相關資訊
overcoming the limitations of 克服限制

guest worker 客座人員
resume 簡歷
academic and professional experiences 學術專業背景
strained financial resources 財務吃緊
innovative approaches 先進的方式
initiated 先行的
transformations 改觀
withstood 忍受
point to the success of 成功的祕訣
expenditure targets 花費的目標金額
strictly adhered to 嚴格遵行
overhead costs 成本
annual average 年平均
restrain 抑制
latest trends 最新流行趨勢

academic advisor 指導老師
disabled elderly 行動不便的長者
implemented 執行
expertise 專長
clinical settings 醫療環境
technology transfer opportunities
技術移轉機會
comprehensive 無所不包的
scope of application 使用範圍
gender 性別
academic advisor 指導老師
proficient 精通的
extensive professional experience
廣泛專業經驗
lack of 缺乏
diligent 勤勉的
diagnose 診斷
widely regarded 廣泛地被認為
a practical context 實際的環境
careful consideration 小心的考慮
as widely anticipated 被大量期望
initiate 發起
globally recognized 全球公認的

specialized training 特殊訓練
population 人口
therapeutic effects 醫療效果
severity 嚴重性
optimal treatment 最佳的治療
clinical effectiveness 醫療效果
elucidated 闡明
unique 特殊
technological expertise 技術專長
National Science Council-sponsored
research projects 國科會補助研究計畫
visiting researcher 客座研究人員
strong background in 強有力的背景
given the opportunity 給予機會
state-of-the-art equipment and facilities
最新的設備
grasp new concepts 了解新觀念
Department of Health 衛生署
equipped 裝配
drafting a resolution 起草法案
clinical implications 醫療牽涉
two decades 二十年
in line with 配合

Situation 1

Situation 2

Situation 3

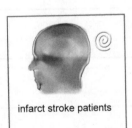

A Write down the key points of the situations on the preceding page, while the instructor reads aloud the script from the Answer Key.

Situation 1

_____

_____

_____

Situation 2

_____

_____

_____

Situation 3

_____

_____

_____

B Oral practice I

Based on the three situations in this unit, write three questions beginning with **How**, and answer them. The questions do not need to come directly from these situations.

Examples

How did Mary secure an administrative position in Taiwan's National Health Insurance organization?

By passing the governmental civil service examination in 1994

How did Mary continue to enhance her administrative skills while working?

By taking courses on management in the medical sector at Yangming University

1. _____

   _____

2. _____

   _____

3. _____

   _____

C Based on the three situations in this unit, write three questions beginning with **What**, and answer them. The questions do not need to come directly from these situations.

Examples

What is the movement disability morbidity model that Jason is developing capable of doing?

Accurately forecasting the population of disabled elderly in Taiwan and overcoming the limitations of the conventional population projection model

What has Jason's graduate school research focused on?

Sociometric Science, with specialized training in Statistics and Gray Mathematical Theory

1. _____

_____

2. _____

_____

3. _____

_____

D Based on the three situations in this unit, write three questions beginning with **Why**, and answer them. The questions do not need to come directly from these situations.

Examples

Why does Jack hope to receive training at a hospital in the latest advances in infarct stroke technology?

Because he is a second year graduate student at the Institute of Medical Imagery at Yuanpei University of Science and Technology (YUST), as well as a full-time radiological technologist at Shin-Kong Wu Ho-Su Memorial Hospital in Taipei

Why does Jack often read supplemental literature in addition to his academic and professional activities?

To remain abreast of the latest technological trends

1. _____

_____

2. _____

_____

3. _____

_____

E Write questions that match the answers provided.

1. _____

_____

A new post in the insurance revenue sector of the National Health Institute

2. _____

_____

Mr. Jeffrey Wu

3. _____

_____

Three

F Listening Comprehension I

Situation 1

1. How has Mary greatly matured as an administrator?

    A. by taking courses on management in the medical sector

    B. through her experience of calculating hospital fees

    C. through her experiences of generating income in the medical sector

2. How did Mary continue to enhance her administrative skills?

    A. by pointing to the success of Germany's national health insurance scheme

    B. by adopting a global budget

    C. by taking courses on management in the medical sector at Yangming University

3. Which country initiated one of the earliest health insurance systems worldwide?

    A. Taiwan   B. Germany   C. the United States

4. What year did Mary pass the Taiwanese governmental civil service examination?

    A. in 1994   B. in 1997   C. in 1991

5. What percent of the total medical cost must hospital inpatients in Germany pay?

    A. only 20%   B. only 25%   C. only 15%

Situation 2

1. What specialized training did Jason receive in graduate school?

    A. in static disability morbidity

    B. in population distribution research

    C. in Statistics and Gray Mathematical Theory

2. What is Jason currently developing?

    A. a population projection model

    B. a movement disability morbidity model

C. a long-term health care model

3. How would Jason's university like him to become familiar with long-term health care systems?

    A. by receiving advanced training

    B. by accurately forecasting the population of disabled elderly in Taiwan

    C. by overcoming the limitations of the conventional population projection model

4. What has Jason's graduate school research focused on?

    A. Statistics   B. Gray Mathematical Theory   C. Sociometric Science

5. What will hopefully give Professor Jones a better idea of Jason's previous academic and professional experiences?

    A. the purpose of his visit

    B. the attached resume

    C. further information on his background

Situation 3

1. Why does Jack often read supplemental literature?

    A. to analyze the feasibility of adopting new technologies

    B. to remain abreast of the latest technological trends

    C. to determine proper medication times and their therapeutic effects

2. What does Jack believe applying the latest technologies will   enable physicians to do?

    A. accurately diagnose diseases in their early stages

    B. collaborate with a local medical instrument manufacturer

    C. investigate differences among infarct stroke patients across races and genders

3. Why does Jack hope to measure the order of severity of the infarct field?

    A. to determine the scope of application of infarct stroke technology in his hospital

B. to enable infarct stroke patients to receive subsequent optimal treatment

C. to integrate the theoretical knowledge acquired at graduate school with his clinical experience in the Radiotechnology Department

4. What will the results of Jack's graduate study help physicians to do?

A. understand how a disease diffuses to the brain area

B. increase the clinical effectiveness of evaluations of patients and curative outcomes

C. determine proper medication times and their therapeutic effects

5. Why does Jack hope to eventually collaborate with a local medical instrument manufacturer?

A. to develop relevant software programs

B. to determine proper medication times and their therapeutic effects

C. to analyze the feasibility of adopting infarct stroke technology

G Reading Comprehension I
Pick the work or expression whose meaning is closest to the meaning of the underlined word or expression in the following passages.

Situation 1

1. I <u>passed</u> the Taiwanese governmental civil service examination in 1994, subsequently securing an administrative position in our country's National Health Insurance organization.

   A. flop   B. successfully completed   C. falter

2. I passed the Taiwanese governmental civil service examination in 1994, <u>subsequently</u> securing an administrative position in our country's National Health Insurance organization.

   A. afterwards   B. beforehand   C. prior to

3. I passed the Taiwanese governmental civil service examination in 1994, subsequently <u>securing</u> an administrative position in our country's National Health Insurance organization.

   A. preserving   B. becoming vulnerable to   C. prone to

4. I passed the Taiwanese governmental civil service examination in 1994, subsequently securing an <u>administrative</u> position in our country's National Health Insurance organization.

   A. subordinate   B. subservient   C. managerial

5. While working, I continued to <u>enhance</u> my administrative skills by taking courses on management in the medical sector at Yangming University.

   A. degrade   B. upgrade   C. deteriorate

6. While working, I continued to enhance my administrative <u>skills</u> by taking courses on management in the medical sector at Yangming University.

A. deficiency   B. insufficiency   C. competency

7. My rich experience in hospital management has <u>familiarized</u> me with formulae for calculating hospital fees.

A. oriented   B. confound   C. bewilder

8. My rich experience in hospital management has familiarized me with formulae for <u>calculating</u> hospital fees.

A. diffusing   B. ciphering   C. implementing

9. I was <u>transferred</u> to a new post in the insurance revenue sector of the National Health Institute in 2003.

A. entrench   B. maneuver   C. ingrain

10. I was transferred to a new <u>post</u> in the insurance revenue sector of the National Health Institute in 2003.

A. eruption   B. assignment   C. explosion

11. I was transferred to a new post in the insurance <u>revenue</u> sector of the National Health Institute in 2003.

A. liquid assets   B. property   C. mechanism

12. My experiences of <u>generating</u> income in the medical sector, and those of monitoring remitted funds in the insurance revenue sector, have greatly matured me as an administrator.

A. shelving   B. triggering   C. putting on ice

13. My experiences of generating income in the medical sector, and those of <u>monitoring</u> remitted funds in the insurance revenue sector, have greatly matured me as an administrator.

A. disregarding   B. shirking   C. supervising

14. My experiences of generating income in the medical sector, and those of monitoring remitted funds in the insurance revenue sector, have greatly <u>matured</u> me as an administrator.

A. ripened   B. puerile   C. juvenile

15. Taiwan's National Health Insurance scheme is currently faced with <u>strained</u> financial resources and societal and political pressures not to raise monthly health insurance premiums.

A. slacken   B. travailed   C. loosen

16. Taiwan's National Health Insurance scheme is currently faced with strained financial resources and <u>societal</u> and political pressures not to raise monthly health insurance premiums.

A. individual   B. familial   C. social

17. Taiwan's National Health Insurance scheme is currently faced with strained financial resources and societal and political <u>pressures</u> not to raise monthly health insurance premiums.

A. unconstrained   B. tensions   C. casual

18. Taiwan's National Health Insurance scheme is currently faced with strained financial resources and societal and political pressures not to raise monthly health insurance <u>premiums</u>.

A. payments   B. benefits   C. advantages

19. <u>Innovative</u> approaches are definitely needed to resolve this dilemma.

A. diffident   B. retrogressive   C. inventive

20. Innovative approaches are definitely needed to resolve this <u>dilemma</u>.

A. opportunity   B. predicament   C. opening

21. Your country <u>initiated</u> one of the earliest health insurance systems worldwide, initiated by Chancellor Bismarck in 1883.

A. embarked   B. terminated   C. wrapped up

22. Given the <u>radical</u> political, social and economic transformations that Germany went through during the First and Second World Wars, and the more recent reunification of Eastern and Western Germany, your country's health insurance

system has withstood many challenges, making it a model worthy of closer examination.

A. extreme　B. mild　C. tempered

23. Given the radical political, social and economic <u>transformations</u> that Germany went through during the First and Second World Wars, and the more recent reunification of Eastern and Western Germany, your country's health insurance system has withstood many challenges, making it a model worthy of closer examination.

A. unyielding　B. constant　C. metamorphosis

24. Given the radical political, social and economic transformations that Germany went through during the First and Second World Wars, and the more recent reunification of Eastern and Western Germany, your country's health insurance system has <u>withstood</u> many challenges, making it a model worthy of closer examination.

A. embraced　B. resisted　C. welcomed

25. Many industrialized countries, including Japan, <u>point to</u> the success of your national health insurance scheme, and especially your adoption of a global budget.

A. waiver　B. imply　C. digress

26. Many industrialized countries, including Japan, point to the success of your national health insurance scheme, and especially your <u>adoption</u> of a global budget.

A. espousal　B. rejection　C. denial

27. <u>Expenditure</u> targets for hospital inpatients are strictly adhered to, and inpatients may pay only 25% of the total cost.

A. aggregate　B. disbursement　C. amass

28. Expenditure targets for hospital inpatients are <u>strictly</u> adhered to, and inpatients

may pay only 25% of the total cost.

A. unbinding   B. rigorously   C. loosely

29. Expenditure targets for hospital inpatients are strictly <u>adhered to</u>, and inpatients may pay only 25% of the total cost.

A. disregarded to   B. turned a blind eye to   C. complied with

30. An expenditure <u>cap</u> has been established to reduce customer fees for outpatient services.

A. upper limit   B. minimum   C. prerequisite

31. Given your <u>aggressive</u> efforts to keep down overhead costs, the average German citizen in 1997 enjoyed an annual average of 11 outpatient services, which was markedly lower than the annual average of 16 in Taiwan.

A. relaxed   B. proactive   C. informal

32. Given your aggressive efforts to keep down <u>overhead</u> costs, the average German citizen in 1997 enjoyed an annual average of 11 outpatient services, which was markedly lower than the annual average of 16 in Taiwan.

A. operating   B. supplemental   C. auxiliary

33. Specifically, we are <u>concerned with</u> how effectively to restrain increases in medical fees.

A. interested in   B. disinterested in   C. disregarding

34. Specifically, we are concerned with how effectively to <u>restrain</u> increases in medical fees.

A. relax   B. constrain   C. loosen up

35. Specifically, we are concerned with how effectively to restrain <u>increases</u> in medical fees.

A. hikes   B. reductions   C. curtailments

36. I hope to visit your organization for three months this year as a visiting researcher to learn about the latest <u>trends</u> in this area.

A. fluctuations　B. tendencies　C. uncertainties

37. My organization will <u>cover</u> my expenses during the stay.

　　A. charge for a service　B. bill for　C. compensate for

38. My organization will cover my <u>expenses</u> during the stay.

　　A. costs　B. discounts　C. rebates

39. I look forward to hearing from you soon as to whether the cooperation I have described would be <u>feasible</u>.

　　A. impractical　B. unrealistic　C. viable

Situation 2

1. Professor Lin Chin Tsai, President of Yuanpei University of Science and Technology, <u>referred me to you</u>.

　　A. spurned you　B. recommended you　C. demoted you

2. My graduate school research has <u>focused on</u> Sociometric Science, with specialized training in Statistics and Gray Mathematical Theory.

　　A. emphasized　B. played down　C. disintegrated

3. My graduate school research has focused on Sociometric Science, with <u>specialized</u> training in Statistics and Gray Mathematical Theory.

　　A. basic　B. standard　C. customized

4. I am currently developing a movement disability morbidity model capable not only of accurately <u>forecasting</u> the population of disabled elderly in Taiwan, but also of overcoming the limitations of the conventional population projection model, which incorporates static disability morbidity.

　　A. projecting　B. generalizing　C. universalizing

5. I am currently developing a movement disability morbidity model capable not only of accurately forecasting the population of disabled elderly in Taiwan, but also of <u>overcoming</u> the limitations of the conventional population projection

model, which incorporates static disability morbidity.

A. subordinate to   B. prevailing over   C. inferior to

6. I am currently developing a movement disability morbidity model capable not only of accurately forecasting the population of disabled elderly in Taiwan, but also of overcoming the <u>limitations</u> of the conventional population projection model, which incorporates static disability morbidity.

A. infinite   B. unbounded   C. confinements

7. I am currently developing a movement disability morbidity model capable not only of accurately forecasting the population of disabled elderly in Taiwan, but also of overcoming the limitations of the <u>conventional</u> population projection model, which incorporates static disability morbidity.

A. atypical   B. traditional   C. novel

8. I am currently developing a movement disability morbidity model capable not only of accurately forecasting the population of disabled elderly in Taiwan, but also of overcoming the limitations of the conventional population projection model, which <u>incorporates</u> static disability morbidity.

A. distances itself from   B. separate itself from   C. embodies

9. The university would like me to receive advanced training that would not only familiarize me with the long-term health care system, but also <u>expose</u> me to population distribution research, including variations among long-term health care systems worldwide.

A. reveal   B. conceal   C. shroud

10. The university would like me to receive advanced training that would not only familiarize me with the long-term health care system, but also expose me to population distribution research, including <u>variations</u> among long-term health care systems worldwide.

A. resistant to change   B. unalterable   C. modifications

11. Your laboratory, a leader in this field of research, could expose me to the latest trends in long-term health care from a global <u>perspective</u>.

    A. viewpoint   B. mandate   C. regulation

12. I hope therefore to join your laboratory for three months this year, preferably from March to June, if <u>convenient</u> for you.

    A. unattainable   B. impractical   C. expedient

13. The proposed <u>format</u> is that of a self-supported guest worker at your laboratory.

    A. structure   B. objective   C. mission

14. The proposed format is that of a <u>self-supported</u> guest worker at your laboratory.

    A. requesting financial support unconditionally

    B. paying one's own expenses

    C. requesting financial support in exchange for a certain amount of work

Situation 3

1. I hope to receive training at your hospital in the latest <u>advances</u> in infarct stroke technology.

    A. reversions   B. digressions   C. progress

2. In addition to my <u>academic</u> and professional activities, I often read supplemental literature to remain abreast of the latest technological trends.

    A. vocational   B. scholarly   C. occupation

3. In addition to my academic and professional activities, I often read <u>supplemental</u> literature to remain abreast of the latest technological trends.

    A. complementary   B. prerequisite   C. necessity

4. In addition to my academic and professional activities, I often read supplemental literature to <u>remain abreast of</u> the latest technological trends.

    A. stay in tune with   B. remain aloof   C. distance oneself from

5. While planning to fulfill my graduate school requirements by June, 2005, I hope

to continue in this field of research to integrate the <u>theoretical</u> knowledge acquired at graduate school with my clinical experience in the Radiotechnology Department.

A. matter-of-fact   B. down-to-earth   C. hypothetical

6. While planning to fulfill my graduate school requirements by June, 2005, I hope to continue in this field of research to integrate the theoretical knowledge acquired at graduate school with my <u>clinical</u> experience in the Radiotechnology Department.

A. laboratory-related   B. hospital-related   C. classroom-related

7. Three associate professors at YUST <u>supervised</u> my graduate school research in magnetic resonance technology.

A. submitted to   B. governed   C. subordinate to

8. I am currently involved in writing computer programs in the field of image quality and resolution, applying the latest technologies to enable physicians accurately to <u>diagnose</u> diseases in their early stages.

A. hide   B. conceal   C. identify

9. I have already <u>drawn up</u> an outline of this project.

A. subtracted   B. drafted   C. extracted

10. I am firstly reviewing <u>pertinent</u> patient histories to obtain large volumes of relevant data, which are then analyzed.

A. conflicting   B. contradictory   C. related

11. I am firstly reviewing pertinent <u>patient histories</u> to obtain large volumes of relevant data, which are then analyzed.

A. medical records   B. medical payment schedule   C. medical services

12. I am firstly reviewing pertinent patient histories to obtain large volumes of <u>relevant</u> data, which are then analyzed.

A. extraneous   B. irrelevant   C. pertinent

13. According to the results <u>generated</u> by my academic advisor's laboratory, less than six hours is required to perform the first diffusion-weighted image (DWI) examination of acute infract patients.

A. extracted   B. produced   C. recorded

14. According to the results generated by my academic advisor's laboratory, less than six hours is required to perform the first diffusion-weighted image (DWI) examination of <u>acute</u> infract patients.

A. recurring   B. regular   C. dire

15. DWI is then conducted on the first, third, fifth, seventh days, and then at one month <u>intervals</u>.

A. period of time   B. length of stay   C. period of scheduled payments

16. The B value infarct region is then measured, and then the time changes in the B value curve are <u>analyzed</u>.

A. glanced over   B. perused   C. scrutinized

17. The results of this study will help physicians to determine proper medication times and their <u>therapeutic</u> effects.

A. curative   B. atrophic   C. degenerative

18. The results of this study will help physicians to determine proper medication times and their therapeutic <u>effects</u>.

A. origin   B. outcomes   C. derivation

19. I hope to <u>measure</u> the order of severity of the infarct field in order to enable infarct stroke patients to receive subsequent optimal treatment.

A. determine   B. confound   C. bewilder

20. I hope to measure the order of severity of the infarct field in order to <u>enable</u> infarct stroke patients to receive subsequent optimal treatment.

A. immobilize   B. incapacitate   C. empower

21. I hope to measure the order of severity of the infarct field in order to enable

infarct stroke patients to receive subsequent <u>optimal</u> treatment.

A. formidable   B. best   C. dreadful

22. Using these programs, <u>clinical</u> physicians can precisely understand how a disease diffuses to the brain area, and increase the clinical effectiveness of evaluations of patients and curative outcomes.

A. hospital-oriented   B. laboratory-oriented   C. focus-oriented

23. Using these programs, clinical physicians can precisely understand how a disease <u>diffuses</u> to the brain area, and increase the clinical effectiveness of evaluations of patients and curative outcomes.

A. disperses   B. coalesce   C. conjugate

24. Using these programs, clinical physicians can precisely understand how a disease diffuses to the brain area, and increase the clinical effectiveness of <u>evaluations</u> of patients and curative outcomes.

A. conclusion   B. resolution   C. assessments

25. In this area, Taiwan currently <u>lacks</u> technology and qualified technological personnel.

A. abounds in   B. is deficient of   C. exceeds in

26. In this area, Taiwan currently lacks technology and <u>qualified</u> technological personnel.

A. incompetent   B. unfit   C. eligible

27. I hope <u>eventually</u> to collaborate with a local medical instrument manufacturer to develop relevant software programs.

A. preliminary   B. ultimately   C. initially

28. Your hospital provides <u>comprehensive</u> and challenging training of individuals who are committed to this area of research and development.

A. thorough   B. exclusive   C. sole

29. Your hospital provides comprehensive and <u>challenging</u> training of individuals

who are committed to this area of research and development.

A. difficult　B. facile　C. effortless

30. Your hospital provides comprehensive and challenging training of individuals who are <u>committed to</u> this area of research and development.

A. devoted to　B. neutral　C. non-aligned

31. In particular, it is <u>distinguished</u> in training highly skilled radiological technologists.

A. enigmatic　B. arcane　C. illustrious

32. In particular, it is distinguished in training highly <u>skilled</u> radiological technologists.

A. proficient　B. inept　C. incompetent

33. I will hopefully be able to determine the <u>scope</u> of application of infarct stroke technology in our hospital.

A. illiterate　B. untimely　C. range

34. The results are used to analyze the <u>feasibility</u> of adopting this technology.

A. unattainable　B. viability　C. impractical

35. The results are used to analyze the feasibility of <u>adopting</u> this technology.

A. espousing　B. nullifying　C. dismissing

36. Our current research direction is to investigate <u>differences</u> among infarct stroke patients across races and genders.

A. similarities　B. uniformity　C. discrepancies

37. Our current research direction is to investigate differences among infarct stroke patients across races and <u>genders</u>.

A. sexes　B. income groups　C. social classes

38. The proposed format, approved by the hospital <u>ethics</u> committee, is that of a self-supported guest worker at your laboratory.

A. impure　B. iniquitous　C. morality

39. For further information regarding my academic and professional <u>expertise</u>, please contact my academic advisor, Dr. Hong-Jue Liu.

A. incapacity   B. adeptness   C. powerlessness

40. His contact information can be found in the <u>accompanying</u> resume.

A. attached   B. lone   C. sole

H Common elements in writing a letter seeking technical training（科技訓練請求信函）by including the following contents:

1. Summarizing one's academic or professional experiences 某人學歷及工作經驗概述
2. Requesting technical training 科技訓練申請
3. Commending the organization to receive technical training from 讚揚提供科技訓練的機構
4. Explaining the details of the technical training 科技訓練細節解釋
5. Expressing optimism in the possibility of technical training 表達對科技訓練機會的樂觀態度

In the space below, write a letter seeking technical training.

_____

_____

_____

_____

_____

Unit one

Seeking Technical Training
科技訓練請求信函

1. Summarizing one's academic or professional experiences
   某人學歷及工作經驗概述

2. Requesting technical training
   科技訓練申請

3. Commending the organization to receive technical training from
   讚揚提供科技訓練的機構

4. Explaining the details of the technical training
   科技訓練細節解釋

5. Expressing optimism in the possibility of technical training
   表達對科技訓練機會的樂觀態度

Look at the following examples of expressing interest in a profession.

Hello,

Allow me to introduce myself. Following graduation from Yuanpei University of Science and Technology (YUST) in 1991, I passed the Taiwanese governmental civil service examination in 1994, subsequently securing an administrative position in our country's National Health Insurance organization. While working, I continued to enhance my proficiency skills in administrative-related tasks by taking courses on management in the medical sector at Yangming University. My rich experience in hospital management has familiarized me with how hospital fees are formulated. I was subsequently transferred to a new post in the insurance revenue sector with the National Health Institute in 2003. My experiences with the medical sector in generating income and the insurance revenue sector with monitoring remitted funds have greatly matured me as an administrator in the medical sector. Taiwan's National Health Insurance scheme is currently faced with the dilemma of strained financial resources as well as societal and political pressure not to raise monthly health insurance premiums. Innovative approaches are definitely needed to resolve this dilemma.

Your country initiated one of the earliest health insurance systems worldwide, as initiated by Chancellor Bismarck in 1883. Given the radical political, social and economic transformations that Germany has gone through with the First and Second World Wars, as well as reunification of Eastern and Western Germany, your country's health insurance system has withstood many challenges, definitely making it a worthwhile model that requires a closer examination. Many industrialized countries, including Japan, point to the success of your national health insurance scheme, especially with your adoption of a global budget. For hospital inpatients, expenditure targets are strictly adhered to maintain expenses, requiring that they pay only pay 25% of the total cost. For outpatient services, an expenditure cap has been established to lower customer fees. Given your aggressive efforts in maintaining overhead costs, the average German citizen in 1997 enjoyed an annual average of eleven outpatient services, which is markedly lower than the annual average of sixteen in Taiwan. Specifically, we are concerned with how to effectively restrain increases in medical fees. I hope to visit your organization as a visiting researcher to learn of the latest trends in this area for three months this year. My organization would cover my expenses during the stay.

Attached please find enclosed my personal resume that describes my professional experiences in the above area. I look forward to hearing from you soon as to whether such cooperation would be feasible. Thanks in advance for your kind assistance.

Sincerely yours,

Dear Professor Coutrakon,

Thank you for you serving as invited speaker at a seminar held recently in the Institute of Medical Imagery at Yuanpei University of Science and Technology (YUST). Three of your lectures for staff of the Radiation Detection Laboratory were highly informative and directly related to our current research direction. Despite Taiwan's lack of clinical experience in proton therapy research, YUST plans to establish a proton spectra laboratory in order to further develop proton treatment methods for clinical applications. Thus, my academic advisor, Professor Hsu, would like me to receive clinical experience in proton therapy technology from the Proton Therapy Center at Loma Linda University, especially in the area of proton microdosimetry spectra. If you allow me to serve as a guest worker in your laboratory, I will send the detailed visiting itinerary shortly.

If given the opportunity, I would like exposure to the following topics:

1. Construction of the shielding of cyclotron to avoid neutron pollution and gamma ray scattering;
2. Operation of the negative ion cyclotron;
3. Blending and design of the shielding material with respect to the half-value layer of lead and concrete;
4. Operating rules of proton spectra analysis facility, with a particular focus on Spread out Bragg Peak (SOBP) analysis; and
5. Clinical information regarding curative doses of proton for different tumor types.

As for my accommodation during the guest stay, I would like to lease a single-room hotel, at range between US$ 50 to US$ 100 daily. Thank you for your generous assistance. I look forward to opportunity for our laboratories to cooperate with each other again.

Sincerely yours,

Hello,

I would like to serve in a self-supported practicum internship in your company. I am drawn to your excellence in data analysis and project planning, as is widely regarded worldwide. I received my undergraduate training in the Healthcare Management at National Taipei College of Nursing (NTCN), with a subsequent Master's degree in

Business Management from Yuanpei University of Science and Technology. Despite the valuable research theory I acquired through graduate studies, I strive to remain abreast of the seemingly endless innovations that appear daily given the significant transformation that has occurred in information technologies. As relevant marketing research methods continuously evolve, I feel somewhat unprepared when implementing data analysis strategies in the workplace. Exposure to the marketing practices and data analysis procedures adopted at your company would orient me on the latest trends in this field. Previously, I participated in projects aimed at assessing the quality of a hospital's medical services and examining the intellectual capital of on-line gaming companies. Under the supervision of my academic advisor, I designed a questionnaire based on research design theory, with the software packages Statistical Package for the Social Science (SPSS) and Expert Choice used to analyze the data. Relevant project experiences have significantly strengthened my independent research capabilities as well as statistical and analytical skills.

The opportunity to work in a practicum internship in your company would provide me with an excellent environment not only to fully realize my career aspirations, but also allow me to implement data analysis methods efficiently. I am especially interested in learning abut the latest data analysis theories and methods, and I will strive to quickly absorb new information. I also hope that I can contribute my previous experience in applying theoretical concepts to survey research and statistics.

Sincerely yours,

Hello,

Professor Lin Chin Tsai, President of Yuanpei University of Science and Technology, referred me to you. I am pursuing a Master's degree in the Institute of Business and Management at Yuanpei University of Science and Technology. My graduate school research has focused on Sociometry Science, with specialized training in Statistics and the Gray System Mathematical Theory. I am currently developing a movement disability morbidity model capable not only of accurately forecasting population trends among the disabled elderly in Taiwan, but also of overcoming the limitations of the conventionally adopted population projection model which incorporates static disability morbidity. I plan to develop such a model in the near future.

Our university would like me to receive advanced training that would not only familiarize me with the long-term health care system, but also expose me to population distribution research in each country, such as the variation among long-term health care systems worldwide. If given the opportunity, your laboratory, one of the leaders in this field of research, could provide me with the exposure to the latest trends in long-term health care from a global perspective, hopefully for three months this year. I would prefer March through June if convenient with you. I am most concerned with how such trends in long-term health care will impact Taiwan. The proposed format is that of a self-supported guest worker at your laboratory.

The attached resume will hopefully give you a better idea of my previous academic and professional experiences. Also, a university classmate of mine (Mr. Jeffrey Wu, tel. (408)1234567) who is currently serving as an administrator in a non-profit healthcare organization near your laboratory could provide you with further clarification as to my background and purpose of my visit.

I would greatly appreciate your comments regarding this proposal. Thanks for your assistance. I look forward to our future cooperation.
Sincerely yours,

Dear Mr. Smith,

I am eager to join your organization as a marketing specialist knowledgeable of integrated information systems that service all departments within an enterprise. I recently received my Master's degree in Business Administration from Yuanpei University of Science and Technology. Marketing has interested me immensely throughout undergraduate and graduate school, as evidenced by my ranking among the top five scholastically in Marketing-related courses. I also acquired knowledge of the latest theories in marketing and market survey. Although lacking formal professional experiences despite a summer internship in the Marketing Department at Pink Technology Corporation, I am diligent and able to adjust to new circumstances.

Somewhat familiar with the scope of activities in your management department, I am confident that my previous academic and professional experiences will prove valuable to any collaborative effort that I belong to in your company. Please find enclosed my personal resume, university academic transcripts and letter of recommendation from our university president. My resume contains additional references, all of whom can give you a better idea of my background and ability to work with others. I would

appreciate it if you arrange for an interview at your earliest convenience.
Sincerely yours,

Dear Dr. Lin,

I would like to serve as a guest worker in your healthcare organization during my upcoming summer vacation. First exposed to hospital management during undergraduate school, I will complete my master's degree requirements from the Institute of Business Management at Yuanpei University of Science and Technology in the spring of 2005. During university, I worked in a hospital practicum internship, focusing on an effective marketing strategy for the domestic cosmetics sector that would enhance the global competitiveness and market share of biotechnology manufacturers.

As is well known, your research group has acquired much experience in developing marketing strategies for the cosmetics sector. The opportunity to serve as a self-supported guest worker in the research group of your organization would equip me with the skills necessary to design and implement marketing strategies for this unique niche sector. After thoroughly reviewing your online literature and promotional materials, I am especially drawn to the marketing strategies that your organization has adopted, which are quite compatible with my current research interests.

I am confident of my ability not only to familiarize myself with your corporate operations, but also to contribute to any effort that I participate in during the guest worker period, as well as share my relevant experiences with Taiwan's cosmetics sector. The attached resume will give you a better idea as to how my personal strengths match the needs of your research group. A six month period as a guest worker would probably be the most appropriate time frame. If my application is accepted, I can start in October, 2005. Please carefully consider my request and inform me of your decision at your earliest convenience. I look forward to our future cooperation.

Sincerely yours,

Dear Sir,

I hope to secure employment in your globally reputed bedding corporation upon successful completion of my graduate school requirements. I am pursuing a Master's degree in Business Management at Yuanpei University of Science and Technology in Taiwan. Advanced knowledge skills acquired during graduate school will allow me to significantly contribute to your corporation's marketing efforts. Among the many management and business-oriented courses I took during undergraduate and graduate school included marketing, finance, information science and research methodology. My graduate school research focused on designing and applying relevant marketing strategies to the bedding franchisee selection model, with those findings submitted to an international journal for publication. I bring to your corporation a solid understanding of research design and methodology that will hopefully contribute to your company's efforts to enhance operational quality.

During a summer vacation, I worked in the Taiwanese branch of your bedding corporation, where I was responsible for creating a customer database and marketing survey. By familiarizing myself with customer service-related issues, I gained further insight into the current market demand in Taiwan. Results generated during my time with your franchise proved most helpful in compiling my master's thesis. I am especially drawn to your corporation's emphasis on customization that orients consumers on the healthy aspect of your products. I am confident that my academic and professional experiences will match the expectations that you hold for marketing personnel. The attached resume will give you a clearer idea of how I have prepared for a marketing-related career, hopefully at your corporation.

As mentioned in the attached resume, Mr. Liu (company chairman of your Taiwanese franchise) and my academic advisor Professor Hsu would be happy to provide you with further details regarding my background and aptitude. Out of a deep respect for the strong market position that your company holds in Europe and abroad, I would immensely enjoy working for your corporation following successful completion of graduate school requirements, hopefully by the summer of 2005. I look forward to your reply.

Sincerely yours,

Dear Mr. Smith,

Given your company's expertise in developing excellent software for medical instrumentation, I would like to receive technical training from your company to understand how we can more effectively implement Amira3.1 and Image J programs. As I will be completing my master's degree requirements in Medical Imagery at Yuanpei University of Science and Technology this summer, my academic advisor recommended that I seek your institution to understand what technology transfer opportunities are available for the local medical instrumentation sector. My master's thesis focused on image fusion in an attempt to demonstrate a larger anatomic slice of the human brain. Importantly, all images displayed abnormal, ischemia and severely acute strokes. The ability to co-register these different slices for image diagnosis is of priority concern. The initial step would be for our two organizations to begin exchanging technological information regarding imaging fusion applications in computer programs. Such a technological collaboration would hopefully lead to a more effective means of confirming brain stroke or ischemia than the conventionally adopted medical procedure offers.

In recent developments, Amira3.1 and Image J computerized programs provide excellent anatomic images of an abnormal brain tissue, especially in irreversible damage tissues. However, we are not exactly sure how to acquire various percentage blood flows in the use of threshold and masked technology. I look forward to your suggestions on how to optimally use this computerized technology as an integral part of this information exchange opportunity. Your academic-oriented computer center has distinguished itself in resolving computer problems. A one month technical training period at your organization appears to be the most effective means of initiating a collaborative research between our two organizations. During this period, I hope to become more proficient in Amira3.1 and Image J programs. I hope that this technical training will pave the way for our two organizations to concentrate efforts to use computer-coregisteration images when diagnosing a human stroke. I look forward to your favorable reply regarding this proposal that will hopefully lead to technological collaboration in the near future.

Sincerely yours,

- -

Dear Professor Wallace,

I hope to receive training at your hospital on the latest advances in infarct stroke technology. As a second year graduate student in the Institute of Medical Imagery at

Yuan-Pei University of Science and Technology (YUST), I am also a full-time radiological technologist of Shin-Kong Wu Ho-Su Memorial Hospital in Taipei. Previously, I received a bachelor's degree in Radiology from the same university. In addition to these academic and professional activities, I often read supplemental literature to remain abreast of the latest technological trends. While tentatively planning to fulfill my graduate school requirements by June, 2005, I hope to continue in this line of research to integrate the theoretical knowledge acquired during graduate school with my clinical experiences in the radiotechnology department.

Three associate professors at YUST closely supervised my graduate school research in magnetic resonance technology. I am currently involved in writing computer program imagery quality and resolution by adopting the latest available technologies so that physicians can accurately diagnose diseases in their early stages. I have already drawn up an outline on how to initiate this project. I first review pertinent patient history to calculate a large volume of pertinent data, followed by analysis. Pertinent research reviewed must have a significant clinical value. Acute infract of brain tumor patients is then studied. According to results generated in my academic advisor's laboratory, not over six hours is required to perform the first diffusion-weighted image (DWI) examination of acute infract patients. Next, DWI is conducted on the first, third, fifth, seventh day and one month intervals. The B value infarct region is then measured, followed by subsequent analysis of the time changes in the B value curve. Results of this study allow physicians to determine proper medication times and their therapeutic effect.

Given my deep interest in this profession, I hope to measure the infarct field range with an order of severity level. Acute infarct stroke patients can subsequently receive optimal treatment. Writing an effective integral diffusion mode map requires taking advantage of the latest programs in which different maps appear in direct relation to different diseases. Using these programs, clinical physicians can precisely understand how a disease diffuses to the brain area, as well as increase clinical effectiveness in evaluating patients and their curative outcome. In this area, Taiwan currently lacks related instrumentation and qualified technology personnel. I hope to eventually collaborate with a local medical instrumentation manufacturer in developing relevant software programs. Your hospital offers comprehensive and challenging training for individuals committed to this area of research and development, having distinguished itself in the training of highly skilled radiological technologists.

Moreover, my research will hopefully be able to determine the extent to which infarct stroke technology can be adopted in our hospital. Data results are used to analyze the feasibility of adopting this technology. Our current research direction is also investigating differences in race and gender among infarct stroke patients. Having received approval from the hospital ethics committee, the proposed format is that of a self-supported guest worker at your laboratory.

For further information regarding my academic and professional expertise, you can contact my academic adviser Dr. Hong-Jue Liu His contact information can be found in the accompanying resume. I would greatly appreciate your comments regarding this proposal. Thank for your kind assistance. I look forward to our future cooperation.

Sincerely yours,

Dear Dr. Huang,

By designating the role of green tea polyphenols in human cell lines as my primary research interest, I hope to work in the lipids research group in Abbott Laboratories as a visiting guest researcher from Yuanpei University of Science and Technology.

Whereas individuals heavily depend on oxygen, oxygen in the air easily contains the reactive oxygen species (ROS) for unknown reasons. As a free radical, ROS can easily contribute to the development of cardiovascular diseases owing to the excess of free radicals in the human body. Additionally, free radicals in the human body are known to induce oxidative stress. Eventually, the human immune system breaks down while attempting to protect against human cells, thus inducing the free radicals. Consequently, oxidative stress occurs if the human body contains an excess of free radicals, eventually leading to cardiovascular diseases and apoplexy of the brain. The presence of many polyphenols in tea is well documented. For instance, polyphenols such as ECg, EGCg, and catechin have excellent antioxidative capabilities to inhibit free radicals in humans. Given my current research direction as to how green tea polyphenols impact human cell lines, e.g. RAW 264.7 cell line and the human breast carcinoma cell line, I have so far observed the ability of green tea polyphenols to inhibit certain reactions.

To facilitate my upcoming stay as a guest researcher in your laboratory, could you please send me the formal application materials for this activity? The opportunity to work in your research program would pave the way for collaborative activities between our two laboratories, based on our mutual interests. I look forward to hearing from you.

Sincerely yours,

Dear Professor Haas,

My academic advisor, Dr. Cheng, recommended that I contact you regarding the possibility of a guest researcher stay in your laboratory, given your progress in microbiology and the H.pylori molecule. As a second year master degree's student in the Institute of Biotechnology at Yuanpei University of Science and Technology in Taiwan, I received my undergraduate degree in Medical Technology at the same institution My current research focus in the laboratory of Professor Jin-Town Wang in the College of Medicine at National Taiwan University is on the modification of H.pylori in relation to several peptic gastric disorders, in which I hope to significantly contribute to efforts to develop novel scientific applications for medicinal purposes.

Having read extensively on your recent research results, I hope to serve as a self-supported guest researcher in your laboratory for a six month period (January through June of 2005), concentrating on the cloning of the H.pylori gene and functional characterization of technologies developed in your laboratory. If possible, I hope to work directly under your supervision. Despite my preferences, I am open to investigating any related topics which you would deem beneficial during my stay.

Given my interest in biotechnology, biochemistry and clinical technology-related topics, I participated in a National Science Council-sponsored research program aimed at clarifying the relation between H.pylori and natural transformation. Having read extensively on the correlation between H.pylori and my current topic in molecular biology, I look forward to consulting with you in your laboratory on current directions in H.pylori research.

Please carefully consider my request. I look forward to your favorable reply.
Sincerely yours,

Dear Dr. Taheri,

I would like to serve as a visiting researcher in your Trauma Burn Center to pave the way for future technological exchanges between our two organizations. I am an emergency care department administrator in En Chu Kong Hospital, originally founded in 1998 by Hsing Tien Buddhist Temple to provide quality medical care to the surrounding community. The twenty-one floor hospital facility has a capacity of 501 beds, including 312 for general patients, 141 for special purposes and forty eight for chronic diseases. The hospital adopts a compassionate approach towards providing quality medical care and integral community services.

While heavily focusing on emergency care and community medical services, En Chu Kong Hospital and its committed staff strive to strengthen its ties to the local community and convey our care through concern for the mental and physical well being of all.

As one of the first dedicated burn units in the United States and the first in Michigan, the Trauma Burn Center of the University of Michigan has distinguished itself globally with its committed burn specialists and researchers whom have led the way in research, care and rehabilitation of burn patients. Moreover, as a Level 1 Pediatric and Adult Trauma Center as well as Burn Center certified by the American College of Surgeons, your organization has much to offer medical professionals in a newly industrialized country such as Taiwan.

Our hospital administrator, Dr. Chen, encouraged me to contact you regarding the possibility of a visiting researcher in your Trauma Burn Center, as En Chu Kong Hospital tentatively plans to open a Trauma Burn Center in October 2006. We have already acquired much experience in research, education, prevention and systemic planning for severely injured patients. Given my decade of nursing experience in an emergency care department, I have received advanced training in advanced trauma care for nurses, registered nursing certification in critical care, advanced cardiac life support and pediatric advanced life support. Patient care includes the initial resuscitation period, daily care, rehabilitation and completion of life care.

This technological exchange will hopefully open doors for further cooperation between our two organizations. Thanks in advance for your kind assistance.
Sincerely yours,

Dr. Smith,

I would like to serve as a self-supported guest researcher in your company's Marketing Department. Allow me to introduce myself. As a graduate student in pursuit of a Master's degree in Business Management at Yuanpei University of Science and Technology in Taiwan, I earlier received my undergraduate training in Healthcare Management from the same institution. Previously, I served in practicum internships in a medical department of Chimei Hospital and an administrative unit of Hsinchu

General Hospital. Following university graduation, I began working in the university's Health Center as an administrative assistant involved in a campus wide anti-smoking campaign. Intensive on-the-job training enabled me to handle various requests and difficult situations, enabling me to resolve problems efficiently. I view myself as a responsible individual that highly prioritizes the need to continuously grow academically and professionally, albeit with a cordial and earnest attitude.

Given my above experiences, I would like to serve in your company's Marketing Department as a self-supported guest researcher for a six month period. Receiving practical training from this department would greatly benefit me in my current career direction. Having spent considerable time in writing marketing proposals, I often peruse through pertinent marketing literature as it seems to develop at an accelerated pace. If given the opportunity to gain exposure to your excellent work environment, I would be able to remain abreast of current trends in marketing research in a practical context.

Thank you for your consideration.

Sincerely yours,

Dear Dr. Drucker,

Professor Lin Chin Tsai, President of Yuanpei University of Science and Technology (YUST), referred me to you regarding the possibility of serving as a self-supported guest worker in your hospital. While pursuing a Master's degree in the Institute of Business Management at YUST, I would like to acquire professional experiences as a guest worker in your hospital during my upcoming summer vacation. As is well known, medical management practices in the United States are revered worldwide. Human resource management heavily relies on talented employees as the crux of a hospital's strategic resources, necessitating that appropriate employees be selected to ensure a medical institution's competitiveness. However, Taiwanese hospitals are deficient in this area, subsequently spurring my interest in how global trends in human resource management can positively impact hospitals island wide.

Having read extensively on results from your recent research efforts, I am quite impressed with your ability to apply the above trends in human resource management in the practical context of hospital operations in your country. I would thus like to serve as a self-supported guest worker in your hospital for a three month period, hopefully January through March of 2006. The opportunity to work in a practicum internship in your hospital would provide me with an excellent environment to fully realize my career aspirations. If possible, I would like to work directly under your supervision, although I am open to any work that is relevant to my research interests.

Please carefully consider my request. I look forward to your favorable reply and appreciate your kind assistance.

Sincerely yours,

Dear Mr. Wang,

Allow me to introduce myself. Having recently obtained my Master's degree in Business Management from Yuanpei University of Science and Technology in Taiwan, I acquired knowledge of the latest theories in marketing research. Earlier, I received undergraduate training in Information Management from Ming Hsin University of Science and Technology, with a special concentration in data analysis and marketing planning. This was followed by six years of work in the semiconductor industry.

Equipped with a solid academic foundation in Business Management and Information Management, I would like to acquire more relevant experiences in this area by serving in a self-supported position as a guest researcher in your company's Marketing Information Department. Such an opportunity would compensate for my lack of formal professional experience in this area. I consider myself to be diligent and would have no problems in adjusting to new circumstances in your highly competitive working environment.

From an article I read in *Business Weekly*, I was quite impressed with the diverse array of projects that your Marketing Information Department has undertaken successfully in recent years. Somewhat familiar with the scope of your company's marketing activities, I am confident that my previous academic and professional experiences will prove valuable to any collaborative effort that I belong to. Please find enclosed my personal resume, academic transcripts from university and graduate school, as well as letters of recommendation from my thesis advisor and university president. I would appreciate it if you would arrange for an interview at your earliest convenience.

Sincerely yours,

Dear Professor Tagamiya,

Professor Lin Chin Tsai, President of Yuanpei University of Science and Technology, suggested that I contact you regarding the possibility of serving as a self-supported guest worker in your research center. Following graduation from Chung Tai Junior College of Medical Technology in 1993, I have worked in Taipei Medical University Municipal Wan Fang Hospital up until now. Despite my professional experiences, I felt that my academic training was lacking, explaining why I received in-service training on the weekends in Healthcare Administration at Yuanpei Institute of Science and Technology. Despite the difficulty in handling the hectic academic and working schedule, I received my bachelor's degree in 2003. Currently pursuing a Master's degree in the Institute of Business and Management at the same institution, I am focusing on medical marketing research.

If given the opportunity to serve as a visiting researcher in the Institute of Business Administration at Keio University, I would receive a practical context for the solid academic fundamentals acquired so far. Widely considered as one of the leaders in the medical marketing field, your Institute would compensate for my lack of formal professional experience in this area. The visiting researcher period will hopefully last fourth months this year. I would prefer April through July if at all possible. Of course, all expenses incurred during this period would be covered by my Institute.

The attached resume will hopefully give you a better idea of my academic background and professional expertise. As for references, a Japanese friend of mine (Miss Ishima Norico) who is currently teaching Organizational Behavior at your university would be happy to provide you with further details of my academic background and purpose of visit. I anxiously look forward to your favorable reply.

Sincerely yours,

Dear Dr. Smith,

Allow me to introduce myself. I am pursuing a Master's degree in the Institute of Business and Management at Yuanpei University of Science and Technology. Given the seemingly unlimited endless possibilities for Internet marketing, my graduate school research focuses on Internet marketing research. Previously, I worked as a franchise manager in Cine-Asia Entertainment Company, a home entertainment enterprise with more than 100 branches located islandwide. This work experience exposed me to the latest theories in marketing and market survey involving Internet marketing.

To build upon the above academic and professional experiences, I would like to serve as a self-supported guest researcher in your company's Management Department for a three month period, hopefully during my upcoming summer vacation. Familiar with the scope of activities that your Department undertakes, I am confident of my ability to contribute to any collaborative effort that I belong to in your company. I am especially interested in acquiring as much knowledge expertise in the latest management strategies and Internet marketing applications. The enclosed resume, academic transcripts and letters of recommendation will hopefully give you further insight into my academic and professional competence in this area. My resume contains additional references from individuals who can shed light on my solid academic training and ability to closely collaborate with others. I hope that you could arrange for a personal interview. Please carefully consider my request and inform me of your decision at your earliest convenience. I look forward to our future cooperation. Sincerely yours,

Hello,

Allow me to introduce myself. As a graduate student in the Master's degree program in Business Management at Yuanpei University of Science and Technology, I have worked as a nurse in Hsinchu General Hospital since 1994. Given your hospital's widely reputed image as adopting the latest approaches to ensure patient safety, I would like to serve in a self-supported practicum internship in your hospital during my upcoming summer vacation.

Taiwan currently faces a dilemma of medical personnel lacking proper motivation, leading to widespread apathy and occasional indifference towards patients. A notable example was the recent death of a hospital patient administered the wrong medicine. Importantly, patients taking medicine should be informed of the medicine's function(s) and its potentially adverse impact. Hospital practices must be adopted island wide to ensure that the patient's welfare is of priority concern, which largely depends on the ability to transform the attitudes of medical personnel.

The opportunity to work in a practicum internship in your hospital would provide me with an excellent environment to understand how medical personnel are oriented in daily routine procedures to ensure patient welfare. I look forward to hearing from you soon as to whether such cooperation would be feasible. Thanks in advance for your kind assistance.

Sincerely yours,

Dear Mr. Smith,

I would like to serve as a self-supported guest researcher in your company's Marketing Department during my upcoming summer vacation. As a graduate student in the Institute of Business Management at Yuanpei University in Taiwan, I am especially interested in researching marketing sales-related topics. Graduate school made me proficient in resolving a wide array of marketing problems, subsequently spurring my creativity and analytical capabilities. When my instructor required that all students to deliver a report weekly, I initially found this teaching style too demanding. However, this intensive training greatly matured me as a researcher in the Business Management field. I now have the confidence to put forward new ideas by myself, which is essential for conducting independent research.

Your company's Marketing Department has distinguished itself globally for its innovative sales promotional efforts. Given our Institute's lack of resources and expertise in this area, I would like to serve as a self-supported guest researcher in your company's Marketing Department during my upcoming summer vacation. Exposure to the way in which your department applies the latest marketing sales concepts in a practical context would give me a clearer direction not only my graduate level research, but also my chosen career path as well. I look forward to hearing your ideas and suggestions on the possibility of this guest researcher opportunity.

Thanks in advance for your careful consideration.

Sincerely yours,

Dr. Smith,

I would like to serve as a self-supported guest researcher in your globally renowned healthcare institution this upcoming summer. After receiving my undergraduate training in nursing in 1985 and following an intensive nationwide civil service examination, I was placed in an administrative position in Hsinchu General Hospital, where I have remained for nearly the past two decades. My work encompasses a wide array of activities, including discharge planning, home care visits, as well as nursing home and community health care. Given my subsequent pursuit of a Master's degree in Business Management from Yuanpei University of Science and Technology, I am interested in implementing an exercise program to activate the psychomotor functions of the elderly.

The market demand for long-term care facilities in Taiwan has increased given the increasing elderly population island wide. In addition to providing necessary medical services, such facilities must enhance the quality of life for their residents. An exercise program to activate the psychomotor functions among the elderly has received considerable attention, especially in Japan with considerable success. The opportunity to serve as a self-supported guest researcher in your healthcare institution would allow me to more thoroughly understand the effectiveness of this activity program in promoting the physical as well as psychological functions of elderly residents in long term care facilities.

Your country has pioneered progressive policies in welfare of its elderly population, including state-of-the-art facilities. I have much to learn from your organization, which would greatly facilitate my graduate level research and current work direction. I would greatly appreciate your comments regarding the possibility of this guest researcher opportunity in your organization for one month this upcoming summer. Thanks in advance for your careful consideration.

Sincerely yours,

Dr. Smith,

Hospital administrator Ms. Nancy Chang of Century Hospital recommended that I contact you regarding the possibility of me serving as a guest researcher in your hospital this upcoming summer. As a graduate student in the Institute of Business Management at Yuanpei University in Taiwan, I am actively involved in a National Science Council-sponsored research project aimed at implementing health promotion activities in regional hospitals. Given your hospital's recent success in holding the 12th International Conference on Health Promotion in Hospitals, I am most interested in learning from your rich experience in this area. The Taiwanese government will, in the near future, legislate health promotion measures to be adopted in hospitals island wide. The opportunity to serve as a self-supported guest researcher in your hospital from June to August of next year would allow me to view firsthand how health promotion activities are implemented in a practical context.

Please carefully consider my request. I look forward to our future cooperation.
Sincerely yours,

Dear Professor Lin,

My master's thesis advisor school suggested that I contact you, given your ample experience in Internet marketing. I would like to serve as a self-supported guest researcher in your laboratory this upcoming summer, hopefully under your supervision with respect to the latest marketing approaches using this unique medium. I am currently involved in a research project that requires collaborating with the advertising design department of an Internet marketing company. Revenues generated from online sales have dramatically increased in Taiwan in recent years, making it important to understand the unique features of this niche consumer market. My graduate school research focuses on identifying the most effective sales strategies aimed at online consumers in Taiwan. Doing so requires careful consideration of ethnic and cultural factors that an Internet marketing company would find most helpful in identifying consumer tastes. I am determined to carefully design marketing strategies that will enhance customer service, ultimately increasing company revenues. Having read extensively on your recent research results, I am encouraged by your developments in this field, explaining why I hope to exchange similar experiences that would hopefully be mutually beneficial to both of our organizations.

Eager to understand the dynamic environment that your work involves, I would like to arrange for summer. Exposure to work in your research program will hopefully pave the way for future collaborative activities between our two organizations. Although I prefer to work directly under your supervision, I am open to any related topics that you would deem beneficial during my stay. The enclosed resume will provide you with a better idea of my academic training and professional experiences. As for references,

you can directly contact my academic advisor, whose address is listed in the accompanying resume. I look forward to your ideas and suggestions regarding this proposal. Please carefully consider my request. I anxiously look forward to your favorable reply.
Sincerely yours,

Hello,
My graduate thesis advisor, Dr. Chen, encouraged me to contact you company regarding the possibility of serving as a visiting researcher in your company. Prior to university graduation from Yuanpei University of Science and Technology in 2003, I became a certified Microsoft service engineer following an intensely competitive nationwide examination in 2000. In addition to my current pursuit of a Master's degree in Business Management at the same institution, I have held several management positions since 1980, especially in sales and marketing. Deeply impressed with the sales marketing strategies that your company adopts, I hope to gain further exposure to relevant marketing research methods. Doing so would definitely benefit my own research interests. Moreover, the opportunity to work in a globally competitive environment such as the one that your company offers would offer me a more practical context for the marketing theories acquired in graduate school. The attached resume will hopefully provide you with a clearer picture of my academic potential and professional experiences. If at all possible, I hope that this three month stay as a visiting researcher in your company will commence once I have fulfilled my graduation requirements in the summer of 2006. I look forward to your reply.
Sincerely yours,

Dear Dr. Kawasaki,
As a recent graduate of the Master's degree program in Business Management from Yuanpei University of Science and Technology in Taiwan, I have learned much of your

agency's efforts to provide quality health care for the elderly in Japan. I am also impressed with your government's efforts to develop innovative welfare and medical service programs for senior citizens, the physically challenged and disadvantaged children. The role that social welfare professionals play in implementing such programs can not be understated.

Given the above needs, the demand for qualified social welfare specialists whom have a solid theoretical foundation and experience in closely collaborating with medical professionals is greater than ever. Such professionals include social workers, nurses, and gerontologists and therapists for physically and mentally challenged individuals, with their services having expanded beyond hospitals and into social welfare facilities and home care.

Given my solid undergraduate training in Nursing and Healthcare Management, as well as postgraduate work in Business Management, I would like to serve as a visiting researcher in your healthcare institution to more thoroughly understand how your country's progressive health care policy differs from that of Taiwan. If given this opportunity, I am especially interested in the following areas of research:

1. How to effectively and efficiently utilize limited resources in the health sector, including human resources;

2. How healthcare services can be more effectively implemented when various medical and health care professionals combine their efforts, especially given the need for medical professionals who must have a solid foundation in health sciences and strong management skills; and

3. How to train specialists to meet the increasing demands of the above areas, which your country's health management professionals have devoted considerable resources.

In addressing some of the above issues, I have much to offer in health and welfare services, areas in which governments in Japan and other industrialized countries highly prioritize. I look forward to your suggestions regarding the possibility of a three month guest researcher stay in your healthcare institution this upcoming summer. The attached resume will hopefully provide you with a clearer picture of my academic potential and professional experiences. If at all possible, please notify me as to which dates are most convenient for you. Thanks in advance for your careful consideration. Sincerely yours,

Dear Professor Smith,

I would like to serve as a self-supported guest researcher in your laboratory this upcoming summer. I am pursuing a Master's degree in Business Management at Yuanpei University of Science and Technology in Taiwan. My graduate school research focuses on human resource management, which is especially relevant given the rapid growth of the knowledge economy in the new century. Given the prevalence of technology in daily life, my professional knowledge skills must be continuously upgraded. I am especially interested in understanding how human resource management can increase worker productivity. I recently read a journal article that identified five major personality characteristics as predictors of an expatriate's desire to terminate an assignment and enhance supervisor-rated performance. These personality characteristics can be used to accurately determine which employees are appropriate for working abroad. Such knowledge would enable a company to reduce overhead costs, subsequently increasing an enterprise's competitiveness. This area of research is especially fascinating to me.

As your laboratory has devoted much time in researching the above topics, I would greatly benefit from the opportunity to work in your laboratory as a self-supported researcher during my upcoming summer vacation. I look forward to your suggestions regarding this proposal. The enclosed resume will provide you with a better idea of my academic training and professional experiences. Thanks in advance for your careful consideration, and I look forward to our future cooperation.

Sincerely yours,

Dear Ms. Wang,

Dr. Chang suggested that I contact you regarding the possibility of serving as a guest worker in your laboratory. He mentioned your instrumental role in the development of the Mass Laboratory at the Polysaccharides Institute. My research in the Mass Laboratory focuses on extracting crude plants for medicinal purposes as I pursue a Master's degree in Medical Imagery at Yuanpei University of Science and Technology in Hsinchu, Taiwan. The attached resume and recommendation letters provide further details of my solid academic background and professional experiences. In addition to the valuable literature on polysaccharides that you sent to our laboratory, I am quite impressed with the GC mass instrumentation purchased from your company.

I am particularly interested in researching topics related to plant polysaccharides. Given the abundant literature on this topic that I have read, I would like to further my knowledge of this area of expertise through a more close analysis of crude plants in your institute.

The opportunity to serve as a guest researcher in your laboratory for three to eight months would allow me to further explore the above research topic. All of the expenses incurred during my stay would be covered by my organization. If possible, I would prefer to begin no earlier than November 11, 2005. Besides the above-mentioned subjects, I hope to spend some time taking assignments directly from you. Please consider my request and inform me of your decision as soon as possible.

Sincerely yours,

Dear Dr. Lin,

Allow me to introduce myself. As a graduate student in the Institute of Medical Imagery at Yuanpei University of Science and Technology (similar to a nuclear science institute), I am also a certified radiation technician with several years of experience. After receiving my junior collage diploma from YUST, I pursued a Bachelor's degree in Radiotechnology at the same institution. In addition to receiveing certification as a radiotechnologist, I also enhanced my knowledge expertise of this field. My current research focuses on radiation oncology, in which I intend to combine simulation with the linac system. Our laboratory would like me to receive advanced training in this technological field, such as its clinical applications in radiation therapy. As a leader in this field of research, your laboratory could allow me to further refine my radiation therapy-related skills. Well aware of your organization's expertise in this area, I hope to acquire clinical practice as well as share with you our relevant research experiences in this field. Specifically, I hope to further my professional knowledge on how to integrate simulation with Linac system technology. Spending two months in your laboratory during the upcoming summer vacation would be sufficient for me to acquire such expertise.

I further hope that this technical training will open the doors of cooperation between our two organizations. Please carefully consider my application. From the above letterhead, you can directly contact me via e-mail or telephone. I look forward to your favorable reply.

Sincerely yours,

Dear Sir,

Having recently received both a Bachelor's degree in Medical Technology and a Master's degree in Biolotechnology from Yuanpei University of Science and Technology, I hope to serve as a research fellow in your company.

Your company has distinguished itself in food research for quite some time, developments that I have closely followed for quite some time. I am confident in my ability to work under your supervision in a research fellowship under your highly skilled research personnel, an opportunity that would greatly advance my competency as a food research biologist.

During undergraduate and graduate school, I acquired much knowledge expertise in a diverse array of topics in food science and related research. In particular, university instructors equipped me with strong academic fundamentals in food science and technology, which further spurred my interest in this area of research. Graduate level courses in food science and biolotechnology are closely related to areas of research that your firm is actively engaged in. My specialization during graduate studies focused on developments in food science related to genetically modified foods. Having devoted considerable time in the laboratory on this topic, I am determined to follow a career in food science by remaining abreast of the latest technological developments in this field.

I hope that you will grant me this opportunity to serve as a research fellow in your company. I would be happy to supply additional information, in addition to that found in the accompanying resume and recommendation letters. I look forward to a personal interview at your earliest convenience.

Sincerely yours,

Dear Professor Lin,

My master's thesis advisor, Professor Chen, suggested that I contact you regarding the possibility of serving as a visiting guest researcher in your laboratory during my upcoming summer vacation in order to enhance my laboratory skills and expertise in biotechnology. Prior to my current pursuit of a Master's degree in Biotechnology at Yuanpei University of Science and Technology, I often heard of your research group's achievements from my undergraduate advisor at National Chiayi University, Dr Liao. As is well known, your research group has made considerable progress in gene expression, regulation and transformation of plant cells, as evidenced by the publishing of your research findings in several internationally renowned journals. I especially enjoyed your recent work involving heat shock proteins in plant cells.

Although my graduate school research in Biotechnology differs from my undergraduate school major in Forestry, my research focus has remained the same, gene expression and transformation in plant cells. Serving as a guest researcher in your laboratory's research group would equip me with the skills necessary to further pursue my research interests. I look forward to your comments regarding this proposal. Thank you in advance for your careful consideration.

Sincerely yours,

Hello,

I would like to serve as a visiting researcher in your laboratory during my upcoming summer vacation. Allow me to briefly introduce myself. After receiving my Bachelors' degree in Radiotechnology from Yuanpei University of Science and Technology (YUST) in 2001, I became a certified radiotechnologist following an intensely competitive, nationwide examination. Besides my current pursuit of a Master's degree in Medical Imagery at the same university, I am departmental leader of radiology technology in the cardiology disease center of a hospital. I specialize in magnetic resonance imagery (MRI), with our research results focusing on its role in combating heart disease, especially the coronary artery.

My current graduate school research at YUST is on enhancing the diagnostic accuracy of heart disease, which will hopefull be the topic of my master's degree thesis. Having read upon your hospital's research findings in the proceedings of several international medical conferences and globally renowned journals, I also am anxious to work in your laboratory as a guest researcher during my upcoming summer vacation.

Please find attached my personal resume and recommendation letters, which will hopefully give you better insight into my academic background and professional expertise. I anxiously look forward to your favorable reply.

Sincerely yours,

Situation 4

Mary Li

dosimetry and microdosimetry-related research

new concepts easily

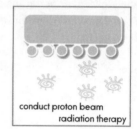

conduct proton beam radiation therapy

Situation 5

Jenny Lin

Bioimage, Java and C++ programs

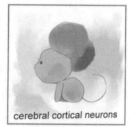

cerebral cortical neurons

firing fluorescence image

Situation 6

Matt Fung

two decades of clinical experience

radiation therapy

learning of new ways

| Write down the key points of the situations on the preceding page, while the instructor reads aloud the script from the Answer Key.

Situation 4

_____

_____

_____

Situation 5

_____

_____

_____

Situation 6

_____

_____

_____

J Oral practice II

Based on the three situations in this unit, write three questions beginning with *What*, and answer them. The questions do not need to come directly from these situations.

Examples

What did Mary's academic advisor, Professor Hsu, suggested that she do?

Contact Professor Tung to ask to work in his laboratory at National Tsing Hua University as a visiting researcher

What clinical experience has Mary acquired?

Four years as a radiographer at a regional hospital

1. _____

_____

2 . _____

_____

3. _____

_____

K Based on the three situations in this unit, write three questions beginning with **Why**, and answer them. The questions do not need to come directly from these situations.

Examples

Why would Jenny like to receive technical training in Professor Dong's laboratory during her upcoming summer vacation?

Because of the laboratory's expertise in developing excellent software for medical instrumentation

Why did Jenny's academic advisor recommend her to work in Professor Dong's laboratory?

To understand what potential technology transfer opportunities are possible in the local medical instrumentation sector

1. _____

_____

2. _____

_____

3. _____

_____

L Based on the three situations in this unit, write three questions beginning with **How**, and answer them. The questions do not need to come directly from these situations.

Examples

How much clinical experience has Matt acquired as a radiology technician?

More than two decades

How has the NYU Clinical Cancer Center distinguished itself?

By its quality of patient care, including privacy, safety and comfort.

1. _____

_____

2. _____

_____

3. _____

_____

M Write questions that match the answers provided.

1. _____

_____

By working in Professor Tung's laboratory

2. _____

_____

Earlier this year

3. _____

_____

The NYU Clinical Cancer Center

N Listening Comprehension II

Situation 4

1. What will Mary be able to do if given the opportunity to work in Professor Tung's laboratory?

    A. determine whether to import proton beam instrumentation from abroad for radiation therapy

    B. research dosimetry, atomic physics, radiation physics and radiation detection physics-related topics

    C. increase her understanding of the dosimetry-related principles

2. Who leads the way in dosimetry and microdosimetry-related research in Taiwan?

    A. Mary's academic advisor and Professor Tung

    B. Yuanpei University of Science and Technology

    C. the Radiation Detection Laboratory

3. Why is the Department of Health drafting a resolution on whether to import proton beam instrumentation from abroad for radiation therapy?

    A. owing to a mandate from Taiwan's Department of Health

    B. owing to Taiwanese governmental legislation on medical treatment

    C. owing to Mary's strong background in engineering mathematics

4. How many years of clinical experience does Mary have as a radiographer at a regional hospital?

    A. four   B. six   C. three

5. When is the planned opening of Hsinchu Biomedical Science Park scheduled?

    A. in 2008   B. in 2006   C. in 2007

Situation 5

1. What does Jenny's academic advisor hope that her working in Professor Dong's

laboratory would help her to do?

A. initiate a long-term collaborative relationship between their two laboratories

B. understand what potential technology transfer opportunities are possible in the local medical instrumentation sector

C. observe quantitatively the formation of functional synapses between cerebral cortical neurons from a mouse

2. What is Jenny's research group involved in?

A. understanding how Bioimage, Java and C++ programs can be more effectively implemented in clinical settings in Taiwan

B. initiating a long-term collaborative relationship between our two laboratories

C. developing an experimental system to observe quantitatively the formation of functional synapses between cerebral cortical neurons from a mouse

3. What did Jenny do following her participation in three National Science Council-sponsored research projects as an undergraduate student?

A. She worked on developing potential technology transfer opportunities in the local medical instrumentation sector.

B. She entered the Master's degree program at the Institute of Medical Imagery at Yuanpei University of Science and Technology

C. She became become more proficient in Bioimage technology and learned how effectively to operate related instruments.

4. Why would Jenny like to receive technical training in Professor Dong's laboratory during her upcoming summer vacation?

A. because of the laboratory's expertise in developing excellent software for medical instrumentation

B. because of the laboratory's expertise in elucidated the interesting phenomenon of synchronous firing

C. because of the laboratory's expertise in more effectively implementing

Bioimage, Java and C++ programs in clinical settings in Taiwan

5. How long would Jenny like to receive technical training in Professor Dong's laboratory?

A. for four months   B. for three months   C. for six months

Situation 6

1. How did Matt become aware of advanced imaging procedures and other diagnostic tests performed at the NYU Clinical Cancer Center to diagnose cancer?

A. in the Radiation Therapy Department at National Taiwan University Hospital

B. in his graduate school courses on advanced imaging processing

C. while developing a radiation therapy planning system that would ensure optimal imaging for diagnosing and treating cancer

2. Why is the NYU Clinical Cancer Center globally recognized?

A. for its new ways to offer patients not only physiological, but also spiritual encouragement

B. for its services that improve the lives of cancer patients

C. for its highly skilled personnel and state-of-the-art equipment and facilities

3. How many articles has Matt's research group published in *Gamma Journal* over the past three years?

A. three   B. two   C. four

4. What is Matt's current research?

A. on the role of magnetic resonance imaging in a herniated inter-vertebral disc

B. on the perfusion function of F-FDG in SPECT

C. on intensity-modulated radiation therapy

5. How much clinical experience has Matt acquired as a radiology technician?

A. nearly two decades   B. more than two decades   C. more than a decade

O Reading Comprehension II
Pick the work or expression whose meaning is closest to the meaning of the underlined word or expression in the following passages.

Situation 4

1. My academic advisor, Professor Hsu, <u>suggested</u> that I contact you to ask to work in your laboratory at National Tsing Hua University as a visiting researcher.

   A. stipulated   B. recommended   C. mandated

2. My academic advisor and you <u>lead the way in</u> dosimetry and microdosimetry-related research in Taiwan.

   A. innovate   B. trail   C. lag behind

3. Having <u>acquired</u> four years of clinical experience as a radiographer at a regional hospital, I am currently pursuing a Master's degree in Medical Imagery at Yuanpei University of Science and Technology, where I am a member of the Radiation Detection Laboratory.

   A. attained   B. relinquished   C. render

4. Having acquired four years of clinical experience as a radiographer at a regional hospital, I am currently pursuing a Master's degree in Medical Imagery at Yuanpei University of Science and Technology, where I <u>am a member of</u> the Radiation Detection Laboratory.

   A. supervise   B. coordinate   C. belong to

5. As well as having a strong <u>background</u> in engineering mathematics, I enjoy researching dosimetry, atomic physics, radiation physics and radiation detection physics-related topics.

   A. inquisitiveness   B. foundation   C. curiosity

6. Despite my <u>lack of</u> a pure science or engineering-related background, I am

confident that my solid logical and statistical skills will prove invaluable to any research effort in which I am involved at your laboratory.

A. deficiency in   B. wealth of   C. profusion of

7. Despite my lack of a pure science or engineering-related background, I am confident that my <u>solid</u> logical and statistical skills will prove invaluable to any research effort in which I am involved at your laboratory.

A. unsound   B. sturdy   C. feeble

8. Despite my lack of a pure science or engineering-related background, I am confident that my solid <u>logical</u> and statistical skills will prove invaluable to any research effort in which I am involved at your laboratory.

A. invalid   B. spurious   C. rational

9. Despite my lack of a pure science or engineering-related background, I am confident that my solid logical and statistical skills will prove <u>invaluable</u> to any research effort in which I am involved at your laboratory.

A. inestimable   B. worthless   C. inexpensive

10. Moreover, I consider myself <u>diligent</u> and able to grasp new concepts easily.

A. unfruitful   B. unproductive   C. industrious

11. Moreover, I consider myself diligent and able to <u>grasp</u> new concepts easily.

A. fathom   B. misconceive   C. misconstrue

12. Proton beam <u>instrumentation</u> has been used in radiation therapy for several years.

A. software   B. machinery   C. data

13. According to Taiwan's Department of Health, only five facilities worldwide are <u>equipped</u> to conduct proton beam radiation therapy.

A. unintentional   B. prepared   C. random

14. Owing to Taiwanese governmental legislation on medical treatment, the Department of Health is <u>drafting</u> a resolution on whether to import proton beam

instrumentation from abroad for radiation therapy.

A. debilitating　B. deconstructing　C. outlining

15. Owing to Taiwanese governmental legislation on medical treatment, the Department of Health is drafting a <u>resolution</u> on whether to import proton beam instrumentation from abroad for radiation therapy.

A. summary　B. proposal　C. resilience

16. Owing to Taiwanese governmental legislation on medical treatment, the Department of Health is drafting a resolution on whether to <u>import</u> proton beam instrumentation from abroad for radiation therapy.

A. bring in　B. send out　C. export

17. As widely <u>anticipated</u>, proton beam radiation therapy has many promising applications in Taiwan, making dosimetry-related principles applicable by medical physicists in radiation therapy.

A. determined　B. expected　C. estimated

18. As widely anticipated, proton beam radiation therapy has many <u>promising</u> applications in Taiwan, making dosimetry-related principles applicable by medical physicists in radiation therapy.

A. sterile　B. potential　C. barren

19. As widely anticipated, proton beam radiation therapy has many promising applications in Taiwan, making dosimetry-related principles <u>applicable</u> by medical physicists in radiation therapy.

A. relevant　B. immaterial　C. extraneous

20. The opportunity to serve as a visiting researcher in your laboratory will allow me more fully to <u>explore</u> the above topics and their clinical implications.

A. drift　B. meander　C. probe

21. The opportunity to serve as a visiting researcher in your laboratory will allow me more fully to explore the above topics and their clinical <u>implications</u>.

A. factors   B. inklings   C. circumstances

22. I look forward to your <u>favorable</u> response.

A. propitious   B. adverse   C. inauspicious

Situation 5

1. Given your laboratory's <u>expertise</u> in developing excellent software for medical instrumentation, I would like to receive technical training in your laboratory during my upcoming summer vacation.

A. mastery   B. amateurish   C. dilettantish

2. Given your laboratory's expertise in developing excellent software for medical instrumentation, I would like to receive technical training in your laboratory during my <u>upcoming</u> summer vacation.

A. preceding   B. delayed   C. approaching

3. I wish to understand how Bioimage, Java and C++ programs can be more effectively <u>implemented</u> in clinical settings in Taiwan.

A. abandoned   B. utilized   C. neglected

4. I wish to understand how Bioimage, Java and C++ programs can be more effectively implemented in clinical <u>settings</u> in Taiwan.

A. conformity   B. congruence   C. environments

5. My academic advisor recommended that working in your laboratory would help me to understand what <u>potential</u> technology transfer opportunities are possible in the local medical instrumentation sector.

A. possible   B. inconceivable   C. impractical

6. My academic advisor recommended that working in your laboratory would help me to understand what potential technology transfer opportunities are possible in the <u>local</u> medical instrumentation sector.

A. worldwide   B. international   C. domestic

7. My academic advisor recommended that working in your laboratory would help me to understand what potential technology transfer opportunities are possible in the local medical instrumentation <u>sector</u>.

A. academic institution　B. industry　C. financial institution

8. Earlier this year, following my participation in three National Science Council-sponsored research projects as an <u>undergraduate</u> student at Tzu Chi College of Technology, I entered the Master's degree program at the Institute of Medical Imagery at Yuanpei University of Science and Technology earlier this year.

A. pursuing a vocational school diploma

B. pursuing a master's degree

C. pursuing a bachelor's degree

9. Specifically, our research group is developing an experimental system to <u>observe</u> quantitatively the formation of functional synapses between cerebral cortical neurons from a mouse.

A. discern　B. avert　C. deviate

10. Specifically, our research group is developing an experimental system to observe <u>quantitatively</u> the formation of functional synapses between cerebral cortical neurons from a mouse.

A. from a broad perspective　B. generally　C. analytically

11. Specifically, our research group is developing an experimental system to observe quantitatively the <u>formation</u> of functional synapses between cerebral cortical neurons from a mouse.

A. establishment　B. liquidation　C. purge

12. Our experimental results have so far <u>elucidated</u> the interesting phenomenon of synchronous firing, whose frequency increases as a function of the culture period.

A. generalized　B. universalized　C. clarified

13. Our experimental results have so far elucidated the interesting <u>phenomenon</u> of synchronous firing, whose frequency increases as a function of the culture period.

    A. unexplained event B. certainty C. assurance

14. Our experimental results have so far elucidated the interesting phenomenon of synchronous firing, whose <u>frequency</u> increases as a function of the culture period.

    A. scarcity B. routine occurrence C. want

15. Our laboratory is developing a <u>unique</u> scanning laser confocal microscope to measure the firing fluorescence image.

    A. paralleled B. rivaled C. incomparable

16. Our laboratory is developing a unique scanning laser confocal microscope to <u>measure</u> the firing fluorescence image.

    A. determine B. evade C. elude

17. However, <u>continuing with</u> this experimentation requires additional instrumentation and technological expertise, which I currently lack.

    A. ceasing B. stalling C. proceeding with

18. However, continuing with this experimentation requires additional instrumentation and technological expertise, which I currently <u>lack</u>.

    A. possess B. deficient of C. retain

19. I would therefore like to receive technical <u>training</u> for four months in your laboratory.

    A. mandate B. legislation C. instruction

20. Unlike <u>ordinary</u> technical training, this four month technical visit will hopefully initiate a long-term collaborative relationship between our two laboratories.

    A. run-of-the-mill B. rare C. atypical

21. Unlike ordinary technical training, this four month technical visit will hopefully

initiate a long-term collaborative relationship between our two laboratories.

A. terminate   B. wrap up   C. embark

22. During this period, I am keen to become more proficient in Bioimage technology
and learn how effectively to operate related instruments.

A. eager   B. hesitant   C. reluctant

23. During this period, I am keen to become more proficient in Bioimage technology
and learn how effectively to operate related instruments.

A. nonprofessional   B. dilettantish   C. masterful

Situation 6

1. The Radiation Therapy Department at National Taiwan University Hospital,
where I have acquired more than two decades of clinical experience as a radiology
technician, would like me to receive advanced training in cancer therapy as a
visiting researcher in your Clinical Cancer Center.

A. bestowed   B. relinquished   C. procured

2. The Radiation Therapy Department at National Taiwan University Hospital,
where I have acquired more than two decades of clinical experience as a radiology
technician, would like me to receive advanced training in cancer therapy as a
visiting researcher in your Clinical Cancer Center.

A. hospital-oriented   B. administrative-oriented   C. finance-oriented

3. I have extensive professional experience, and am now pursuing a Master's degree
in Medical Imagery at Yuapei University of Science and Technology.

A. confining   B. cramped   C. expansive

4. I have extensive professional experience, and am now pursuing a Master's degree
in Medical Imagery at Yuapei University of Science and Technology.

A. unethical   B. adept   C. amateurish

5. Given the opportunity, I will perform advanced research at the NYU Clinical

Cancer Center, which has highly skilled personnel and state-of-the-art equipment and facilities.

   A. impediment   B. hindrance   C. opening

6. Given the opportunity, I will perform <u>advanced</u> research at the NYU Clinical Cancer Center, which has highly skilled personnel and state-of-the-art equipment and facilities.

   A. progressive   B. retrogressive   C. reverted

7. It is globally <u>recognized</u> for its services that improve the lives of cancer patients.

   A. unaccredited   B. shunned   C. accepted

8. It is globally recognized for its services that <u>improve</u> the lives of cancer patients.

   A. degrade   B. elevate   C. deteriorate

9. Given the opportunity, I will perform advanced research at the NYU Clinical Cancer Center, which has <u>highly skilled</u> personnel and state-of-the-art equipment and facilities.

   A. inadequate   B. incapable   C. competent

10. The NYU Clinical Cancer Center has <u>distinguished itself</u> by its quality of patient care, including privacy, safety and comfort.

   A. denigrated itself   B. made a mark for itself   C. downgraded itself

11. The NYU Clinical Cancer Center has distinguished itself by its quality of patient care, including privacy, safety and <u>comfort</u>.

   A. hardship   B. rigor   C. ease

12. In my graduate school courses on advanced imaging processing, I became <u>aware</u> of advanced imaging procedures and other diagnostic tests performed at the NYU Clinical Cancer Center to diagnose cancer.

   A. cognizant   B. oblivious   C. uninformed

13. <u>Working in</u> your organization would give me a practical context for the concepts learned in class.

A. Supervising　B. employed by　C. coordinating

14. One of our articles <u>addressed</u> the preservation of hearing in nasal and pharyngeal cancer patients who had received post-irradiation treatment.

A. digressed from　B. neglected　C. confronted

15. One of our articles addressed the <u>preservation</u> of hearing in nasal and pharyngeal cancer patients who had received post-irradiation treatment.

A. degeneracy　B. protection　C. atrophy

16. As the NYU Clinical Cancer Center is widely <u>regarded</u> as having the best radiation therapy planning system for cancer treatment worldwide, I hope that my above research interests are in line with those of your research group.

A. viewed　B. obstructed　C. concealed

17. As the NYU Clinical Cancer Center is widely regarded as having the <u>best</u> radiation therapy planning system for cancer treatment worldwide, I hope that my above research interests are in line with those of your research group.

A. undistinguished　B. mediocre　C. optimal

18. As the NYU Clinical Cancer Center is widely regarded as having the best radiation therapy planning system for cancer treatment worldwide, I hope that my above research interests are <u>in line with</u> those of your research group.

A. compatible　B. incongruent　C. inconsistent

19. More specifically, I am interested in developing a radiation therapy planning system that would <u>ensure</u> optimal imaging for diagnosing and treating cancer.

A. guarantee　B. dispute　C. discredit

20. I am also interested in learning of new ways to offer patients not only <u>physiological</u>, but also spiritual encouragement.

A. Intellectual　B. anatomical　C. cerebral

21. I am also interested in learning of new ways to offer patients not only physiological, but also <u>spiritual</u> encouragement.

A. religious   B. materialistic   C. masterly

22. I am also interested in learning of new ways to offer patients not only physiological, but also spiritual <u>encouragement</u>.

A. inspiration   B. dissatisfaction   C. discontent

P Matching Exercise

1. Each sentence in the following is commonly used to seek technical training: summarizing one's academic or professional experiences 科技訓練請求信函：某人學歷及工作經驗概述. Each phrase on the left should be matched with one on the right in order to complete the sentence. Match a number on the left with a letter on the right.

1. The attached resume and recommendation letters provide	a. handle various requests and difficult situations, enabling me to resolve problems efficiently.
2. Relevant project experiences have significantly strengthened my	b. the need to continuously grow academically and professionally, albeit with a cordial and earnest attitude.
3. I received my undergraduate training in the Healthcare Management at National Taipei College of Nursing (NTCN),	c. personal resume, university academic transcripts and letter of recommendation from our university president.
4. Intensive on-the-job training enabled me to	d. I often read supplemental literature to remain abreast of the latest technological trends.
5. University instructors equipped me with strong academic fundamentals in food science and technology,	e. further details of my solid academic background and professional experiences.
6. I view myself as a responsible individual that highly prioritizes	f. more receptive to accepting new challenges.
7. Please find enclosed my	g. which further spurred my interest in this area of research.
8. Performing independent research has definitely made me	h. independent research capabilities as well as statistical and analytical skills.
9. In addition to these academic and professional activities,	i. to how my personal strengths match the needs of your research group.
10. The attached resume will give you a better idea as	j. with a subsequent Master's degree in Business Management from Yuanpei University of Science and Technology.

2. Seeking technical training: summarizing one's academic or professional experiences 科技訓練請求信函：某人學歷及工作經驗概述

1. My graduate school research focused on designing and applying relevant marketing strategies to the bedding franchisee selection model,	a. the latest methods and theories involving clinical examination, including clinical biochemistry, clinical microbiology, clinical immunology and clinical hematology.
2. My resume contains additional references from individuals	b. all of whom can give you a better idea of my background and ability to work with others.
3. Study at the graduate and undergraduate levels has fully oriented me on	c. I have prepared for a marketing-related career, hopefully at your corporation.
4. Graduate school made me proficient in resolving a wide array of marketing problems,	d. by taking courses on management in the medical sector at Yangming University.
5. My resume contains additional references,	e. as evidenced by my ranking among the top five scholastically in Marketing-related courses.
6. I passed the Taiwanese governmental civil service examination in 1994,	f. I will complete my master's degree requirements from the Institute of Business Management at Yuanpei University of Science and Technology in the spring of 2005.
7. The attached resume will give you a clearer idea of how	g. with those findings submitted to an international journal for publication.
8. Marketing has interested me immensely throughout undergraduate and graduate school,	h. subsequently securing an administrative position in our country's National Health Insurance organization.
9. While working, I continued to enhance my proficiency skills in administrative-related tasks	i. subsequently spurring my creativity and analytical capabilities.
10. First exposed to hospital management during undergraduate school,	j. who can shed light on my solid academic training and ability to closely collaborate with others.

3. Seeking technical training: requesting technical training 科技訓練請求信函：科技訓練申請

1. My academic advisor, Dr. Cheng,	a. a three month stay in your laboratory as a self-supported guest researcher, hopefully this upcoming summer.
2. Eager to strengthen my knowledge expertise in this field,	b. to pave the way for future technological exchanges between our two organizations.
3. I hope to visit your organization	c. clinical experience in proton therapy technology from your research center.
4. I would like to serve as a visiting researcher in your Trauma Burn Center	d. would allow me to further explore the above research topic.
5. Eager to understand the dynamic environment that your work involves, I would like to arrange for	e. as a visiting researcher to learn of the latest trends in this area for three months this year.
6. The opportunity to serve in a self-supported guest researcher position in your laboratory would	f. your company's Management Department for a three month period, hopefully during my upcoming summer vacation.
7. My academic advisor, Professor Hsu, would like me to receive	g. further orient me on how to become more proficient in this line of research.
8. The opportunity to serve as a guest researcher in your laboratory for three to eight months	h. recommended that I contact you regarding the possibility of a guest researcher stay in your laboratory.
9. To build upon the above academic and professional experiences, I would like to serve as a self-supported guest researcher in	i. knowledgeable of integrated information systems that service all departments within an enterprise.
10. I am eager to join your organization as a marketing specialist	j. I hope to serve in your laboratory as a guest worker to compensate for my lack of training and practical laboratory experiences in this area.

4. Seeking technical training: requesting technical training 科技訓練請求信函：科技訓練申請

1. A one month technical training period at your organization appears to be	a. explaining why I would like to receive technical training over a four month period in your laboratory.
2. If you allow me to serve as a guest worker in your laboratory, I will	b. a guest worker in your healthcare organization during my upcoming summer vacation.
3. Continuing further with this experimentation requires additional instrumentation and technological expertise,	c. a self-supported practicum internship in your company.
4. I hope to receive training at your hospital	d. your recent research results, I hope to serve as a self-supported guest researcher in your laboratory for a six month period (January through June of 2005).
5. I would like to serve as	e. recommended that I contact you regarding the possibility of a guest researcher stay in your laboratory.
6. Upon the recommendation of my master's thesis advisor, Professor Hsu, I hope to receive training in biopharmaceuticals in your research group	f. upon successful completion of my graduate school requirements.
7. I hope to secure employment in your globally reputed bedding corporation	g. as a visiting guest worker, hopefully during my upcoming summer vacation.
8. I would like to serve in	h. the most effective means of initiating a collaborative research between our two organizations.
9. Having read extensively on	i. on the latest advances in infarct stroke technology.
10. My academic advisor, Dr. Cheng,	j. send the detailed visiting itinerary shortly.

5. Seeking technical training: commending the organization to receive technical training from 科技訓練請求信函：讚揚提供科技訓練的機構

1. As your laboratory has devoted much time in researching the above topics, I would greatly benefit from	a. your findings published in international journals.
2. As a leader in this field of research,	b. food research for quite some time, developments that I have closely followed for quite some time.
3. While searching for pertinent research literature in my field, I often come across	c. as evidenced by the publishing of your research findings in several internationally renowned journals.
4. As is well known, your research group has	d. the most appropriate place.
5. From your laboratory's online introduction, I am impressed with	e. as well as its globally recognized services for improving the lives of cancer patients.
6. Your company has distinguished itself in	f. in researching cardiological intervention-related topics.
7. As is well known, your research group has made considerable progress in gene expression, regulation and transformation of plant cells,	g. the opportunity to work in your laboratory as a self-supported researcher during my upcoming summer vacation.
8. Your division is widely recognized as a leader	h. the comprehensive strategies that you adopt in clinical practice.
9. Given my research interests, your laboratory appears to be	i. your laboratory could allow me to further refine my radiation therapy-related skills.
10. I hope to perform advanced research in your center owing to its highly skilled personnel, state-of-the-art equipment and facilities,	j. devoted considerable time and resources to researching biopharmaceutical-related topics.

6. Seeking technical training: commending the organization to receive technical training from 科技訓練請求信函：讚揚提供科技訓練的機構

1. After reviewing your online brochure and research findings published in international journals, I am quite impressed with	a. my graduate level research and current work direction.
2. As your center is widely regarded as having	b. your Marketing Information Department has undertaken successfully in recent years.
3. I have much to learn from your organization, which would greatly facilitate	c. in holding the 12th International Conference on Health Promotion in Hospitals, I am most interested in learning from your rich experience in this area.
4. Your hospital offers comprehensive and challenging training	d. the best radiation therapy planning system for cancer treatment worldwide, I hope that my above research interests are in line with those of your research group.
5. From an article I read in *Business Weekly*, I was quite impressed with the diverse array of projects that	e. which are quite compatible with my current esearch interests.
6. After thoroughly reviewing your online literature and promotional materials, I am especially drawn to the marketing strategies that your organization has adopted,	f. to work in your laboratory as a guest researcher during my upcoming summer vacation.
7. Having read upon your hospital's research findings in the proceedings of several international medical conferences and globally renowned journals, I also am anxious	g. orients consumers on the healthy aspect of your products.
8. Given your hospital's recent success	h. your laboratory's facilities and the wide scope of activities that you are engaged in.
9. I am especially drawn to your corporation's emphasis on customization that	i. progressive policies in welfare of its elderly population, including state-of-the-art facilities.
10. Your country has pioneered	j. for individuals committed to this area of research and development, having distinguished itself in the training of highly skilled radiological technologists.

7. Seeking technical training: explaining the details of the technical training 科技訓練請求信函：科技訓練細節解釋

1. Specifically, we are concerned with	a. at a range between US$50 to US$100 daily.
2. If given the opportunity, I would like exposure	b. under your supervision.
3. As for my accommodation during the guest stay, I would like to lease a single-room hotel,	c. about the latest data analysis theories and methods.
4. If granted this opportunity, I am open to	d. to the following topics:
5. If possible, I hope to work directly	e. the most appropriate time frame.
6. I am especially interested in learning	f. clinical practice as well as share with you our relevant research experiences in this field.
7. A six month period as a guest worker would probably be	g. of a self-supported guest worker at your laboratory.
8. Well aware of your organization's expertise in this area, I hope to acquire	h. how to effectively restrain increases in medical fees.
9. The proposed format is that	i. investigating related topics with your highly skilled staff.
10. To facilitate my upcoming stay as a guest researcher in your laboratory, could you please send me	j. the formal application materials for this activity?

8. Seeking technical training: explaining the details of the technical training 科技訓練請求信函：科技訓練細節解釋

1. I am most concerned with	a. this profession, I hope to measure the infarct field range with an order of severity level.
2. Despite my preferences, I am open to	b. in the latest management strategies and Internet marketing applications as possible.
3. I am especially interested in acquiring as much knowledge expertise	c. in addition to that found in the accompanying resume and recommendation letters.
4. Given my deep interest in	d. investigating related topics with your highly skilled staff.
5. Of course, all expenses incurred	e. more thoroughly discuss my academic background and professional experiences, as well as the topics to be covered during my stay at your hospital.
6. If granted this opportunity, I am open to	f. you can directly contact my academic advisor Dr. T.G Zhu for further details.
7. As for references, you can directly contact	g. how such trends in long-term health care will impact Taiwan.
8. I would be happy to supply additional information,	h. during this period would be covered by my Institute.
9. I hope that you could arrange for a personal interview so that we can	i. investigating any related topics which you would deem beneficial during my stay.
10. After reviewing my academic background and professional competency in the attached resume,	j. my academic advisor, whose address is listed in the accompanying resume.

9. Seeking technical training: expressing optimism in the possibility of technical training 科技訓練請求信函：表達對科技訓練機會的樂觀態度

1. I look forward to hearing from you soon as to whether	a. matches that of your research group, I am anxious to look for potentially collaborative activities that would be mutually beneficial.
2. I am confident in my ability to work under your supervision in a research fellowship	b. with an excellent environment not only to fully realize my career aspirations, but also to upgrade my own technological expertise.
3. The opportunity to work in a practicum internship in your company would provide me	c. an asset to any effort that I belong to in your laboratory.
4. Exposure to the way in which your department applies the latest marketing sales concepts in a practical context would	d. context for the concepts learned in class.
5. My previous experience in applying theoretical concepts to analysis and related applications will hopefully prove to be	e. give me a clearer direction not only my graduate level research, but also my chosen career path as well.
6. Given that the research direction of our laboratory closely	f. as an aspiring researcher in this field, as I search for a more practical context for the academic concepts taught in class.
7. Working in your organization would give me a practical	g. such cooperation would be feasible.
8. The opportunity to work in your laboratory would mature me	h. in applying theoretical concepts to survey research and statistics.
9. More than the opportunity to receive technical training, this four month technical visit	i. with your highly skilled research personnel, an opportunity that would greatly advance my competency as a food research biologist.
10. I hope that I can contribute my previous experience	j. will hopefully initiate a long-term collaborative relationship between our two laboratories.

10. Seeking technical training: expressing optimism in the possibility of technical training 科技訓練請求信函：表達對科技訓練機會的樂觀態度

1. If granted this opportunity, I am confident of my ability not only	a. practical context for the marketing theories acquired in graduate school.
2. Given my considerable laboratory experience in this area, I am confident of my ability to	b. to any collaborative effort that I belong to in your company.
3. The opportunity to work in a globally competitive environment such as the one that your company offers would offer me a more	c. research design and methodology that will hopefully contribute to your company's efforts to enhance operational quality.
4. If given the opportunity to gain exposure to your excellent work environment, I would be able to remain abreast	d. excellent environment to fully realize my career aspirations.
5. The opportunity to work in a practicum internship in your company would provide me with an	e. for my lack of formal professional experience in this area.
6. Somewhat familiar with the scope of your company's marketing activities, I am confident that my previous	f. regarding this proposal.
7. Such an opportunity would compensate	g. to understand the clinical applications of this field, but also to integrate a theoretical and practical understanding as well.
8. I would greatly appreciate your comments	h. academic and professional experiences will prove valuable to any collaborative effort that I belong to.
9. I am confident that my previous academic and professional experiences will prove valuable	i. contribute to the development of a more innovative experimental design.
10. I bring to your corporation a solid understanding of	j. of current trends in marketing research in a practical context.

11. Seeking technical training: expressing optimism in the possibility of technical training 科技訓練請求信函：表達對科技訓練機會的樂觀態度

1. I am diligent and	a. this proposal that will hopefully lead to technological collaboration in the near future.
2. I consider myself to be diligent and would have no problems	b. would equip me with the skills necessary to design and implement marketing strategies for this unique niche sector.
3. I look forward to your favorable reply regarding	c. in adjusting to new circumstances in your highly competitive working environment.
4. I would appreciate it if you arrange for an	d. as a visiting researcher in your laboratory will allow me to more fully understand the latest trends in magnetic transfer images.
5. The opportunity to serve as a self-supported guest worker in the research group of your organization	e. the expectations that you hold for marketing personnel.
6. I hope that this technical training will pave the way	f. but also to contribute to any effort that I participate in during the guest worker period.
7. I am confident of my ability not only to familiarize myself with your corporate operations,	g. of your decision at your earliest convenience.
8. Building upon this solid academic foundation and clinical experiences in the MRI field, I hope that serving	h. able to adjust to new circumstances.
9. Please carefully consider my request and inform me	i. for our two organizations to concentrate efforts to use computer-coregisteration images when diagnosing a human stroke.
10. I am confident that my academic and professional experiences will match	j. interview at your earliest convenience.

Unit Two

Becky Ko
Germany on May 2005

patents

visit

Sam Long
look forward to

differentiate the infarction area

exchange data and experiences

Exchanging Information

資訊交流信函

Vocabulary and related expressions 相關字詞

exhibition 展示
information exchange relationship
資訊交換合作關係
elderly individuals 年長者
technology transfer 技術移轉
joint venture 合資企業
aggressive marketing strategy
有幹勁的市場策略
collaborating with 和某人合作
committed significant resources to
指定重大的資源給
published 被發表的
attenuated（使）變（稀）薄
ulcers 潰瘍
incidence rates 發生事故比率
infection 傳染

look forward to an opportunity to
期待一個機會去
the extent to which 在某程度上
accurately predict 準確預測
incidence 影響範圍
characterization（對人或物的）特性描述
tentative plans 試驗性的計畫
exchange technological information
交換科技資訊
induce 引誘
Intellectual Property Office 經濟部智慧財產局
Ministry of Economic Affairs 經濟部
consumer trends 消費趨勢
has distinguished itself 使本身顯出特色
niche 合適的職務（或地位等）
collaborative relationship 合作關係

purifying 使純淨

areas of mutual interest 相互利益

open doors to 對……開放

future collaboration 相互合作

innovative 創新的

technology transfer 技術移轉

strives 努力

appears to be unlimited 顯示出無限制的

is committed to 作出保證

boost international competitiveness
促進國際競爭力

exchange of experiences 經驗交換

convenient 便利的

concern over 影響到

long-term collaborative ties
長期合作關係

clinical experience 臨床經驗

radiation therapy 放射線治療

focusing on 集中精神

acquired 養成的

aspiring 有抱負的

strive 奮鬥

therapeutic planning system
有療效計畫系統

dissemination 宣傳

highly qualified technical personnel
高度合格的科技人員

continued success 接連的成功

research personnel 研究人員（總稱）

therapeutic treatment 有療效的治療

state-of-the-art technology 先進的技術

advanced expertise 先進的專門知識

stroke-related factors 中風相關因素

long-lasting cooperative relationships
長遠合作關係

satisfy consumer demand 滿足客戶需求

maturation 成熟

open sharing 分享

tentative plans 試驗性的計畫

organizational scope 組織領域

committed significant resources
指定重大的資源給

two decades 二十年

resolve 解決

innovation 創新

firmly believe 堅定的相信

publication 出版

integration 整合

joint collaboration 合資合作

Chinese herbal medicine 中藥

extraction 抽出

wide-reaching organizations 目標廣大的機構

fuelled by 被……激起

feasibility 可能性

assessment 評估

Situation 1

Becky Ko

Situation 2

Sam Long

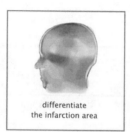

Situation 3

Amy Huang

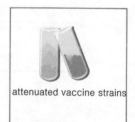

A Write down the key points of the situations on the preceding page, while the instructor reads aloud the script from the Answer Key.

Situation 1

_____

_____

_____

Situation 2

_____

_____

_____

Situation 3

_____

_____

_____

B Oral practice I

Based on the three situations in this unit, write three questions beginning with **How**, and answer them. The questions do not need to come directly from these situations.

Examples

How has the Taiwanese branch of this bedding company increased its number of business units?

By pursuing an aggressive marketing strategy since 2000

How has the R&D Division of the Taiwanese branch responded to the rapid growth of Taiwan's elderly population?

By committing significant resources to designing bedding customized for elderly individuals

1. _____

_____

2. _____

_____

3. _____

_____

C Based on the three situations in this unit, write three questions beginning with ***What***, and answer them. The questions do not need to come directly from these situations.

Examples

What position does Sam hold at S.W.M Memorial Hospital?

A member of the technical staff of the Nuclear Medicine Department

What does Sam's work involve?

Various stages of the therapeutic treatment of acute stroke patients

1. _____

_____

2. _____

_____

3. _____

_____

D Based on the three situations in this unit, write three questions beginning with **Why**, and answer them. The questions do not need to come directly from these situations.

Examples

Why would Amy like to visit Mr. Haas's organization?

To exchange technological information regarding gene expression, the assay function of proteins and related transformation mechanisms

Why is Amy collaborating with her professor in a National Science Council-sponsored research project?

To generate a mutant library from a clinical isolate of Helicobacter pylori

1. _____

_____

2. _____

_____

3. _____

_____

E Write questions that match the answers provided.

1. _____

_____

A new factory next year

2. _____

_____

Nearly 100

3. _____

_____

Producing an antiserum, preparing membranes and purifying proteins from inclusion bodies

F Listening Comprehension I

Situation 1

1. What does the Taiwanese branch office tentatively plan to do?

    A. pursue an aggressive marketing strategy

    B. advance the latest technological developments in bedding comfort, the marketing of these products, and consumer relations in this niche

    C. construct a new factory next year and broaden its organizational scope

2. What has the R&D Division of the Taiwanese branch committed significant resources to?

    A. meeting with departmental managers and research personnel

    B. emphasizing electrically heated bedding and customized pillows

    C. designing bedding customized for elderly individuals

3. What kind of information exchange relationship is Becky proposing?

    A. regarding a technology transfer

    B. regarding the sleeping needs of elderly individuals

    C. regarding a joint venture opportunity

4. What is Becky requesting prior to the visit to the company?

    A. materials regarding the company's technological developments and marketing strategies in this area

    B. samples of electrically heated bedding and customized pillows

    C. patent information

5. What has grown rapidly in recent years?

    A. the Intellectual Property Office of the Ministry of Economic Affairs

    B. Taiwan's elderly population

    C. technological developments and marketing strategies in this area

Situation 2

1. How many stroke patients do neurological departments in Taiwan admit weekly for clinical treatment?

   A. nearly 150   B. nearly 100   C. over 100

2. What has S.W.M Memorial Hospital spent considerable resources to do?

   A. exchange data and experiences in the field of brain stroke patients

   B. improve continuously expertise in medical diagnosis

   C. reduce the risk of stroke and solve problems that involve blood flow in the brain

3. How could collaboration between Mr. Push's and Sam's organizations be mutually beneficial?

   A. It would allow them to differentiate the infarction area in irreversibly damaged tissue.

   B. It would allow both of their organizations to improve continuously expertise in medical diagnosis.

   C. It would allow them to emphasize stroke-related factors leading to mortality.

4. What does S.W.M. Hospital's advanced PET technological capacity enable it to do?

   A. reduce the incidence of stroke

   B. identify abnormal sites in the infarct area

   C. determine the extent to which tracer uptake reduction can accurately predict neurological recovery

5. How did Sam learn how Mr. Push's laboratory has reduced semihemisphere bleeding using coregisteration technology?

   A. while sharing and exchanging relevant experiences

   B. while discussing areas of common knowledge

   C. while reading the January 2003 issue of *Nuclear Medicine Journal*

Situation 3

1. Why would Mary like to visit Mr. Haas's organization?

   A. to produce an antiserum, preparing membranes and purify proteins from inclusion bodies

   B. to identify associated proteins

   C. to exchange technological information regarding gene expression, the assay function of proteins and related transformation mechanisms

2. How does Amy hope to be able to identify areas of mutual interest?

   A. through characterization of genes and their role in the natural transformation of Helicobacter pylori

   B. through a technological information exchange

   C. through the development of an effective and safe vaccine

3. What opens the possibility of prevention through the development of an effective and safe vaccine?

   A. the fact that the incidence rates of women and men are nearly identical

   B. the fact that proteins are purified from inclusion bodies

   C. the fact that most ulcers are caused by an infection with *Helicobacter pylori*

4. How many Americans suffer from an ulcer during their lifetimes?

   A. nearly 25 million　B. over 25 million　C. over 20 million

5. Who can get ulcers?

   A. individuals of all ages　B. mostly women　C. mostly men

G Reading Comprehension I
Pick the work or expression whose meaning is closest to the meaning of the underlined word or expression in the following passages.

Situation 1

1. Thank you for your message sent via e-mail and dated December 31, 2004, inviting our Taiwanese branch office to <u>exhibit</u> its innovative bedding and pillow products in Cologne, Germany on May 2005.

   A. obscure   B. display   C. shroud

2. Thank you for your message sent via e-mail and dated December 31, 2004, inviting our Taiwanese branch office to exhibit its <u>innovative</u> bedding and pillow products in Cologne, Germany on May 2005.

   A. lifeless   B. lackluster   C. ingenious

3. Before <u>participating in</u> the exhibition, I would like to propose an information exchange relationship between our two organizations regarding the sleeping needs of elderly individuals, hopefully leading to a technology transfer or joint venture opportunity in the near future.

   A. disenfranchising   B. engaging in   C. withdrawing from

4. Before participating in the exhibition, I would like to propose an information exchange relationship between our two organizations regarding the sleeping needs of <u>elderly</u> individuals, hopefully leading to a technology transfer or joint venture opportunity in the near future.

   A. adolescents   B. juveniles   C. senior citizens

5. Before participating in the exhibition, I would like to propose an information exchange relationship between our two organizations regarding the sleeping needs of elderly individuals, hopefully leading to a technology transfer or <u>joint</u> venture

opportunity in the near future.

　A. cooperative　B. autonomous　C. solitary

6. Before participating in the exhibition, I would like to propose an information exchange relationship between our two organizations regarding the sleeping needs of elderly individuals, hopefully leading to a technology transfer or joint <u>venture</u> opportunity in the near future.

　A. undertaking　B. regulation　C. mandate

7. The Taiwanese <u>branch</u> of this bedding company has increased its number of business units by pursuing an aggressive marketing strategy since 2000.

　A. firm　B. corporation　C. subsidiary

8. The Taiwanese branch of this bedding company has increased its number of business units by <u>pursuing</u> an aggressive marketing strategy since 2000.

　A. abstain from　B. desist from　C. contending for

9. The Taiwanese branch of this bedding company has increased its number of business units by pursuing an <u>aggressive</u> marketing strategy since 2000.

　A. inactive　B. assertive　C. insipid

10. It has more than 20 units across the island and has <u>seen</u> a dramatic increase in sales volume.

　A. enshrouded　B. witnessed　C. obscured

11. It has more than 20 units across the island and has seen a <u>dramatic</u> increase in sales volume.

　A. significant　B. diminutive　C. slight

12. The branch office <u>tentatively</u> plans to construct a new factory next year and broaden its organizational scope.

　A. speculatively　B. unquestionably　C. indisputably

13. The branch office tentatively plans to <u>construct</u> a new factory next year and broaden its organizational scope.

A. cancel   B. terminate   C. assemble

14. The branch office tentatively plans to construct a new factory next year and underline broaden its organizational scope.

    A. expand   B. confine   C. constrain

15. Franchises are helped to outperform the competition, as evidenced by our development of several bedding and pillow types and emphasis on electrically heated bedding and customized pillows.

    A. surpass   B. lag behind   C. wane

16. Franchises are helped to outperform the competition, as evidenced by our development of several bedding and pillow types and emphasis on electrically heated bedding and customized pillows.

    A. conjectured   B. attested   C. assumed

17. Franchises are helped to outperform the competition, as evidenced by our development of several bedding and pillow types and emphasis on electrically heated bedding and customized pillows.

    A. dilapidation   B. disrepair   C. stress

18. Franchises are helped to outperform the competition, as evidenced by our development of several bedding and pillow types and emphasis on electrically heated bedding and customized pillows.

    A. standard   B. tailored   C. conventional

19. Taiwan's elderly population has grown rapidly in recent years, and the bedding market has generated considerable revenues.

    A. inhabitants   B. emigrants   C. refugees

20. Taiwan's elderly population has grown rapidly in recent years, and the bedding market has generated considerable revenues.

    A. awkwardly   B. sluggishly   C. expeditiously

21. Given this trend, the R&D Division of the Taiwanese branch has committed

significant resources to designing bedding customized for elderly individuals.

A. diverted   B. withdrawn   C. relegated

22. Given this trend, the R&D Division of the Taiwanese branch has committed significant resources to designing bedding customized for elderly individuals.

A. marginal   B. substantial   C. peripheral

23. Given this trend, the R&D Division of the Taiwanese branch has committed significant <u>resources</u> to designing bedding customized for elderly individuals.

A. assets   B. liabilities   C. deficits

24. The Intellectual Property Office of the Ministry of Economic Affairs has already <u>granted</u> the relevant patents.

A. approved   B. turned down   C. rebuffed

25. Given our headquarters' <u>vast</u> knowledge of consumer trends and technological developments in this area, we would like to exchange product information and manufacturing technology expertise with your R&D unit.

A. circumscribed   B. immense   C. confined

26. Given our headquarters' vast knowledge of <u>consumer trends</u> and technological developments in this area, we would like to exchange product information and manufacturing technology expertise with your R&D unit.

A. purchasing patterns   B. selling patterns   C. investment patterns

27. Germany has <u>distinguished itself</u> in the latest technological developments in bedding comfort, the marketing of these products, and consumer relations in this niche.

A. denigrated itself   B. made a reputation for itself   C. played down itself

28. Germany has distinguished itself in the latest technological developments in bedding comfort, the marketing of these products, and consumer relations in this <u>niche</u>.

A. corner of the market   B. development of the market   C. potential of the market

29. To <u>initiate</u> this collaborative relationship, five colleagues from the Taiwan branch (including myself) would like to visit your R&D unit, this upcoming January, hopefully to meet with your departmental managers and research personnel.

A. trigger   B. curtail   C. retrench

30. To initiate this <u>collaborative</u> relationship, five colleagues from the Taiwan branch (including myself) would like to visit your R&D unit, this upcoming January, hopefully to meet with your departmental managers and research personnel.

A. agitated   B. hostile   C. cooperative

31. To initiate this collaborative relationship, five colleagues from the Taiwan branch (including myself) would like to visit your R&D unit, this upcoming January, hopefully to meet with your departmental managers and research <u>personnel</u>.

A. management   B. staff   C. board of directors

32. Let me know which dates would be the most <u>convenient</u> for such a visit.

A. burdensome   B. expedient   C. annoying

33. I look forward to this <u>mutually</u> beneficial, cooperative effort.

A. personally   B. autonomously   C. reciprocally

34. I look forward to this mutually <u>beneficial</u>, cooperative effort.

A. inopportune   B. advantageous   C. onerous

Situation 2

1. As a member of the technical <u>staff</u> of the Nuclear Medicine Department at S.W.M Memorial Hospital, I am involved in various stages of the therapeutic treatment of acute stroke patients.

A. employees   B. supervisors   C. administrators

2. As a member of the technical staff of the Nuclear Medicine Department at S.W.M Memorial Hospital, I am involved in various stages of the <u>therapeutic</u> treatment of

acute stroke patients.

A. impaired　B. debilitative　C. curative

3. As a member of the technical staff of the Nuclear Medicine Department at S.W.M Memorial Hospital, I am involved in various stages of the therapeutic treatment of acute stroke patients.

A. mild　B. severe　C. subdued

4. Given your institution's state-of-the-art technology and advanced expertise in neurology, I would like to propose a technological information exchange between our two hospital departments on the subject of treating patients with brain ischemia and acute brain stroke.

A. rudimentary　B. primal　C. cutting edge

5. Given your institution's state-of-the-art technology and advanced expertise in neurology, I would like to propose a technological information exchange between our two hospital departments on the subject of treating patients with brain ischemia and acute brain stroke.

A. formative　B. preliminary　C. progressive

6. Given your institution's state-of-the-art technology and advanced expertise in neurology, I would like to propose a technological information exchange between our two hospital departments on the subject of treating patients with brain ischemia and acute brain stroke.

A. adeptness　B. imperfection　C. inferiority

7. Medical research in Taiwan heavily emphasizes stroke-related factors leading to mortality.

A. atypically　B. scarcely　C. profoundly

8. Medical research in Taiwan heavily emphasizes stroke-related factors leading to mortality.

A. negates　B. plays down　C. punctuates

9. Medical research in Taiwan heavily emphasizes stroke-related factors leading to <u>mortality</u>.

A. life expectancy   B. death   C. birthrate

10. Our hospital has spent considerable resources to reduce the <u>risk</u> of stroke and solve problems that involve blood flow in the brain.

A. safeness   B. invulnerability   C. peril

11. As growth in the medical technology sector appears to be <u>unlimited</u>, the neurological department of our hospital is committed to overcoming stroke-related illnesses and reducing the incidence rate of strokes in Taiwan.

A. boundless   B. finite   C. hemmed in

12. As growth in the medical technology sector appears to be unlimited, the neurological department of our hospital is committed to overcoming stroke-related illnesses and reducing the <u>incidence</u> rate of strokes in Taiwan.

A. probability   B. prevalence   C. likelihood

13. <u>Progress</u> in this area depends on the ability of medical institutions to share and exchange relevant experiences — and we look forward to an opportunity to do the same with you.

A. advances   B. relapses   C. recessions

14. Progress in this area depends on the ability of medical institutions to share and <u>exchange</u> relevant experiences — and we look forward to an opportunity to do the same with you.

A. dictate   B. impose   C. reciprocate

15. Your ability to <u>differentiate</u> the infarction area in irreversibly damaged tissue is a respectable achievement.

A. blend   B. combine   C. distinguish

16. Your ability to differentiate the infarction area in <u>irreversibly</u> damaged tissue is a respectable achievement.

A. reverberation　B. recurrence　C. irrevocably

17. Your ability to differentiate the infarction area in irreversibly <u>damaged</u> tissue is a respectable achievement.

A. injured　B. rejuvenated　C. regenerated

18. Your ability to differentiate the infarction area in irreversibly damaged tissue is a <u>respectable</u> achievement.

A. infamous　B. disrepute　C. laudable

19. HMPAO SPECT can be used to determine <u>the extent to which</u> tracer uptake reduction can accurately predict neurological recovery and various programming languages can be used to write software to identify abnormal sites in the infarct area.

A. how　B. which　C. why

20. HMPAO SPECT can be used to determine the extent to which tracer uptake reduction can accurately <u>predict</u> neurological recovery and various programming languages can be used to write software to identify abnormal sites in the infarct area.

A. miscalculate　B. forecast　C. undervalue

21. HMPAO SPECT can be used to determine the extent to which tracer uptake reduction can accurately predict neurological <u>recovery</u> and various programming languages can be used to write software to identify abnormal sites in the infarct area.

A. retrieval　B. irreclaimable　C. irreparable

22. HMPAO SPECT can be used to determine the extent to which tracer uptake reduction can accurately predict neurological recovery and various programming languages can be used to write software to identify <u>abnormal</u> sites in the infarct area.

A. conventional　B. prevailing　C. deviant

101

23. Given our hospital's <u>advanced</u> PET technological capacity to reduce the incidence of stroke, such collaboration would be mutually beneficial, allowing both of our organizations to improve continuously expertise in medical diagnosis.

    A. retrospective   B. forward-looking   C. reflective

24. Given our hospital's advanced PET technological capacity to reduce the <u>incidence</u> of stroke, such collaboration would be mutually beneficial, allowing both of our organizations to improve continuously expertise in medical diagnosis.

    A. irrelevance   B. frequency   C. insignificance

25. Given our hospital's advanced PET technological capacity to reduce the incidence of stroke, such collaboration would be mutually beneficial, allowing both of our organizations to improve <u>continuously</u> expertise in medical diagnosis.

    A. interruptedly   B. incoherently   C. incessantly

Situation 3

1. Thank you for your letter dated 10 Nov 2003, which included your article, "<u>Isolation</u> and characterization of functions of genes essential for DNA transformation in *Helicobacter pylori*".

    A. consolidation   B. separation   C. integration

2. Thank you for your letter dated 10 Nov 2003, which included your article, "Isolation and <u>characterization</u> of functions of genes essential for DNA transformation in *Helicobacter pylori*".

    A. concealment   B. camouflaging   C. identification

3. Thank you for your letter dated 10 Nov 2003, which included your article, "Isolation and characterization of functions of genes essential for DNA

<u>transformation</u> in *Helicobacter pylori*".

   A. mutation　B. transgression　C. encroachment

4. In <u>response</u> to your invitation, I would like to visit your organization to exchange technological information regarding gene expression, the assay function of proteins and related transformation mechanisms.

   A. disregard　B. neglect　C. reply

5. In response to your <u>invitation</u>, I would like to visit your organization to exchange technological information regarding gene expression, the assay function of proteins and related transformation mechanisms.

   A. departure　B. summons　C. parting

6. The results from our laboratory on *Helicobacter pylori*, have demonstrated that some gene mutants <u>induce</u> dramatic natural transformation.

   A. impede　B. instigate　C. obstruct

7. The results from our laboratory on *Helicobacter pylori*, have demonstrated that some gene mutants induce <u>dramatic</u> natural transformation.

   A. bland　B. emotive　C. insipid

8. The article attempted to <u>characterize</u> genes and their role in the natural transformation of *Helicobacter pylori*.

   A. elucidate　B. extract　C. induce

9. The experimental results <u>obtained</u> in this project have already greatly helped Taiwan's development of attenuated vaccine strains of *Helicobacter pylori*.

   A. dismissed　B. refuted　C. acquired

10. The experimental results obtained in this project have already greatly helped Taiwan's development of <u>attenuated</u> vaccine strains of *Helicobacter pylori*.

   A. strengthened　B. enhanced　C. weakened

11. The <u>incidence</u> rates of women and men are nearly identical.

   A. prevalence　B. deficiency　C. scarcity

12. The incidence rates of women and men are nearly <u>identical</u>.

    A. different   B. disparate   C. indistinguishable

13. Over 25 million Americans <u>suffer from</u> an ulcer during their lifetimes.

    A. profit from   B. benefit from   C. are inflicted with

14. Fortunately, most ulcers are caused by an infection with *Helicobacter pylori*, opening the possibility of prevention through the development of an effective and safe <u>vaccine</u>.

    A. nutritional supplement   B. immunization   C. toxic

15. The results will be helpful in <u>producing</u> an antiserum, preparing membranes and purifying proteins from inclusion bodies.

    A. generating   B. deteriorating   C. declining

16. The results will be helpful in producing an antiserum, preparing membranes and <u>purifying</u> proteins from inclusion bodies.

    A. spoiling   B. denigrating   C. sanitizing

17. Your <u>recognized</u> expertise in this area would greatly benefit our own research efforts.

    A. infamous   B. respected   C. disreputable

18. Your recognized <u>expertise</u> in this area would greatly benefit our own research efforts.

    A. ineptness   B. incompetence   C. deftness

19. Thank you in advance for your careful <u>consideration</u>.

    A. inattention   B. thoughtfulness   C. negligence

20. I hope that this information exchange opportunity will <u>open doors</u> to future collaboration between our two organizations.

    A. create opportunities   B. establish barriers   C. set up obstacles

H Common elements in writing a letter to exchange information（資訊交流信函）include the following contents:

1. Proposing an information exchange relationship 資訊流通關係的提呈
2. Introducing one's professional experience or that of one's organization in relation to the proposed information exchange relation 為資訊流通而提供個人或機構經驗
3. Commending the organization or individual to exchange information with 為資訊流通而讚揚某機構或某人
4. Outlining details of the information exchange relation 資訊流通關係的細節詳述
5. Expressing optimism in the anticipated information exchange relation 表達對資訊流通關係的樂觀態度
6. Initiating the information exchange relation 開始資訊流通關係

In the space below, write a letter on exchanging information with another organization.

_____

_____

_____

_____

Unit two

Exchanging Information
資訊交流信函

1. Proposing an information exchange relationship
   資訊流通關係的提呈

2. Introducing one's professional experience or that of one's organization in relation to the proposed information exchange relation
   為資訊流通而提供個人或機構經驗

3. Commending the organization or individual to exchange information with
   為資訊流通而讚揚某機構或某人

4. Outlining details of the information exchange relation
   資訊流通關係的細節詳述

5. Expressing optimism in the anticipated information exchange relation
   表達對資訊流通關係的樂觀態度

6. Initiating the information exchange relation
   開始資訊流通關係

Look at the following examples of letters on exchanging information with another organization.

Dear Mr. Smith,

Thank you for your letter dated 16 October 2004 regarding the status of long term healthcare in Taiwan. In response, I'd like to propose an academic information exchange regarding the global long-term health care system and population distribution research in Taiwan and the United States.

We are currently involved in a research effort entitled "Forecasting the Market Supply and Demand of Long-term Care in Taiwan," which is a critical issue facing countries with aging populations. This research focuses mainly on accurately forecasting the growth trends of the disabled elderly population and bed capacity in healthcare institutions in Taiwan. The results generated so far in this research have already been most helpful in strategic planning for Taiwan's long-term care system.

The rapidly growing disabled elderly population in Taiwan has severely strained available medical personnel and facilities. Ke (2002) indicated that 30-40% of all relatives taking care of disabled family members suffer from low job performance evaluations, with 9.1% - 26.6% of them eventually quitting their jobs. To alleviate this burden upon family members, government, industry, and research organizations have conferred that accurately forecasting the demand and supply of long-term care is the initial step for planning effective social welfare policies.

I look forward to hearing your ideas or suggestions regarding this information exchange opportunity. I would also like to arrange for a three-month academic visit to your organization this upcoming November as the initial step of our cooperation. If at all possible, please notify me as to which dates are most convenient for you. A tentative visiting schedule would also be appreciated. Thanks in advance for your careful consideration; I look forward to our future cooperation.

Sincerely yours,

Dear Dr. Brown,

I belong to the Cancer Center at National Taiwan University Hospital, the first medical institute and teaching hospital in Taiwan. As a governmental supported research organization, our Center maintains state-of-the-art instrumentation for clinical use. We have recently began adopting intraoperative radiotherapy (IORT) in treating cancer patients, which allows physicians to deliver a high radiation dose to the tumor site during surgery. As is well known, one-time IORT is more convenient than traditional radiotherapy and minimizes the risk of exposing healthy tissues to radiation. Moreover, IORT increases the dose delivered to the target organ more effectively and precisely than conventional methods do. However, we lack sufficient experience in adopting this new therapeutic method. As the Cancer Center of Stanford University is globally renowned for its pioneering cancer therapy, especially in the IORT method, we would like to seek your expertise on this matter. Therefore, we would like to develop a partner relation with your Center to exchange related experiences in radiation therapy. We believe that such a relation would be a mutually beneficial one, like addressing differences between IORT and CRT or differences in therapeutic treatment between the East and the West. Through this relationship, we could freely exchange our views and approaches towards achieving the best therapeutic outcome for our patients. I look forward to your thoughts regarding the possibility of such collaboration.

Sincerely yours,

Dear Mr. Jones,

As an administrator in the Rehabilitation Department of ABC Hospital in Taiwan, I have received your publication "Hospital Marketing" regularly for quite some time, finding it to provide valuable information for my profession. As a non-governmental, non-profit organization, ABC Hospital strives to rehabilitate patients in order to achieve full recovery from an injury or illness.

Enclosed please find a document that will hopefully give further insight into the missions of ABC Hospital and our Department. The project that we are currently engaged in focuses on providing relevant information that would facilitate a patient's recovery and well being. Doing so includes encouraging physical fitness and mental well being through a quarterly publication that describes recuperative measures for patients and dissemination of a hospital management project. The work results generated so far in this project have yielded numerous benefits for Taiwanese undergoing therapy through physical fitness.

Since our goals closely match those of your organization, we would like to develop a partner relationship with you, for information exchange and for possible future collaboration. Would you please send me introductory information as well as any other relevant publications that describe your methodology, achievements and future objectives? We also anticipate the possibility of our organizations collaborating in the near future. Please let me know if you have any comments regarding this information. Also, please contact me if I can be of any further assistance.

If possible, please notify of me as to which dates are most convenient for you for us to visit your organization. A tentative visiting schedule would also be appreciated. Thanks in advance for your careful consideration for possible. I look forward to hearing your thoughts regarding this information exchange opportunity. Again, I look forward to our future cooperation.

Sincerely yours,

Dear Mr. Smith,

Miss Hu recommended that I contact you regarding the possibility of an information exchange opportunity with your company with respect to your biotechnology products and potential technology transfer opportunities between our two organizations. As a globally renowned nonprofit bioresearch center that provides biological products, technical services, and educational programs to the private sector, government and academic organizations worldwide, your company specializes in researching and developing biotechnology products and services.

We are interested in what opportunities for technological cooperation are available between our two organizations in the area of advanced biotechnology product development. Established in 1998, our company strives to develop inexpensive yet high quality bio-medical products for clinical diagnosis. In line with consumer demand, we continuously improve upon and streamline biological research methods and clinical diagnostic procedures.

Our biochip development program hopes to attract overseas partners who can either develop biochip products or engage in a technical cooperative program with biomedical manufacturers in Taiwan such as ours. The major items to be developed in this biochip development program comprise the following:

1. Measure the poisonous contents of organic substances precisely and analyze efficiently how noxious substances influencethe human body;
2. Increase the accuracy and speed of inspecting a biochip; and

3. Screen medicines at minimum cost and time.

Thanks in advance for your careful consideration; I look forward to our future cooperation.

Sincerely yours,

Dear Mr. Smith,

Thank you for your invitation via e-mail dated December 31, 2004 for our Taiwanese branch office to exhibit its innovative bedding and pillow products in Cologne, Germany on May 2005. Before participating in the exhibition, I would like to propose an information exchange relation between our two organizations regarding the sleeping needs of elderly individuals, hopefully leading to a technology transfer or joint venture opportunity in the near future.

The Taiwanese branch of this bedding company has extended its number of business units by pursuing an aggressive marketing strategy since 2000, with more than twenty units currently island wide and a dramatic increase in business volume. The branch office tentatively plans to construct a new factory next year and broaden its organizational scope. Franchise employees are encouraged to perform their best, as evidenced by our development in several bedding and pillow types and emphasis on electrically heated bedding and customized pillows.

Taiwan's elderly population has grown rapidly in recent years, with the bedding market generating considerable revenues. Given this trend, the R&D Division of the Taiwanese branch has committed significant resources to designing bedding customized for elderly individuals, with the Intellectual Property Office of the Ministry of Economic Affairs having already granted patents in this area. With the headquarters' vast knowledge of consumer trends and technological developments in this area, we would like to exchange product information and manufacturing technology expertise with your R&D unit. Germany has distinguished itself in the latest technological developments in bedding comfort, marketing promotion and consumer relations in this market niche.

To initiate this collaborative relation, five colleagues from the Taiwan branch (including myself) would like to visit your R&D unit this upcoming January 2005, hopefully meeting with your departmental managers and research personnel. Let me know which dates would be the most convenient for such a visit. Prior to our visit, it would also be appreciated if you would forward to us any relevant materials regarding your company's technological developments and marketing strategies in this area. I look forward to hearing your ideas or suggestions regarding this information exchange opportunity. Thanks in advance for your careful consideration; I look forward to this mutually beneficial, cooperative effort.

Sincerely yours,

Dear Mr. Smith,

Your recent publication *Customer Behavior* has been extremely helpful in my graduate school research in the Institute of Business Management at Yuanpei University (Taiwan), especially your unique perspective on analyzing consumer behavior. Since my current research direction closely resembles that of your organization, I would like to develop a partner relationship with you by exchanging pertinent information that would hopefully lead to future collaboration in this field of study. While you could provide valuable information on current trends in consumer behavior analysis, I could offer relevant data from Taiwan and the Southeast Asian region. I am especially interested in analyzing consumers in terms of what psychological factors influence their purchasing behavior so that managers can draw up appropriate marketing strategies. Given my considerable research in consumer behavior and my university's solid reputation in medical imagery and quantitative analysis, I believe that you would find our collaboration as an asset in applying scientific analysis to consumer trends and behavioral patterns.

Given your corporation's solid expertise in qualitative analysis and related approaches, I hope that you find the above information as an opportunity for our two organizations to collaborate with each other in a joint venture in the near future. I look forward to hearing your ideas or suggestions regarding this information exchange opportunity. Also, would you please send me introductory information as well as other pertinent literature that analyzes consumer behavior in the above areas?

I anxiously look forward to your favorable reply.

Sincerely yours,

Dear Mr. Push,

As a member of the technical staff in the Nuclear Medicine Department at S.W.M Memorial Hospital, I am involved in various stages of therapeutic treatment of acute stroke patients. Given your institution's state-of-the-art technology and advanced expertise in neurology, I would like to propose a technological information exchange between our two hospital departments with respect to treating patients suffering from brain ischemia and acute brain stroke. Medical research in Taiwan heavily emphasizes stroke-related factors leading to mortality.

We are anxious to develop long-lasting cooperative relationships with an institution such as yours. Neurological departments in Taiwan take in nearly 100 stroke patients for clinical treatment on a weekly basis. In terms of resolving problems involving blood flow in the brain, our hospital has spent considerable resources in reducing the risk of stroke. As growth of the medical technology sector appears to be unlimited, the neurological department in our hospital is committed to overcoming stroke-related illnesses and reducing the incidence rate of strokes in Taiwan. Progress in this area depends on the ability of medical institutions to share and exchange relevant experiences, an opportunity which we look forward to having with you. From the January 2003 issue of *Nuclear Medicine Journal*, I learned how your laboratory decreased semihemisphere bleeding using coregisteration technology. Your ability to differentiate the infarction area in irreversibly damaged tissue is a respectable achievement, through the use of HMPAO SPECT, the extent to which tracer uptake reduction can accurately predict neurological recovery and adoption of various computer program languages to identify the abnormal sites of infarct area. I hope that our staff will have the opportunity to exchange data and experiences in the field of brain stroke patients. Given our hospital's advanced PET technological capabilities to reduce the incidence rate of stroke patients, such collaboration would be mutually beneficial in both of our organizations' efforts to continuously upgrade expertise in medical diagnosis.

We look forward to hearing your ideas or suggestions regarding this technological information exchange involving your work in voxel-based correlations in stroke patients and our research efforts on advanced ischemic damaged tissue. With your consent, I would like to arrange for a fourteen-day technical visit to your department this upcoming October as the initial step of our cooperation. Please let me know if there are any areas of common interest you would like to discuss.

Sincerely yours,

Dear Mr. Hass,

Thank you for your letter dated 10 Nov 2003 that included your article "Isolation and functional characterization of genes for DNA transformation in *Helicobacter pylori*". In response to your invitation, I would like to visit your organization to exchange technological information regarding gene expression, the assay function of proteins and related transformation mechanisms.

As a graduate student in the Institute of Biotechnology Research at Yuanpei University of Science and Technology in Hsinchu, Taiwan, I am collaborating with my professor in a National Science Council-sponsored research project aimed at generating a mutant library from clinical isolate Helicobacter pylori. With our laboratory's efforts concentrated on investigating *Helicobacter pylori*, our results have so far demonstrated that some gene mutants that dramatically induce natural transformation. Our recent findings have been published in a monthly JBC magazine, in which we attempted to characterize genes and their role in the natural transformation of Helicobacter pylori. The experimental results generated in this project have already been most helpful in Taiwan's development of attenuated vaccine strains of *Helicobacter pylori*.

Individuals of all ages can suffer from ulcers, with the incidence rate among women and men nearly identical. Over 25 million Americans suffer from an ulcer during their lifetime. Fortunately, most ulcers are caused by an infection with *Helicobacter pylori*, opening the possibility of resolving this project through the development of effective and safe vaccine. Our research is focused mainly on identifying proteins that may be associated, results of which will be helpful in producing an antiserum, preparing membranes and purifying proteins from inclusion bodies. Your recognized expertise in this area would greatly benefit our own research efforts. I hope that through our technological information exchange, we will be able to identify areas of mutual interest, possibly leading to a technology transfer or joint venture.

I anxiously look forward to your response to some of the above points that I have raised concerning this information exchange opportunity. Visiting your laboratory for a two week period to exchange ideas of mutual interest would appear to be the first step of our cooperation. Let me know which dates would be the most convenient for you. Thanks in advance for your careful consideration. I hope that this information exchange opportunity will open the doors for future collaboration between our two organizations.

Sincerely yours,

Dear Mr. Jones,

Thank you for your letter dated November 28, 2004 containing the apoplectic correlation technology-related data requested earlier. I'd like to propose a technological information exchange between our two organizations regarding ROI technological applications for stroke patients and advanced software programs.

We are currently involved in a long-term project entitled, "Evaluating the extent of damage incurred by hyper-acute infarction strokes." Hyper-acute infarction stroke patients from a nearby community hospital have already participated in our prospective study for over two months. Our objective is to adopt MRI in those patients to avoid early damage of brain tissue. The experimental results generated in this project have already been most helpful in our efforts to understand the incidence of hyper-acute infarction stroke among our hospital's patients.

The incidence of strokes in Taiwan is on the increase. Infarction strokes may occur regardless of an individual's age, with death often occurring in middle age or later life. The effectiveness of clinically diagnosing and treating stroke patients, as well as investigating the underlying pathophysiology of the disease, hinges on inferences from the anatomy of the stroke lesion. Treatment has focused on reestablishing the flow after occlusion and increasing tissue tolerance to ischemia. Additionally, MRI can roughly estimate stroke topography and size with respect to numerous aspects. Coordinated diffusion and perfusion studies provide a more detailed view of the evolution of stroke contour in relation to a perimeter of relative hypoperfusion. Despite its limited quantitative applications, MRI is appropriate for a volumetric study of stroke patients and subsequent brain damage incurred.

The conventional means of diagnosing acute cerebral infarctions, in which clinical physicians review the medical history of patients and current condition as well as subjectively assess stroke cases for diagnostic purposes, normally makes it impossible not only to diagnose patients with an acute stroke the first time, but also to identify the type and regional geography of such a stroke accurately. Therefore, our laboratory has recently developed a quantitative measurement method that can reconstruct and analyze a 3D infarct field range.

I look forward to hearing your ideas or suggestions regarding this information exchange opportunity. I would like to arrange a visit to your hospital for one month as a self-supported guest researcher as the initial step of cooperation between our two organizations. If you find such an arrangement agreeable, please notify me as to which dates are most convenient for you. A tentative visiting schedule would also be appreciated. Thanks in advance for your careful consideration of this collaborative activity. Sincerely yours,

Dear Dr. Huang,

Thank you for your encouraging letter dated January 11, 2004. In response, I would like to propose a technological information exchange to further explore how green tea polyphenols affect human intestine cell, e.g. the Caco-2 cell line.

As a graduate student in the Institute of Biotechnology at Yuanpei University of Science and Technology, I participate in a National Science Council-sponsored research project aimed at exploring the impact of green tea polyphenols, which has been underway for the past two years. This long-term project focuses on inhibiting inflammatory responses and increasing anti-oxidant responses of green tea polyphenols. This effort involves analyzing not only the effect of green tea polyphenols on RAW 264.7 cell line,but also the proteins in food or human cell by Western blotting and spray drying. The experimental results generated so far in this project have already been most helpful in more thoroughly understanding the excellent anti-oxidant properties of green tea polyphenols. Continued success of this project depends on our ability to exchange relevant experiences with similar organizations such as yours.

I look forward to hearing your ideas or suggestions regarding this information exchange opportunity. I would also like to arrange for a one week technical visit to your organization in order to discuss some of the above topics in more detail. If at all possible, please notify me as to which dates are most convenient for you. A tentative visiting schedule would also be appreciated. Thanks in advance for your careful consideration.

Sincerely yours,

Dear Dr. Wu,

Given your laboratory's innovative research in product marketing strategies, I would like to propose an information exchange relationship between our two organizations, hopefully beginning with my visit to your laboratory this upcoming July. Allow me to briefly introduce myself. Having recently acquired my Master`s degree in Business Management from Yuanpei University of Science and Technology in Taiwan, I am a product sales manager at Bu Ting Company. Before that, I received my Bachelor's degree in Healthcare Management from the same institution. My work entails developing marketing strategies for the company's extensive line of products and services.

Scientific and technological advances have dramatically transformed Taiwanese society, as it gradually evolved from an agricultural-based economy into turn into an industrial-oriented and, more recently, a knowledge-based economy. Previously, product commercialization in most Taiwanese companies did not consider consumer concerns, thus making marketing strategies incomplete. However, given the emphasis on consumer demand in the current business climate, an increasing number of businesses adopt various strategies to attract customers. For instance, Internet marketing is a viable strategy to draw customers online.

As I am actively involved in marketing strategy, the opportunity to share our professional experiences in this area could be mutually beneficial for both of our companies, perhaps leading to a joint venture in the near future. I look forward to your ideas on how to initiate such a cooperative relation.

Sincerely yours,

Dear Mr. Wang,

94.10 Thank you for your invitation via e-mail dated November 8, 2004 for the branch office in Taiwan to exhibit our innovative TFT-LCD products in New York this upcoming March. Before participating in this exhibition, I would like to propose an information exchange relation between our two organizations regarding the material development of TFT-LCD products, hopefully leading to a technology transfer in the near future.

As TFT-LCD technology continuously advances, our branch office strives to offer a line of quality products to satisfy consumer demand, both locally and abroad. Such innovativeness contributes to the maturation of Taiwan's recently emerging electronics sector, subsequently accelerating technological efforts that boost international competitiveness of the industry. The Taiwanese branch of this TFT-LCD company has extended its number of business units to ten by pursuing an aggressive marketing strategy since 1995, subsequently increasing generated revenues. The branch office tentatively plans to construct a new production facility next year and broaden its organizational scope.

Taiwan TFT-LCD products have grown rapidly in recent years, with related products generating considerable profits. The Taiwan branch has committed significant resources to designing TFT-LCD products, with the Intellectual Property Office of the Ministry of Economic Affairs granting several patents so far. To continue with our progress, we would like to exchange product-related information and manufacturing technology expertise with your R&D unit, possibly leading to a joint venture once ties are established.

To initiate this collaborative relation, ten colleagues from the Taiwan branch would like to visit your R&D unit next year, hopefully meeting with your departmental managers and research personnel. Let me know which dates will be the most convenient for this visit. Taiwan's TFT-LCD manufacturers focus mainly on producing small- and medium-sized panels. Establishing long-term collaborative ties with renowned manufacturers such as yours reflects our resolve to ensure innovativeness in Taiwan's TFT-LCD products.

I look forward to hearing your suggestions regarding this information exchange opportunity. Thanks in advance for your careful consideration. I firmly believe that such a cooperative relation would mutually benefit both of our organizations.
Sincerely yours,

Dear Professor Anzai,
Professor Qiu Wonder, Superintendent of Municipal Wan Fang Hospital at Taipei Medical University, suggested that I contact you regarding the possibility of establishing an information exchange relation between our two organizations. Allow me to introduce myself. Following graduation from Chung Tai Junior College of Medical Technology in 1993, I began working in the Wan Fang Municipal Hospital at Taipei Medical University, where I have remained until now. Given my excellent performance over the past seven years, I was promoted to Administrator of the Registration and Finance Department in 2004. Despite my professional experiences, I felt that my academic training was lacking, explaining why I am pursuing a Master's degree in Business Management at Yuanpei University of Science and Technology. My graduate school research focuses on adopting medical marketing practices to maintain the competitiveness of hospitals in the intensely competitive medical sector.

Thank you for the description of your hospital's products and services, which is a valuable reference for our own efforts to increase consumer satisfaction in Taiwan. Your mottos of "Quality is our pride", "Quality coincides with customer's expectations" and "Quality is seeking the best treatment available" set the standard for quality that our hospital should strive for in offering medical treatment. Doing so would not only enhance our competitiveness domestically, but also help promote our activities abroad.

Keio University Hospital has distinguished itself as a global leader among medical service providers, explaining why we want to initiate this information exchange opportunity in order to remain abreast of the latest developments in this field. A visit by our administrative staff to your hospital would appear to be the appropriate next step to initiate this collaborative relation. If convenient, please let us know which times for such a visit would be the most agreeable with you. Please find enclosed an introductory DVD of Wanfang Hospital for your reference.

I anxiously look forward to your favorable reply.

Sincerely yours,

- - - - - - - - - - - - - - - - - - - -

Dear Mr. Lin,

Our organization is eager to collaborate with your marketing department given our similar research interests. Exchanging related information, e.g., methodologies, strategies, corporate missions and objectives, would appear to be the starting point for such cooperation, followed by visits to each other's marketing departments and, eventually, collaboration on a joint venture. Having received my Master's degree in Business Administration from Yuanpei University of Science and Technology, I focused on Internet marketing research. The Internet provides seemingly unlimited opportunities to market one's products and services without conventional constraints of time, location or resources. Our two organizations are aggressively pursuing Internet marketing strategies, an area that I hope we can develop further collaboratively. Findings of my graduate school research were published in *The Journal of Marketing*. I hope to continue with this line of research by applying the knowledge expertise acquired in graduate school to the work place. Given your company's solid reputation in marketing, researching related topics in collaboration with your company would be an immense boost to my determination to acquire the latest knowledge skills in this field.

Familiar with the scope of activities in your marketing department, I am confident that our organization's similar methodologies and strategies will enable us to easily engage in a collaborative effort in the near future. Please carefully consider my request and inform me of your decision at your earliest convenience. I look forward to our

future cooperation.
Sincerely yours,

Dear Mr. Braun,
The manager of our company's marketing department, Shi-Pi Fang, suggested I contact you regarding the possibility of establishing an information exchange relation with your company's marketing department to share relevant marketing strategies and methodologies. As is well known, your company has distinguished itself in online auctioning of its goods and services. Online auctioning is especially attractive given its ability to concert its marketing efforts according to different regional preferences and characteristics. Our collaborative relation would hopefully allow us to share information on the latest advances in online auctioning for marketing segmentation purposes.

Having recently received a Master's degree in Business Management from Yuanpei University of Science and Technology (YUST), I spent considerable time in researching online auctioning-related topics. Exchanging marketing information in this area with your company would not only give me a more practical context for the theoretical concepts taught in graduate school, but also allow me to more effectively contribute to marketing efforts in Taiwan.

I look forward to hearing your suggestions on how to initiate this information exchange relation, perhaps a visit to your marketing department to discuss relevant strategies and areas of mutual interest. Please find enclosed our company brochure, in which corporate missions, goals, strategies and methodologies are briefly introduced. Sincerely yours,

---

Dear Mr. Smith,
Thank you for your letter dated January 16, 2005 regarding your positive response to the idea of our two organizations collaborating together. I suggest that we exchange pertinent information on global efforts to promote the physiological and mental well

being of elderly residents in long term care facilities in Taiwan and Japan.

Our current research focus is on assessing the effectiveness of an exercise program aimed at enhancing the physiological and psychological well being of elderly residents of long term care facilities. Results of this study will hopefully provide a valuable reference for strategic planning of long-term care facilities in Taiwan.

A visit to your organization in order to more fully discuss some of the above topics and areas of mutual interest would appear to be the best way of initiating this information exchange relation. A tentative visiting schedule would also be appreciated. Thanks in advance for your preparation. I look forward to our future cooperation.

Sincerely yours,

Dear Mr. Jones,

Given the tremendous global presence of your corporation in more than fifty countries and revenues exceeding $US 5,747,000,000 in 1999, our company would like to establish a mutually beneficial information exchange relation with your organization to learn of the novel management practices in your daily operations, as well as share our own experiences in this field. As a graduate student in the Institute of Business Management at Yuanpei University of Science and Technology, I am actively involved in customer relationship management-related research.

The information exchange between our two organizations will hopefully allow us to share pertinent data involving risk assessment, customer loan policies, database management and the transfer of business capital. I believe that such cooperation could be mutually beneficial if the goals are clearly set at the outset. A visit to your organization would appear to be the best way of initiating this information exchange opportunity so that we exchange ideas on how to implement activities that could perhaps to lead to a joint venture in the near future. Following your careful consideration, please let me know which dates are the most convenient to discuss some of the above topics in more detail. I look forward to our future cooperation.

Sincerely yours,

Dear Professor Lin,

Your recent research on Internet marketing has been extremely helpful in my graduate school research in the Institute of Business Management at Yuanpei University, especially your unique strategies adopted to analyze the market potential for online commerce. Given your prestige in this field of research, I would like to develop a mutually beneficial partnership that would allow us to exchange pertinent information, leading to future collaboration such as co-authoring of a research article or even a joint venture between our two organizations. While you could provide valuable information on current trends in network marketing analysis, I could offer relevant data from Taiwan and the Asian region.

I am especially interested in analyzing which parameters influence consumer purchases online, providing a valuable reference for managers devising online sales strategies. Our Institute has devoted considerable time to examining the psychological behavior of consumers when shopping online. Your recognized expertise in this area would greatly benefit our own research efforts. I hope that through our information exchange relation, we will be able to identify areas of mutual interest, possibly leading to fruitful results for online marketing companies.

I look forward your ideas and suggestions regarding the above proposal as to whether we have areas of mutual interest for this information exchange opportunity. Visiting your laboratory for a week period to further discuss some of the above topics would appear to be the first step of our cooperation. If possible, please let me know which dates would be the most convenient. Thanks in advance for your careful consideration. I hope that this information exchange opportunity will open the doors of cooperation between our two organizations.

Sincerely yours,

Dear Mr. Smith,

Thank you for your letter dated December 18, 2004 containing the publication *Advanced Medical Knowledge*. In response, I'd like to propose an information exchange relation between our two organizations on integrating digital image processing, biochemistry and medical technologies for extraction of Chinese herbal medicine. As a graduate student in the Institute of Biotechnology at Yuanpei University of Science and Technology (YUST) in Hsinchu, Taiwan, I am currently involved in a project on Chinese herbal medicine extracts, which is a joint collaboration between our research institute and the Institute of Nuclear Science at National Tsing Hua University. Specifically, this project focuses on generating pertinent data from Chinese herbal medicine extracts. Our major work includes publication of a bimonthly magazine that describes the extraction and dissemination of Chinese herbal medicine compounds for commercialization. The experimental results generated in this project have already been most helpful in efforts to identify Chinese herbal medicine compounds.

The potential to integrate digital image processing, biochemistry and medical technology could further contribute to Taiwan's rapid economic growth, as fueled by the development of many innovative technologies. Chinese herbal medicine been extensively used among Chinese and Taiwanese for centuries. Given advances in laboratory facilities, instrumentation and available technologies, educational institutions in Taiwan now employ highly qualified technical personnel capable of engaging in advanced research on Chinese herbal medicine-related topics.

Many such projects currently focus on studying the feasibility of integrating digital image processing with biochemistry assessment, molecular biology technologies and extraction of Chinese herbal medicine. We recognize that ensuring the continued success of our efforts in Taiwan depends on the open sharing and exchange of related experiences with other similar organizations. Enclosed please find an introductory brochure of the Institute of Biotechnology at YUsT, which will hopefully provide further details regarding our missions, methodologies and current research directions.

I look forward to hearing your ideas or suggestions regarding this information exchange opportunity. I would also like to arrange for a fifteen-day technical visit to your organization this upcoming January as the initial step of our cooperation. If at all possible, please notify me as to which dates are most convenient for you. A tentative visiting schedule would also be appreciated. Thanks in advance for your careful consideration.

Sincerely yours,

Dear Mr. Smith,

Mr. Yau proposed that I contact you about your company's radiation therapy products and the possibility of exchanging data with your research division on the latest advances in intensity modulated radiation therapy (IMRT), including recent developments in product technology. As our department actively engages in National Science Council-sponsored research in this area, we hope that the exchanging of relevant data between our two organizations will lead to a joint venture aimed increasing the efficiency of both radiation therapy and three-dimensional conformal radiation therapy in a hospital's oncology department.

We are involved in a development program for clinical applications, aimed at seeking overseas partners who are proficient in developing radiation therapy strategies or are capable of engaging in a joint venture to enhance the level of intensity modulated radiation therapy and three-dimensional conformal radiation therapy in a hospital's oncology department. For example, the ionizing chamber and other detectors, as well as the multi-leaf collimator (MLC), simulation software for therapeutic treatment and other instrumentation must adhere to stringent quality control standards. The line of products and services introduced in your company brochure will be most helpful to the smooth implementation of our radiation therapy project. This information exchange opportunity will hopefully lead to further technical cooperation through licensing or a joint venture.

I anxiously look forward to your favorable reply. You can contact me directly at the below e-mail address or telephone numbers. Thanks in advance for your attention to this matter.

Sincerely yours,

Dear Dr. Chang,

Thank you for your encouraging letter dated September 12, 2004. I suggest that our laboratories begin exchanging information on how anthocyanins and other phenolic compounds inhibit nitric oxide production in LPS/IFN-γ-activated RAW 264.7 macrophages. As a graduate student in the Institute of Biotechnology at Yuanpei University of Science and Technology, I work under the direction of my master's thesis advisor in a National Science Council-sponsored research project on the above topic. Already underway for the past two years, this long-term project focuses on the potential of flavonoids to lower oxidative stress and alleviate the impact of cardiovascular diseases and chronic inflammatory diseases associated with nitric oxide (NO). Our investigation also examined how common phenolic compounds found in fruits, including phenolic acids, flavonols, isoflavones, and anthocyanins, affect NO production in LPS/IFN-γ-activated RAW 264.7 macrophages. Anthocyanin-rich crude extracts and concentrates of selected berries were also assayed, in which their inhibitory effects on NO production were significantly correlated with total phenolic and anthocyanin contents. To our knowledge, this is the first study to examine how anthocyanins and berry phenolic compounds inhibit NO production. The experimental results generated so far in this project have already been most helpful in more thoroughly understanding these excellent phenolic compounds. Nevertheless, continued success of this project depends on our ability to exchange data with laboratories such as yours. I look forward to hearing your ideas or suggestions regarding this information exchange opportunity. I would also like to arrange for a technical visit to your organization in order to discuss some of the above topics in more detail. If at all possible, please notify me as to which dates are most convenient for you. A tentative visiting schedule would also be appreciated. Thanks in advance for your careful consideration.

Sincerely yours,

Dear Mr. Lin,

Thank you for your encouraging letter of November 25, 2004 that included your recent article " Developmental expression of three mung bean Hsc70s and substrate binding specificity of the encoded proteins." As our laboratories share common research interests, I hope that we could exchange information on how Hsc70s developmental expression affects the mung bean. I am especially interested in the possibility that *de novo* synthesized HSC70s may be required to escort the large amount of newly synthesized proteins during germination in the mung bean (*Vigna radiata*).

As a graduate student in the Institute of Biotechnology at Yuanpei University of Science and Technology in Hsinchu, Taiwan, I am collaborating with my master's thesis advisor in research on Chinese herbal medicine-related topics. The healing properties of Chinese herbal medicine have received increasing attention among medical researchers worldwide. Our project currently underway focuses on gene expression in response to temperature and/or water stress. This explains why I would like to propose a mutually beneficial information exchange between our two organizations on potential applications of gene expression in plant cells and advanced software programs. The experimental results generated so far in our research have already shed light on the excellent medical properties of Chinese herbal medicine

I look forward to hearing your ideas or suggestions regarding this information exchange opportunity. I would also like to arrange a visit to your organization in order to discuss some of the above topics in more detail for two weeks as a self-supported guest researcher as the initial step of cooperation between our two organizations. If you find such an arrangement agreeable, please notify me as to which dates are most convenient for you. A tentative visiting schedule would also be appreciated. Thanks in advance for your careful consideration.

Sincerely yours,

Dear Mr. Wang,

It is a pleasure to make contact with you again. Much appreciation for the invitation you're your hospital extended to us during your recent visit. The achievements that your closely knit staff has achieved are quite impressive. Given our many areas of mutual interest, I suggest that our organizations begin exchanging information that would enhance the quality of clinical practice in daily operations.

As a medical imagery specialist in the Department of Cardiology Surgery, I constantly strive to upgrade the quality of instrumentation in accurately diagnosing heart diseases. Although progress has been made in heart transplant images, the same can hopefully be made for liver blood vessel images. While visiting your hospital, I was most impressed with the expertise of your staff in capturing concise images of liver blood vessels, which is a rather complex procedure.

I look forward to hearing your ideas or suggestions on how to initiate this information exchange relation between our two hospitals. As for understanding precise medical imagery of liver blood vessels, we are especially interested not only how these images compare with those of different organs in the human body, but also how to identify similar blood vessels in the livers of different individuals. We also hope to share our professional diagnostic skills in medical imagery of heart blood vessels.

I am confident that such collaboration will ultimately benefit patients in both of our hospitals whom require advanced diagnostic techniques.

Sincerely yours,

Dear Professor Smith,

Quite some time has passed since we made contact with each other. As you recall, I am a graduate student in the Institute of Medical Imagery at Yuanpei University presenting Taiwan. After reviewing your online brochure and research findings of your laboratory published in numerous international journals, I was quite impressed with your facilities and wide scope of research activities that you are engaged in, especially the development of drug resistance cells. Given our similar interests in this field of research, we would like to exchange related information on some of the areas outlined below. We also anticipate the possibility of a cooperative venture between our two laboratories in the near future.

As a private, non-profit organization, our laboratory currently focuses on developing a method capable of producing a cancer resistant cell. I was pleased to learn of your interest in our current programs from your recent correspondence. Let me briefly let you in on our ongoing projects, which are largely concerned with how to produce a drug that resists cancer cells based on the following characteristics:

1. Administer an anticancer drug such as Taxol that resists cancer cells.
2. Adopt a method that utilizes low pressure, high temperatures or other chemical materials.
3. Ensure that the likelihood of damage to normal cells in the human body is minimal, based on a physics-based therapeutic method for cancer patients.

This information exchange opportunity would allow our two laboratories to share pertinent data on the latest advances in cancer treatment. Would you please send me introductory information that briefly outlines your strategies, methodologies, achievements and future objectives? I look forward to your comments regarding the above areas of mutual interest.

Sincerely yours,

Dear Mr. Smith,

Thank you for your encouraging letter dated January 10, 2003. In response, I would like to propose a technological information exchange to further explore mutual areas of interest such as gene expression, assay function of proteins and related transformation mechanisms. Established in 1995, our company strives to develop inexpensive, yet high quality bio-medical products for clinical diagnosis. In line with consumer demand, we continuously improve upon and streamline biological research methods and clinical diagnostic procedures. Your recognized expertise in this area would greatly benefit our own research efforts.

This information exchange opportunity between our two organizations would allow us to identify areas of mutual interest, possibly leading to a technology transfer or joint venture in the near future. I look forward to hearing your ideas or suggestions. To initiate this mutually beneficial relation, I would like to arrange for a week technical visit to your organization in order to discuss some of the above topics in more detail. If you find such an arrangement agreeable, please notify me as to which dates are most convenient for you. A tentative visiting schedule would also be appreciated. I look forward to our future cooperation.

Sincerely yours,

Dear Dr. Mitsudo,

Dr. Cheng Jun-Jack highly recommended your hospital for its expertise in cardiac intervention, suggesting that I contact you regarding the possibility of exchanging information with your organization on the latest technological trends. As a radiology technologist in the Cardiac Cath Unit of Shin Kong Hospital (SKH) in Taiwan, I am especially intrigued with your specialization in chronic total occlusion (CTO), which your hospital is renowned for in Asia.

The Cardiac Cath Unit largely focuses on providing excellent PTCA treatment for patients with coronary artery disease by continuously training highly skilled personnel and adopting the latest instrumentation and skills. However, the incidence of mortality from chronic total occlusion syndrome remains high. As your institution collaborated with SKH a few years ago in stent implantation, angioplasty, and atheromabectomy, we would like to extend this cooperation to sharing pertinent data on the incidence of CTO among patients and appropriate therapeutic treatment. To initiate this information exchange relation, we suggest not only that our personnel receive intern training in treatment of CTO in your institution, but also that your staff offer lectures and clinical demonstrations in Taiwan. As for the intern position offered at your hospital on an annual basis, training will hopefully include use of the new guiding wire, triple-wire technique and implantation of drug eluting stents.

The opportunity to exchange information on the latest CTO therapeutic skills would pave the way for future collaboration between Japanese and Taiwanese researchers in this field. Thanks in advance for your careful consideration. We look forward to your favorable reply.

Sincerely yours,

Dear Professor Tung,

I appreciate your valuable instruction that you provided during my brief stay as a visiting researcher in the Institute of Nuclear Science at National Tsing Hua University, an opportunity which has made me further resolute to pursue a radiotechnology-related career. I would like to continue with our collaboration by exchanging information with your laboratory regarding the planning of proton radiation treatment and minimization of biological effects.

As is well known, cancer often occurs long before a diagnosis is performed, making it difficult to treat and cure. Therapeutic treatment is occasionally so extensive that patients fear it as much as the disease itself. As the most accurate form of advanced radiation treatment available for certain cancers and the other diseases, proton therapy minimizes the likelihood of harm to surrounding tissues owing to its accuracy. All individuals receiving treatment are treated as outpatients, allowing them to continue with normal activities without minimal or no side effects from therapy. Moreover, proton radiation treatment offers the potential of effectively managing localized cancer.

The accelerated growth of medical physics worldwide has greatly enhanced clinical practice. To keep pace with global trends in proton radiation treatment, the Hsinchu Biomedical Science Park will establish a Proton Therapy Center in 2007 as Taiwan's first hospital-based treatment facility. This facility is widely anticipated to spearhead research trends in proton therapy in medical physics-related field. Heavily involved in dosimetry-related research, my academic advisor, Professor Hsu, spoke highly of you as a leading authority in Taiwan on microdosimetry-related research for proton therapy applications. Given the numerous advantages of proton therapy, I am anxious to consult with you and share pertinent laboratory data on the latest advances in this field. Would you please send me introductory information as well as any other pertinent publications that describe your current microdosimetry-related applications to proton therapy? If convenient, I would like to discuss with you in person some of the above

topics. I anxiously look forward to your reply.
Sincerely yours,

Dear Professor Smith,

Thank you for your letter dated November 10, 2004 on how to purify and characterize an interleukin enzyme family protease that activates cysteine protease. I look forward to exchanging laboratory data with your laboratory as part of a collaborative venture on protein purification and apoptosis mechanisms.

Our laboratory is currently attempting to understand cysteine protease in cell apoptosis mechanisms, a self-destructive biochemical process in our cells. In doing so, we hope to identify the precise defects of this fundamental biological process in human diseases, e.g., cancer, and design strategies to combat such diseases based on the knowledge acquired from our laboratory results. A variety of technical approaches have been adopted in our research, including state-of-the-art technologies in biochemistry, molecular biology and cellular biology.

During our information exchange, we hope to collaborate with your laboratory in exploring the biochemical pathway of apoptosis in mammalian systems, hopefully enabling us to identify areas of mutual interest that would lead to a technology transfer or joint venture.

I look forward to hearing your ideas or suggestions regarding this information exchange opportunity. If convenient, I would like to visit your laboratory for a two week period as the initial step of our cooperation. Thanks in advance for your careful consideration.

Sincerely yours,

Dear Mr. White,

Mr. Brine suggested that I contact you regarding the possibility of sharing our experience in protein purification as part of an information exchange relation with your laboratory that will hopefully lead to a joint venture in the near future. As widely known, your company has developed much expertise in purifying proteins and developing a baculovirus expression system. I believe that this opportunity would allow us to identify areas of common interest that would be mutually beneficial for both of our laboratories.

As a graduate student in the Institute of Biotechnology at Yuanpei University of Science and Technology in Taiwan, I belong to a research group committed to developing biochemistry-related technologies. We are currently involved in a bio-chemical development program aimed at seeking foreign partners who can either provide technologies already under patent protection or cooperate with our laboratory in a joint venture.

If you are interested in the above information exchange opportunity, we would like to visit you for further consultation. Please inform us of the appropriate time for such a visit. I look forward to hearing from you soon.

Sincerely yours,

Dear Professor Dong,

94.10 Thank you for allowing myself to visit to your laboratory. Our visiting group looks forward to meeting with you at MIT. As mentioned in my previous letter, I would like to meet with members of your laboratory group regarding the details of our joint venture, as well as tour your facilities.

Currently involved in the study of neural networks, I am especially interested in transgenic technology. In preparation for our upcoming joint venture, I am trying to become proficient in the following areas in the next four months:

1. Familiarizing myself with how a confocal scanning microscope operates to perform transgenic experiments efficiently.

2. Enhancing my computer programming skills to design experimental procedures. Doing so would allow me to conserve laboratory resources.

3. More completely understanding the principles of biological imagery.

Preparing myself in the above areas will hopefully make me more proficient in collaboration with your research group.

Sincerely yours,

Dear Mr. Johnson,

My supervisor in the X-ray Department at Lihsin Hospital, Dr. Lee, suggested that I contact you regarding the possibility of exchanging diagnosis-related information in MR imaging. Given your hospital's specialty in MR pulse sequence in neurology, we are anxious to collaborate with you in varying the pulse sequence to more closely distinguish the gray and white matter from the disease. Doing so would enable us to select accurate parameters for evaluation. We are especially interested in your currently utilized pulse sequence and specific parameters.

Li-Shin Hospital in northern Taiwan, where I work, is a teaching hospital. The MR instrumentation used in our facility is a Signa 0.5T GE system, which examines 150 patients monthly, most of whom have a neurological disorder.

As stated above, our current focus is on identifying the optimal pulse sequence for patients in the acute stage of a stroke. Each patient suspected of having a stroke initially underwent examination via the CT perfusion procedure. All of the patients then underwent MR examination under the following pulse sequence: transverse TI weighted image, transverse T2 weighted image, transverse PD weighted image, as well as coronal T2 weighted and DWI; the total scan time was 25 minutes. Next, the information provided by CT perfusion imaging was utilized to access the cerebral flow and total volume of blood. Traditional MR imaging was used mainly to evaluate the brain tissue morphology, while DW imaging was performed to evaluate the cerebral parenchyma, including the gray and white matter. Unfortunately, we did not achieve the anticipated sensitivity and accuracy rate. Based on your clinical experience, the injection volume of the contrast medium could influence the ability to accurately diagnose the likelihood of an acute stroke.

Please let me know if there are any mutual areas of interest in some of the above areas that we could collaborate on together.

Sincerely yours,

Dear Mr. Smith,

Thank you for your letter dated Nov 30, 2004. Given our common research interests, I would like to exchange information regarding gene knockout, assay function of pacemaker channel and the physiological role that may lead to disease.

As a graduate student in the Institute of Biotechnology at Yuanpei University of

Science and Technology in Taiwan, I work under the supervision of my master's thesis advisor in researching why mice lacking the pacemaker channel may display certain diseases. Of priority concern is hyperpolarization-activated cation (HCN) channels that may generate cardiac pacemaker depolarizations, as well as play a role in the control of neuronal excitability and plasticity. Our initial process was generated HCN-deficient mice. A whole-cell patch clamp was used to analyze neurons and use the Powerlab machine for physiological signal applications. The Powerlab machine can accumulate sixteen channel physiology signals simultaneously, including electrocardiograms, electroencephalograph and blood pressure. Our recent findings have been published in *The EMBO Journal* , in which the diverse physiological roles in which the channel functions were characterized.

Your recognized expertise and state-of-the-art technology would greatly benefit of our own research efforts. I look forward to hearing your ideas regarding this information exchange opportunity, as we hope to exchange relevant experiences of similar interest. To initiate this relation, I would like to visit your laboratory for a two week period in order to exchange ideas that would be mutually beneficial and accumulate pertinent data. If at all possible, please notify me which dates would be the most appropriate. Thanks in advance for your careful consideration.

Sincerely yours,

Dear Dr. Jones,

Upon the recommendation of my master's thesis advisor, I would like to exchange information with your laboratory regarding your widely recognized expertise in the atomic force microscope for purposes of Alzheimer's disease-related research. Belonging to a group that researches nanotechnology-related topics at National Nano Device Laboratories in Taiwan, I am especially interested in the role of the localized surface plasmon resonance (LSPR) nanosensor based on the optical properties of Ag nanotriangles in clarifying how amyloid β-derived diffusible ligands (ADDL) and the anti-ADDL antibody interact with each other, molecules that possibly lead to the formation of Alzheimer's disease.

I am especially concerned with how to demonstrate the nature of true nanotriangles. Doing so requires use of the atomic force microscope. As the leading cause of dementia among individuals over age 65, Alzheimer's disease inflicts an estimated 120,000 people in Taiwan. In addition to the difficulty of estimating social costs incurred from this disease, a reliable, an alternative method is unavailable to examine

Alzheimer's disease. Detecting this disease in the early stages would enable early treatment, subsequently decreasing social costs. Therefore, to compensate for this need, a LSPR nanosensor must be developed.

Given your expertise in the atomic force microscope, the opportunity to exchange information with your laboratory in the above area would greatly facilitate our research efforts. Please find enclosed pertinent statistics on Alzheimer's disease in Taiwan. I look forward to hearing from you.

Sincerely yours,

Dear Dr. Curtin,

Given our concern over upgrading the quality of universal medical and teaching facilities worldwide, our organization, National Taiwan University Hospital, we would like to apply for membership in your society. Having acquired more than two decades of clinical experience in radiation therapy at National Taiwan University Hospital, the first medical institute and teaching hospital in Taiwan and Asia, I believe that such an opportunity would be mutually beneficial for both of our organizations.

While focusing on teaching, research and service, National Taiwan University Hospital has accumulated the best medical personnel and technologists in Asia, explaining the strong emphasis on teaching. Pedagogical activities advance not only medical knowledge, but also the quality of health care. While aspiring to become a leading medical and teaching hospital worldwide, our hospital hopes to participate in the activities of universal medical and teaching hospital organizations. More than providing medical services, we also strive to enhance the quality of medical techniques and medical research. For instance, the hospital's Clinical Cancer Center has recently implemented a therapeutic planning system for cervical cancer, i.e., the most common cancer among women worldwide. Via this novel system, we can more efficiently locate the target organ and require fewer dosages for normal tissues.

Continuing with the success of our organization by further upgrading our medical and teaching capabilities depends on our ability to participate in universal organizations such as yours, subsequently elevating the quality of medical care in Asia. The opportunity to join your organization would allow us to openly exchange related experiences with other medical and teaching hospitals worldwide.

Sincerely yours,

Situation 4

Jason Wu

innovative TFT-LCD products

visit your R&D

cooperative

Situation 5

Sally Lin

Medical Knowledge

Chinese herbal medicine extracts

digital image processing biochemistry

Situation 6

Max Bai

National Taiwan University Hospital

beneficial

teaching, research

service

exchange experiences with other medical and teaching hospitals worldwide

| Write down the key points of the situations on the preceding page, while the instructor reads aloud the script from the Answer Key.

Situation 4

_____

_____

_____

Situation 5

_____

_____

_____

Situation 6

_____

_____

_____

J Oral practice II

Based on the three situations in this unit, write three questions beginning with **What**, and answer them. The questions do not need to come directly from these situations.

Examples

What does Jason's branch office strive to offer?

A line of quality products that satisfy consumer demand, both locally and abroad

What has the Taiwanese branch of this TFT-LCD company increased?

Its number of business units to ten

1. _____

   _____

2. _____

   _____

3. _____

   _____

K Based on the three situations in this unit, write three questions beginning with *Why*, and answer them. The questions do not need to come directly from these situations.

Examples

Why is Sally's research institute and the Institute of Nuclear Science at National Tsing Hua University jointly collaborating on a project?

To generate data regarding Chinese herbal medicine extracts.

Why have the experimental results generated in this project been beneficial?

They have greatly helped efforts to identify Chinese herbal medicine compounds.

1. _____

_____

2. _____

_____

3. _____

_____

L Based on the three situations in this unit, write three questions beginning with **How**, and answer them. The questions do not need to come directly from these situations.

Examples

How is National Taiwan University Hospital concerned over the need to upgrade the quality of universal medical and teaching facilities worldwide?

Owing to its intention to apply for membership in Dr. Curtin's society

How is National Taiwan University Hospital qualified for membership in Dr. Curtin's society?

By its more than two decades of clinical experience in radiation therapy

1. _____

_____

2. _____

_____

3. _____

_____

M Write questions that match the answers provided.

1. _____

_____

To initiate this collaborative relationship

2. _____

_____

At the Institute of Biotechnology at Yuanpei University of Science and Technology (YUST) in Hsinchu, Taiwan

3. _____

_____

Max's hospital

N Listening Comprehension II

Situation 4

1. What has the Taiwanese branch committed significant resources to?

    A. producing small and medium-sized panels

    B. exchanging product-related information and manufacturing technology expertise

    C. designing TFT-LCD products

2. How can Taiwan's TFT-LCD manufacturers maintain innovation in the production of TFT-LCD in Taiwan?

    A. by accelerating technological efforts that boost international competitiveness

    B. by establishing long-term collaborative ties with renowned

    C. by offering a line of quality products that satisfy consumer demand, both locally and abroad

3. What do Taiwan's TFT-LCD manufacturers focus on?

    A. producing small and medium-sized panels

    B. meeting with departmental managers and research personnel

    C. maintaining innovation in the production of TFT-LCD in Taiwan

4. What has grown rapidly in recent years?

    A. significant resources to designing TFT-LCD products

    B. establishment of long-term collaborative ties with renowned manufacturers

    C. the range of TFT-LCD products manufactured in Taiwan

5. What does Jason hope that the information exchange will lead to?

    A. a new production facility

    B. a technology transfer

    C. establishment of collaborative ties

Situation 5

1. What does the joint collaboration between Sally's research institute and the Institute of Nuclear Science at National Tsing Hua University focus on?

   A. openly sharing and exchanging experiences with other similar organizations

   B. generating data regarding Chinese herbal medicine extracts

   C. extracting and disseminating Chinese herbal medicine compounds for commercialization

2. How long have Chinese and Taiwanese extensively used Chinese herbal medicine?

   A. for a thousand years   B. for thousands of years   C. for centuries

3. What do many Chinese herbal medicine-related projects currently focus on?

   A. the potential integration of digital image processing, biochemistry and medical technology?

   B. the feasibility of integrating digital image processing with biochemical assessment, molecular biology technologies and the extraction of Chinese herbal medicine from natural substances

   C. Chinese herbal medicine extracts

4. Why can educational institutions in Taiwan employ highly qualified technical personnel to conduct advanced research on Chinese herbal medicine-related topics?

   A. advances in laboratory facilities, instrumentation and available technologies

   B. integration of digital image processing, biochemistry and medical technologies for extraction of Chinese herbal medicine from natural substances

   C. extraction and dissemination of Chinese herbal medicine compounds for commercialization

5. What has fueled Taiwan's rapid economic growth?

   A. information exchange opportunities

B. the development of many innovative technologies

C. publication of a bimonthly magazine that describes the extraction and dissemination of Chinese herbal medicine compounds for commercialization

Situation 6

1. What is the most common cancer among women worldwide?

A. lung cancer   B. breast cancer   C. cervical cancer

2. How is the hospital's Clinical Cancer Center able to more efficiently locate the target organ and use lower dosages of radiation for normal tissues?

A. using a therapeutic planning system for cervical cancer

B. using clinical experience in radiation therapy

C. a strong focus on teaching, research and service

3. How has National Taiwan University Hospital acquired the best medical personnel and technologists in Asia?

A. by exchanging experiences with other medical and teaching hospitals worldwide

B. by focusing on teaching, research and service

C. by further upgrading its medical and teaching capabilities

4. What has the hospital's Clinical Cancer Center recently implemented?

A. a therapeutic planning system for cervical cancer

B. pedagogical activities

C. lower dosages of radiation for normal tissues

5. As well as providing medical services, what has National Taiwan University Hospital strived to do?

A. upgrade the quality of universal medical and teaching facilities worldwide

B. further upgrade its medical and teaching capabilities

C. improve medical techniques and medical research

O Reading Comprehension II
Pick the work or expression whose meaning is closest to the meaning of the underlined word or expression in the following passages.

Situation 4

1. Thank you for your message sent <u>via</u> e-mail and dated November 8, 2004 inviting the branch office in Taiwan to exhibit our innovative TFT-LCD products in New York this upcoming March.

   A. of B. by C. on

2. Thank you for your message sent via e-mail and dated November 8, 2004 inviting the <u>branch</u> office in Taiwan to exhibit our innovative TFT-LCD products in New York this upcoming March.

   A. subsidiary B. headquarters C. main office

3. Thank you for your message sent via e-mail and dated November 8, 2004 inviting the branch office in Taiwan to <u>exhibit</u> our innovative TFT-LCD products in New York this upcoming March.

   A. obscure B. conceal C. unveil

4. Thank you for your message sent via e-mail and dated November 8, 2004 inviting the branch office in Taiwan to exhibit our <u>innovative</u> TFT-LCD products in New York this upcoming March.

   A. substandard B. revolutionary C. below par

5. As TFT-LCD technology <u>advances</u>, our branch office strives to offer a line of quality products that satisfy consumer demand, both locally and abroad.

   A. progresses B. retrogrades C. declines

6. As TFT-LCD technology advances, our branch office <u>strives</u> to offer a line of quality products that satisfy consumer demand, both locally and abroad.

A. emote   B. downgrade   C. set one's sight on

7. As TFT-LCD technology advances, our branch office strives to offer <u>a line of</u> quality products that satisfy consumer demand, both locally and abroad.

A. a range of   B. boundary   C. confines

8. Such <u>innovation</u> contributes to the maturation of Taiwan's recently emerging electronics sector, accelerating technological efforts that boost international competitiveness.

A. par   B. paradigm   C. novelty

9. Such innovation contributes to the <u>maturation</u> of Taiwan's recently emerging electronics sector, accelerating technological efforts that boost international competitiveness.

A. greenness   B. incipiency   C. evolution

10. Such innovation contributes to the maturation of Taiwan's recently <u>emerging</u> electronics sector, accelerating technological efforts that boost international competitiveness.

A. retracting   B. emanating   C. rescinding

11. Such innovation contributes to the maturation of Taiwan's recently emerging electronics sector, <u>accelerating</u> technological efforts that boost international competitiveness.

A. precipitating   B. wind down   C. de-escalate

12. Such innovation contributes to the maturation of Taiwan's recently emerging electronics sector, accelerating technological efforts that boost international <u>competitiveness</u>.

A. rivalry   B. assent   C. concurrence

13. The Taiwanese branch of this TFT-LCD company has increased its number of business units to ten by <u>pursuing</u> an aggressive marketing strategy since 1995, increasing revenues.

A. forestalling　B. precluding　C. contending for

14. The Taiwanese branch of this TFT-LCD company has increased its number of business units to ten by pursuing an <u>aggressive</u> marketing strategy since 1995, increasing revenues.

A. vigorous　B. stand-offish　C. aloof

15. The <u>branch</u> office tentatively plans to construct a new production facility next year and to broaden its organizational scope.

A. subsidiary　B. main office　C. corporate headquarters

16. The branch office <u>tentatively</u> plans to construct a new production facility next year and to broaden its organizational scope.

A. positively　B. unequivocally　C. temporarily

17. The branch office tentatively plans to construct a new production facility next year and to <u>broaden</u> its organizational scope.

A. hone down　B. distend　C. dwindle

18. The branch office tentatively plans to construct a new production facility next year and to broaden its organizational <u>scope</u>.

A. spectrum　B. diffusion　C. dispersion

19. The <u>range</u> of TFT-LCD products manufactured in Taiwan has grown rapidly in recent years; such products have generated considerable profits.

A. dissemination　B. propagation　C. scope

20. The range of TFT-LCD products manufactured in Taiwan has grown rapidly in recent years; such products have generated considerable <u>profits</u>.

A. liabilities　B. revenues　C. arrears

21. The Taiwanese branch has <u>committed</u> significant resources to designing TFT-LCD products, and the Intellectual Property Office of the Ministry of Economic Affairs has granted several patents.

A. relegated　B. retracted　C. receded

22. The Taiwanese branch has committed significant <u>resources</u> to designing TFT-LCD products, and the Intellectual Property Office of the Ministry of Economic Affairs has granted several patents.

A. indebtedness   B. impediment   C. assets

23. The Taiwanese branch has committed significant resources to designing TFT-LCD products, and the Intellectual Property Office of the Ministry of Economic Affairs has <u>granted</u> several patents.

A. conferred   B. nullified   C. disputed

24. The Taiwanese branch has committed significant resources to designing TFT-LCD products, and the Intellectual Property Office of the Ministry of Economic Affairs has granted several <u>patents</u>.

A. published article in a journal

B. inventions

C. published article in the proceedings of a conference or symposium

25. To continue this <u>progress</u>, we would like to exchange product-related information and manufacturing technology expertise with your R&D unit, possibly leading to a joint venture once ties are established.

A. ascent   B. plunge   C. subsidence

26. To continue this progress, we would like to exchange product-related information and manufacturing technology expertise with your R&D unit, possibly leading to a joint <u>venture</u> once ties are established.

A. maltreatment   B. undertaking   C. persecution

27. To continue this progress, we would like to exchange product-related information and manufacturing technology expertise with your R&D unit, possibly leading to a joint venture once <u>ties</u> are established.

A. bonds   B. disunion   C. dissension

28. To <u>initiate</u> this collaborative relationship, ten colleagues from the Taiwanese

branch would like to visit your R&D unit next year, hopefully meeting with your departmental managers and research personnel.

A. curtail   B. halt   C. pioneer

29. To initiate this collaborative relationship, ten colleagues from the Taiwanese branch would like to visit your R&D unit next year, hopefully meeting with your departmental managers and research <u>personnel</u>.

A. staff   B. subordinates   C. superiors

30. <u>Establishing</u> long-term collaborative ties with renowned manufacturers such as yours reflects our resolve to maintain innovation in the production of TFT-LCD in Taiwan.

A. disintegrating   B. composing   C. dissecting

31. Establishing long-term collaborative ties with <u>renowned</u> manufacturers such as yours reflects our resolve to maintain innovation in the production of TFT-LCD in Taiwan.

A. iniquitous   B. despicable   C. venerable

32. Establishing long-term collaborative ties with renowned manufacturers such as yours reflects our <u>resolve</u> to maintain innovation in the production of TFT-LCD in Taiwan.

A. determination   B. dubiousness   C. diffidence

Situation 5

1. Thank you for your letter dated December 18, 2004, containing the <u>publication</u> *Advanced Medical Knowledge*.

A. brochure   B. journal   C. newspaper

2. In response, I'd like to propose an information <u>exchange</u> between our two organizations, on the integration of digital image processing, biochemistry and medical technologies for extracting Chinese herbal medicine from natural

substances.

A. directive   B. mandate   C. interchange

3. In response, I'd like to propose an information exchange between our two organizations, on the <u>integration</u> of digital image processing, biochemistry and medical technologies for extracting Chinese herbal medicine from natural substances.

A. quarantine   B. consolidation   C. confinement

4. In response, I'd like to propose an information exchange between our two organizations, on the integration of digital image processing, biochemistry and medical technologies for <u>extracting</u> Chinese herbal medicine from natural substances.

A. discharging   B. extricating   C. dispensing

5. The project is a <u>joint</u> collaboration between our research institute and the Institute of Nuclear Science at National Tsing Hua University, and focuses on generating data regarding Chinese herbal medicine extracts.

A. concerted   B. self-reliant   C. self-governing

6. The project is a joint collaboration between our research institute and the Institute of Nuclear Science at National Tsing Hua University, and focuses on <u>generating</u> data regarding Chinese herbal medicine extracts.

A. demolishing   B. pulverizing   C. procreate

7. Our important work includes <u>publishing</u> a bimonthly magazine that describes the extraction and dissemination of Chinese herbal medicine compounds for commercialization.

A. revising   B. printing   C. proofreading

8. Our important work includes publishing a bimonthly magazine that describes the <u>extraction</u> and dissemination of Chinese herbal medicine compounds for commercialization.

A. insertion　B. instillation　C. removal

9. Our important work includes publishing a bimonthly magazine that describes the extraction and <u>dissemination</u> of Chinese herbal medicine compounds for commercialization.

A. censure　B. promulgation　C. reproof

10. Our important work includes publishing a bimonthly magazine that describes the extraction and dissemination of Chinese herbal medicine compounds for <u>commercialization</u>.

A. of buying and selling

B. of coordinating and organizing

C. of managing and consulting

11. The experimental results generated in this project have already greatly helped efforts to <u>identify</u> Chinese herbal medicine compounds.

A. camouflage　B. recognize　C. cloak

12. The experimental results generated in this project have already greatly helped efforts to identify Chinese herbal medicine <u>compounds</u>.

A. components　B. all-inclusive　C. aggregate

13. The <u>potential</u> integration of digital image processing, biochemistry and medical technology could contribute to Taiwan's rapid economic growth, fuelled by the development of many innovative technologies.

A. retroactive　B. reflective　C. prospective

14. The potential <u>integration</u> of digital image processing, biochemistry and medical technology could contribute to Taiwan's rapid economic growth, fuelled by the development of many innovative technologies.

A. consolidation　B. partition　C. fragmentation

15. The potential integration of digital image processing, biochemistry and medical technology could contribute to Taiwan's rapid economic growth, <u>fuelled by</u> the development of many innovative technologies.

A. deprecated by   B. belittled by   C. empowered by

16. Chinese and Taiwanese have <u>extensively</u> used Chinese herbal medicine for centuries.

A. narrowly   B. confining   C. expansively

17. Chinese and Taiwanese have extensively used Chinese herbal medicine for <u>centuries</u>.

A. hundreds of years   B. several years   C. several decades

18. Given advances in laboratory facilities, instrumentation and available technologies, educational institutions in Taiwan now <u>employ</u> highly qualified technical personnel to conduct advanced research on Chinese herbal medicine-related topics.

A. offer internships to

B. offer investment opportunities to

C. offer work to

19. Given advances in laboratory facilities, instrumentation and available technologies, educational institutions in Taiwan now employ highly <u>qualified</u> technical personnel to conduct advanced research on Chinese herbal medicine-related topics

A. competent   B. inept   C. clumsy

20. Many such projects currently focus on the <u>feasibility</u> of integrating digital image processing with biochemical assessment, molecular biology technologies and the extraction of Chinese herbal medicine from natural substances.

A. inefficacy   B. inoperability   C. practicality

21. Many such projects currently focus on the feasibility of <u>integrating</u> digital image processing with biochemical assessment, molecular biology technologies and the extraction of Chinese herbal medicine from natural substances.

A. bisecting   B. blending   C. subdividing

22. Many such projects currently focus on the feasibility of integrating digital image

processing with biochemical <u>assessment</u>, molecular biology technologies and the extraction of Chinese herbal medicine from natural substances.

A. appraisal   B. negation   C. rejection

23. We recognize that ensuring the <u>continued</u> success of our efforts in Taiwan depends on the open sharing and exchange of experiences with other similar organizations.

A. linear   B. interrupted   C. incoherent

24. We recognize that ensuring the continued success of our efforts in Taiwan depends on the <u>open sharing</u> and exchange of experiences with other similar organizations.

A. interaction   B. censure   C. denunciation

Situation 6

1. Given our <u>concern over</u> upgrading the quality of universal medical and teaching facilities worldwide, our organization, National Taiwan University Hospital (NTUH), would like to apply for membership in your society.

A. disregard of   B. emphasis on   C. neglect of

2. Given our concern over <u>upgrading</u> the quality of universal medical and teaching facilities worldwide, our organization, National Taiwan University Hospital (NTUH), would like to apply for membership in your society.

A. demoting   B. debasing   C. ameliorating

3. Having gained more than <u>two decades</u> of clinical experience in radiation therapy, NTHUH is the first medical institute and teaching hospital in Asia.

A. two hundred years   B. twenty months   C. twenty years

4. Having gained more than two decades of <u>clinical</u> experience in radiation therapy, NTHUH is the first medical institute and teaching hospital in Asia.

A. hospital-oriented   B. administrative-oriented   C. executive-oriented

5. <u>Pedagogical</u> activities advance not only medical knowledge, but also the quality

of health care.

A. occupational   B. learning   C. teaching (correct answer)

6. While <u>aspiring</u> to become a leading medical and teaching hospital worldwide, we hope to participate in the activities of other medical and teaching hospital organizations.

A. pausing   B. yearning   C. procrastinating

7. While aspiring to become a <u>leading</u> medical and teaching hospital worldwide, we hope to participate in the activities of other medical and teaching hospital organizations.

A. pioneering   B. unsuccessful   C. substandard

8. For instance, the hospital's Clinical Cancer Center has recently <u>implemented</u> a therapeutic planning system for cervical cancer, which is the most common cancer among women worldwide.

A. quell   B. terminate   C. put into effect

9. For instance, the hospital's Clinical Cancer Center has recently implemented a <u>therapeutic</u> planning system for cervical cancer, which is the most common cancer among women worldwide.

A. degenerative   B. restorative   C. retrogressive

10. Continuing with the success of our organization by further upgrading our medical and teaching <u>capabilities</u> depends on our ability to be involved with in wide-reaching organizations such as yours, with a view to improving medical practice in Asia.

A. aptitudes   B. weak points   C. infirmities

11. Continuing with the success of our organization by further upgrading our medical and teaching capabilities depends on our ability to be involved with in wide-reaching organizations such as yours, with a view to improving medical <u>practice</u> in Asia.

A. profession   B. entertainment   C. leisure

P Matching Exercise

1. Each sentence in the following is commonly used to exchange information: proposing an information exchange relationship 資訊交流信函：資訊流通關係的提呈. Each phrase on the left should be matched with one on the right in order to complete the sentence. Match a number on the left with a letter on the right.

1. I'd like to propose an academic information exchange	a. we would like to develop a partner relationship with you, for information exchange and for possible future collaboration.
2. Given your laboratory's innovative research in product marketing strategies, I would like to propose an information exchange relationship	b. your marketing department given our similar research interests.
3. Since our goals closely match those of your organization,	c. of a collaborative venture on protein purification and apoptosis mechanisms.
4. Miss Hu recommended that I contact you regarding	d. between our two organizations, hopefully beginning with my visit to your laboratory this upcoming July.
5. I look forward to exchanging laboratory data with your laboratory as part	e. of which can hopefully be published in a renowned international journal such as *Science*.
6. Exchanging data with your laboratory on pertinent developments would provide a valuable frame of reference for our own developments, results	f. exchanging information with your organization on the latest technological trends.
7. As our laboratories share common research interests, I hope that we could	g. regarding the global long-term health care system and population distribution research in Taiwan and the United States.
8. Dr. Cheng Jun-Jack highly recommended your hospital for its expertise in cardiac intervention, suggesting that I contact you regarding the possibility of	h. the possibility of an information exchange opportunity with your company with respect to your biotechnology products and potential technology transfer opportunities between our two organizations.
9. Our organization is eager to collaborate with	i. exchange information on how Hsc70s developmental expression affects the mung bean.

2. Exchanging information: proposing an information exchange relationship 資訊交流信函：資訊流通關係的提呈

1. Continuing with the success of our organization by further upgrading our medical and teaching capabilities depends on our ability	a. leading to future collaboration such as co-authoring of a research article or even a joint venture between our two organizations.
2. We would like to seek	b. the physiological and mental well being of elderly residents in long term care facilities in Taiwan and Japan.
3. I suggest that we exchange pertinent information on global efforts to promote	c. your Center to exchange related experiences in radiation therapy.
4. Given your prestige in this field of research, I would like to develop a mutually beneficial partnership that would allow us to exchange pertinent information,	d. manufacturing technology expertise with your R&D unit, possibly leading to a joint venture once ties are established.
5. We would like to develop a partner relation with	e. of the novel management practices in your daily operations, as well as share our own experiences in this field.
6. To continue with our progress, we would like to exchange product-related information and	f. exchanging information that would enhance the quality of clinical practice in daily operations.
7. Our company would like to establish a mutually beneficial information exchange relation with your organization to learn	g. to participate in universal organizations such as yours, subsequently elevating the quality of medical care in Asia.
8. Given our many areas of mutual interest, I suggest that our organizations begin	h. with similar organizations such as yours.
9. Continued success of this project depends on our ability to exchange relevant experiences	i. your expertise on this matter.

3. Exchanging information: introducing one's professional experience or that of one's organization in relation to the proposed information exchange relation 資訊交流信函：為資訊流通而提供個人或機構經驗

1. I belong to the Cancer Center at National Taiwan University Hospital,	a. maintains state-of-the-art instrumentation for clinical use.
2. In line with consumer demand, we continuously improve	b. patients in order to achieve full recovery from an injury or illness.
3. As a governmental supported research organization, our Center	c. developing a process model by mining text-based information that will optimize management of customer relations.
4. While aspiring to become a leading medical and teaching hospital worldwide, our hospital hopes	d. for the company's extensive line of products and services.
5. As a non-governmental, non-profit organization, ABC Hospital strives to rehabilitate	e. began working in the Wan Fang Municipal Hospital at Taipei Medical University, where I have remained until now.
6. I am currently involved in a research effort aimed at	f. the first medical institute and teaching hospital in Taiwan.
7. My work entails developing marketing strategies	g. in which corporate missions, goals, strategies and methodologies are briefly introduced.
8. Following graduation from Chung Tai Junior College of Medical Technology in 1993, I	h. to participate in the activities of universal medical and teaching hospital organizations.
9. Please find enclosed our company brochure,	i. upon and streamline biological research methods and clinical diagnostic procedures.

4. Exchanging information: introducing one's professional experience or that of one's organization in relation to the proposed information exchange relation 資訊交流信函：為資訊流通而提供個人或機構經驗

1. While focusing on teaching, research and service, National Taiwan University Hospital has accumulated	a. my professor in a National Science Council-sponsored research project aimed at generating a mutant library from clinical isolate Helicobacter pylori.
2. As a graduate student in the Institute of Biotechnology Research at Yuanpei University of Science and Technology in Hsinchu, Taiwan, I am collaborating with	b. improve upon and streamline biological research methods and clinical diagnostic procedures.
3. The project that we are currently engaged in focuses on	c. I am involved in various stages of therapeutic treatment of acute stroke patients.
4. In line with consumer demand, we continuously	d. have yielded numerous benefits for Taiwanese undergoing therapy through physical fitness.
5. As a member of the technical staff in the Nuclear Medicine Department at S.W.M Memorial Hospital,	e. which are largely concerned with how to produce a drug that resists cancer cells based on the following characteristics:
6. Enclosed please find a document that will hopefully give	f. to develop inexpensive yet high quality bio-medical products for clinical diagnosis.
7. Let me briefly let you in on our ongoing projects,	g. the best medical personnel and technologists in Asia, explaining its strong emphasis on teaching.
8. The work results generated so far in our project	h. branch office strives to offer a line of quality products to satisfy consumer demand, both locally and abroad.
9. Established in 1998, our company strives	i. providing relevant information that would facilitate a patient's recovery and well being.
10. As TFT-LCD technology continuously advances, our	j. further insight into the missions of ABC Hospital and our Department.

5. Exchanging information: commending the organization or individual to exchange information with 資訊交流信函：為資訊流通而讚揚某機構或某人

1. The Cancer Center of Stanford University is globally renowned	a. are quite impressive.
2. Given your institution's state-of-the-art technology	b. expertise in imagery analysis and project planning, which is widely regarded worldwide.
3. Given your headquarters' vast knowledge of consumer trends and technological developments in this area,	c. and advanced expertise in neurology,
4. The achievements that your closely knit staff has achieved	d. is a respectable achievement.
5. Your recent research on Internet marketing has been extremely helpful in my graduate school research in the Institute of Business Management at Yuanpei University of Science and Technology,	e. exceeding $US 5,747,000,000 in 1999,
6. Your ability to differentiate the infarction area in irreversibly damaged tissue	f. spoke highly of you as a leading authority in Taiwan on microdosimetry-related research for proton therapy applications.
7. Your research on medical imagery analysis is quite impressive, especially your	g. especially your unique strategies adopted to analyze the market potential for online commerce.
8. Given the tremendous global presence of your corporation in more than fifty countries and revenues	h. benefit our own research efforts.
9. Heavily involved in dosimetry-related research, my academic advisor, Professor Hsu,	i. for its pioneering cancer therapy.
10. Your recognized expertise in this area would greatly	j. we would like to exchange product information and manufacturing technology expertise with your R&D unit.

6. Exchanging information: commending the organization or individual to exchange information with 資訊交流信函：為資訊流通而讚揚某機構或某人

1. After reviewing your online brochure and research findings of your laboratory published in numerous international journals, I was quite impressed	a. researching related topics in collaboration with your company would be an immense boost to my determination to acquire the latest knowledge skills in this field.
2. While visiting your hospital, I was most impressed with the expertise	b. researching and developing biotechnology products and services.
3. As a globally renowned nonprofit bioresearch center that provides biological products, technical services, and educational programs to the private sector, government and academic organizations worldwide, your company specializes in	c. among medical service providers, explaining why we want to initiate this information exchange opportunity in order to remain abreast of the latest developments in this field.
4. Given your company's solid reputation in marketing,	d. with your facilities and wide scope of research activities that you are engaged in, especially the development of drug resistance cells.
5. Keio University Hospital has distinguished itself as a global leader	e. set the standard for quality that our hospital should strive for in offering medical treatment.
6. Your recent publication *Customer Behavior* has been extremely helpful in my	f. of *Nuclear Medicine Journal*, I learned how your laboratory decreased semihemisphere bleeding using coregisteration technology.
7. Your mottos of "Quality is our pride", "Quality coincides with customer's expectations", and "Quality is seeking the best treatment available"	g. of your staff in capturing concise images of liver blood vessels, which is a rather complex procedure.
8. From the January 2003 issue	h. graduate school research in the Institute of Business Management at Yuanpei University (Taiwan), especially your unique perspective on analyzing consumer behavior.

7. Exchanging information: outlining details of the information exchange relation 資訊交流信函：資訊流通關係的細節詳述

1. Through this relationship, we could	a. training will hopefully include use of the new guiding wire, triple-wire technique and implantation of drug eluting stents.
2. As for the intern position offered at your hospital on an annual basis,	b. the latest advances in online auctioning for marketing segmentation purposes.
3. We are interested in what opportunities for technological cooperation are available between	c. hopefully enabling us to identify areas of mutual interest that would lead to a technology transfer or joint venture.
4. During our information exchange, we hope to collaborate with your laboratory in exploring the biochemical pathway of apoptosis in mammalian systems,	d. but also how to identify similar blood vessels in the livers of different individuals.
5. Our collaborative relation would hopefully allow us to share information on	e. our two organizations in the area of advanced biotechnology product development.
6. As for understanding precise medical imagery of liver blood vessels, we are especially interested not only how these images compare with those of different organs in the human body,	f. I could offer relevant data from Taiwan and the Asian region.
7. While you could provide valuable information on current trends in network marketing analysis,	g. freely exchange our views and approaches towards achieving the best therapeutic outcome for our patients.
8. Our two organizations are aggressively	h. pursuing Internet marketing strategies, an area that I hope we can develop further collaboratively.

8. Exchanging information: outlining details of the information exchange relation 資訊交流信函；資訊流通關係的細節詳述

1. To initiate this information exchange relation, we suggest not only	a. to share pertinent data involving risk assessment, customer loan policies, database management and the transfer of business capital.
2. As our department actively engages in National Science Council-sponsored research in this area, we hope that the exchanging of relevant data between our two organizations will lead to	b. diagnostic skills in medical imagery of heart blood vessels.
3. The information exchange between our two organizations will hopefully allow us	c. a joint venture aimed increasing the efficiency of both radiation therapy and three-dimensional conformal radiation therapy in a hospital's oncology department.
4. We hope to share our professional	d. of mutual interest, possibly leading to a technology transfer or joint venture.
5. I hope that our staff will have the opportunity to exchange	e. I could offer relevant data from Taiwan and the Southeast Asian region.
6. While you could provide valuable information on current trends in consumer behavior analysis,	f. that our personnel receive intern training in treatment of CTO in your institution, but also that your staff offer lectures and clinical demonstrations in Taiwan.
7. I hope that through our technological information exchange, we will be able to identify areas	g. data and experiences in the field of brain stroke patients.

9. Exchanging information: expressing optimism in the anticipated information exchange relation 資訊交流信函：表達對資訊流通關係的樂觀態度

1. with the scope of activities in your marketing department,	a. mutually beneficial one.
2. We believe that such a relation would be a	b. acquire new perspectives towards the experimental process.
3. We are anxious to develop	c. regarding the possibility of such collaboration.
4. I look forward to your thoughts	d. to identify areas of common interest that would be mutually beneficial for both of our laboratories.
5. Such an exchange would enable us to	e. I am confident that our organization's similar methodologies and strategies will enable us to easily engage in a collaborative effort in the near future.
6. Your recognized expertise	f. of our hospitals whom require advanced diagnostic techniques.
7. I believe that this opportunity would allow us	g. cooperative effort.
8. I am confident that such collaboration will ultimately benefit patients in both	h. in this area would greatly benefit our own research efforts.
9. I look forward to this mutually beneficial,	i. of mutual interest, possibly leading to fruitful results for online marketing companies.
10. I hope that through our information exchange relation, we will be able to identify areas	j. long-lasting cooperative relationships with an institution such as yours.

10. Exchanging information: expressing optimism in the anticipated information exchange relation 資訊交流信函：表達對資訊流通關係的樂觀態度

1. Exchanging marketing information in this area with your company would not only	a. the doors for future collaboration between our two organizations.
2. I was pleased to learn of your interest	b. I believe that you would find our collaboration as an asset in applying scientific analysis to consumer trends and behavioral patterns.
3. Establishing long-term collaborative ties with renowned manufacturers such as yours	c. as an opportunity for our two organizations to collaborate with each other in a joint venture in the near future.
4. I firmly believe that such a cooperative relation woul	d. give me a more practical context for the theoretical concepts taught in graduate school, but also allow me to more effectively contribute to marketing efforts in Taiwan.
5. I hope that this information exchange opportunity will open	e. to share our professional experiences in this area could be mutually beneficial for both of our companies, perhaps leading to a joint venture in the near future.
6. We also anticipate the possibility	f. reflects our resolve to ensure innovativeness in Taiwan's TFT-LCD products.
7. Given my considerable research in consumer behavior and my university's solid reputation in medical imagery and quantitative analysis,	g. in our current programs from your recent correspondence.
8. I hope that you find the above information	h. would be mutually beneficial in both of our organizations' efforts to continuously upgrade expertise in medical diagnosis.
9. Given our hospital's advanced PET technological capabilities to reduce the incidence rate of stroke patients, such collaboration	i. of our organizations collaborating in the near future.
10. As I am actively involved in marketing strategy, the opportunity	j. mutually benefit both of our organizations.

11. Exchanging information: initiating the information exchange relation 資訊交流信函：開始資訊流通關係

1. Would you please send me introductory information	a. inform me of your decision at your earliest convenience.
2. Exchanging related information, e.g., methodologies, strategies, corporate missions and objectives, would	b. as to which dates are most convenient for you.
3. Please carefully consider my request and	c. there are any areas of common interest you would like to discuss.
4. I look forward to hearing your suggestions on how to initiate this information exchange relation,	d. ten colleagues from the Taiwan branch would like to visit your R&D unit next year, hopefully meeting with your departmental managers and research personnel.
5. If you find such an arrangement agreeable, please notify me	e. of our organizations collaborating in the near future.
6. With your consent, I would like to arrange for a fourteen-day technical visit	f. as well as other pertinent literature that analyzes consumer behavior in the above areas?
7. Please let me know if	g. would also be appreciated.
8. A tentative visiting schedule	h. appear to be the starting point for such cooperation, followed by visits to each other's marketing departments and, eventually, collaboration on a joint venture.
9. We also anticipate the possibility	i. perhaps a visit to your marketing department to discuss relevant strategies and areas of mutual interest.
10. To initiate this collaborative relation,	j. to your department this upcoming October as the initial step of our cooperation.

163

Unit Three

Making Technical Visits Overseas

科技訪問信函

Vocabulary and related expressions　相關字詞

expended considerable effort 花費相當的努力	collaborative ties 合作關係
state-of-the-art instrumentation 最先進的儀器設備	severely lacks 嚴重缺乏
latest technological developments 最新的科技發展	strongly desire 強烈的渴望
aggregation 聚集	research capacity 研究能力
a large degree of freedom 相當自由	currently engaged in 目前忙於……的
significant role 重要的角色	successful adopted 成功的採用
extensively adopted 廣泛地採用	integrate 使合併
exploited 利用	unique aspects 獨特的觀點
cooperative venture 合作企業	itinerary 旅程
state-of-the-art design 最先進的設計	accommodation 膳宿
pave the way 鋪路	expenses incurred 導致的花費
exchange of data 資料交換	accompany 陪同
technological capabilities 科技能力	memorandum of understanding 備忘錄
	state-of-the-art technologies 最先進的科技
	delay 使延期

as evidenced by 被引為證據
turning point 轉捩點
remain abreast of 跟上時代
lack of expertise 缺乏專業知識
brand awareness 品牌知名度
market share 市場占有率
roundtrip airfare 來回飛機票價
strengthen the cooperative ties
加強合作關係
health care facilities 保健設施
hotel reservation 旅館預訂
registered under the names of
登記在……名下
globally renowned 有全球聲譽的
prevalent 盛行的
nurturing 培育的
exchange relevant experiences
交換有關的經驗
diverse array 多變化的列陣
medical care 醫療照護
visiting schedule 訪問行程
sufficient time 足夠的時間
pose the following questions
提出以下問題

anniversary 週年紀念日
procuring （努力）取得
priority 優先
integrating 整合
design concept 設計觀念
our clinical needs 臨床需求
clinical experience 臨床經驗
plenty of time 充分的時間
itinerary 旅程
observe firsthand 直接地觀察
clarify our concerns 澄清我們關心的事
potential areas of collaboration
合作的可能空間
therapeutic treatment 有療效的治療
reputation 名譽
upcoming visit 即將來臨的訪問
forefront 最前線
safeguarding 為……提供防護措施
state-of-the-art 最先進的
highly supportive environment 高度支援的環境
slight change 微小的改變
book his flight 預訂班機

Situation 1

Larry

brain ischemia-related problems

appreciated

Larry Wang

Mr. Push

provide me with useful information

Situation 2

Mary Lu

MOU

technical cooperation

TFT-LCD products

participate technology transfer

Situation 3

Jim Lin

?!

severely lacks

visit your laboratory

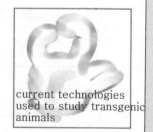

current technologies used to study transgenic animals

A Write down the key points of the situations on the preceding page, while the instructor reads aloud the script from the Answer Key.

Situation 1

_____

_____

_____

Situation 2

_____

_____

_____

Situation 3

_____

_____

_____

B Oral practice I

Based on the three situations in this unit, write three questions beginning with **What**, and answer them. The questions do not need to come directly from these situations.

Examples

What department at Kaohsiung Medical College does Larry belong to?

The Department of Nuclear Medicine

What has Mr. Push's research group expended considerable effort in doing?

Treating stroke patients using state-of-the-art instrumentation to solve brain ischemia-related problems

1. _____

_____

2. _____

_____

3. _____

_____

C Based on the three situations in this unit, write three questions beginning with **Why**, and answer them. The questions do not need to come directly from these situations.

Examples

Why did Mary invite Mr. Wang to accompany representatives of the Taiwan branch office of DISPLAY Corporation to Korea?

To explore potential product development opportunities

Why is the signing of this memorandum of understanding (MOU) important?

It will allow the two companies to engage in technical cooperation.

1. _____

_____

2. _____

_____

3. _____

_____

D Based on the three situations in this unit, write three questions beginning with *How*, and answer them. The questions do not need to come directly from these situations.

Examples

How does Mr. Smith's laboratory have much to offer Taiwan as it attempts to increase its research capacity in this area?

As a global leader in the development of medical instrumentation

How are these nonlinear complex systems extensively adopted?

In materials science and exploited in particular technologies used in industrial applications

1. _____

   _____

2. _____

   _____

3. _____

   _____

E Write questions that match the answers provided.

1. _____

   _____

   By integrating the advances of your medical research program with unique aspects of image fusion

2. _____

   _____

   Owing to its ability to remain abreast of the latest technologies that leaders in the field adopted to ensure continued growth, research and development of products, and product innovation

3. _____

   _____

   The synchronization firing of neural networks and their aggregation in the dictyostelium system

F Listening Comprehension I

Situation 1

1. How has Mr. Push's research group expended considerable effort in treating stroke patients?

 A. by integrating the advances of medical research program with unique aspects of image fusion

 B. by using state-of-the-art instrumentation to solve brain ischemia-related problems

 C. through continuous advances in computer software programs

2. Who has recently formed a research group to learn of the latest medical technologies available to combat brain ischemia?

 A. Dr. Smith　B. Larry Wang　C. Mr. Push

3. How is it possible to ensure continuous advances in computer software programs to alleviate brain ischemia?

 A. successful treatments that have reduced the likelihood of strokes

 B. specialists in the field of nuclear medicine

 C. aggressive efforts to reduce the incidence of failure during brain operations

4. What can greatly reduce examination time?

 A. the latest computer software

 B. considerable effort in treating stroke patients using state-of-the-art instrumentation

 C. unique aspects of image fusion would significantly reduce the incidence of stroke

5. How can one significantly reduce the incidence of stroke at Larry's hospital?

 A. by ensuring continuous advances in computer software programs to alleviate brain ischemia

B. the ability to integrate the advances of your medical research program with unique aspects of image fusion

C. successful treatments that have reduced the likelihood of strokes

Situation 2

1. What evidence proves that the employees at Mary's company are highly motivated?

   A. potential product development opportunities

   B. brand awareness and market share

   C. the recent development of several TFT-LCD products

2. What would the signing of this MOU at the Korean headquarters of DISPLAY Corporation allow the Taiwan branch to do?

   A. explore potential product development opportunities

   B. develop state-of-the-art technologies by continually upgrading the company's technological capabilities and innovation in product design

   C. participate in a technology transfer to help develop some of the above product technologies

3. What are the 6.4W and 10.4W inch offerings intended for?

   A. DVD, automobile navigation, portable TV, entertainment products and digital TV cameras

   B. industrial products

   C. developing TFT-LCD materials

4. What are notable examples of the latest technologies that leaders in the field adopted to ensure continued growth, research and development of products, and product innovation?

   A. 10.4-inch TFT-LCD products, as well as 2.45W and 3.5W-inch products for digital cameras, pocket TVs and TV cameras

B. 5W, 6.4W, 6.5W, 7W, 8W and 10W inch offerings

C. 6.4W and 10.4W inch offerings

5. Where will the signing of this MOU be held?

A. at the American headquarters of DISPLAY Corporation

B. at the Taiwan headquarters of DISPLAY Corporation

C. at the Korean headquarters of DISPLAY Corporation

Situation 3

1. What does Jim believe that the opportunity to visit Mr. Smith's laboratory will lead to?

A. synchronization firing of neural networks and their aggregation in the dictyostelium system

B. a large degree of freedom in which cooperative effects play a significant role

C. a technology transfer and/or a cooperative venture in the near future

2. Who is a global leader in the development of medical instrumentation?

A. Mr. Smith's laboratory   B. Jim's laboratory   C. Mr. Lin's laboratory

3. What is Taiwan attempting to increase?

A. its research capacity in medical instrumentation

B. its research capacity in bioimaging instruments

C. its research capacity in advanced computer software

4. What can save Jim's laboratory considerable resources?

A. nonlinear complex systems

B. advanced medical instrumentation

C. state-of-the-art design program applications could automate a part of the experimental procedure

G Reading Comprehension I
Pick the work or expression whose meaning is closest to the meaning of the underlined word or expression in the following passages.

Situation 1

1. I belong to the Department of Nuclear Medicine at Kaohsiung Medical College.

   A. am a supervisor in   B. am an employee of   C. am a consultant to

2. Your research group has <u>expended</u> considerable effort in treating stroke patients using state-of-the-art instrumentation to solve brain ischemia-related problems.

   A. spent   B. sustained   C. preserved

3. Your research group has expended considerable effort in treating stroke patients using <u>state-of-the-art</u> instrumentation to solve brain ischemia-related problems.

   A. subordinate   B. second-rate   C. cutting edge

4. Although I <u>strongly</u> desire to undergo extensive training from your medical group on the latest technological developments in this area, arranging the required large block of time is impossible given my hectic schedule at work.

   A. sensitively   B. intensely   C. temperately

5. Although I strongly desire to undergo extensive training from your medical group on the latest technological developments in this area, arranging the required large <u>block of time</u> is impossible given my hectic schedule at work.

   A. time period   B. capacity   C. quantity

6. Although I strongly desire to undergo extensive training from your medical group on the latest technological developments in this area, arranging the required large block of time is impossible given my <u>hectic</u> schedule at work.

   A. placid   B. slack   C. busy

7. However, I would like to arrange for a five-day technical visit with the Head of

your Nuclear Medicine Department, Dr. Smith, and his recently <u>formed</u> research group, to learn of the latest medical technologies available to combat brain ischemia.

A. dissolved　B. established　C. dispersed

8. However, I would like to arrange for a five-day technical visit with the Head of your Nuclear Medicine Department, Dr. Smith, and his recently formed research group, to learn of the latest medical technologies available to <u>combat</u> brain ischemia.

A. facilitate　B. make amends with　C. fight

9. I am especially interested in learning about your successful treatments that have reduced the <u>likelihood</u> of strokes.

A. incredibility　B. probability　C. unavailability

10. I am very <u>impressed with</u> the medical software program developed by your research group, which has been successful adopted at UCLA.

A. encouraged by　B. discouraged with　C. despondent

11. At graduate school, I attempted to <u>elucidate</u> the actual mechanism that operates during ischemia.

A. perplex　B. clarify　C. baffle

12. At graduate school, I attempted to elucidate the actual mechanism that <u>operates</u> during ischemia.

A. functions　B. malfunctions　C. breaks down

13. The ability to <u>integrate</u> the advances of your medical research program with unique aspects of image fusion would significantly reduce the incidence of stroke at our hospital.

A. disengage　B. uncouple　C. combine

14. The ability to integrate the advances of your medical research program with <u>unique</u> aspects of image fusion would significantly reduce the incidence of

stroke at our hospital.

A. mediocre   B. unparalleled   C. humdrum

15. The ability to integrate the advances of your medical research program with unique aspects of image fusion would significantly reduce the <u>incidence</u> of stroke at our hospital.

A. occurrence   B. misconception   C. fallacy

16. A five-day technical visit to your institution would provide me with <u>useful</u> information on the latest computer software that could greatly reduce examination time.

A. defective   B. insufficient   C. functional

17. A five-day technical visit to your institution would provide me with useful information on the latest computer software that could greatly <u>reduce</u> examination time.

A. amplify   B. aggrandize   C. alleviate

18. <u>Specialists</u> in the field of nuclear medicine are well aware that ensuring continuous advances in computer software programs to alleviate brain ischemia depends on aggressive efforts such as those that are currently being made by your research group, to reduce the incidence of failure during brain operations.

A. connoisseurs   B. dabblers   C. novices

19. Specialists in the field of nuclear medicine are <u>well aware</u> that ensuring continuous advances in computer software programs to alleviate brain ischemia depends on aggressive efforts such as those that are currently being made by your research group, to reduce the incidence of failure during brain operations.

A. oblivious   B. cognizant   C. unconscious

20. Specialists in the field of nuclear medicine are well aware that ensuring <u>continuous</u> advances in computer software programs to alleviate brain ischemia depends on aggressive efforts such as those that are currently being made by

your research group, to reduce the incidence of failure during brain operations.

A. successive   B. obstructed   C. hindered

21. Specialists in the field of nuclear medicine are well aware that ensuring continuous advances in computer software programs to <u>alleviate</u> brain ischemia depends on aggressive efforts such as those that are currently being made by your research group, to reduce the incidence of failure during brain operations.

A. increase the likelihood of

B. lower the likelihood of

C. stabilize the likelihood of

22. Specialists in the field of nuclear medicine are well aware that ensuring continuous advances in computer software programs to alleviate brain ischemia depends on aggressive efforts such as those that are currently being made by your research group, to reduce the incidence of <u>failure</u> during brain operations.

A. accomplishment   B. fiasco   C. affluence

23. A suggested itinerary would also be most appreciated, including time for discussion, and a tour of research facilities and <u>accommodation</u>.

A. conference arrangements

B. consulting arrangements

C. living arrangements

24. Of course, all expenses <u>incurred</u> during the visit will be covered by my organization.

A. created   B. paid for   C. written off

25. Of course, all expenses incurred during the visit will be <u>covered by</u> my organization.

A. paid for   B. sold to   C. invested by

Situation 2

1. I hope that you received my letter dated May 30, 2004 in which I invited you to <u>accompany</u> representatives of the Taiwan branch office of DISPLAY Corporation to Korea, to explore potential product development opportunities.

   A. refute   B. go along with   C. resist

2. I hope that you received my letter dated May 30, 2004 in which I invited you to accompany representatives of the Taiwan branch office of DISPLAY Corporation to Korea, to <u>explore</u> potential product development opportunities.

   A. disavow   B. scrutinize   C. disclaim

3. I hope that you will be present for the signing of this <u>memorandum</u> of understanding (MOU) that would allow our two companies to engage in technical cooperation.

   A. postponement   B. delay   C. reminder

4. I hope that you will be present for the signing of this memorandum of understanding (MOU) that would allow our two companies to <u>engage in</u> technical cooperation.

   A. participate in   B. abstain from   C. desist from

5. Our R&D Department <u>strives</u> to develop state-of-the-art technologies by continually upgrading our technological capabilities and innovation in product design.

   A. subdues   B. subjugates   C. aims

6. Our R&D Department strives to develop <u>state-of-the-art</u> technologies by continually upgrading our technological capabilities and innovation in product design.

   A. retrogressive   B. progressive   C. reactionary

7. Our R&D Department strives to develop state-of-the-art technologies by <u>continually</u> upgrading our technological capabilities and innovation in product

design.

A. incessantly　B. intermittently　C. sporadically

8. Our R&D Department strives to develop state-of-the-art technologies by continually upgrading our technological capabilities and <u>innovation</u> in product design.

A. relic　B. antiquity　C. modernization

9. Our employees are highly <u>motivated,</u> as evidenced by our recent development of several TFT-LCD products.

A. intimidated　B. impelled　C. daunted

10. Our employees are highly motivated, <u>as evidenced by</u> our recent development of several TFT-LCD products.

A. as ridiculed by　B. as proven by　C. as refuted by

11. Our <u>turning point</u> in corporate growth arose from our ability to remain abreast of the latest technologies that leaders in the field adopted to ensure continued growth, research and development of products, and product innovation.

A. decisive moment　B. inconclusive　C. unsettled

12. Our turning point in corporate growth arose from our ability to <u>remain abreast of</u> the latest technologies that leaders in the field adopted to ensure continued growth, research and development of products, and product innovation.

A. lose interest in　B. lose touch with　C. keep in tune with

13. While 5W, 6.4W, 6.5W, 7W, 8W and 10W inch <u>offerings</u> are for DVD, automobile navigation, portable TV, entertainment products and digital TV cameras, the 6.4W and 10.4W inch offerings are for industrial products.

A. available products　B. inefficacious products　C. futile products

14. Given our <u>lack of</u> expertise in developing TFT-LCD materials, this cooperative agreement will ultimately increase our brand awareness and market share.

A. bounty of　B. plentitude of　C. deficiency in

15. Given our lack of expertise in developing TFT-LCD materials, this cooperative agreement will ultimately increase our <u>brand</u> awareness and market share.

    A. product type   B. software type   C. hardware type

16. Again, your presence at this signing would be <u>meaningful</u> to both of our organizations given your expertise in this area.

    A. irrelevant   B. immaterial   C. portentous

17. Again, your presence at this signing would be meaningful to both of our organizations given your <u>expertise</u> in this area.

    A. immaturity   B. proficiency   C. wet-behind-the-ears

18. Your <u>prompt</u> reply regarding the details of this upcoming visit would be most appreciated.

    A. deliberate   B. punctual   C. careful

19. Your prompt reply regarding the <u>details</u> of this upcoming visit would be most appreciated.

    A. particulars   B. ambiguities   C. vagueness

Situation 3

1. As I mentioned in earlier <u>correspondence</u>, as a researcher at the Bioimage Laboratories at Yuanpei University of Science and Technology in Taiwan, I am concerned with upgrading the precision of bioimaging instruments, which Taiwan severely lacks.

    A. communiqué   B. visit   C. training

2. As I mentioned in earlier correspondence, as a researcher at the Bioimage Laboratories at Yuanpei University of Science and Technology in Taiwan, I am concerned with upgrading the <u>precision</u> of bioimaging instruments, which Taiwan severely lacks.

    A. inaccuracy   B. exactness   C. ambiguousness

3. As a global leader in the development of medical instrumentation, your laboratory <u>definitely</u> has much to offer our country as we attempt to increase our research capacity in this area.

A. impervious　B. disputably　C. unequivocally

4. As a global leader in the development of medical instrumentation, your laboratory definitely has much to offer our country as we attempt to increase our research <u>capacity</u> in this area.

A. magnitude　B. encounter　C. address

5. Allow me to <u>brief</u> you on our ongoing projects.

A. skirt the issue　B. summarize　C. avoid the topic of discussion

6. Allow me to brief you on our <u>ongoing</u> projects.

A. current　B. preceding　C. onetime

7. We are currently <u>engaged in</u> the synchronization firing of neural networks and their aggregation in the dictyostelium system.

A. refraining from　B. abstaining from　C. participating in

8. We are currently engaged in the synchronization firing of neural networks and their <u>aggregation</u> in the dictyostelium system.

A. dispersion　B. accumulation　C. dissemination

9. Often exhibiting <u>unusual</u> and physically interesting phenomena, these nonlinear complex systems are extensively adopted in materials science and exploited in particular technologies used in industrial applications.

A. extraordinary　B. habitual　C. routine

10. Often exhibiting unusual and physically interesting <u>phenomena</u>, these nonlinear complex systems are extensively adopted in materials science and exploited in particular technologies used in industrial applications.

A. verification　B. occurrences　C. confirmation

11. Often exhibiting unusual and physically interesting phenomena, these nonlinear

complex systems are extensively <u>adopted</u> in materials science and exploited in particular technologies used in industrial applications.

A. taken out　B. held back　C. utilized

12. Often exhibiting unusual and physically interesting phenomena, these nonlinear complex systems are extensively adopted in materials science and <u>exploited</u> in particular technologies used in industrial applications.

A. capitalized on　B. disregarded　C. overlooked

13. <u>State-of-the-art</u> design program applications could automate a part of the experimental procedure, saving us considerable laboratory resources.

A. obsolete　B. outmoded　C. cutting edge

14. I am confident that the upcoming visit to your laboratory will <u>pave the way</u> for a further exchange of data on the aforementioned program developments.

A. terminate　B. open doors　C. abort

H Common elements in making technical visits overseas（科技訪問信函）include the following contents:

1. Requesting permission to make a technical visit 科技訪問許可申請

2. Stating the purpose of the technical visit 闡述科技訪問的目的

3. Introducing one's qualifications or one's organizational experiences 介紹某人的能力或機構經驗

4. Commending the organization to be visited 對訪問機構的讚揚

5. Outlining details of the technical visit 詳述科技訪問的細節

6. Requesting confirmation for approval of the technical visit 科技訪問核准的確認申請

Write a letter to make a technical visit overseas.

_____

_____

_____

_____

Unit three

Making Technical Visits Overseas
科技訪問信函

1. Requesting permission to make a technical visit
科技訪問許可申請

2. Stating the purpose of the technical visit
闡述科技訪問的目的

3. Introducing one's qualifications or one's organizational experiences
介紹某人的能力或機構經驗

4. Commending the organization to be visited
對訪問機構的讚揚

5. Outlining details of the technical visit
詳述科技訪問的細節

6. Requesting confirmation for approval of the technical visit
科技訪問核准的確認申請

Look at the following examples of letters on making technical visits overseas.

Dear Mr. Wang,

Thank you for your enthusiasm in working with me to set up a collaborative relationship between our hospitals in the form of a memorandum of understanding (MOU) to be signed later this year in a formal ceremony. Our hospital administrators are fully supportive of this collaborative agreement and anticipate the possibility of joint venture projects in the future. Recently, I have been arranging the detailed schedule for our collaboration and would like to sum up what progress has been made.

In preparation for our meeting next month, I have been working on the details of how we can evaluate diseases by adopting the latest imagery procedures for purposes of liver and heart transplantation. Hopefully, those evaluation results can enable both of our hospitals to produce concise images of the liver before the transplantation procedure. Prior to our meeting next month, I hope that you could supply some medical images from case studies involving different liver diseases, such as images of a normal liver vessel, a congenital liver vessel and an abnormal disease or acquired liver disease. As per your request, I have prepared heart transplantation-related images. The ability to exchange information that would ultimately enhance diagnostic accuracy prior to surgery would definitely benefit administrative procedures in both of our hospitals.

As we have been preparing the details of this cooperative agreement for the past two months, I am pleased with the way in which we have been able to openly exchange information that will enhance the quality of medical care in both of our hospitals. Any additional information that you could supply me regarding the above topics would be most appreciated. I look forward to seeing you at next month's meeting.

Sincerely yours,

Dear Mr. Push,

I belong to the Department of Nuclear Medicine at Kaohsiung Medical College. Your research group has expended considerable effort in treating stroke patients by state-of-the-art instrumentation aimed at resolve brain ischemia-related problems. Although I strongly desire to receive an extensive period of training from your medical group on the latest technological developments in this area, arranging such a large block of time is impossible given my hectic schedule at work. However, I would like to arrange for a five day technical visit with your Nuclear Medicine Department chief, Dr. Smith, and his recently formed research group to learn of the latest medical technologies available to combat brain ischemia. I am especially interested in learning of your successful cases of treatment to reduce the likelihood of a stroke from occurring. I am also highly impressed with the medical software program developed in your research group, which has been successful adopted at UCLA. My graduate school research attempted to elucidate the actual mechanism that is present during ischemia. The ability to integrate the advances of your medical research program with the unique aspects of image fusion would significantly decrease the rate of stroke victims in our hospital.

A five-day technical visit to your institution would hopefully provide me with relevant information on the latest computer software that can reduce examination time as much as possible. Specialists in the nuclear medicine field are well aware that ensuring continuous advances in computer software programs to alleviate brain ischemia depends on aggressive efforts such as those in your research group to reduce the incidence of failure during brain operations.

If this visit is agreeable with you, please notify me which dates are convenient for you. A suggested itinerary would also be most appreciated, including our discussion time, tour of research facilities and accommodations. Of course, all expenses incurred during this visit will be covered by my organization. I look forward to your favorable reply.

Sincerely yours,

Dear Professor Smith,

We are pleased to have had you working in our laboratory as a guest researcher this past month. During the International Conference on Three-dimensional Medical Images on Oct 29, you mentioned your radiology department's capabilities in processing three-dimensional images. Given our interest in your technological developments in this field, we would like to visit your hospital to more thoroughly understand the progress that you have made.

I hope the following information aptly describes the nature of this proposed technical visit:

1. Purpose: To visit your hospital's radiological department in order to more thoroughly understand the capabilities of three-dimensional digital imaging processing in your laboratory to display pertinent patient data. We are especially interested in how a medical image's quality is related to image space, as well as the latest medical breakthroughs in this area.

2. The visiting group will comprise administrative officials from the Taiwanese Association of Medical Imagery, , surgeons in this field of expertise, radiologists and medical personnel from other leading hospitals in Taiwan.

Quite some time has passed since I originally proposed the idea of our technical visit to your country without any response from you so far. I would be most grateful if you could advise us on the status of this proposed technical visit so that we can begin making the necessary travel arrangements.

Thanks in advance for your kind assistance.

Sincerely yours,

Dear Mr. Smith,

Thank you for allowing us to visit to your center. Our visiting group looks forward to meeting you in Helsinki. As a research unit of Biomedicum Helsinki, your research center (Biomedicum Biochip Center) is renowned for its efforts to develop biochip technologies for post-genomic era biomedical research. We are especially interested in the high throughput screening of genomes, transcriptase and proteome coupled with cell-based functional screening. We are also impressed with your innovativeness in performing bioinformatics-based analyses of biochip data, while applying the results of these research efforts to eradicate complex diseases such as cancer. More specifically, during our upcoming trip, we hope to discuss the following topics in detail:

1. Biochip technology developments, including SNP, cDNA, oligo, lysate and cell microarrays;

2. Use of biochips to identify novel drug targets for cancer;

3. Novel bioinformatics-related procedures to analyze microarray data;

4. Microarray-related applications in studying complex diseases; and

5. Available microarray services that your core facility provides for academic and commercial purposes.

The above topics will hopefully give you a clearer idea of the topics we want to cover during the upcoming visit so that you can make necessary preparations beforehand.

We look forward to meeting you.
Sincerely yours,

Dear Ms. Smith,

Thank you for your prompt reply to my query regarding your research efforts to understand how genes and the natural transformation of Helicobacter pylori are related. I am especially interested in efforts underway in Germany to elucidate the role of Helicobacter pylori. From your press release dated November 10, 2005 on recent developments to identify protein functions, I greatly benefited from your findings on how Helicobacter pylori can be used in vaccines and medicinal applications. I would like to arrange a three day technical visit to discuss some of the above topics with you in more detail.

As is well known, exactly how *H. pylori* spreads remains unknown. Roughly 20% of all children inflicted with peptic ulcers experience bleeding, subsequently leading to hematemesis or melena. Diagnosing this condition in children with peptic ulcers may be more difficult owing to the lack of clear cut symptoms as compared to those found in adolescents. Therefore, given the difficulty of prevention, efforts such as those in both of our laboratories are underway to develop a vaccine that would prevent infection. In the near future, we hope to obtain gene knockout strains to ultimately develop an effective vaccine.

I look forward to your ideas regarding this proposed visit and some of the above issues raised. The opportunity to consult with you in person will hopefully yield mutually beneficial results for both of our laboratories.
Sincerely yours,

Dear Mr. Brown,

Thank you for allowing Dr. Lin and myself to visit ABC Laboratory at 9:00 AM on November the 12th. As mentioned in my previous letter, we would like to meet with members of your working group regarding details of our cooperative agreement, as well as tour your facilities.

I would like to pose the following questions before our discussion on November 12 so that you will have sufficient time to prepare your responses:

1. What sampling procedures or software program does your laboratory adopt to reduce sampling error, especially when the samples come from different countries?

2. How does your laboratory develop or implement a forecasting model based on an incomplete database, particularly in developing countries?

3. As is well known, governments normally publish only a portion of their statistical data. What procedures or standard operational procedures does your laboratory adopt in accumulating detailed data?

4. Each country has its own unique standard of classifying its long-term health care facilities, as well as different services provided. What standard does your laboratory adopt to classify long-term health care facilities in different countries? Also, what is your rationale for adopting such a standard?

I hope that the above questions will give you a clearer idea of some of the topics we hope to cover during the upcoming visit. I look forward to meeting you on November 12.

Sincerely yours,

Dear Mr. Jones,

I am a graduate student in the Yuanpei University of Science and Technology. I am currently involved in a research effort aimed at developing a process model by mining text-based information that will optimize management of customer relations. I am also studying the characteristics of various mining technologies adopted in statistics process control.

Professor Lin, the President of Yuanpei University of Science and Technology, recommended that we visit your renowned institute and find some time to discuss our needs with you, as well as learn of some of your own related experiences. Therefore, we hope to visit you in the latter part of March.

Please let me know if it is convenient for us to visit on March 7. If so, could you arrange for a tour of your facilities? I look forward to hearing from you.

Sincerely yours,

Dear Dr. Jones,

My colleague, Mr. Wang, suggested that I contact you regarding the possibility of a technical visit to your company given your excellent product quality and strong commitment to adopting advanced environmental protection practices in your manufacturing processes. As is well known, your company pioneered the use of natural plant oil to refine crude oil for use in daily goods and appliances. We are particularly impressed with your company's extensive line of more than one hundred family and health products and appliances through the refining of natural oil via natural plants. Your products conform to the most stringent environmental standards through use of ingredients that are phosphate-free and environmentally friendly. We are further impressed with the number of patented technologies that you hold for manufacturing your natural products that adopt the latest scientific and technological advances, as well as quality assurance standards.

Our company's Product Development Division is committed to adhering to the Taiwannese government's aggressive policy towards promoting the use of environmentally friendly practices in manufacturing. Given your company's expertise in this area, we would like to arrange for a technical visit next month to tour your facilities and share our related experiences in product development using the refinement of natural oil via natural plants. I will be accompanies by two environmental protection experts in this area: Mr. Chen, a biologist who is studying how certain organisms and the surrounding environment are related and Mr. Lee, also a biologist who is studying natural product applications that do not endanger the environment. Our discussions will hopefully be mutually beneficial, perhaps leading to technology transfer or joint venture opportunities between our two companies. Please find enclosed our company brochure that briefly introduces our product line. If this is agreeable with you, please contact me at your earliest convenience so that we can make the necessary travel arrangements.

Sincerely yours,

Dear Mr. Lion,

Allow me to introduce myself. I am currently an administrative manager in the Product Development Division of ABC Company. Having recently acquired my

Master's degree in Business Management from Yuanpei University of Science and Technology in Taiwan, I received my undergraduate training in Healthcare Management at National Taipei College of Nursing (NTCN).

Rapid economic growth in Taiwan has incurred alarming levels of air, water and environmental pollution. . In response, the Taiwanese government has implemented an aggressive environmental policy aimed at integrating the efforts of local industry and various research and technology organizations to alleviate the threat posed to the island's 23 million inhabitants. With aspirations of becoming a "Green Silicon Island", Taiwan has actively encouraged its enterprises in recent years with numerous incentives to be more socially responsible in its manufacturing practices.

Given your corporation's committing to adopting the most advanced environmental protection technologies in your manufacturing processes, I would like to arrange for a three day technical visit to your product development division to learn of the operational aspects and theoretical applications that you adopt in production. In addition to your pioneering efforts in environmental protection, I am also interested in how to maintain production efficiency, as well as related marketing strategies, implementation and problem solving measures.

I would like to arrange for a ten day technical visit to your company and other pertinent places this upcoming December. If this visit is agreeable with you, please notify me which dates are convenient for you. A suggested itinerary would also be most appreciated, i.e., discussion time, plant tour schedule and accommodations. I look forward to your favorable reply.

Sincerely yours,

Dear Dr. Wu,

Thank you for the opportunity to serve as a visiting guest researcher in your laboratory this upcoming June. Given my concern with the role of Internet commerce in sales-related research, I hope to directly consult with you on my current research direction.

Hopefully, my upcoming research stay will allow me to achieve the following objectives:

1. Understand the current status of Internet commerce in the Philippines.
2. Understand the availability of the Internet to consumers in the Philippines.

3. Discuss my research methodology for an Internet marketing project with Dr. Wu.

To arrange for the upcoming research visit in order to consult with you on the above topics, I need to set up an itinerary and time schedule to report to my superiors. I would appreciate it if you could list the details of this visit in an itinerary form for processing of an overseas visit that my organization requires I look forward to meeting you in anticipation of our future collaboration.

Sincerely yours,

Dear Mr. Lin,

We look forward to visiting your organization next year. Prior to our visit, we would appreciate any introductory information that you could pass on to us regarding transportation arrangements and a list of hotels near our meeting place. If possible, we hope to meet with you on the morning of January the 12th. During our discussion, we are especially interested in the following areas:

1. Operating procedures of your organization in terms of implementing Internet marketing-related strategies;

2. Specific strategies that your organization adopts in marketing its products and services online;

3. Time schedules and other considerations made when establishing Internet marketing-related goals; and

4. Distinguishing features of your organization's Internet marketing practices in contrast to those of other companies.

I hope that the above questions will give you a clearer idea of our interests and allow you sufficient time to prepare any relevant materials beforehand. Thanks for the arrangements that you have already made in preparation for this visit. I look forward to meeting you this upcoming January. If you are ever in the Far East, I hope that you will have the opportunity to visit our organization as well.

Sincerely yours,

Dear Ms. Smith,

Thank your for the opportunity to your organization. Our visiting group is anxious to meet your working group, as well as tour your hospital facilities. I would like to point out our areas of concern that can hopefully be included in our discussion on December the 24th beforehand so that you will have sufficient time to prepare your responses:

1. Procedure for establishing a safety treatment environment during personnel training;
2. Blood transfusion process that your hospital follows;.
3. Identification procedure for returning outpatients and patients to be admitted to the hospital; and
4. Overview of your hospital's main medical procedures.

I hope that the above topics of discussion will give you sufficient time to prepare any relevant materials or handouts. Thanks in advance for your careful arrangements. I look forward to meeting you and hope that, in the near future, you will have the opportunity to visit our facilities in Taiwan.

Sincerely yours,

Dear Mr. Smith,

Thank you for the opportunity to receive intensive training in your laboratory during my upcoming winter vacation. I am confident that I will learn much that will benefit my current research direction. Hopefully, this opportunity will pave the way for further exchanges between our laboratories. I would appreciate if you would forward any pertinent information that will make my visit more productive, such as transportation arrangements and a list of nearby hotels. Of course, all expenses will be covered by my organization.

As I mentioned previously, as a graduate student in the Institute of Business Management at Yuanpei University of Science and Technology in Taiwan, I have become increasingly proficient in resolving a wide array of marketing problems, subsequently spurring my creativity and analytical capabilities. I am especially fascinated with how technological advances in quantitative analysis and computer software have greatly facilitated our laboratory's efforts in researching marketing approaches adopted in the global network and their implications for marketing strategies aimed at the Greater China sector. As is well known, gaining greater access to markets online is exposure. Advertisers must constantly come up with innovative ways to draw in customers to their websites and hold their attention until goods or services are purchased online. Effective strategies incorporate local and regional considerations, thus highlighting the need for informative market Surveys. In this area, your laboratory has acquired much expertise and relevant data, explaining why I am eager to join your laboratory for this intensive training course.

Thanks in advance for your assistance. I hope that this training will eventually lead to a collaborative relationship between our two laboratories that would allow us to share pertinent data based on our mutual scientific research interests.

Sincerely yours,

Dear Mr. Smith,

Thank you for allowing us to visit your research center. Our visiting group looks forward to meeting you in Japan. Given your country's progressive welfare policies for the elderly population (including state-of-the-art facilities), we can learn much from your organization. During our visit, we hope to discuss the following topics in detail:

1. Distribution of medical personnel in nursing home facilities and some of the current challenges;
2. Salary scale structure and insurance coverage for medical personnel in nursing home facilities;
3. Activity exercise schedule for residents in nursing home facilities; and
4. Adoption and implementation of quality control standards in nursing home facilities.

The above topics will hopefully give you a clear idea of the topics we would like to cover during the upcoming visit. Thanks in advance for making necessary preparations beforehand. We look forward to meeting you.

Sincerely yours,

Dear Mr. Duke,

Thank you for your favorable reply on December the 7th in agreement with our research team visiting your organization early next year. Given the pivotal role that your organization plays in the World Health Organization, we are eager to learn of your expertise in handling global health issues, especially promotion-related activities. I would like to pose the following questions prior to our arrival so that you would have a better idea of our current direction:

1. How does your organization assist local governmental authorities in implementing health promotion activities?
2. What role does your organization play in devising the government's health promotion policies?
3. What communication channel does your organization have with local governmental authorities when promoting health issues nationwide?
4. What health promotion strategies do you hope to develop in the future?

I hope that posing these questions in advance will make our discussion a more productive one. Thanks in advance for preparing materials relevant to the above questions. I also hope that this meeting will allow our two organizations to freely exchange information on a mutually beneficial basis, perhaps through the signing a memorandum of understanding (MOU) in the near future. I look forward to your ideas or suggestions for such a collaborative arrangement. See you on January the 25th. Sincerely yours,

Dear Professor Lin,

Allow me to introduce myself. Having recently acquired my Master's degree in Business Management from Yuanpei University of Science and Technology in Taiwan, I am currently working with a travel agency in devising marketing strategies for promoting domestic tour packages island wide. With its multi-faceted purposes, tourism requires further development for Taiwan to reach its potential in this area As tourism generates an influx of foreign currency into the local economy, some countries are aggressively devising strategies to develop tourism as a means of spurring economic growth. For Taiwan, local tourism is more than just increasing foreign currency exchange, but also enabling others to understand the island's contributions to the international community.

Given my above interests, I would visit your research laboratory and discuss with you some of the above topics in more detail. If this visit is agreeable with you, please notify me which dates are convenient for you. A suggested itinerary would also be most appreciated, including our discussion time, tour of research facilities and accommodations. Of course, all expenses incurred during this visit will be covered by my organization.

I look forward to your ideas regarding this proposed visit and some of the above issues raised. Thanks in advance for your assistance. Hopefully, this visit will lead to some form of collaboration in the near future that would allow us to share pertinent data based on our mutual areas of research interest.

Sincerely yours,

Dear Mr. Smith,

Thank you for allowing us to visit to your laboratory. Dr. Chang, Mrs. Li and myself would like to thank you in advance for meeting us at the Biochemical Laboratories at Yuanpei University of Science and Technology in Hsinchu on January the 8th at 9 AM. As mentioned in our previous correspondence, we would like to visit your new computer testing facilities, as well as discuss the details of our cooperative agreement. I would like to pose the following questions to allow you time to prepare your responses before our discussion:

1. As extracting Chinese herbal medicine in Taiwan is quite expensive, would it be possible to supply advanced extraction machinery.

2. Operating advanced computer machinery to treat plant systems takes approximately 150 hours weekly, including 100 hrs for operation, twelve hours for start-up, with the remaining time for maintenance and clean-up. It is possible to extend the operating period? If not, is a batch operation performed weekly?

3. Owing to extensive variety of Chinese herbal medicines available, we must select specific Chinese herbal medicines for discussion.

4. What is the oxygen content of the discharged gas following extraction? Also, what is the temperature of the steam generated by the cooling water or the heat exchanger?

5. Could your laboratory provide detailed information on cost analysis for our production plant's reference, especially for Chinese herbal medicine?

6.To extract Chinese herbal medicine component we need new technology information for GC ?

7. How were you able to macerate and sieve extraction products containing solids to produce a particle size less than 0.2cm? Also, how did you measure particle sizes less than 0.2 cm?

I hope that the above questions give you a clearer idea of some of the topics we hope to cover during the upcoming visit. I look forward to meeting you on January

Sincerely yours,

Dear Mr. Sky,

It was a pleasure having you with us in Taiwan this past July. While meeting with you in the Loma Linda University Medical Center for Science and Technology on July 22, I mentioned the possibility of our hospital's Intensity Modulated Radiation Therapy (IMRT) Group scheduling a visit to your facility in the United States. During this visit, we hope that you could personally lecture our colleagues on radiation treatment in this field. Hoping that you could make the necessary arrangements for this event, I hope that the following information for our visiting group will be helpful:

Purpose: to evaluate successful cases and the current status of radiation therapy in the United States with respect to technologies adopted, setting and IMRT related-information.

Participants: hospital administrators of medical centers in Taiwan and medical personnel, including radiation therapy physicians.

Two months have passed without any news regarding this technical visit. I would be most appreciative if you could let us know the current status of the visit so that we can to begin making necessary arrangements. Thanks in advance for your kind assistance.

Sincerely yours,

Dear Dr. Chen,

Thank you for allowing us to visit ABC Corporation. Dr. Chang and Mr. Lin have asked me to express our appreciation for meeting with us and preparing appropriate materials for discussion.

To give you time to prepare in advance for our discussion, I would like to briefly summarize some of the points which we hope to cover during our time together. We are investigating how anthocyanins and berry phenolic compounds inhibit NO production. As well known, flavonoids can lower oxidative stress and impede cardiovascular diseases and chronic inflammatory diseases associated with nitric oxide (NO). We are especially in investigations that examined how phenolic compounds found in fruits, including phenolic acids, flavonols, isoflavones and anthocyanins, affect NO production in LPS/IFN-γ-activated RAW 264.7 macrophages. In particular, phenolic compounds in quantities of 16-500 μM that inhibited NO production by more than 50% without showing cytotoxicity included flavonols quercetin and myricetin, isoflavone daidzein, anthocyanins/anthocyanidins, pelargonidin, cyanidin, delphinidin, peonidin, malvidin, malvidin 3-glucoside and malvidin 3,5-diglucosides. Notably, anthocyanins significantly inhibited NO production. Anthocyanin-rich crude extracts and concentrates of selected berries were also assayed, in which their inhibitory effects on NO production were significantly correlated with total phenolic and anthocyanin contents. Given your technical expertise in the above area, I hope that we can share information that would be mutually beneficial for both of our laboratories.

I hope that the above areas that I have outlined will give you a clearer idea of some of the topics we hope to cover during the upcoming visit. Thanks again for agreeing to meet with us, and I look forward to meeting you on August 28.

Sincerely yours,

Dear Dr. Smith,

As a graduate student in the Institute of Medical Imagery at Yuanpei University of Science and Technology in Taiwan, I am researching the development of cancer resistant cells. As I will be attending the 2005 Medical Meeting of the Society of Biotechnology in New York with my colleague next month, we would like to visit the ABC Research Center in Los Angeles on February 15. In addition to touring your facilities, we hope to discuss with you some potential areas of mutual interest, as outlined below. I would appreciate it if you could arrange an itinerary schedule for this visit and e-mail it to me at your earliest convenience.

During our visit, we hope to consult with you on the following topics:

1. How does one distinguish the different characteristics of cancer resistant cells, as well as the various responses produced after using different anticancer drugs?

2. What are some of the latest methods available to investigate the various responses of cancer resistant cells under the influence of various drugs?

3. What are some effective strategies for treating cancer patients whose normal cells have been slightly damaged during therapy?

4. How can comparing all of the chemical and physical properties in a cancer cell lead to a more effective therapeutic treatment?

Please let me know if February the 15th would be convenient for us to visit you. I look forward to hearing from you.

Sincerely yours,

Dear Dr. Mitsudo,

Much appreciation for arranging for our colleagues to visit the Cardiac Cath Laboratory in Kurashiki Central Hospital. As I mentioned in my previous e-mail, we would like observe a clinical demonstration of the latest procedures adopted in your laboratory, followed by a discussion of specific medical instrumentation and potential collaborative activities. I would like to pose the following questions before our discussion on December the 25th to allow you sufficient time to prepare your responses:

1. Intern training of CTO in your institution: Despite the many patients treated with CAD in our laboratory annually, we are often unsuccessful at CTO. Your clinical expertise is required to train our staff in this area;

2. As for the unique instrumentation that your laboratory adopts for CTO, we are interested in its accurate use and whether such instrumentation could be exported to Taiwan; and

3. Given that both of our hospitals hold live demonstrations of laboratory procedures annually, we are interested in signing a memorandum of understanding (MOU) with you that would allow both organizations to mutually provide technical support

for each other.

Hopefully, the above concerns will give us some common areas of discussion during the upcoming visit. I look forward to meeting you on December the 25th.

Sincerely yours,

Dear Professor Coutrakon,

Thank you for permitting us to visit to Proton Treatment Center at Loma Linda University. I am confident that this visit will further enhance my theoretical knowledge of proton therapy in a practical context. My academic advisor, Professor Hsu, who is actively engaged in research of the microdosimetry spectra in proton therapy in Taiwan, asked me to convey his appreciation for meeting us at the Medical Center at 8:30 AM on December 22 (Following the meeting, we will return to Taiwan the following day). Would you reserve hotel accommodations for us within walking distance of Loma Linda University? Also, would you arrange for a taxi to pick us up at the airport?

During our visit, we hope to consult with you on the following topics:

1. The experimental layout for microdosimetry measurements;

2. The horizontal beam room in your facility;

3. Measurement of microdosimetry spectra of the Loma Linda proton beam to assess its relative biological effectiveness;

4. Analysis of microdosimetry spectra for cobalt and protons;

5. Current bottlenecks in proton therapy development;

6. Merits and limitations of proton therapy, heavy charged particle therapy, fast neutron therapy and boron neutron capture therapy (BNCT); and

7. Potential technology transfer opportunities for the Proton Therapy Center at Hsinchu Biomedical Science Park in Taiwan.

I hope that the above questions give you a clearer idea of some of the topics we hope to cover during the upcoming visit. Thanks in advance for preparations made so far for the upcoming visit. I look forward to meeting you next month.

Sincerely yours,

Dear Professor Smith,

Thank you for your prompt reply regarding my query on how to purify and characterize cysteine protease. I am interested mainly in the role of cysteine protease in cell apoptosis mechanisms. Given your laboratory's considerable research in the structural and functional characterization of cystatins, I hope to arrange a five day technical visit to your laboratory in order to consult with you on related research topics.

As you are well aware, cystatins, a superfamily of cysteine protease inhibitors, play a pivotal role in regulating the activities of endogeneous cysteine protease during seed development and germination. Also capable of protecting plants from pathogens, cystatins are implicated in apoptosis, making them highly promising for agricultural and medicine-related applications. As our laboratory largely focuses on isolating the DNA of plant cystatins from sesame seed, we would like to share our experiences with your working group in exploring how cystatin and cystatin protease interact with each other. Arranging for a five day technical visit to your laboratory would appear to be the best way of beginning this discussion. I look forward to your ideas and suggestions on how such a discussion could possibly lead to collaborative activities in the future.

Thanks in advance for your careful consideration; I look forward to our future cooperation.

Sincerely yours,

Dear Dr. White,

Allow me to introduce myself. I am a Senior Researcher at Union Chemical Laboratories of Industrial Technology Research in Taiwan, where I focus mainly on protein purification. Accompanied by my colleague, Miss Tseng, I will be attending the 2004 Regional Bio-chemical Conference on Protein Purification in Singapore. While in Singapore, we would like to visit the Wan-Da Research Center on December 8 (with the conference ending on December 7, we will leave on the evening of December 9). We would appreciate it if you could arrange a visiting program for us.

During our visit, we hope to consult with you on the following topics:

1. The latest software developed in your laboratory to purify proteins;

2. Details on how to use this software in purifying and analyzing proteins; and

3. Future directions that your laboratory is taking in developing advanced software for purposes of protein purification.

203

I hope that the above areas that I have outlined will give you a clearer idea of some of the topics we hope to cover during the upcoming visit. Please let me know visiting your laboratory on December 8 would be convenient. If possible, a visiting itinerary would be most appreciated. I look forward to hearing from you.

Sincerely yours,

Dear Mr. Smith,

Thank you for allowing us to visit to your laboratory on December the 28th. As I mentioned in the previous correspondence, as a researcher in the Bioimage Laboratories at Yuanpei University of Science and Technology in Taiwan, I am concerned with upgrading the level of precise instrumentation in bioimagery, which Taiwan severely lacks. As a global leader in developing medical instrumentation, your laboratory definitely has much to contribute to our country's efforts to elevate its research capacity in this area.

Let me brief you on our ongoing projects. We are currently engaged in the synchronization firing of neural networks and their aggregation in the dictyostelium system. These nonlinear complex systems have a large degree of freedom in which cooperative effects play a significant role. Often exhibiting unusual and physically interesting phenomena, these nonlinear complex systems are extensively adopted in materials science and related technologies for industrial applications. Hopefully, the opportunity to visit your laboratory and more thoroughly understand our organizational needs will lead to a technology transfer and/or a cooperative venture in the near future.

Having recently received training in how to use advanced computer software to operate the confocal scanning microscope in order to more thoroughly understand the nature of nerve cells, I am most impressed with your laboratory's development of computer software compatible with Linux and IDL. State-of-the-art design program applications could automate a portion of the experimental procedure, thus saving us considerable laboratory resources. We are especially interested in discussing this concern with you, particularly the current technological status of investigating transgenic animals.

I am confident that the upcoming visit to your laboratory will pave the way for a further exchange of related data in the above-mentioned program developments. We are intent on establishing a long-term collaborative relation with your laboratory. I look

forward to meeting you in December.
Sincerely yours,

Dear Mr. Wilson,

Apologies for the delay in responding to your fax. In addition to preparing for our hospital's tenth anniversary, I have been assigned the task of procuring advanced MRI instrumentation for our hospital. In particular, I am evaluating the feasibility of using the 1.5 Tesla MRI in performing as many patient examinations as possible on a daily basis. During such examinations, determining the pulse sequences for various diseases is of priority concern. Importantly, integrating the MRI and PACS systems heavily depends on the communication gateway. Given the different MRI system designs from manufacturers such as Philips, Siemens and GE, I must determine which design concept is the most appropriate for our hospital's needs.

As arranged by GE, I will travel to the United States next month and consult with its research group on our clinical needs. As I understand, your hospital uses the MRI and PACS systems manufactured by GE; the PACS system in your hospital is the same as the one in our hospital. Therefore, on the final two days of my trip, I would like to visit your hospital and learn of your clinical experiences in using this instrumentation. I have two specific concerns. First, as for the patient's work-list generated by the PACS server, I am interested in how to connect the broker to the MRI system through the hospital's Intranet. Second, as for GE's MRI system in which varying pulse sequences are developed (including multi-IR pulse sequence and DW imaging), I hope to learn of the correct parameter settings and the chosen optimal coil.

I hope that this trip will strengthen the cooperative ties between our hospitals. I am open to any suggestions you might have regarding the itinerary or any materials you would like me to prepare prior to my visit.
Sincerely yours,

Dear Mr. Chu,

Thank you for quick response to my query regarding your AFM research group in the Atomic Force Department. From your press release, dated April 15, 2002, on your recently formed research group , I learned how important AFM applications are for Taiwan. I am eager to learn of its potential implications for ongoing research efforts already underway island wide.

Given the recent formation of this research group, I would like to arrange for twenty days of technical instruction and consultation on the latest trends in AFM in your department. Accompanying me would be Mr. Yo, a researcher with National Nano Device Laboratories and Mr. Zang, an instructor at Yuanpei Institute of Science and Technology (our organizations will cover all expenses incurred during the visit). If this visit is agreeable with you, please notify me which dates are the most convenient. A suggested itinerary would also be most appreciated, i.e., discussion time, plant tour schedule, accommodations. I look forward to your reply.

Also, given AFM's success in applications involving the detection of nanotriangles, Mr. Yo can clarify any questions you might have regarding this area of research.

Please do not hesitate to contact me if I can be of any further assistance.

Sincerely yours,

Dear Dr. Curtin,

Thank you for allowing us to observe firsthand some of the latest advances in research at the New York Clinical Cancer Center during our upcoming visit. Also, much appreciation for meeting with us at the Seasons Hotel at 10:00 on December the 20th, where we hope to clarify our concerns for research in this area and potential areas of collaboration between our two organizations.

The New York Clinical Cancer (N.Y.C.C) Center is globally renowned for the best therapeutic treatment of cancer, especially in radiation therapy. As treatment planning for all forms of cancer has advanced, the N.Y.C.C Center has perfected therapeutic strategy for breast cancer, cervical cancer as well as head and neck cancer. In Taiwan, head and neck cancer is the second leading form of cancer. Unfortunately, irradiation treatment for head and neck cancer may damage normal tissues and incur hearing loss, thus highlighting the necessity for precise treatment planning. In addition to NYCC Center's reputation as having the highest survival rate for cancer, its patients also receive nurturing care following irradiation treatment. Such care is essential to elevating the quality of living for those patients. Hopefully, our upcoming visit will allow us to exchange relevant experiences on how not only to handle side effects caused from treatment, but also to provide better nurturing care for those patients.

As is well known, a medical technician stands in the forefront of safeguarding a patient's health and well-being. Additionally, a hospital offers a diverse array of services and support staff to effectively address the emotional, physical and societal challenges that patients might encounter when receiving cancer therapy. Besides providing state-of-the-art medical care, medical technicians actively encourage patients undergoing therapeutic treatment in a highly supportive environment to ensure the most productive outcome.

We hope that this upcoming visit will open doors for future cooperation between our two hospitals.

Sincerely yours,

Dear Dr. Wang,

Thank you for allowing me to visit to your department at 11:30 AM on January the 15th. As mentioned in my previous correspondence, I am impressed with your radiology department's capabilities in analyzing digital images. I would like to consult with your research group on the most effective use of the Picture Archiving and Communication System (PACS).

I would like to pose my questions before our meeting to allow you sufficient time to prepare a response:

1. How can one control the quality of a digital image?
2. How can one select the most effective computer monitor in PACS?
3. How long does it require to achieve quality control for a computer monitor ?
4. What is the most effective and confidential means of communicationonline?
5. Which skill is the most important to reserve a database for operations?

I hope that the above questions will give you a clearer idea of topics we hope to cover during our meeting.

Thanks in advance for your kind assistance.

Sincerely yours,

Mr. Lin,

Thank you for your fax dated December 1. I plan to arrive in New York on December the 26th at 9:15 A.M. on Flight No. UA888. Would you please reserve hotel accommodations (within driving distance of your company, about $US 100 per night) for me? Also, please arrange for a taxi to pick me up at the airport. Thank you for your help. Credit card information is provided as follows.

I will visit your laboratory at 9:00 on December 27. I hope that you can arrange a travel itinerary program for this event. I hope to achieve the following during the upcoming visit:

1. Learn of the Cortisol antibody manufacturing method that your laboratory has developed;
2. Learn more about HRP dilution multiple;3. Use both Cortisol antibody and HRP dilution to achieve standard curve conditions;
4. Attempt to characterize the standard curve diagram;
5. Exchange information on the latest mensuration techniques for cortisol;
6. Identify problems that commonly arise during experimentation and the most effective means of resolving these problems collaboratively; and
7. Understand the latest research trends in Cortisol research.

I hope that the above questions will give you a clearer idea of some of the topics we hope to cover during the upcoming visit. Please let me know if it is convenient for us to visit at 9:00 on December 27. Thanks in advance for your kind assistance.
Sincerely yours,

Situation 4

Karen Su

delay

hospital

design concept

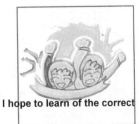

I hope to learn of the correct

Situation 5

Mark Wang

appreciated

N.Y.C.C

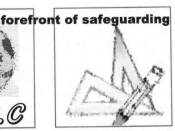

forefront of safeguarding

Situation 6

Mary Lin

slight change

our visiting schedule

prepare your responses

note

Mr. Ting, Mrs. Lin, Mr. Lin and Ms. Chi

I Write down the key points of the situations on the preceding page, while the instructor reads aloud the script from the Answer Key.

Situation 4

_____

_____

_____

Situation 5

_____

_____

_____

Situation 6

_____

_____

_____

J Oral practice II

Based on the three situations in this unit, write three questions beginning with **Why**, and answer them. The questions do not need to come directly from these situations.

Examples

Why did Karen delay in responding to Mr. Wilson's fax?

In addition to preparing for her hospital's tenth anniversary, she has been assigned the task of procuring advanced MRI instrumentation for her hospital.

Why is Karen interested in the patient's work-list generated by the PACS server? To learn how to connect the broker to the MRI system through the hospital's Intranet

1. _____

_____

2. _____

_____

3. _____

_____

K Based on the three situations in this unit, write three questions beginning with **What**, and answer them. The questions do not need to come directly from these situations.

Examples

What is the New York Clinical Cancer (N.Y.C.C) Center globally renowned for?

Its therapeutic treatment of cancer, especially in the field of radiation therapy

What concerns does Mark hope to clarify?

Concerns over research in this area and potential areas of collaboration between the two organizations

1. _____

_____

2. _____

_____

3. _____

_____

L Based on the three situations in this unit, write three questions beginning with *How*, and answer them. The questions do not need to come directly from these situations.

Examples

How can Mr. Slater help Mary's colleagues to receive their visas?

By providing an itinerary for their visit

How will Mary's colleagues have sufficient time to obtain American visas?

By pushing back the tour

1. _____

    _____

2. _____

    _____

3. _____

    _____

M Write questions that match the answers provided.

1. _____

_____

During such examinations

2. _____

_____

In Taiwan

3. _____

_____

Whether May 14-16 would be acceptable to Mr. Slater?

N Listening Comprehension II

Situation 4

1. What has Karen been assigned to do?

    A. learn of the correct parameter settings and the optimal coil

    B. connect the broker to the MRI system through the hospital's Intranet

    C. procure advanced MRI instrumentation for her hospital

2. What is Karen evaluating the feasibility of?

    A. using the 1.5 Tesla MRI in performing as many patient examinations daily

    B. determining the pulse sequences for various diseases

    C. connecting the broker to the MRI system through the hospital's Intranet

3. What does integrating the MRI and PACS systems depend strongly on?

    A. varying pulse sequences

    B. the communication gateway

    C. the patient's work-list generated by the PACS server

4. What is Karen's purpose in evaluating the feasibility of using the 1.5 Tesla MRI?

    A. to learn of the correct parameter settings and the optimal coil

    B. to perform as many patient examinations daily

    C. to determine the pulse sequences for various diseases

5. What occurs in GE's MRI system?

    A. varying pulse sequences are developed

    B. the broker is connected to the MRI system through the hospital's Intranet

    C. the MRI and PACS systems are integrated

Situation 5

1. What does Mark hope to clarify in his meeting with Dr. Curtin at the Seasons Hotel?

215

A. concerns regarding research in this area and potential areas of collaboration between their two organizations

B. concerns regarding therapeutic treatment of cancer, especially in the field of radiation therapy

C. concerns regarding the side effects of treatment

2. Why is the New York Clinical Cancer Center globally renowned?

A. for its irradiation treatment for head and neck cancer that may damage normal tissues and cause loss of hearing

B. for a diverse array of services and support staff to effectively address the emotional, physical and societal challenges

C. for its therapeutic treatment of cancer, especially in the field of radiation therapy

3. What is the second most prevalent cancer in Taiwan?

A. cervical cancer   B. head and neck cancer   C. breast cancer

4. Why is it important for patients to receive nurturing care following irradiation treatment?

A. to highlight the necessity for precise treatment planning

B. to exchange relevant experience of not only handling the side effects of treatment, but also providing better nurturing care to patients

C. to elevate the quality of living for those patients

5. Why has NYCC Center built an excellent reputation?

A. Its cancer patients have the highest survival rate, and receive nurturing care following irradiation treatment.

B. Medical technicians actively encourage patients who are undergoing therapeutic treatment in a highly supportive environment to ensure the most productive outcome.

C. Precise treatment planning is necessary.

Situation 6

1. What does Mary hope will not inconvenience Mr. Slater?

   A. not enough time to obtain American visas

   B. a slight change made in the visiting schedule

   C. an itinerary that is received too late for Mary's colleagues to receive their visas

2. What is Mary concerned with the Medical Center's laboratory can develop or implement?

   A. a forecasting animal model based on a treatment database

   B. treatment planning software programs

   C. a proton treatment center

3. What will Taiwan be establishing in the near future?

   A. long-term health care facilities in different countries

   B. treatment plan data

   C. a proton treatment center

4. What does Taiwan need more of?

   A. long-term health care facilities, providing different services

   B. standard services to classify long-term health care facilities in different countries

   C. forecasting animal models based on a treatment database

5. When will Taiwan establish a proton treatment center?

   A. next month   B. in the near future   C. next year

O Reading Comprehension II
Pick the work or expression whose meaning is closest to the meaning of the underlined word or expression in the following passages.

Situation 4

1. I <u>apologize</u> for the delay in responding to your fax.

   A. boast   B. beg pardon   C. pat oneself on the back

2. I apologize for the <u>delay</u> in responding to your fax.

   A. extension   B. branching   C. procrastination

3. In addition to preparing for our hospital's tenth anniversary, I have been <u>assigned</u> the task of procuring advanced MRI instrumentation for our hospital.

   A. allocated   B. negated   C. nullified

4. In addition to preparing for our hospital's tenth anniversary, I have been assigned the task of <u>procuring</u> advanced MRI instrumentation for our hospital.

   A. selling   B. purchasing   C. developing

5. In particular, I am <u>evaluating</u> the feasibility of using the 1.5 Tesla MRI in performing as many patient examinations daily.

   A. overlooking   B. snubbing   C. approximating

6. In particular, I am evaluating the <u>feasibility</u> of using the 1.5 Tesla MRI in performing as many patient examinations daily.

   A. hopelessness   B. inefficaciousness   C. practicality

7. Importantly, <u>integrating</u> the MRI and PACS systems depends strongly on the communication gateway.

   A. uncoupling   B. disengaging   C. merging with

8. GE has arranged for me to travel to the United States next month and <u>consult</u> its research group on our clinical needs.

   A. seek funds   B. seek advice   C. seek data

9. Therefore, on the final two days of my trip, I would like to visit your hospital and learn of your clinical experience of using this <u>instrumentation</u>.

    A. program applications　B. software　C. machinery

10. Second, with respect to GE's MRI system in which <u>varying</u> pulse sequences are developed (including multi-IR pulse sequence and DW imaging), I hope to learn of the correct parameter settings and the optimal coil.

    A. altering　B. uniform　C. immutable

11. Second, with respect to GE's MRI system in which varying pulse sequences are developed (including multi-IR pulse sequence and DW imaging), I hope to learn of the correct parameter settings and the <u>optimal</u> coil.

    A. mediocre　B. best　C. preferred

Situation 5

1. Thank you for allowing us to observe <u>firsthand</u> some of the latest research at the New York Clinical Cancer Center during our upcoming visit.

    A. via a videoconference call　B. in person　C. through the Internet webcam

2. We also greatly appreciated your agreeing to meet us at the Seasons Hotel at 10:00 on December 20th, where we hope to <u>clarify</u> our concerns regarding research in this area and potential areas of collaboration between our two organizations.

    A. disavow　B. disclaim　C. illuminate

3. The New York Clinical Cancer (N.Y.C.C) Center is globally <u>renowned</u> for its therapeutic treatment of cancer, especially in the field of radiation therapy.

    A. dishonorable　B. peerless　C. infamous

4. As treatment planning for all forms of cancer has advanced, the N.Y.C.C Center has <u>perfected</u> a therapeutic strategy for breast cancer, cervical cancer and head and neck cancer.

    A. demoted　B. degraded　C. cultivated

5. In Taiwan, head and neck cancer is the second most <u>prevalent</u> cancer.

A. common   B. rare   C. atypical

6. <u>Unfortunately</u>, irradiation treatment for head and neck cancer may damage normal tissues and cause loss of hearing, highlighting the necessity for precise treatment planning.

A. opportune   B. prosperous   C. inauspicious

7. Unfortunately, irradiation treatment for head and neck cancer may <u>damage</u> normal tissues and cause loss of hearing, highlighting the necessity for precise treatment planning.

A. inflict   B. restore   C. heal

8. Unfortunately, irradiation treatment for head and neck cancer may damage normal tissues and cause loss of hearing, <u>highlighting</u> the necessity for precise treatment planning.

A. downplaying   B. accentuating   C. downgrading

9. NYCC Center has a <u>reputation</u> built on the fact that its cancer patients have the highest survival rate, and receive nurturing care following irradiation treatment.

A. color   B. space   C. distinction

10. NYCC Center has a reputation built on the fact that its cancer patients have the highest survival <u>rate</u>, and receive nurturing care following irradiation treatment.

A. level   B. velocity   C. amount

11. NYCC Center has a reputation built on the fact that its cancer patients have the highest survival rate, and receive <u>nurturing</u> care following irradiation treatment.

A. erosive   B. abrasive   C. maternal

12. Hopefully, our upcoming visit will allow us to exchange relevant experience of not only handling the <u>side effects</u> of treatment, but also providing better nurturing care to patients.

A. adverse impacts   B. merits   C. beneficial aspects

13. As is well known, a medical technician stands at the <u>forefront</u> of safeguarding a patient's health and well-being.

A. decay　B. dilapidation　C. welfare

14. As is well known, a medical technician stands at the forefront of <u>safeguarding</u> a patient's health and well-being.

A. protecting　B. inhibiting　C. hindering

15. A hospital offers a <u>diverse</u> array of services and support staff to effectively address the emotional, physical and societal challenges that patients might encounter while they receive cancer therapy.

A. uniform　B. homogeneous　C. heterogeneous

16. A hospital offers a diverse array of services and support staff to effectively address the emotional, physical and societal <u>challenges</u> that patients might encounter while they receive cancer therapy.

A. advantages　B. provocations　C. benefits

17. Besides providing <u>state-of-the-art</u> medical care, medical technicians actively encourage patients who are undergoing therapeutic treatment in a highly supportive environment to ensure the most productive outcome.

A. customary　B. pioneering　C. conventional

18. Besides providing state-of-the-art medical care, medical technicians actively encourage patients who are undergoing therapeutic treatment in a highly <u>supportive</u> environment to ensure the most productive outcome.

A. disheartened　B. dispirited　C. encouraging

19. Besides providing state-of-the-art medical care, medical technicians actively encourage patients who are undergoing therapeutic treatment in a highly supportive environment to ensure the most <u>productive</u> outcome.

A. resourceful　B. valueless　C. ineffectual

Situation 6

1. Unfortunately, a <u>slight</u> change has been made in our visiting schedule, which will hopefully not inconvenience you.

A. significant   B. diminutive   C. substantial

2. Unfortunately, a slight change has been made in our visiting schedule, which will hopefully not <u>inconvenience</u> you.

A. promote   B. contribute to   C. disturb

3. If so, Dr. Jones can <u>book</u> his flight to arrive in the United States on May the 14th.

A. cancel   B. reserve   C. reschedule

4. Accordingly, could you please provide an <u>itinerary</u> that would allow our colleagues to receive their visas?

A. payment plan   B. investment plan   C. schedule

5. I would like to <u>pose</u> the following questions before our discussion on May 14, to give you plenty of time to prepare your responses:

A. ask   B. refer   C. consult with

6. How does your Medical Center laboratory develop or <u>implement</u> a forecasting animal model based on a treatment database?

A. delay   B. postpone   C. put into effect

7. How does your Medical Center laboratory develop or implement a <u>forecasting</u> animal model based on a treatment database?

A. prediction   B. software   C. database

8. What <u>standard</u> services does your Proton Treatment Center offer to classify long-term health care facilities in different countries?

A. modern   B. unique   C. conventional

9. What standard services does your Proton Treatment Center offer to <u>classify</u> long-term health care facilities in different countries?

A. implement   B. categorize   C. execute

10. If you could provide the travel <u>party</u> with an itinerary, I would like to make a hotel reservation for three single rooms (for two nights) from May 14 to May 16, 2005, and another single room (for one night) from May 15 to May 16, 2005.

A. group   B. festival   C. meeting

P Matching Exercise

1. Each sentence in the following is commonly used to make a technical visit overseas: requesting permission to make a technical visit 科技訪問信函：科技訪問許可申請. Each phrase on the left should be matched with one on the right in order to complete the sentence. Match a number on the left with a letter on the right.

1. Although I strongly desire to receive an extensive period of training from your medical group on the latest technological developments in this area,	a. to more thoroughly understand the progress that you have made.
2. As I will be attending the 2005 Medical Meeting of the Society of Biotechnology in New York with my colleague next month,	b. on the morning of January the 12th.
3. Given our interest in your technological developments in this field, we would like to visit your hospital	c. members of your working group regarding details of our cooperative agreement, as well as tour your facilities.
4. Arranging for a five day technical visit to your laboratory would appear to be	d. we would like to visit the ABC Research Center in Los Angeles on February 15.
5. We would like to meet with	e. your working group, as well as tour your hospital facilities.
6. If possible, we hope to meet with you	f. a technical visit to your company.
7. We would appreciate it if you could arrange	g. of your clinical experiences in using this instrumentation.
8. On the final two days of my trip, I would like to visit your hospital and learn	h. arranging such a large block of time is impossible given my hectic schedule at work. I would therefore like to arrange a three day visit to your laboratory next month.
9. Our visiting group is anxious to meet with	i. a visiting program for us.
10. My colleague, Mr. Wang, suggested that I contact you regarding the possibility of	j. the best way of beginning this discussion.

2. Making a technical visit overseas: requesting permission to make a technical visit 科技訪問信函：科技訪問許可申請

1. Given the recent formation of this research group, I would like to arrange	a. discuss with you some of these topics in more detail.
2. Given my above interests, I would visit your research laboratory and	b. to tour your facilities and share our related experiences in product development using the refinement of natural oil via natural plants.
3. I will be accompanied by	c. technical visit with the technical staff. in your Nuclear Medicine Department.
4. Given your corporation's committing to adopting the most advanced environmental protection technologies in your manufacturing processes,	d. for twenty days of technical instruction and consultation on the latest trends in AFM in your department.
5. I would like to arrange for a five day	e. as well as discuss the details of our cooperative agreement.
6. Given your company's expertise in this area, we would like to arrange for a technical visit next month	f. two environmental protection experts in this area.
7. As mentioned in our previous correspondence, we would like to visit your new computer testing facilities,	g. I would like to arrange for a three day technical visit to your product development division to learn of the operational aspects and theoretical applications that you adopt in production.

3. Making a technical visit overseas: stating the purpose of the technical visit 科技訪問信函：闡述科技訪問的目的

1. We would like observe a clinical demonstration of	a. for ongoing research efforts already underway island wide.
2. The ability to integrate the advances of your medical research program	b. with you some potential areas of mutual interest, as outlined below.
3. In addition to touring your facilities, we hope to discuss	c. lead to a technology transfer and/or a cooperative venture in the near future.
4. The opportunity to consult with you	d. to handle side effects caused from treatment, but also to provide better nurturing care for those patients.
5. I am eager to learn of the potential implications of this new technology	e. with the unique aspects of image fusion would significantly decrease the rate of stroke victims in our hospital.
6. A five-day technical visit to your institution would hopefully provide me with relevant information on	f. describes the nature of this proposed technical visit:
7. Hopefully, the opportunity to visit your laboratory and more thoroughly understand our organizational needs will	g. the latest computer software that can reduce examination time as much as possible.
8. Hopefully, our upcoming visit will allow us to exchange relevant experiences on how not only	h. the latest procedures adopted in your laboratory, followed by a discussion of specific medical instrumentation and potential collaborative activities.
9. I hope the following information aptly	i. we are eager to learn of your expertise in handling global health issues, especially promotion-related activities.
10. Given the pivotal role that your organization plays in the World Health Organization,	j. in person will hopefully yield mutually beneficial results for both of our laboratories.

4. Making a technical visit overseas: stating the purpose of the technical visit 科技訪問信函：闡述科技訪問的目的

1. Hopefully, my upcoming research stay will allow me	a. perhaps leading to technology transfer or joint venture opportunities between our two companies.
2. I hope that the upcoming technical visit will eventually	b. to achieve the following objectives:
3. Our discussions will hopefully be mutually beneficial,	c. establishing a long-term collaborative relation with your laboratory.
4. I hope that this meeting will allow our two organizations to freely exchange information on a	d. mutually beneficial basis, perhaps through the signing a memorandum of understanding (MOU) in the near future.
5. We are intent on	e. lead to a collaborative relationship between our two laboratories that would allow us to share pertinent data based on our mutual scientific research interests.

5. Making a technical visit overseas: introducing one's qualifications or one's organizational experiences 科技訪問信函：介紹某人的能力或機構經驗

1. Our company's Product Development Division is committed	a. on our ongoing projects.
2. Let me brief you	b. encouraged its enterprises in recent years with numerous incentives to be more socially responsible in its manufacturing practices.
3. Technological advances in quantitative analysis and computer software have greatly facilitated our laboratory's	c. to elucidate the actual mechanism that is present during ischemia.
4. My graduate school research attempted	d. to adhering to the Taiwannese government's aggressive policy towards promoting the use of environmentally friendly practices in manufacturing.
5. With aspirations of becoming a "Green Silicon Island", Taiwan has actively	e. increasingly proficient in resolving a wide array of marketing problems, subsequently spurring my creativity and analytical capabilities.
6. Please find enclosed our company brochure	f. efforts in researching marketing approaches adopted in the global network and their implications for marketing strategies aimed at the Greater China sector.
7. As a graduate student in the Institute of Business Management at Yuanpei University of Science and Technology in Taiwan, I have become	g. that briefly introduces our product line.

6. Making a technical visit overseas: commending the organization to be visited 科技訪問信函：對訪問機構的讚揚

1. Your research group has expended considerable effort	a. for its efforts to develop biochip technologies for post-genomic era biomedical research.
2. I found the results from your recent article, "Effect of Green Tea Polyphenols on RAW 264.7"	b. definitely has much to contribute to our country's efforts to elevate its research capacity in this area.
3. As is well known, your company pioneered	c. to be extremely helpful to my own research direction.
4. As a global leader in developing medical instrumentation, your laboratory	d. with the report on your radiology department's capabilities in processing three-dimensional images.
5. In this area, your laboratory has acquired much expertise and relevant data, explaining why I am	e. hold for manufacturing your natural products that adopt the latest scientific and technological advances, as well as quality assurance standards.
6. Given your excellent product quality and strong commitment to	f. benefited from your findings on how Helicobacter pylori can be used in vaccines and medicinal applications.
7. During the International Conference on Three-dimensional Medical Images on Oct 29, I was impressed	g. in treating stroke patients by state-of-the-art instrumentation aimed at resolve brain ischemia-related problems.
8. Your products conform to the most stringent environmental standards through the use of ingredients	h. eagerly looking forward to this upcoming technical visit.
9. As a research unit of Biomedicum Helsinki, your research center (Biomedicum Biochip Center) is renowned	i. the use of natural plant oil to refine crude oil for use in daily goods and appliances.
10. We are most impressed with the number of patented technologies that you	j. of biochip data, while applying the results of these research efforts to eradicate complex diseases such as cancer.
11. From your press release dated November 10, 2005 on recent developments to identify protein functions, I greatly	k. adopting advanced environmental protection practices in your manufacturing processes,
12. We are also impressed with your innovativeness in performing bioinformatics-based analyses	l. that are phosphate-free and environmentally friendly.

7. Making a technical visit overseas: outlining details of the technical visit 科技訪問信函：詳述科技訪問的細節

1. I am especially interested in learning	a. summarize some of the points which we hope to cover during our time together.
2. To give you time to prepare in advance for our discussion, I would like to briefly	b. particularly the current technological status of investigating transgenic animals.
3. I would like to pose the following questions before our discussion on November 12	c. discussion during the upcoming visit.
4. We are especially interested in discussing this concern with you,	d. questions in advance will make our discussion a more productive one.
5. I am open to any suggestions you might have	e. during the upcoming visit so that you can make necessary preparations beforehand:
6. I would like to point out our areas of concern	f. of your successful cases of treatment to reduce the likelihood of a stroke from occurring.
7. More specifically, during our upcoming trip,	g. that can hopefully be included in our discussion on December the 24th.
8. The following topics will hopefully give you a clearer idea of the topics we want to cover	h. so that you will have sufficient time to prepare your responses:
9. I hope that posing the following	i. we hope to discuss the following topics in detail:
10. Hopefully, the above concerns will give us some common areas of	j. regarding the itinerary or any materials you would like me to prepare prior to my visit.

8. Making a technical visit overseas: requesting confirmation for approval of the technical visit 科技訪問信函：科技訪問核准的確認申請

1. If this visit is agreeable with you, please notify me	a. proposed the idea of our technical visit to your country without any response from you so far.
2. To arrange for the upcoming research visit in order to consult with you on the above topics,	b. on the status of this proposed technical visit so that we can begin making the necessary travel arrangements.
3. Quite some time has passed since I originally	c. on to us regarding transportation arrangements and a list of hotels near our meeting place.
4. Prior to our visit, we would appreciate any introductory information that you could pass	d. of an overseas visit that my organization requires.
5. A suggested itinerary would also be most appreciated,	e. as to which dates are convenient for you.
6. I would be most grateful if you could advise us	f. including our discussion time, tour of research facilities and accommodations.
7. I would appreciate it if you could list the details of this visit in an itinerary form for processing	g. I need to set up an itinerary and time schedule to report to my superiors.

Unit Four

Inviting Speakers and Consultants

演講者邀請信函

Vocabulary and related expressions 相關字詞

constantly strives 不斷地奮鬥
growing elderly population
漸漸變多的老年人口
reimbursement 退款
tax levy 徵收稅
lecture on 向……演講
recent advances in 近期的發展
population 人口
emerged（事實）暴露
irreversible 不可逆的
strain 使勁
relies on 依賴
medical instrumentation 醫療設備
renowned research 有名的研究
allot extra time 分配多餘的時間
memorandum of understanding 備忘錄

selected publications 精選的出版物
curriculum vitae 履歷
lack of confidence 缺乏自信
extensive experience 廣泛的經驗
consultant 顧問
governmental authorities 政府當局
implement 工具
practitioners 開業者（尤指醫生、律師）
consultancy period 顧問服務時段
sufficient time 足夠的時間
reimbursed 歸還
speech honorarium 演講謝禮
In light of 從……觀點
renowned 有聲譽的
serve as 供……使用
collaborative activities 合作的活動

developmental trends 發展的趨勢

expert 專家

expertise 專門技術

proficiency 熟練

facilitating 使容易的

fluent 流暢的

your earliest convenience
您方便的時間

technical service fee 技術服務費用

recent trends and developments
最新的趨勢及發展

tentative schedule 暫時性的行程

cultural attractions 文化吸引力

itinerary 旅程

traditional Chinese medicine 中藥

accommodation 膳宿

average price 平均價格

reimbursement 退款

eminence（地位、成就）卓越

rescheduling 再安排

related handouts 有關的印刷品

in touch with you 跟您聯絡

Situation 1

'Suzy Chen

quality of medical care

recommend a consultant

Situation 2

Marvin Lu

National Taiwan University in Taipei

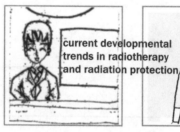

current developmental trends in radiotherapy and radiation protection

Situation 3

Christi Fung

brain stroke

younger population

the role of SPECT and PET Scan

airfare ticket

A Write down the key points of the situations on the preceding page, while the instructor reads aloud the script from the Answer Key.

Situation 1

_____

_____

_____

Situation 2

_____

_____

_____

Situation 3

_____

_____

_____

B Oral practice I

Based on the three situations in this unit, write three questions beginning with **What**, and answer them. The questions do not need to come directly from these situations.

Examples

What does Suzy's hospital constantly strive to do?

Promote its long-term care facilities and services

What does the growing elderly population require?

Urgent medical treatment daily, with efficient follow-up services, including discharge planning, respiratory care, nursing facilities and home care as part of a visiting nursing program

1. _____

_____

2. _____

_____

3. _____

_____

C Based on the three situations in this unit, write three questions beginning with **Why**, and answer them. The questions do not need to come directly from these situations.

Examples

Why does Marvin want to formally invite Dr. Lin to serve as an Invited Speaker at the upcoming Radiotherapy Oncology Conference?

In light of his renowned research and contributions in the field of treatment planning systems

Why is a discussion to be held on April 25, 2004?

On how to assess current developments in proton therapy

1. _____

   _____

2. _____

   _____

3. _____

   _____

D Based on the three situations in this unit, write three questions beginning with **Which**, and answer them. The questions do not need to come directly from these situations.

Examples

Which part of the population in Taiwan has the incidence of brain strokes increased?
The younger population

Which technologies have emerged, aimed at resolving salvageable tissue and irreversible damage?
Medical ones

1. _____

_____

2. _____

_____

3. _____

_____

E Write questions that match the answers provided.

1. _____

_____

Two hours

2. _____

_____

A discussion of the current developmental trends in radiotherapy and radiation

protection

3. _____

_____

In light of his renowned research on the role of SPECT and PET scan in nuclear

medicine and pharmaceutical-based nuclear medicine

F Listening Comprehension I

Situation 1

1. Why does Suzy's hospital constantly strive to promote its long-term care facilities and services and offer medical treatment?

   A. to control the quality of long term care services

   B. to implement long-term care national policies

   C. to meet the demands of the growing elderly population

2. Why does Suzy want Mr. Smith to recommend a consultant who could instruct her hospital staff?

   A. because of his organization's extensive experience in implementing long-term care programs

   B. because of his organization's efficient follow-up services, including discharge planning, respiratory care, nursing facilities and home care as part of a visiting nursing program

   C. because of his organization's ability to promote its long-term care facilities and services

3. What is Suzy's interest in national health insurance?

   A. how it is integrated into the provision of long term care services

   B. how it can be adopted to control the quality of long term care services

   C. how it can be used to assess the various levels of long-term care services provided to the nation's elderly

4. What is Suzy's interest in the role of practitioners?

   A. how they implement long-term care national policies

   B. how they control the quality of long term care services

   C. how they assess the various levels of long-term care services provided to the nation's elderly

5. How long will each lecture last?

   A. three hours   B. two hours   C. two and a half hours

Situation 2

1. When will a discussion be held on how to assess current developments in proton therapy?

   A. April 23, 2004   B. April 25, 2004   C. April 26, 2004

2. When will Dr. Lin sightsee Taipei's cultural attractions, as arranged by the faculty and the staff at National Taiwan University?

   A. April 28 2004   B. April 29 2004   C. April 26 2004

3. How much is the tax levy for a technical service fee?

   A. 30%   B. 25%   C. 20%

4. When should Dr. Lin send his lecture topics to Dr. Ting?

   A. before February 25, 2004

   B. before February 28, 2004

   C. before February 29, 2004

5. When will Dr. Lin return to the United States?

   A. April 28 2004   B. April 26 2004   C. April 27 2004

Situation 3

1. What has increased in Taiwan?

   A. recent advances in diagnosing severe ischemia

   B. the incidence of brain strokes among the younger population

   C. salvageable tissue and irreversible damage

2. How does Taiwan's national defense heavily rely on its youth?

   A. All males perform nearly two years of compulsory military service.

   B. All females perform nearly two years of compulsory military service.

C. All males and females perform nearly two years of compulsory military service.

3. What requires expensive medical instrumentation?

A. medical insurance coverage that is too expensive for most young people

B. diagnosing cardiac-vessel-cerebral disease

C. the incidence of brain strokes among the younger population

4. What will Dr. Jones lecture on in Taiwan next month?

A. diagnosis of cardiac-vessel-cerebral disease

B. SPECT and PET scan in nuclear medicine and pharmaceutical-based nuclear medicine

C. recent advances in diagnosing severe ischemia

5. What do increases in ischemia or severe brain strokes strain?

A. economic resources

B. the island's national defense

C. younger population

G Reading Comprehension I
Pick the work or expression whose meaning is closest to the meaning of the underlined word or expression in the following passages.

Situation 1

1. Our hospital <u>constantly</u> strives to promote its long-term care facilities and services, and offers medical treatment to meet the demands of the growing elderly population.

   A. sporadically   B. intermittently   C. perpetually

2. Our hospital constantly <u>strives</u> to promote its long-term care facilities and services, and offers medical treatment to meet the demands of the growing elderly population.

   A. aspires   B. renounces   C. relinquishes

3. Our hospital constantly strives to promote its long-term care facilities and services, and offers medical treatment to meet the demands of the growing <u>elderly</u> population.

   A. adolescent   B. aging   C. younger

4. They require <u>urgent</u> medical treatment daily, with efficient follow-up services, including discharge planning, respiratory care, nursing facilities and home care as part of a visiting nursing program.

   A. immediate   B. discontinued   C. postponed

5. They require urgent medical treatment daily, with efficient follow-up services, including discharge planning, <u>respiratory</u> care, nursing facilities and home care as part of a visiting nursing program.

   A. nervous system-related   B. circulatory   C. breathing

6. Despite our <u>aspirations</u>, our hospital is lacking in many of the above areas,

explaining the lack of confidence among patients and their relatives in the quality of medical care offered by Taiwanese hospitals.

A. hesitations　B. intentions　C. reservations

7. Despite our aspirations, our hospital is lacking in many of the above areas, explaining the <u>lack</u> of confidence among patients and their relatives in the quality of medical care offered by Taiwanese hospitals.

A. absence　B. surplus　C. glut

8. How do governmental <u>authorities</u> in your country implement long-term care national policies?

A. registrants　B. participants　C. lawmakers

9. What <u>measures</u> can be adopted to control the quality of long term care services?

A. characters　B. steps　C. qualities

10. Once final arrangements are made, please advise us of the consultant's flight <u>details</u> so that we can meet him/her at the airport.

A. specifics　B. inferences　C. suggestions

11. Each lecture will last two hours, and the consultant will be <u>reimbursed</u> with a speech honorarium.

A. billed　B. charged for　C. refunded

12. Each lecture will last two hours, and the consultant will be reimbursed with a speech <u>honorarium</u>.

A. payment for transportation

B. payment for lecture

C. payment for accommodations

Situation 2

1. We hope your lecture will include a discussion of the current <u>developmental</u> trends in radiotherapy and radiation protection.

A. established   B. permanent   C. evolving

2. The following is a <u>tentative</u> schedule for your visit.

A. permanent   B. under consideration   C. nailed down

3. Arrival in Taiwan at Chiang Kai Shek International, and <u>transit</u> to hotel accommodation

A. stop   B. curtail   C. traverse

4. Any comments or suggestions regarding the above <u>itinerary</u> or topics of discussion would be most appreciated.

A. schedule   B. message   C. communication

5. We will then have <u>sufficient</u> time to make copies and appropriate arrangements.

A. inferior   B. flawed   C. adequate

6. Please pay in advance for your roundtrip airfare and other <u>incidental</u> expenses, and hold onto those receipts for reimbursement prior to your departure from Taiwan.

A. substantial   B. inconsequential   C. significant

7. Please pay in advance for your roundtrip airfare and other incidental expenses, and hold onto those receipts for <u>reimbursement</u> prior to your departure from Taiwan.

A. repayment   B. reinstatement   C. replacement

8. According to our government's tax system, a technical service fee is subject to a 20% tax <u>levy</u>.

A. loan   B. fee   C. rebate

Situation 3

1. We are pleased to hear that you will be returning to Taiwan next month to <u>lecture on</u> recent advances in diagnosing severe ischemia.

A. avert   B. address   C. prevent

2. We are pleased to hear that you will be returning to Taiwan next month to lecture

on recent <u>advances</u> in diagnosing severe ischemia.

    A. regresses   B. setbacks   C. progress

3. The <u>incidence</u> of brain strokes among the younger population has increased in Taiwan.

    A. rise   B. occurrence   C. failing

4. Many medical technologies have <u>emerged</u>, aimed at resolving salvageable tissue and irreversible damage.

    A. retrograded   B. receded   C. appeared

5. Many medical technologies have emerged, aimed at resolving salvageable tissue and <u>irreversible</u> damage.

    A. irrevocable   B. replicable   C. repetitive

6. Let me briefly describe the <u>severity</u> of strokes among the younger aged population.

    A. light side   B. gravity   C. optimistic view

7. The younger population <u>dominates</u> the country's economic activities, so increases in ischemia or severe brain strokes strain economic resources.

    A. substantiates   B. subverts   C. reigns over

8. Additionally, the island's national defense heavily relies on its youth: all males perform nearly two years of <u>compulsory</u> military service.

    A. voluntary   B. mandatory   C. volitional

9. Your presence at this event would indeed be an <u>honor</u> for us.

    A. esteem   B. disgrace   C. scandal

10. I hope that you can <u>allot</u> extra time to see some of the cultural wonders of Taiwan.

    A. decrease   B. cut back   C. allocate

11. I hope that you can allot extra time to see some of the cultural <u>wonders</u> of Taiwan.

    A. marvels   B. doldrums   C. eye sore

H Common elements in letters inviting speakers and consultants（演講者邀請信函）include the following:
1. Inviting a speaker 邀請演講者
2. Describing the purpose of the lecture 描述演講目的
3. Explaining details of the lecture 詳述演講的細節
4. Describing transportation and accommodation details 詳述交通及住宿的細節
5. Instructing the speaker what to prepare before the visit 演講者行前必知指導
6. Emphasizing the importance of the upcoming visit 對演講者強調訪問的重要性

In the space below, write a letter inviting a speaker or consultant.

_____

_____

_____

_____

_____

_____

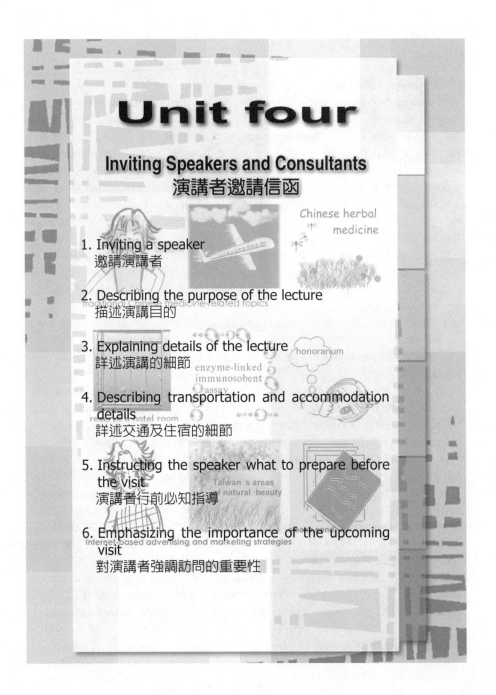

Unit four

Inviting Speakers and Consultants
演講者邀請信函

Chinese herbal medicine

1. Inviting a speaker
   邀請演講者

2. Describing the purpose of the lecture
   描述演講目的

3. Explaining details of the lecture
   詳述演講的細節

honorarium

enzyme-linked immunosobent assay

4. Describing transportation and accommodation details
   詳述交通及住宿的細節

5. Instructing the speaker what to prepare before the visit
   演講者行前必知指導

6. Emphasizing the importance of the upcoming visit
   對演講者強調訪問的重要性

Look at the following examples of letters inviting a speaker or consultant.

Dear Mr. Smith,

Our hospital constantly strives to promote its long-term care facilities and services, with medical treatment urgently required to fulfill the demands of the growing elderly population. Such urgent medical treatment is required on a daily basis, with efficient follow-up services such as discharge planning, respiratory care, nursing facilities and home care through a visiting nursing program. Despite the above aspirations, our hospital is lacking in many of the above areas, explaining the lack of confidence among patients and their relatives in the quality of medical care offered in Taiwanese hospitals. Given your organization's extensive experience in implementing long-term care programs, we hope that you could recommend a consultant that could instruct our hospital staff on the following topics:

1. How do governmental authorities in your country implement long-term care policies nationwide?
2. How do practitioners assess the various levels of long term care services provided to the nation's elderly?
3. What measures can be adopted to control the quality of long term care services?
4. How is national health insurance integrated into the provision of long term care services?

We will provide roundtrip airfare and accommodations during the consultancy period. I advise that the consultant stay here for an additional week or so to enjoy some of the sights that Taiwan has to offer. Once final arrangements are made, please advise us of the consultant's flight details so that we can meet him/her at the airport. Please ask your consultant to send us his/her lecture titles and related handouts before January 10, 2005 so that we will have sufficient time to make copies and appropriate arrangements. I also need his/her curriculum vitae, with contents to include: NAME, DATE OF BIRTH, PLACE OF BIRTH, NATIONALITY, MARITAL STATUS, ACADEMIC QUALIFICATIONS, PROFESSIONAL EXPERIENCE, SCIENTIFIC ACHIEVEMENTS, CURRENT SCIENTIFIC ACTIVITIES, OTHER SCIENCE-RELATED ACTIVITIES, AND SELECTED PUBLICATIONS.

Each lecture will last two hours, with the consultant reimbursed with a speech honorarium. The consultancy period will hopefully begin before February of 2005. We welcome any suggestions or comments that you might have regarding the above proposal.

Sincerely yours,

Dear Professor Huang,

Given your renowned research and contributions in the field of cell culture technologies, we would like to formally invite you to serve as an Invited Speaker at the upcoming Food Health Symposium. This symposium is to be held at Yuanpei University of Science and Technology (Hsinchu, Taiwan) on January 30, 2005. We hope your lecture will cover recent trends and developments in tea polyphenols, antiinflammation and flow cytometer.

Please let us know as soon as possible if you will be able to accept our invitation. If so, please send us the text of your talk before December 10, 2004. I look forward to hearing from you soon. My colleagues will contact you regarding details of the symposium and travel arrangements. Your contribution to the symposium would definitely benefit all of the participants.

Sincerely yours,

Dear Professor Wu,

Given your eminent research and contributions in the field of long term care, we would like to formally invite you to serve as an Invited Speaker at an upcoming seminar on this topic in Taiwan. The symposium is to be held at Yuanpei University of Science and Technology (Hsinchu, Taiwan) on February 25, 2005. We hope your lecture will examine how developmental trends in the growth of the disabled population and Manton's dynamic equilibrium model are related. This topic is particularly relevant given that Taiwan ranks second worldwide in the growth rate of elderly individuals.

We will provide roundtrip airfare and accommodations during your stay in Taiwan. I advise you to stay here for one week (if at all possible) so that you can enjoy some of Taiwan's spectacular sights. Please advise us of your flight details so that we can meet you at the Chiang Kai Shek International Airport upon your arrival.

Please send us your lecture title and outline, along with related handouts, before January 31, 2005. We will then have sufficient time to make copies and appropriate arrangements. I also need your curriculum vitae, including the following contents: NAME, DATE OF BIRTH, PLACE OF BIRTH, NATIONALITY, ACADEMIC QUALIFICATIONS, PROFESSIONAL EXPERIENCE, SCIENTIFIC ACHIEVEMENTS, CURRENT SCIENTIFIC ACTIVITIES, OTHER SCIENCE-RELATED ACTIVITIES,

AND SELECTED PUBLICATIONS.

Please do not hesitate to let me know if you have any concerns and/or suggestions. Your contribution to this symposium will definitely benefit all of the participants.

Sincerely yours,

Dear Miss Chen,

Given the progressive decline in customer satisfaction, understanding their needs and maintaining their loyalty are essential to sustained commercial success. An enterprise's ability to retain its customers depends on the ability to closely interact with them to ensure a lasting partnership.

In light of your renowned research and contributions in the field of customer relationship management, we would like to formally invite you to serve as an Invited Speaker at the upcoming Customer Relationship Management Symposium. This symposium is to be held at National Health Insurance Bureau in Taipei, Taiwan on December 24, 2004. We hope that your lecture will include telephone courtesy, protocol during official ceremonies and the nature of a customer's needs.

As for compensation of this event, please pay in advance for the roundtrip airfare ticket, and other incidental expenses. Retain the receipts or invoices, for which, you will be reimbursed (by check) prior to your departure of Taiwan. Taiwan is a beautiful island, originally known as Formosa. We suggest you stay a week to enjoy some of the island's natural attractions. Incidentally, hotel accommodations in Taipei for a single room averages between DM$ 130 to DM$250 daily.

Please e-mail us your curriculum vitae and course materials before December 24, 2004. Please e-mail all your materials to me on time so that we will have sufficient time for translation and printing.

Your contribution to the symposium will definitely benefit all of the participants. If you have any questions or suggestions, please do not hesitate to contact us at fax number 886-3-4381810. I look forward to meeting you.

Sincerely yours,

Dear Dr. Chang,

In light of your renowned research and contributions in medical science education, we would like to formally invite you to serve as an Invited Speaker at the upcoming Medical Science Education Symposium, which is to be held at Union ABC Hospital in Hsinchu, Taiwan on May 15, 2005. Your lecture will hopefully include a summary of recent developmental trends in medical science, relevant governmental policy and current status of medical education.

Please send us your lecture title and outline, along with related handouts, before February 30, 2005. We will then have a sufficient amount of time to make copies and appropriate arrangements. Your curriculum vitae will hopefully include the following information: NAME, DATE OF BIRTH, PLACE OF BIRTH, NATIONALITY, MARITAL STATUS, ACADEMIC QUALIFICATIONS, PROFESSIONAL EXPERIENCE, SCIENTIFIC ACHIEVEMENTS, CURRENT SCIENTIFIC ACTIVITIES, OTHER SCIENCE-RELATED ACTIVITIES and SELECTED PUBLICATIONS.

In addition to an honorarium for your lecture, the organizing committee will also provide a roundtrip train ticket and hotel accommodations in Hsinchu for the evening of May the 15th. Please inform us of your arrival time to the Hsinchu train station so that we can meet you.

Please let us know as soon as possible whether you will be able to accept our invitation.

Your contribution to this symposium would definitely benefit all of the participants.

Yours respectfully,

Chen-Yin Wang

Dear Smith,

I hope that my letter dated October 30, 2004 reached you, in which I invited you to accompany our representatives of the Asian branch office of TED Corporation to Switzerland in order to explore potential product development opportunities. TED Corporation has strived to develop bedding materials that contain anti dust mite and anti microbial fiber properties for many decades, such as in bedspreads, bed sheets and pillowcases. Such properties are particularly desirable for Asian countries during weather conditions. TED Corporation has subsequently requested me to sign a contract in its Switzerland headquarters that would allow our Taiwanese branch to receive this technology transfer. Therefore, I would like to invite you to this signing of technical cooperation in Switzerland next month. Our employees are highly committed, as evidenced by the recent development of several mattress and pillow types as well as a particularemphasis on electrically heated bedding and customized pillows. However, given our lack of research in developing bedspread materials, we anxiously look forward to this technical cooperation agreement with TED Corporation that would ultimately increase our brand awareness and market share. As the time for our trip draws near, we need to arrange a convenient time for the signing of this agreement. This trip will hopefully strengthen the collaborative ties between our organizations. Your speedy reply regarding the details of this upcoming visit would be most appreciated. Sincerely yours,

Dear Dr. Push,

We are pleased to hear that you will be returning to Taiwan next month to lecture on recent advances in diagnosing severe ischemia. Given the increasing incidence of brain strokes among the younger population in Taiwan, many medical technologies have emerged, aimed at resolving salvageable tissue and irreversible damage. Let me briefly describe the severity of strokes among the younger aged population. As the younger population plays a predominant role in the country's economic activities, an increase in ischemia or severe brain strokes would strain economic resources. Additionally, the island's national defense heavily relies on its youth, among which all males serve nearly two years of compulsory military service. Moreover, diagnosing cardiac-vessel-cerebral disease requires expensive medical instrumentation, with related medical insurance coverage too expensive for most young people.

In light of your renowned research on the role of SPECT and PET Scan in nuclear medicine and pharmaceutical-based nuclear medicine, we would like to invite you to serve as an Invited Speaker at National Taiwan University, which is to be held on December 15, 2004. Your lecture will hopefully cover recent trends in SPECT and PET-CT technologies. Your presence at this event would indeed be an honor. As for compensation, we will provide a roundtrip airfare ticket and accommodations during your stay in Taiwan. I hope that you can allot extra time to see some of the cultural wonders that Taiwan offers. Please advise us of your flight number so that we can meet you at the Chiang Kai Shek International Airport In Taoyuan. Please send us your lecture title and outline, along with belated references, so that we will have sufficient time to make copies. I look forward to hearing from you soon.

Sincerely yours,

Dear Professor Haas,

The Society of Biochemists of the R.O.C. will hold a seminar on molecular biology, which will be held in Taipei Taiwan on November 16, 2005. The seminar will focus on recent advances in molecular biology-related technologies. Given your distinguished research on the Helicobacter pylori full genome, I would like to speak at the upcoming Ninth Symposium on Recent Advances in Cellular and Molecular Biology. We hope that your lecture will discuss efforts to (1) achieve natural transformation that encompasses the entire procedure (including DNA binging, uptake and transformation for final DNA recombination) (2) develop an effective vaccine for Helicobacter pylori and (3) decrease antibiotic resistance of Helicobacter pylori patients.

The organizing committee will provide a roundtrip airfare ticket and accommodations during your stay. I also suggest that you allot extra time to visit some of Taiwan's natural wonders and cultural places of interest. Please advise us of your flight number so that we can meet you at the airport. If you can accept our invitation, let us know as soon as possible so that we can make necessary preparations. Your contribution will definitely benefit all of the participants.

Sincerely yours,

Dear Professor Smith,

In light of your renowned research, we would to like to invite you to speak at an upcoming seminar to be held in Taiwan. We hope your lecture will include how to analyze chitin and chitosan, as well as their practical implementation. We will provide a roundtrip train ticket and hotel accommodations during your stay. Please send us your lecture handouts at your earliest convenience. After this seminar, I hope to receive training in your laboratory with my colleagues on the latest trends in this field. This opportunity would give me a clearer idea of my own research direction, along with the most effective methods available.

If you can attend this seminar, your contribution will definitely benefit all of the participants. I would be more than happy to meet you at the train station upon your arrival. Let us know at your earliest convenience whether you will be able to participate in this seminar.

Sincerely yours,

Dear Mr. Wang,

I hope that you received my letter dated May 30, 2004 in which I invited you to accompany representatives of the Taiwan branch office of DISPLAY Corporation to Korea in order to explore potential product development opportunities. I hope that you will be present for the signing of this memorandum of understanding (MOU) that would allow our two companies to engage in technical cooperation.

Our R & D Department strives to develop state-of-the-art technologies by continually upgrading our technological capabilities and innovativeness in products striving design. Our employees are highly motivated, as evidenced by our recent development of several TFT-LCD products. The turning point is success for corporate growth arose from our ability to remain abreast of the latest technological trends that leaders in the field adoptor us to keep growing and grasp in research and development of the products, as well as in product innovation. Notable examples include 10.4-inch TFT-LCD products, as well as 2.45W and 3.5W-inch products for digital cameras, pocket TVs and TV cameras. While 5W, 6.4W, 6.5W, 7W, 8W, and 10W inch offerings are for DVD, automobile navigation, portable TV, entertainment products and digital TV cameras, the 6.4W and 10.4W inch offerings are for industrial products.

The signing of this MOU in the Korean headquarters of DISPLAY Corporation would allow our Taiwan branch to receive a technology transfer for some of the above product technology developments. Given our lack of expertise in developing TFT-LCD materials, this cooperative agreement will ultimately increase our brand awareness and market share. Again, your presence at this signing would be most meaningful for both of our organizations given your expertise in this area.

We will provide roundtrip airfare and accommodations during your stay in Korea.

Please let us know of a convenient time for the signing of this agreement. This trip will hopefully strengthen the collaborative ties between our organizations. Your speedy reply regarding the details of this upcoming visit would be most appreciated.
Sincerely yours,

Dear Dr. Chang,

Quite some time has passed since you visited our laboratories in June of 2004. I hope that all is going well at your institute. As to the scientific and non-scientific collaboration progress between China and Taiwan, R.O.C., as outlined in our joint signing of a memorandum of understanding (MOU) between our two organizations on the research of traditional Chinese medicine-related topics, the time seems right for Yuanpei University of Science and Technology research Institute and National Tsing Hua University to begin collaborative activities. As I mentioned in our earlier conversation, we could began by exchanging scientific experts. I would thus like to propose the following.

Please recommend one scientific expert to serve as a short term consultant at Yuanpei University of Science and Technology. Naturally, we would like someone whose expertise is highly relevant to the following subjects:

1. proficiency in the latest technologies involving traditional Chinese medicine.
2. solid background in designing and integrating approaches in traditional Chinese medicine to facilitate commercial applications.

This expert must also be fluent in English and Chinese (and hopefully have a fundamental grasp of the Taiwanese dialect). During his or her roughly two week stay in our laboratory, we also hope that he/she could lecture on the following topics:

1. Recent advances in the research of Chinese herbal medicine at Yuanpei University of Science and Technology (2 hours)
2. Technological advances in traditional Chinese pharmacology (3 hours)
3. Introduction to chemical components in Chinese herbal medicine (3 hours)
4. GC mass machine-related applications in Chinese herbal medicine

As for compensation of this event, we will offer round-trip airfare from China to Taipei, as well as accommodations in Taiwan during the consultancy period. An honorarium will also be provided for the seminars. If you have such a candidate available or if you should have any comments regarding this proposal, please let us

know at your earliest convenience.
Sincerely yours,

Dear Dr. Smith,

In light of your innovative research in the field of proton therapy, we would like to invite you to serve as an Invited Speaker at the upcoming 2005 Symposium on Proton Therapy Applications in Oncology. The symposium will be held at the Physical Sciences Laboratories of Yuanpei University of Science and Technology in Hsinchu, Taiwan on July 22, 2005. Hopefully, your lecture will cover current directions in clinical, biopsy and oncology treatment.

For your participation, we will provide roundtrip airfare and accommodations during the symposium. I recommend that you stay in Taiwan for up to a week after the symposium so that you can enjoy some of the island's natural and cultural wonders. Once your flight is confirmed, please let us know your arrival time so that we can meet you at the airport.

Please send us your lecture title and abstract, along with related handouts before May 31, 2005. This will give us sufficient time to make copies and necessary preparations. I also need your curriculum vitae, with its contents to include the following: name, date of birth, place of birth, nationality, address, e-mail address, telephone number, marital status, academic qualifications, professional experience, scientific achievements, current scientific activities, other science-related activities, and selected publications.

Please do not hesitate to contact us if you have any questions about the above details. Your contribution to this symposium would definitely benefit all of the participants.
Sincerely yours,

Dear Dr. Chen,

I am pleased to announce that a seminar on DNA mutation, methylation, repair and recombination will be held at Yuanpei University of Science and Technology in July of 2005. Given your distinguished research in this field, as evidenced by your numerous publications in several internationally renowned journals, we would like to invite you to give a talk at this seminar. This event will hopefully coincide with your return to Taiwan. As for your lecture title, you can choose from among the following topics:(1)mutability and repair of DNA;(2)role of mismatch repair in eliminating errors undetected during proofreading; (3)DNA damage; (4)repair of DNA damage; and (5)homologous recombination.

Please let us know as soon as possible if you will be able to accept our invitation and which of the above topics you would be interested in speaking on. If so, please send us the text of your talk before December 5. We will then have a sufficient amount of time to make copies and appropriate arrangements. I look forward to hearing from you soon.

Sincerely yours,

Professor Wang,

Our hospital's Cardiac Department would like to invite you to speak at our upcoming seminar on the role of medical imagery in evaluating the success rate of heart transplantations. The seminar will begin punctually at 9 AM in our hospital's conference room on December the 31st, which is a Friday. With more than 200 practitioners and academics anticipated to attend, participants hope to learn of the latest medical imagery trends in this area. If you are able to attend this event, we need your confirmation before December the 24th, along with your title, abstract and related handouts in both printed out A4 size form and electronic file. Let us know if you have any special requirements prior to your presentation or on the day of the seminar.

To reserve your air ticket and hotel accommodations at the Taipei Spring Leisure Resort, I need your formal name, current address and passport number. I also need your departure date from Taiwan. Please retain all receipts for incidental expenses incurred during your stay. We will pay you in cash for your speech honorarium and also reimburse you for any incidental expenses.

Please let us know at your earliest convenience whether you will be able to participate in this event.

Sincerely yours,

Dear Professor Smith,

A biotechnology seminar on drug resistant cancer cells will be held in Hsinchu on October the 16th. Specifically, this seminar will focus on the relation between a cancer cell's resistance to anticancer drugs and the sequelae form in patients after the drug resistant cancer cell is produced. The seminar will also address appropriate medicine and therapeutic approaches for such cancer cells.

Given your eminent research of cancer cells, I would like to invite you to speak at this seminar on biotechnological applications of drug resistant cancer cells in therapeutic treatment. Your participation in this event would make the event a truly memorable experience. If you have other commitments during this time, could you recommend another qualified speaker, preferably a researcher who is familiar with anticancer drug properties (e.g., taxol or cisplanting series) and the role of high temperature or high pressure in the responses of drug resistant cancer cells?

If you can participate in this symposium, please let us know at your earliest convenience. Then, my colleague will contact you regarding details of the symposium and travel arrangements. Your contribution to the symposium would definitely benefit all of the participants.

I look forward to hearing from you.

Sincerely yours,

Dear Professor Kawasaki,

In light of your renowned research and contributions in protein expression and secretion, we would like to formally invite you to serve as an Invited Speaker at the upcoming 2005 Biology Technology Symposium, which is to be held at Yuanpei University of Science and Technology in Hsinchu, Taiwan on February 7, 2005. We hope that your lecture will cover recent trends and technological developments in this field.

We will provide roundtrip airfare and accommodations during your stay in Taiwan. I advise you to stay here for one week (if at all possible) so that you can enjoy some of Taiwan's spectacular sights. Please advise us of your flight number so that we can meet you at the Chiang Kai Shek International Airport upon your arrival.

If you can participate in this event, please e-mail us your curriculum vitae and lecture handouts before December 7, 2004 so that we will have sufficient time for translation and printing. Please do not hesitate to let me know if you have any concerns and/or suggestions. Thanks again for your participation in this event. Your contribution will definitely benefit all of the participants.

Sincerely yours,

Dear Professor Smith,

Given your renowned research and contributions in the field of protein purified technologies, we would like to formally invite you to serve as an Invited Speaker at a symposium to be held at Yuanpei University of Science and Technology (Hsinchu, Taiwan) on May 20, 2005. We hope that your lecture will include a discussion of trends and current developments in cysteine protease for polysaccharids-related applications.

We will provide roundtrip airfare and accommodations during your stay in Taiwan. If you can accept our invitation, please advise us of your flight number so that we can meet you at the Chiang Kai Shek International Airport upon your arrival.

If you have any question or suggestions, please do not hesitate to contact us. Your contribution to this symposium will definitely benefit all of the participants.

Sincerely yours,

Dear Dr. Tseng,

Given your significant contributions in the field of protein purification, we would like to invite you to serve as an Invited Speaker at the upcoming Biology Technology Symposium to be held at Yuanpei University of Science and Technology (Hsinchu, Taiwan) on February 15, 2005. We hope your lecture will focus on current efforts to select appropriate raw materials, extraction methods, extraction media, purification methods and sequence of chromatography for purposes of protein purification.

We will provide roundtrip airfare and accommodations during your stay. I hope that you can stay here for one week to enjoy some of the island's natural wonders and cultural sights. Once you have made flight reservations, please inform us of the details so we can meet you at the airport. Please let me know if you have any concerns or suggestions. Your contribution to the conference would definitely benefit all the participants.

Sincerely yours,

Dear Mr. Lin,

We are planning a seminar on J2EE software Applications for customer relationship management, which will be held in Hsinchu, Taiwan on February 14. This seminar will focus on how to handle the channels of communication between customers and call centers. The properties, application and technology of information technologies will also be discussed.

We have learned that you are a representative of A Corporation in Taiwan. We would be very pleased if you could participate in this event. Perhaps you could also recommend a speaker who could discuss the features of Internet-based technology applications. If you have such a candidate available or if you should have any comments about this seminar, please let us know at your earliest convenience.

Sincerely yours,

Dear Mr. Tsai,

We are planning a seminar to be held in Lishin Hospital on October 21 on recent emerging technologies to examine the human body. This seminar will focus on abdomen imaging by utilizing various instrumentation, including MRI, computed tomography and conventional x-ray examination. Given your renowned research and contributions in multi-slice computed tomography, we hope that you could give a talk at an upcoming seminar, in which you could present your relevant experiences in CT angiography for diagnosing liver diseases. Your participation in this seminar would be most meaningful for all of the attendees.

We will provide roundtrip airfare and accommodations during your stay. I advise you to stay here for one week to enjoy some of Taiwan's cultural and natural attractions.

Following adjournment of the seminar, we hope that you will join in the celebration activities for our hospital's tenth anniversary. Once final arrangements have been made, please advise us of your flight number so that we can meet you at the Chiang Kai Shek International Airport.

Our Public Relations Department will supply you with a detailed travel itinerary for the event. Your contribution to the seminar would definitely benefit all of the participants.

Sincerely yours,

Dr. Thomas Meyer,

Given your prominent research in analyzing neurophysiological signals, we would like to formally invite you to serve as an Invited Speaker at the upcoming Cardiovascular Symposium to be held at Yuanpei University of Science and Technology (Hsinchu, Taiwan) on December 30, 2004. We hope your lecture will cover recent trends and developments in amplifying physiological signals from PowerLab systems.

Please let us know as soon as possible if you will be able to accept our invitation. If so, please send us your lecture title and outline, along with related handouts before December 10, 2004. We will then have sufficient time to make copies and appropriate arrangements. We look forward to hearing from you soon.

Please do not hesitate to let me know if you have any enterprise and/or suggestions. We will contact you regarding details of the symposium and travel arrangements. Your contribution to the symposium would definitely benefit all of the participants.

Sincerely yours,

Dear Dr. Chang,

In light of your renowned research and contributions in medical science education, we would like to formally invite you to serve as an Invited Speaker at the upcoming Medical Science Education Symposium, which is to be held at Union ABC Hospital in

Hsinchu, Taiwan on May 15, 2005. Your lecture will hopefully include a summary of recent developmental trends in medical science, relevant governmental policy and current status of medical education.

Please send us your lecture title and outline, along with related handouts, before February 30, 2005. We will then have a sufficient amount of time to make copies and appropriate arrangements. Your curriculum vitae will hopefully include the following information: NAME, DATE OF BIRTH, PLACE OF BIRTH, NATIONALITY, MARITAL STATUS, ACADEMIC QUALIFICATIONS, PROFESSIONAL EXPERIENCE, SCIENTIFIC ACHIEVEMENTS, CURRENT SCIENTIFIC ACTIVITIES, OTHER SCIENCE-RELATED ACTIVITIES and SELECTED PUBLICATIONS.

In addition to an honorarium for your lecture, the organizing committee will also provide a roundtrip train ticket and hotel accommodations in Hsinchu for the evening of May the 15th. Please inform us of your arrival time to the Hsinchu train station so that we can meet you. Please let us know as soon as possible whether you will be able to accept our invitation. Your contribution to this symposium would definitely benefit all of the participants.

Sincerely yours,

Dear Professor Kennison,

Given your renowned research and your contributions in the field of CVC chambers, we would like to formally invite you to serve as an Invited Speaker at the upcoming CVC Principles Symposium to be held at Yuanpei University (Hsinchu, Taiwan) on May 27, 2005. We hope your lecture will include a discussion of CVC principles and applications.

We will provide roundtrip airfare, a chauffer and accommodations during your stay. I advise you to stay here for one week (if at all possible) so that you can enjoy some of the sights that Taiwan has to offer. Please advise us of your flight number so that we can meet you at the airport.

Please send us your lecture title and outline, along with related handouts, before January 31, 2005. We will then have a sufficient amount of time to make copies and appropriate arrangements. I also need your curriculum vitae, with contents to include name, date of birth, nationality, marital status, academic qualifications, professional experiences, scientific achievements and publications.

Please do not hesitate to let me know if you have any concerns and/or suggestions.

Your contribution to this symposium would definitely benefit all the participants.
Sincerely yours,

Dear Mr. Lin,

Thank you for your encouraging e-mail response regarding the cooperation between our two organizations, as well as confirmation that you will be able to serve as an Invited Speaker at the upcoming Health Management Symposium to be held in Taiwan on May 15, 2004.

Please purchase your roundtrip airfare ticket and retain all receipts. We will reimburse you prior to your departure of Taiwan. We will also provide five-star hotel accommodations during your stay. In addition to the symposium, we will arrange several trips so that you can see some of Taiwan's scenic spots and places of historical significance. If you have any questions or suggestions regarding the itinerary of the upcoming, please do not hesitate to contact me.

Sincerely yours,

Dear Dr. Wang,

I am pleased to inform you that our administrators have approved your application to visit Mackay Memorial Hospital as a guest researcher. Our hospital is especially interested in your expertise in the Picture Archiving and Communication System. Given our lack of time to make necessary preparations, please pay in advance for your roundtrip airfare ticket and other incidental expenses. Retain the receipts and, upon your departure of Taiwan, our hospital will reimburse you.

As per your request, the average price of single room hotel accommodations in Taipei ranges from 150USD to 200USD daily. Once the schedule has been finalized, I will reserve a room for your colleagues and yourself. On January the 10th, I will meet you at the Chiang Kai Shek International Airport in transit to your hotel and dinner thereafter.

Please don't hesitate to contact us if any questions should arise.

Sincerely yours,

Dear Dr. Lin,

In light of your renowned research and your contributions in the field of treatment planning systems, we would like to formally invite you to serve as an Invited Speaker at the upcoming Radiotherapy Oncology Conference. We hope your lecture will include a discussion of the current developmental trends in radiotherapy and radiation protection. This conference is to be held at the International Conference Hall in National Taiwan University in Taipei, Taiwan on April 23, 2004.

The following is a tentative agenda for Dr. Lin's visit:

April 23, 2004: Arrival in Taiwan at Chiang Kai Shek International in transit to hotel accommodations

April 24, 2004: Tour of Proton Therapy Cancer Center

Lecture on a special topic in radiotherapy and radiation protection: 2 to 3 hrs

April 25, 2004: Discussion on how to assess current developments in proton therapy

April 26, 2004: Discussion on how to further improve the quality of medicine in proton therapy

April 27, 2004: Discussion on the role of radiation protection in proton therapy

April 28 2004: Sightseeing of Taipei's cultural attractions, asarranged by faculty and staff of National Taiwan University

April 28 2004: Return to the United States

Any comments or suggestions regarding the above itinerary or topics of discussion would be most appreciated. If you find the above itinerary acceptable, please send your lecture topics to Dr. Ting, before February 28, 2004. We will then have sufficient time to make copies and appropriate arrangements. I also need your curriculum vitae, with contents to include name, date of birth, nationality, academic qualifications, professional experiences, scientific achievements, current scientific activities, other science-related activities, other science-related activities, and selected publications.

Please pay in advance for your roundtrip airfare and other incidental expenses; hold onto those receipts for reimbursement prior to your departure of Taiwan. According to our government's tax system, a technical service fee is subject to a 20% tax levy. You must make a copy of the receipt and the counterfoil for us to reimburse you for the transportation fee.

Please do not hesitate to let me know if you have any concerns and suggestions. Your contribution to this conference would definitely benefit all of the participants.

Sincerely yours,

Dear Professor Yang,

Given your solid background in biotechnology research, we would like to formally invite you to serve as an Invited Speaker at the upcoming Purification Enzyme Symposium. We also hope that you could chair a roundtable discussion on a related topic. The symposium will be held at Yuanpei University of Science and Technology on October 25,2004. We hope that your lecture will include a discussion of a maltotriose-producing α-amylase from *Thermobifida fusca*.

As the Symposium will coincide with the Christmas holidays, we will also arrange a special Christmas dinner and related activities. For your participation, we will provide roundtrip airfare and accommodations. Please advise us of your flight number so that we can meet you at the airport. Please send us your lecture title and outline, along with related handouts, before October 18, 2004 so that we will have sufficient time to prepare promotional materials for the event.

If you have any concerns or suggestions regarding the above details, please do not hesitate to contact me. Our entire staff and student body look forward to your participation.

Sincerely yours,

Dear Professor Smith,

Having extensively read upon your published research on chitin, I find these results most helpful to my own research direction. Therefore, I would like to invite you to visit our laboratory and share your expertise in this field with research staff. Hopefully, your two day visit will include a seminar on related topics that you could lecture on. The theme of this seminar will coincide with efforts to develop product technologies in this area. Each lecture topic will last roughly one hour. If you are in agreement, I am confident that your participation will greatly benefit our colleagues. All accommodation and transportation arrangements will be made in advance.

I need to know which dates are the most convenient for such a visit. If you have any suggestions regarding the above preparations, please feel free to contact me. I firmly believe that the opportunity for you to share your expertise with our colleagues will lead to a mutually beneficial relation, possibly collaborative activities in the near future.

Sincerely yours,

Dear Dr. Wu,

Thank you for your encouraging reply on recent trends in Internet marketing research. Given your eminent research and contributions in this field, we want to formally invite you lecture our research staff on the latest research trends in Internet marketing. At a special conference to be held at Yuanpei University of Science and Techonlogy on March 15, 2005, we hope that you can serve as the keynote speaker, lecturing on trends in Internet marketing and novel sales approaches. Besides providing accommodations and transportations arrangements during your stay, we would also like to show you some of Taiwan's cultural and historical places of interest. Therefore, please allot extra time besides your involvement in the conference to enjoy some of the island's cultural and natural wonders.

Once final arrangements have been made, let us know of your flight details so that we can meet you at the Chiang Kai Shek International Airport in transit to your hotel accommodations. I also need your lecture title and handouts by March 1, 2005, as well as your curriculum vitae, with its contents including your name, date of birth, nationality, academic qualifications, professional experiences, scientific achievements, current scientific activities, other science-related activities, other science-related activities and selected publications. Please do not hesitate to contact me if you have any suggestions regarding the upcoming visit.

Sincerely yours,

Dear Dr. Beatrice,

In light of your renowned research and your contributions in the field of evidence-based nursing, we would like to formally invite you to serve as an Invited Speaker at the upcoming Symposium on Implications for Clinical Practice and Management, which is to be held in the Main Auditorium at Taipei Medical University on July 15, 2005. We hope that your lecture will include a discussion of clinical practice and related management practices in evidence-based nursing.

We will provide roundtrip airfare and accommodations during your stay, along with a honorarium of $US 1,000 for a four hour lecture. I also advise you to stay here for an extra three days or so following the symposium so that you can enjoy some of the sights that Taiwan has to offer. Once your reservations are confirmed, please advise us of your flight number so that we can meet you at the airport.

Please send us your lecture title and outline, along with related handouts, before July 1, 2005. We will then have sufficient time to print the lecture handouts. Please do not hesitate to let me know if you have any concerns. Your contribution to this symposium would definitely benefit all of the participants.

Sincerely yours,

Dear Professor Lin,

Given your eminent research in marketing, we would like to formally invite you to serve as an Invited Speaker at the upcoming Internet Marketing Symposium to be held at Yuanpei University of Science and Technology (Taiwan) on February 10, 2005. We hope that your lecture will cover recent trends and developments in Internet-based advertising and marketing strategies.

As February is normally a busy month in preparation for the Chinese New Years holiday, I would suggest rescheduling the symposium for March the 22nd. I advise you to lengthen your visit until March 26 so that you will be able to tour some of Taiwan's natural scenery.

As for compensation, the organizing committee will provide roundtrip airfare, hotel accommodations and a speech honorarium for your lecture. Please let us know as soon as possible whether you will be able to accept our invitation and if this change in dates is agreeable with you. If so, please send us your lecture topic and related handouts before December 31, 2004. Also, I will be in touch with you shortly regarding further details of the symposium and travel arrangements. Your contribution to the symposium would definitely benefit all of the participants.

I anxiously look forward to your favorable reply.

Sincerely yours,

Situation 4

Marty Wang

Chinese herbal medicine

traditional Chinese medicine-related topics

Situation 5

Christine Huang

reserve a hotel room

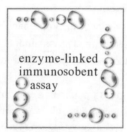

enzyme-linked immunosobent assay

honorarium

Situation 6

John Su

Taiwan's areas of natural beauty

please send

Internet-based advertising and marketing strategies

I Write down the key points of the situations on the preceding page, while the instructor reads aloud the script from the Answer Key.

Situation 4

_____

_____

_____

Situation 5

_____

_____

_____

Situation 6

_____

_____

_____

J Oral practice II
Based on the three situations in this unit, write three questions beginning with *How*, and answer them. The questions do not need to come directly from these situations.

Examples

How long has it been since Dr. Chang visited Marty's laboratories?

Quite some time

How was the scientific and non-scientific collaboration between China and Taiwan, R.O.C. initiated?

By the signing of a memorandum of understanding (MOU) between the two organizations

1. _____

_____

2. _____

_____

3. _____

_____

K Based on the three situations in this unit, write three questions beginning with **What**, and answer them. The questions do not need to come directly from these situations.

Examples

What will Christine do once the schedule has been finalized?

She will reserve a hotel room for Dr. Lin.

What is the range for the average price of a single hotel room in Hsinchu?

From US$100 to US$150

1. _____

_____

2. _____

_____

3. _____

_____

L Based on the three situations in this unit, write three
   questions beginning with **Why**, and answer them. The
   questions do not need to come directly from these
   situations.

Examples

Why does John want to invite Professor Lin to participate as an Invited Speaker at
the upcoming Internet Marketing Symposium?

Because of his eminence in the field of marketing

Why is February normally a busy month?

Everyone is preparing for Chinese New Year.

1. _____

   _____

2. _____

   _____

3. _____

   _____

M Write questions that match the answers provided.

1. _____

   _____

   The latest technologies related to traditional Chinese medicine

2. _____

   _____

   Quite some time

3. _____

   _____

   Roundtrip airfare, hotel accommodation and a speech honorarium for his lecture

N Listening Comprehension II

Situation 4

1. When was the last time that Dr. Chang visited Marty's laboratories?

   A. April of 2004   B. May of 2004   C. June of 2004

2. What research area does the memorandum of understanding (MOU) between the two organizations cover?

   A. GC mass machine-related applications

   B. traditional Chinese medicine-related topics

   C. traditional Chinese pharmacology

3. How many hours will the lecture on recent advances in research on Chinese herbal medicine at Yuanpei University of Science and Technology last?

   A. 2 hours   B. 3 hours   C. 1 hour

4. What will Marty's organization provide Dr. Chang for the seminars?

   A. round-trip airfare from China to Taipei

   B. accommodation in Taiwan

   C. an honorarium

5. What must the short-term consultant be proficient in?

   A. traditional Chinese pharmacology

   B. the latest technologies related to traditional Chinese medicine

   C. GC mass machine-related applications

Situation 5

1. What general topic will Marty's organization consult with Dr. Lin during his stay in Taiwan?

   A. enzyme-linked immunosobent assay

   B. cortisol antibody

C. biotechnology

2. What have Dr. Lin's previous research collaborations involved?

A. the medical sector　B. the chemical sector　C. the biotech sector

3. What is the average price range for a single room in Hsinchu?

A. from US$ 200 to US$ 250

B. from US$ 100 to US$ 150

C. from US$ 300 to US$ 350

4. When did Dr. Lin last visit Christine's laboratories?

A. in December 2004　B. in November 2004　C. in January 2004

5. What should Dr. Lin purchase in advance before arriving to Taiwan?

A. insurance　B. a hotel room　C. a roundtrip ticket (business class)

Situation 6

1. In what field is Professor Lin known for his eminent research?

A. finance　B. marketing　C. cost-benefit analysis

2. What is the theme of the symposium to be held at Yuanpei University of Science and Technology?

A. Global Commerce

B. Cost-Benefit Analysis in Marketing

C. Internet Marketing

3. Why is the symposium rescheduled to March 22nd?

A. since February is normally a busy month as everyone prepares for Chinese New Year

B. owing to a conflict in schedules

C. owing to a previous commitment

4. What does John hope that Professor Lin's lecture will cover?

A. recent trends and developments in finance

B. recent trends and developments in cost-benefit analysis

C. recent trends and developments in Internet-based advertising and marketing strategies

5. Why does John want Professor Lin to extend his visit until March 26?

A. to consult with researchers at Yuanpei University of Science and Technology on Internet marketing

B. to give him time to tour some of Taiwan's areas of natural beauty

C. to give additional lectures following the symposium on Internet-based advertising and marketing strategies

○ Reading Comprehension II
Pick the work or expression whose meaning is closest to the meaning of the underlined word or expression in the following passages.

Situation 4

1. With regard to the scientific and non-scientific <u>collaboration</u> between China and Taiwan, R.O.C., as outlined in our signing of a memorandum of understanding (MOU) between our two organizations on research into traditional Chinese medicine-related topics, the time seems right for the Yuanpei University of Science and Technology Research Institute and National Tsing Hua University to begin collaborative activities.

   A. competition   B. synergy   C. conflict

2. With regard to the scientific and non-scientific collaboration between China and Taiwan, R.O.C., as outlined in our signing of a memorandum of understanding (MOU) between our two organizations on research into <u>traditional</u> Chinese medicine-related topics, the time seems right for the Yuanpei University of Science and Technology Research Institute and National Tsing Hua University to begin collaborative activities.

   A. conventional   B. unique   C. cutting edge

3. As I mentioned in our earlier conversation, we could begin by <u>exchanging</u> scientific experts.

   A. hoarding   B. amassing   C. reciprocating

4. As I mentioned in our earlier conversation, we could begin by exchanging scientific <u>experts</u>.

   A. novices   B. protégés   C. specialists

5. Naturally, we would like someone whose <u>expertise</u> is highly relevant to the

following subjects.

   A. imperfection   B. skillfulness   C. shallowness

6. <u>Proficiency</u> in the latest technologies related to traditional Chinese medicine.

   A. adeptness   B. ineptness   C. incompetent

7. Solid background in designing and <u>integrating</u> approaches to facilitating commercial applications of traditional Chinese medicine.

   A. disentangle   B. consolidating   C. disengage

8. Solid background in designing and integrating approaches to <u>facilitating</u> commercial applications of traditional Chinese medicine.

   A. paving the way for   B. inhibiting   C. hindering

Situation 5

1. Once the <u>schedule</u> has been finalized, I will reserve a hotel room for you.

   A. hardware   B. agenda   C. software

2. Once the schedule has been <u>finalized,</u> I will reserve a hotel room for you.

   A. conclusive   B. tentative   C. in the trial stages

3. Once the schedule has been finalized, I will <u>reserve</u> a hotel room for you.

   A. recant   B. retract   C. book

4. If you decide to come, please purchase your roundtrip ticket (business class) in advance and save the receipt for <u>reimbursement</u>.

   A. incorporation   B. addition   C. remuneration

5. I should also mention that Taiwan's government <u>levies</u> a technical service fee tax of 20%.

   A. gather   B. refunds   C. rebates

6. How to <u>ameliorate</u> a defect in enzyme-linked immunosobent assay (ELISA)

   A. aggravate   B. exacerbate   C. heal

7. An <u>honorarium</u> for the seminars will also be given.

A. payment for lecture

B. payment for accommodations

C. payment for interview

Situation 6

1. Given your <u>eminence</u> in the field of marketing, we would like formally to invite you to participate as an Invited Speaker at the upcoming Internet Marketing Symposium to be held at Yuanpei University of Science and Technology (Taiwan) on February 10, 2005.

   A. infamy　B. notoriety　C. esteem

2. We hope that your lecture will cover <u>recent</u> trends and developments in Internet-based advertising and marketing strategies.

   A. primeval　B. primordial　C. up-to-the-minute

3. We hope that your lecture will cover recent <u>trends</u> and developments in Internet-based advertising and marketing strategies.

   A. inclinations　B. relapses　C. reversals

4. I advise you to <u>extend</u> your visit until March 26 to give you time to tour some of Taiwan's areas of natural beauty.

   A. curtail　B. condense　C. elongate

5. If so, please send us your lecture title and <u>related</u> handouts before December 31, 2004.

   A. dissimilar　B. affiliated　C. divergent

6. I will be in <u>touch</u> with you shortly regarding further details of the symposium and travel arrangements.

   A. line　B. place　C. contact

7. Your contribution to the symposium would <u>definitely</u> benefit all of the participants.

A. inconclusively B. indisputably C. indecisively

8. Your contribution to the symposium would definitely <u>benefit</u> all of the participants.

A. avail B. impede C. frustrate

P Matching Exercise

1. Each sentence in the following is commonly used to invite speakers for a conference, symposium or lecture: inviting a speaker 演講者邀請信函：邀請演講者. Each phrase on the left should be matched with one on the right in order to complete the sentence. Match a number on the left with a letter on the right.

1. Given your renowned research and contributions in the field of cell culture technologies,	a. chair a roundtable discussion on a related topic.
2. Having extensively read upon your published research on chitin, I find these results most helpful to my own research direction.	b. to speak at the upcoming Ninth Symposium on Recent Advances in Cellular and Molecular Biology.
3. We also hope that you could	c. long-term care programs, we hope that you could recommend a consultant that could instruct our hospital staff on the following topics:
4. Given your distinguished research on the Helicobacter pylori full genome, I would like to invite you	d. as an Invited Speaker at the upcoming Health Management Symposium to be held in Taiwan on May 15, 2004.
5. Given your organization's extensive experience in implementing	e. on March 15, 2005, we hope that you can serve as the keynote speaker, lecturing on trends in Internet marketing and novel sales approaches.
6. Given your distinguished research in this field,	f. we would like to formally invite you to serve as an Invited Speaker at the upcoming Food Health Symposium.
7. At a special conference to be held at Yuanpei University of Science and Techonlogy	g. at the upcoming Purification Enzyme Symposium.
8. Thank you for your confirmation that you will be able to serve	h. Therefore, I would like to invite you to visit our laboratory and share your expertise in this field with research staff.
9. Given your solid background in biotechnology research, we would like to formally invite you to serve as an Invited Speaker	i. as evidenced by your numerous publications in several internationally renowned journals, we would like to invite you to give a talk at this seminar.

2. Inviting speakers for a conference, symposium or lecture: describing the purpose of the lecture 演講者邀請信函：描述演講目的

1. Your lecture will hopefully include a summary of recent developmental trends	a. and current status of medical education.
2. Your lecture will hopefully include a summary of recent developmental trends in medical science, relevant governmental policy	b. aimed at resolving salvageable tissue and irreversible damage.
3. The theme of this seminar will coincide	c. explaining the lack of confidence among patients and their relatives in the quality of medical care offered in Taiwanese hospitals.
4. Despite the above aspirations, our hospital is lacking in many of the above areas,	d. second worldwide in the growth rate of elderly individuals.
5. With more than 200 practitioners and academics anticipated to attend the symposium, participants hope	e. with them to ensure a lasting partnership.
6. The seminar will focus	f. in medical science, relevant governmental policy and current status of medical education.
7. This topic is particularly relevant given that Taiwan ranks	g. essential to sustained commercial success.
8. Given the progressive decline in customer satisfaction, understanding their needs and maintaining their loyalty are	h. on recent advances in molecular biology-related technologies.
9. An enterprise's ability to retain its customers depends on the ability to closely interact	i. with efforts to develop product technologies in this area.
10. Given the increasing incidence of brain strokes among the younger population in Taiwan, many medical technologies have emerged,	j. in developing TFT-LCD materials, this cooperative agreement will ultimately increase our brand awareness and market share.
11. Given our lack of expertise	k. to learn of the latest medical imagery trends in this area.

3. Inviting speakers for a conference, symposium or lecture: explaining details of the lecture 演講者邀請信函：詳述演講的細節

1. Each lecture will last two hours,	a. will be held at Yuanpei University of Science and Technology in July of 2005.
2. The Society of Biochemists of the R.O.C. will hold a seminar on molecular biology,	b. for the Chinese New Years holiday, I would suggest rescheduling the symposium for March the 22nd.
3. I am pleased to announce that a seminar on DNA mutation, methylation, repair and recombination	c. and developments in tea polyphenols, antiinflammation and flow cytometer.
4. This symposium is to be held at Yuanpei University of Science and Technology (Hsinchu, Taiwan)	d. on January 30, 2005.
5. If you have other commitments during this time, could you recommend another qualified speaker,	e. details of the symposium and travel arrangements.
6. As February is normally a busy month in preparation	f. in the celebration activities for our hospital's tenth anniversary.
7. Perhaps you could also recommend a speaker	g. with the consultant reimbursed with a speech honorarium.
8. We hope your lecture will cover recent trends	h. preferably a researcher who is familiar with anticancer drug properties (e.g., taxol or cisplanting series) and the role of high temperature or high pressure in the responses of drug resistant cancer cells?
9. My colleagues will contact you regarding	i. we will also arrange a special Christmas dinner and related activities.
10. As the Symposium will coincide with the Christmas holidays,	j. which will be held in Taipei Taiwan on November 16, 2005.
11. Following adjournment of the seminar, we hope that you will join	k. who could discuss the features of Internet-based technology applications.
12. I need to know which dates	l. are the most convenient for you to give this lecture.

283

4. Inviting speakers for a conference, symposium or lecture: describing transportation and accommodation details 演講者邀請信函：詳述交通及住宿的細節

1. We will provide	a. to enjoy some of the sights that Taiwan has to offer.
2. Besides providing accommodations and transportations arrangements during your stay,	b. in The Regent Formosa Taipei ranges between JPY ￥17000 to JPY ￥24000 daily.
3. All accommodation and transportation arrangements	c. for which, you will be reimbursed (by check) prior to your departure of Taiwan.
4. I advise that you stay here for an additional week or so	d. we would also like to show you some of Taiwan's cultural and historical places of interest.
5. In addition to the symposium, we will arrange several trips	e. provide roundtrip airfare, hotel accommodations and a speech honorarium for your lecture.
6. Once final arrangements are made, please advise	f. We suggest you stay a week to enjoy some of the island's natural attractions.
7. As for compensation, the organizing committee will	g. so that you can see some of Taiwan's scenic spots and places of historical significance.
8. The average price of a deluxe room	h. roundtrip airfare and accommodations during your visit.
9. Retain the receipts or invoices,	i. us of the flight details so that we can meet you at the airport.
10. Taiwan is a beautiful island, originally known as Formosa.	j. will be made in advance.

5. Inviting speakers for a conference, symposium or lecture: describing transportation and accommodation details 演講者邀請信函：詳述交通及住宿的細節

1. As for compensation of this event, please pay	a. for a single room averages between DM$ 130 to DM$250 daily.
2. Please allot extra time besides your involvement in the conference	b. I need your formal name, current address and passport number.
3. To reserve your air ticket and hotel accommodations at the Taipei Spring Leisure Resort,	c. a roundtrip train ticket and hotel accommodations in Hsinchu for the evening of May the 15th.
4. In addition to an honorarium for your lecture, the organizing committee will also provide	d. that you will be able to tour some of Taiwan's natural scenery.
5. Incidentally, hotel accommodations in Taipei	e. in advance for the roundtrip airfare ticket, and other incidental expenses.
6. Please inform us of your arrival time to the Hsinchu	f. reserve a room for you and your wife.
7. I hope that you can allot extra time to see some	g. of the cultural wonders that Taiwan offers.
8. Once your schedule is confirmed, I will	h. to enjoy some of the island's cultural and natural wonders.
9. I advise you to lengthen your visit until March 26 so	i. train station so that we can meet you.

6. Inviting speakers for a conference, symposium or lecture: instructing the speaker what to prepare before the visit 演講者邀請信函：演講者行前必知指導

1. Please send us your lecture titles and related handouts before January 10, 2005	a. of your talk before December 5.
2. Please e-mail us your curriculum vitae and course materials	b. marital status, academic qualifications, professional experience, scientific achievements, current scientific activities, other science-related activities, and selected publications.
3. I need your curriculum vitae, with contents to include the following name, date of birth, place of birth, nationality, address, e-mail address, telephone number,	c. so that we will have sufficient time to make copies and appropriate arrangements.
4. Please send us the text	d. to your presentation or on the day of the seminar.
5. Let us know if you have any special requirements prior	e. before December 24, 2004 so that we will have sufficient time for translation and printing.

Unit Five

Connie Li

dosimetry related research

Laboratory at YUST

collaborative opportunities

Donald Wang

Radiology Technologists

enjoy traditional Chinese tea

IMRT

3 ? questions

Arranging Travel Itineraries

旅行安排信函

Vocabulary and related expressions 相關字詞

eminent scholars 卓越的學者
keynote speakers 主旨演講者
developmental trends 發展的趨勢
clinical experiences 臨床經驗
tentative schedule 暫時性的行程
collaborative opportunities 合作機會
hesitate 猶豫
reimburse 賠償
consultation 諮詢
impressed with 給……極深的印象
intention 意圖
distinguished contributions 著名的貢獻
accommodation 膳宿
consultation topics 諮詢的主題
feedback 反饋的信息

current trends 最近的趨勢
roundtable discussion 大眾參與的討論
options 選擇
flight details 班機細節
ample time 充裕的時間
marital status 婚姻狀態
positive reply 肯定的回覆
technical seminar 科技專題討論會
modified 修改的
a major highlight（主要最精彩）的部分
state-of-the-art 最先進的
latest developments in 最新的發展
itinerary 旅行計畫
tentative 暫時性的
concentrate on 集中

product life cycle 產品的生命週期　　speech honorarium 演講報酬
celebrated research 馳名的研究　　invited speaker 受邀演講者

Situation 1

Connie Li

dosimetry related research

Laboratory at YUST

collaborative opportunities

Situation 2

Donald Wang

Radiology Technologists

enjoy traditional Chinese tea

IMRT

3 ? questions

Situation 3

Jessamine Su

IMRT

airport

Radiological Technologists

Chinese New Year

A Write down the key points of the situations on the preceding page, while the instructor reads aloud the script from the Answer Key.

Situation 1

_____

_____

_____

Situation 2

_____

_____

_____

Situation 3

_____

_____

_____

B Oral practice I

Based on the three situations in this unit, write three questions beginning with **What**, and answer them. The questions do not need to come directly from these situations.

Examples

What has Professor Coutrakon agreed to participate as?

An invited speaker at the upcoming seminar to be held in the Institute of Medical Imagery at Yuanpei University of Science and Technology (YUST)

What area is Professor Coutrakon an eminent scholar in?

Dosimetry-related research

1. _____

_____

2. _____

_____

3. _____

_____

> **C** Based on the three situations in this unit, write three
> questions beginning with **Why**, and answer them. The
> questions do not need to come directly from these
> situations

Examples

Why is Donald inviting Dr. Curtin to come to Taiwan?

For consultation

Why is Donald writing Dr. Curtin?

He is responsible for arranging the details of his visit.

1. _____

_____

2. _____

_____

3. _____

_____

D Based on the three situations in this unit, write three questions beginning with **How**, and answer them. The questions do not need to come directly from these situations.

Examples

How has Dr. Kawasaki contributed to the efforts of radiological technologists?

In the field of IMRT

How would Jessamine like Dr. Kawasaki to participate at the upcoming meeting of the Chinese Association of Radiological Technologists?

As an Invited Speaker

1. _____

_____

2. _____

_____

3. _____

_____

E Write questions that match the answers provided.

1. _____

_____

Professor Hsu

2. _____

_____

Mr. Curtin's address to members of The Association of Radiology Technologists
of the Republic of China

3. _____

_____

The above itinerary and consultation topics

F Listening Comprehension I

Situation 1

1. Who will serve as keynote speakers at the upcoming seminar to be held in the Institute of Medical Imagery at Yuanpei University of Science and Technology?

   A. Professor Smith, Professor Hsu and Professor Tung

   B. Professor Hsu, Professor Tung and Professor Coutrakon

   C. Professor Hsu, Professor Jones and Professor Tung

2. What comparison is made during proton beam treatment?

   A. fast neutron therapy and boron neutron capture therapy

   B. microdosimetry spectra and proton therapy

   C. microdosimetry spectra and biological efficacy

3. When will Professor Coutrakon deliver a lecture on the current status of proton therapy research?

   A. Dec. 27, 2004   B. Dec. 25, 2004   C. Dec. 28, 2004

4. When will Professor Coutrakon spend free time sightseeing at Hsinchu Science-based Industrial Park?

   A. Dec. 30, 2004   B. Dec. 27, 2004   C. Dec. 28, 2004

5. Who is Connie's academic advisor?

   A. Professor Tung   B. Professor Coutrakon   C. Professor Hsu

Situation 2

1. What does Donald's hospital intend to implement?

   A. advanced cancer therapeutic treatments

   B. a state-of-the-art therapeutic planning system

   C. an IMRT system

2. When are the clinical implications for implementing the latest advances in IMRT

considered?

A. when improving other therapeutic planning systems

B. when diagnosing and treating cancer

C. when treating breast and head and neck cancer

3. At what university is Dr. Curtin expected to share his experiences of diagnosing and treating cancer?

A. Stanford University

B. National Taiwan University

C. Yuanpei University of Science and Technology

4. When will Mr. Curtin deliver the keynote speech at the Annual Meeting of The Association of Radiology Technologists of the Republic of China?

A. 1/11　B. 1/12　C. 1/13

5. When will Mr. Curtin tour the northern coast of Taiwan and enjoy some traditional Chinese tea?

A. 1/13　B. 1/12　C. 1/16

Situation 3

1. Why is Jessamine inviting Dr. Kawasaki to participate as an Invited Speaker at the upcoming meeting of the Chinese Association of Radiological Technologists?

A. owing to his distinguished contributions in the field of radiation treatment

B. owing to his distinguished contributions in the field of IMRT

C. owing to his distinguished contributions in the field of radiological technology

2. What does Jessamine hope that Dr. Kawasaki's lecture will include a discussion of?

A. the latest developments in reciprocity-related topics

B. the latest developments in radiological technology

C. the latest developments in radiation treatment used in IMRT

3. When will Dr. Kawasaki arrive in Taiwan at Chiang Kai International Airport and meet colleagues for transit to hotel?

A. Feb. 6, 2005　B. Feb. 8, 2005　C. Feb. 10, 2005

4. When will Dr. Kawasaki meet with CART staff members and discuss his schedule?

A. Feb. 5, 2005　B. Feb. 17, 2005　C. Feb. 7, 2005

5. In what area can the two organizations discuss potential collaborative activities?

A. IMRT　B. radiation treatment　C. radiological technology

G Reading Comprehension I
Pick the work or expression whose meaning is closest to the meaning of the underlined word or expression in the following passages.

Situation 1

1. As <u>eminent</u> scholars in dosimetry-related research, my academic advisor Professor Hsu, Professor Tung and you, will be the keynote speakers for this event.

    A. contentious B. controversial C. revered

2. As eminent <u>scholars</u> in dosimetry-related research, my academic advisor Professor Hsu, Professor Tung and you, will be the keynote speakers for this event.

    A. luminaries B. apprentices C. greenhorns

3. As eminent scholars in dosimetry-related research, my academic advisor Professor Hsu, Professor Tung and you, will be the <u>keynote</u> speakers for this event.

    A. subordinate B. secondary C. main

4. If you have any <u>suggestions</u> regarding the above schedule and lecture topics, please do not hesitate to contact me.

    A. reprisals B. retributions C. recommendations

5. If you have any suggestions regarding the above schedule and lecture topics, please do not <u>hesitate</u> to contact me.

    A. hasten B. drag one's feet C. precipitate

6. Keep your receipts so that we can <u>reimburse</u> you prior to your departure from Taiwan.

    A. refund B. send a statement to C. charge

7. Keep your receipts so that we can reimburse you <u>prior to</u> your departure from Taiwan.

    A. after B. before C. during

Situation 2

1. Thank you for accepting our invitation to come to Taiwan for <u>consultation</u> on our latest research efforts.

 A. repudiation　B. counsel　C. renunciation

2. Thank you for accepting our invitation to come to Taiwan for consultation on our latest research <u>efforts</u>.

 A. undertakings　B. retractions　C. contradictions

3. I was most <u>impressed with</u> the lecture you delivered during The Annual Meeting of Radiology Therapy in 1998.

 A. touched by　B. appalled by　C. disheartened by

4. Your address to members of The Association of Radiology Technologists of the Republic of China will be a major <u>highlight</u> of the upcoming event.

 A. periphery　B. fringe　C. core

5. In particular, we will <u>raise</u> the following questions during our meeting.

 A. repress　B. ask (correct answer)　C. impede

6. I hope that the above questions will give you a clearer idea of our <u>intention</u> to improve medical services at our hospital and implement a state-of-the-art therapeutic planning system.

 A. pointlessness　B. purpose (correct answer)　C. futileness

7. I hope that the above questions will give you a clearer idea of our intention to <u>improve</u> medical services at our hospital and implement a state-of-the-art therapeutic planning system.

 A. demote　B. debase　C. rectify (correct answer)

Situation 3

1. Recognizing your <u>distinguished</u> contributions in the field of IMRT, we would like formally to invite you to participate as an Invited Speaker at the upcoming

meeting of the Chinese Association of Radiological Technologists.

A. discredited   B. celebrated   C. censured

2. We hope that your lecture will include a discussion of the <u>latest</u> developments in radiation treatment used in IMRT.

A. archaic   B. obsolete   C. up-to-the-minute

3. Thank you for your faxed response regarding <u>cooperation</u> between our two organizations.

A. concerted effort   B. autonomous effort   C. sel-reliant effort

4. Discuss <u>potential</u> collaborative activities of our two organizations in the area of radiation treatment.

A. feasible   B. inoperative   C. inutile

5. The above <u>itinerary</u> and consultation topics are only tentative.

A. estimate   B. price list   C. schedule

6. The above itinerary and consultation topics are only <u>tentative</u>.

A. in the trial stages   B. fixed   C. established

7. We welcome your <u>feedback</u> if you feel any changes should be made.

A. command   B. directive   C. response

8. Any comments or suggestions regarding the <u>aforementioned</u> proposal would be greatly appreciated.

A. discussed earlier   B. discussed later   C. discussed now

H Common elements in arranging travel itineraries（旅行安排信函）include the following contents:
1. Listing details of the travel itinerary 行程細節列表
2. Welcoming suggestions about the proposed itinerary 對行程細節列表的建議

In the space below, write a letter arranging the travel itinerary for an upcoming visit.

_____

_____

_____

_____

_____

_____

_____

_____

Look at the following examples of letters arranging travel itineraries for upcoming visits.

Dear Mr. Smith,

Thank you for your response regarding Mr. Smith's visit to our Taiwan branch office. Although contents of the proposal seem fine, we hope to change the date of Mr. Smith's visit to February of 2005 given that January is extremely busy with the upcoming Chinese New Year holiday. Accordingly, a tentative agenda for Mr. Smith's ten day visit is summarized below:

Feb. 6, 2005 (Sun): Pick up Mr. Smith at Chiang-Kai Shek International Airport in Taoyuan.

Feb. 7, 2005 (Mon): Meet with R&D staff in the Taiwan branch office and discuss Mr. Smith's schedule.

Feb. 8, 2005 (Tue): Oversee the mattress and pillow manufacturing process.

Feb. 9, 2005 (Wed): Oversee the manufacturing process in the factory of a collaborative partner.

Feb. 10, 2005 (Thu): Meet with R&D staff and discuss relevant manufacturing technologies.

Feb. 11, 2005 (Fri): Tour cultural attractions, as arranged by the General Affairs Section of the Taiwan branch office.

Feb. 12, 2005 (Sat): Tour cultural attractions, as arranged by the General Affairs Section of the Taiwan branch office.

Feb. 13, 2005 (Fri): Discuss areas of cooperation in developing innovative product technologies.

Feb. 14, 2005 (Fri): Continue with discussion on areas of cooperation between our two organizations.

Feb. 15, 2005 (Sat): Return to Germany.

The agenda and consulting topics can be changed, if necessary. Any comments or suggestions regarding the aforementioned proposal would be highly appreciated. We look forward to your response to the above itinerary.

Sincerely yours,

Dear Mr. Ross,

Thanks for your recent reply that Mr. Robbins has agreed to participate in our academic discussion on intellectual capital-related topics in Taiwan. As February marks the end of our school term, we suggest changing the date of Mr. Robbins' visit to January. Please find below a tentative agenda of Mr. Robbins' visit:

Jan. 12, 2005 (Sun): Pick up Mr. Robbins at Chiang-Kai Shek International Airport in transit to Hsinchu.

Jan. 13, 2005 (Mon): Meet with academic staff at Yuanpei University of Science and Technology (YUST) and discuss Mr. Robbins' schedule.

Jan. 14, 2005 (Tue): Chair a roundtable discussion on intellectual capital (2 to 3 hrs).

Jan. 15, 2005 (Wed): Tour the campus of YUST.

Jan. 16, 2005 (Thu): Chair a roundtable discussion on measuring intellectual capital (2 to 3 hrs).

Jan. 17, 2005 (Fri): Tour cultural attractions of Hsinchu.

Jan. 18, 2005 (Sat): Chair a roundtable discussion on intellectual capital-related professions (2 to 3 hrs).

Jan. 19, 2005 (Sun): Spend free time sightseeing Taipei.

Jan. 20, 2005 (Mon): Chair a roundtable discussion on managing intellectual capital (2 to 3 hrs).

Jan. 21, 2005 (Tue): Discuss the possibilities for collaborative academic activities in the future.

Jan. 22, 2005 (Fri): Return to the United States.

The agenda and consulting topics can be changed, if necessary. Any comments or suggestions regarding the aforementioned proposal would be highly appreciated. If the proposal is acceptable, please send us Dr. Robbins' presentation topics and curriculum vitae as soon as possible.

Sincerely yours,

Dear Mr. Smith,

Thank you for agreeing to serve as an invited speaker at the upcoming seminar to be held at Yuanpei University of Science and Technology, November 22-30, 2004. The seminar will focus on two topics: (a) quantitative methodology and Statistical Package for Social Science (SPSS) related applications and (b) theoretical concepts involving society and science. A tentative schedule for the seminar schedule is as follows:

Nov. 22	10:00－12:00	Introduction to quantitative methodology (with an emphasis on data collection and the data matrix)
	13:00－15:00	Laboratory practicum using SPSS
Nov. 23	10:00－12:00	Description of variables
	13:00－15:00	Laboratory practicum using SPSS
Nov. 24	10:00－12:00	Simple relationships between simple variables (with an emphasis on analysis of tables)
	13:00－15:00	Laboratory practicum using SPSS
Nov. 25	10:00－12:00	Random or systematic variation (with an emphasis on statistical inference)
	13:00－15:00	Laboratory practicum using SPSS
Nov. 26	10:00－12:00	Relationship between quantitative variables (with an emphasis on correlation and regression analysis)
	13:00－15:00	Laboratory practicum using SPSS
Nov. 27	10:00－12:00	Implications of Theory and Method
	13:00－15:30	Durkheim's Theory on Suicide
Nov. 28	10:00－12:00	Weber Merton Thesis and Kuhns Theory of Scientific Revolutions
	13:00－15:30	Harts' Inverse Health Care Law
Nov. 29	10:00－12:00	Tragedy of The Commons
	13:00－15:30	Placebo Effect and Hawthorne Effect
Nov. 30	10:00－12:00	Cross Pressure Hypothesis
	13:00－15:30	Two Step Flow of Communication

As for compensation, the organizational committee will provide a roundtrip airfare ticket (business class), a speech honorarium for each lecture and accommodations during your stay. Let us know if you have any suggestions regarding the above schedule. Thanks again for your participation in this event. Your contribution will definitely benefit all of the participants.

Sincerely yours,

Dear Professor Coutrakon,

Thank you for agreeing to serve as an invited speaker at the upcoming seminar to

305

be held in the Institute of Medical Imagery at Yuanpei University of Science and Technology (YUST) on December 22-31, 2004. As eminent scholars in dosimetry-related research, my academic advisor, Professor Hsu, Professor Tung, and you will be the keynote speakers for this event. The seminar will focus on three topics: (a) comparison of microdosimetry spectra during proton beam treatment, along with its biological efficacy; (b) developmental trends in proton therapy, heavy charged particles therapy, fast neutron therapy and boron neutron capture therapy; and (c) relevant clinical experiences of the Proton Therapy Center at Loma Linda University.

A tentative agenda of your visit is summarized below:

Dec. 22, 2004 (Wed): Arrive in Taiwan and meet Mr. Chang at Chiang Kai Shek International Airport in transit to Hsinchu.

Dec. 23, 2004 (Thu): Tour the Institute of Medical Imagery at YUST.

Dec. 24, 2004 (Fri): Tour the Institute of Nuclear Science at National Tsing Hua University.

Dec. 25, 2004 (Sat): Attend the seminar held in the International Conference Hall at YUST. Deliver an introductory lecture on cyclotron and synchrotron.

Dec. 26, 2004 (Sun): Spend free time sightseeing cultural attractions in Taipei.

Dec. 27, 2004 (Mon): Attend a seminar in the Radiation Detection Laboratory at YUST. Deliver a lecture on the current status of proton therapy research.

Dec. 28, 2004 (Tue): Attend a seminar in the Radiation Detection Laboratory at YUST. Deliver a lecture covering a clinical case report involving proton therapy research.

Dec. 29, 2004 (Wed): Attend a seminar in the Radiation Detection Laboratory at YUST. Discuss collaborative opportunities in dosimetry-related research between the Proton Therapy Center at Loma Linda University and the Institute of Medical Imagery at YUST.

Dec. 30, 2004 (Thu): Spend free time sightseeing Hsinchu Science-based Industrial Park.

Dec. 31, 2004 (Fri): Return to the United States.

If you have any valuable suggestions regarding the above agenda and lecture topics, please do not hesitate to contact me. Moreover, the average price of single room hotel accommodations in Hsinchu ranges between U.S$200~U.S$250 daily. Hold to your receipts so that we can reimburse prior to your departure of Taiwan. I look forward to meeting you.

Sincerely yours,

Dear Professor Tung,

Given your renowned research and contributions in bioimagery, we would like to formally invite you to serve as an Invited Speaker at the upcoming 9th Symposium on Recent Advances in Biophysics. This symposium is to be held at National Sun Yat-Sen University (Kaohsiung, Taiwan) on January 29, 2005.As is well known, life science applications have been made in seemingly unrelated disciplines. Academics and researchers from a wide array of disciplines have converged on investigating physics-related topics. Your participation in this event will highlight the interaction among symposium participants on recent scientific and technological trends in the field.

For the day symposium, below is a tentative agenda of Professor Tung's visit:

Jan. 29, 2005 (Sat):

10:00－12:00 Meet Professor Tung at Kaohsiung International Airport in transit to National Sun Yat-Sen University.

12:20－13:30 Have dinner with symposium participants and discuss Professor Tung's schedule.

14:00－17:00 Tour the facilities at National Sun Yat-Sen University.

Jan. 30, 2005(Sun):

8:30－10:30 Lecture on structural genomics.

10:50－11:50 Lecture on protein networks.

12:00－13:30 Have lunch.

13:40－14:40 Lecture on nucleic acid and protein interaction.

15:00－16:50 Lecture on drug discovery in biophysics.

Jan. 31, 2005(Mon):

8:30－9:30 Lecture on nano biophysics.

9:50－10:50 Lecture on imaging and biosensors.

11:00－12:00 Lecture on computational biophysics.

If you have any questions or suggestions, please do not hesitate to contact us. We look forward to hearing your ideas or suggestions regarding the above itinerary.

Sincerely yours,

Dear Mr. Curtin,

Thank you for accepting our invitation to come to Taiwan for consultation on our latest research efforts. I was most impressed with the lecture you delivered during The

Annual Meeting of Radiology Therapy in 1998. Your address to members of The Association of Radiology Technologists of the Republic of China will be a major highlight of the upcoming event. I am responsible for arranging the details of your visit.

The following is a tentative schedule for your upcoming visit to Taiwan:

1/10: Arrive at the Chiang Kai Shek International Airport in Taoyuan in transit to your accommodations in the Hyatt Hotel in Taiwan.

1/11: Meet with Dr. Chen and myself at 10:00 am in the hotel lobby.

1/12: Deliver the keynote speech at the Annual Meeting of The Association of Radiology Technologists of the Republic of China.

1/13: Tour the northern coast of Taiwan and experience the island's art of drinking tea.

1/14: Lecture the staff and researchers in the Institute of Medical Imagery at Yuanpei University of Science and Technology on recent advances in IMRT for breast cancer as well as head and neck cancer.

1/15: Return to the United States on China Airlines at 3:00 pm.

We are interested in your recent research on the latest advances in IMRT for breast cancer as well as head and neck cancer. We also hope that there will be sufficient time to discuss advanced cancer therapeutic treatments. In particular, we will raise the following questions during our meeting:

1. Could you share your expertise at Stanford University in diagnosing and treating cancer?

2. How are the latest advances in IMRT preferable to other therapeutic planning systems?

3. What are the clinical implications for implementing the latest advances in IMRT when treating breast and head and neck cancer?

I hope that the above questions will give you a clearer idea of our intentions to elevate the quality of medical services in our hospital and implement a state-of-the-art therapeutic planning system.

Sincerely yours,

Dear Dr. Kawasaki,

Owing to your distinguished research and contributions in the field of IMRT technique, we would like to formally invite you to serve as an Invited Speaker at the upcoming Chinese Association of Radiological Technologists. We hope that your lecture will include a discussion of the latest developmental trends in the radiation treatment of IMRT. We will provide roundtrip airfare and accommodations during your stay. I advise that you stay here for one week (if at all possible) so that you can enjoy some of the sights that Taiwan has to offer. Please advise us of your flight number so that we can meet you at the airport.

Thank you for your fax response regarding bilateral cooperation between our two organizations. We generally agree with your proposal. However, I would suggest that your visit be in February of 2005 because we are usually quite busy during the month of January in preparation for the Chinese New Years holiday. A tentative agenda of Dr. Brown's visit is summarized below:

Feb. 6, 2005(Sun): Arrive in Taiwan at Chiang Kai International Airport and meet colleagues in transit to hotel accommodations

Feb. 7, 2005(Mon): Meet with CART staff members and discuss Mr. Brown's schedule.

Feb. 8, 2005(Tue): Consult with staff of Radiation Treatment Laboratory consultation on reciprocity-related topics.

Feb. 9, 2005 (Wed): Lecture on quality control of IMRT.

Feb. 10, 2005(Thu) to Feb. 11, 2005(Fri): Tour cultural and historical sites in Taiwan, as arranged by staff members.

Feb. 12, 2005(Sat): Discuss potential collaborative activities between our two organizations in radiation treatment.

Feb. 13, 2005 (Sun): Return to Japan

The above itinerary and consulting topics are only tentative. We welcome your feedback if you feel any changes should be made. Any comments or suggestions regarding the aforementioned proposal would be highly appreciated. If the proposal is acceptable, please send us your presentation topics and curriculum vitae as soon as possible.

Sincerely yours,

Dear Mr. Wang,

Thank you for agreeing to serve as an invited speaker at the upcoming seminar to be held at Yuanpei University of Science and Technology, May 20-24, 2005.

The seminar will focus on exactly what TFT-LCD Encompasses and the role of (b) TFT-LCD manufacturers.

The following is a tentative schedule for the seminar schedule:

May 20(Mon):

10:00－12:00 Introduction to TFT-LCD

13:00－15:00 TFT-LCD - Electronic aspects of LCD TVs and LCD monitors

May 21(Tue):

10:00－12:00 Potential TFTLCD applications

13:00－15:00 Display features of the matrix driving method

May 22(Wed):

10:00－12:00 Direct vs. multiplex driving mechanisms of LCD TVs

13:00－15:00 Role of the TFT-LCD sector in a hypercompetitive global industry

May 23(Thu):

10:00－12:00 Competitive advantages of the TFT-LCD industries of Taiwan, Japan and South Korea

13:00－15:00 Core competence as the most important strategic resource in development of the TFT-LCD industries

May 24(Fri):

10:00－12:00 Position of LCD-TVs as the largest niche market in the future

13:00－15:00

The seminar will heavily emphasize how the Taiwanese and Japanese TFT-LCD manufacturers can integrate their efforts through use of the diamond model of cooperation. As for compensation, the organizational committee will provide roundtrip airfare, hotel accommodations and a speech honorarium for each lecture during your stay.

Let us know if you have any suggestions regarding the above schedule. Thanks again for your participation in this event. We also need your curriculum vitae and course handouts via e-mail before March 20, 2005 so that we have sufficient time for translation and printing. Your contribution to the symposium will definitely benefit all of the participants. Again, please do not hesitate to contact me if you have any questions or suggestions. I look forward to meeting you.

Sincerely yours,

Dear Professor Yosada,

On behalf of the Institute of Business and Management at Yuanpei University of Science and Technology in Hsinchu, Taiwan, we would like to invite you to lecture our graduate students on December the 1st regarding the role of Internet marketing in Taiwan's business management practices. Your professional expertise in this area would definitely allow us to acquire further insight into the dynamics of this field. As is well known, our company, Trend Micro Corporation, has distinguished itself for its effective marketing strategies that create added product value through its Internet promotional activities. We are especially interested in learning of your approaches and experiences in dealing with the "Trend Micro".

A tentative schedule for your visit is as follows:

December 12, 2005:

Arrive at Chiang Kai-Shek International Airport in transit to the Ambassador Hotel in Hsinchu.

December 13, 2005:

9:00 am Arrive at Yuanpei University of Science and Technology.

9:00 am－10:00 am Visit with university president and tour school facilities.

10:00 am noon Deliver first presentation in lecture series

Noon—1:20 pm Have lunch

1:30 pm－3:20 pm Deliver second presentation in lecture series

3:30 pm－5:00 pm Deliver third presentation in lecture series.5:30 pm Return to Ambassador Hotel for dinner and rest.

December 14, 2005:

9:00 am－11:00 am Tour Hsinchu City

12:30 pm－2:00 pm Have lunch at Ambassador Hotel-Taipei

5:00 pm Departure from Chiang Kai-Shek International Airport in return to Japan.

Once your arrival and departure times are confirmed, we can reserve your airplane ticket and hotel accommodations. Let us know your arrival and departure times at your earliest convenience. Thanks again for your participation in this event. Your contribution will definitely benefit all of the participants.

Sincerely yours,

Dear Mr. Armstrong,

Thank you for agreeing to serve as an invited speaker at the upcoming marketing seminar to be held at Yuanpei University of Science and Technology on March 9, 2005. The seminar will concentrate on: (a) effective management strategies to achieve marketing goals and (b) advanced product development strategies and the product life cycle. A brief itinerary of the seminar is as follows:

Date	Morning agenda 9 am – noon	Afternoon agenda 1:30 pm—4:30 pm	Evening agenda 7 pm—9 pm
January the 3rd (Monday)	Overseas and local scholars arrive for registration		Taiwanese Film Festival
January the 4th (Tuesday)	First lecture: Rey Chow	First lecture: Nancy Armstrong	Taiwanese Film Festival
January the 5th (Wednesday)	Second lecture: Rey Chow	Rey Chow responds to questions: chaired by Shi Pi-fang and Wu Chen-zu	Taiwanese Film Festival
January the 6th (Thursday)	Third lecture: Nancy Armstrong speech	Nancy Armstrong responds to questions: chaired by Shi Pi-fang and Wu Chen-zu	Taiwanese Film Festival
January the 7th (Friday)	First lecture: Meaghan Morris	First lecture: Kaja Silverman	Taiwanese Film Festival
January the 8th (Saturday)	Free activity		Taiwanese Film Festival
January the 9th (Sunday)	Conclusion and Adjournment		Taiwanese Film Festival

As for compensation, the organizing committee will provide round trip air fare (business class), hotel accommodations during your stay and a speech honorarium for each lecture. Let me know if you have any questions regarding the above itinerary. t the above schedule. Thanks again for yours participation this event. Your contribution will definitely beneficial all of the participants.
Sincerely yours,

Dear Professor Daming,
Given your celebrated research and contributions in the field of medical quality

management, we would like to formally invite you to serve as an Invited Speaker at a symposium to be held in Taiwan on current trends in medical quality management. The symposium will be held in the International Conference Hall of the Municipal WanFang Hospital in Taipei on January the 15th, 2005. The following describes your itinerary for the upcoming symposium:

Time	
08:30—09:00	Registration
09:00—09:20	Professor Daming delivers the opening address.
09:20—10:20	A discussion is held on the systematic monitoring of medical quality systems.
10:20—10:30	Roundtable discussion (Q&A)
10:30—10:50	Refreshments.
10:50—11:50	Lecture on the role of medicine and disease in providing quality care
11:50—12:00	Roundtable discussion (Q & A)
12:00—1:30	Lunch
1:30—2:20	Lecture on a monitoring system for health insurance premiums
2:20—2:30	Roundtable discussion (Q & A)
2:30—3:20	Lecture on medical quality control and patient security
3:20—3:30	Roundtable discussion (Q & A)
3:30—3:50	Refreshments
3:50—4:40	Lecture on recent trends in Taiwanese medical quality control
4:40—4:50	Final roundtable discussion (Q & A)
4:50	Adjournment

As for compensation of the event, we will provide roundtrip airfare and accommodations during your stay. I suggest you that stay in Taiwan following adjournment of the symposium to enjoy some of the natural and cultural wonders that the island offers. Once you have made final confirmations, let us know your flight details so we can meet you at the airport upon your arrival.

Please mail me your lecture title and related handouts by December the 30th, 2004 so that we will have ample time for translation. Also, please send us your curriculum vitae, with its contents to include your name, date of birth, nationality, marital status, academic qualifications, professional experiences, scientific achievements and selected publications.

I look forward to seeing you.

Sincerely yours,

Dear Mrs. Perez,

Thanks for your positive reply to our invitation of Dr. Kanbinsky as a guest speaker at the PIDA technical seminar on current trends in laser technology. A tentative agenda for this upcoming trip is as follows:

Jan. 30, 2005 (Sun): Dr. Kanbinsky and Mrs. Kanbinsky arrive at Chiang-Kai Shek International
Airport (Flight details: CX461, 21:00)

Jan. 31, 2005 (Mon): Meet with PIDA employees and discuss seminar topics

Feb. 1, 2005 (Tue): Deliver lecture on current trends in display technologies

Feb. 2, 2005 (Wed): Deliver morning lecture on difficulties & solution in blue light productions.
Deliver after afternoon lecture on laboratory achievement

Feb. 3, 2005 (Thu): Deliver morning lecture on TFT-LCD panel applications
Deliver afternoon lecture on special topic

Feb. 4, 2005 (Fri): Deliver morning lecture on LED - backlight source for cellular phones
Participate in afternoon panel discussion

Feb. 5, 2005 (Sat.): Sightseeing (arranged by PIDA staff members)

Feb. 6, 2005 (Sun): Sightseeing (arranged by PIDA staff members)

Feb. 7, 2005 (Mon): Visit PIDA Labor at Ming Chuan E. Rd., Taipei

Feb. 8, 2005 (Tue): Meet with PIDA president Dr. Shih on future cooperation opportunities

Feb. 9, 2005 (Wed): Dr. Kanbinsky and Mrs. Kanbinsky return to Holland (CX759, 12:00)

The agenda and topics can be modified, if necessary. Any comments or suggestions regarding the proposal would be highly appreciated. If the proposal is acceptable, please send us the presentation contents and curriculum vitae for our reference.

Sincerely yours,

P.S.: Options for the entertainment program: As Feb. 8 will be Chinese New Year, we highly recommend that Dr. Kanbinsky & Mrs. Kanbinsky can stay for two or more days to experience traditional Asian culture firsthand.

Situation 4

Shane Huang

marketing seminar

development strategies

product life cycle

honorarium

roundtrip airfare

hotel.......

Situation 5

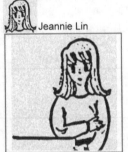

Jeannie Lin

medical quality management

Q&A

enjoy

Situation 6

Jim Wu

Dr. Kanbinsky and Mrs. Kanbinsky

current trends in laser technology

International Airport

experience traditional Asian culture firsthand

I Write down the key points of the situations on the preceding page, while the instructor reads aloud the script from the Answer Key.

Situation 4

_____

_____

_____

Situation 5

_____

_____

_____

Situation 6

_____

_____

_____

J Oral practice II

Based on the three situations in this unit, write three questions beginning with **When**, and answer them. The questions do not need to come directly from these situations.

Examples

When will Nancy Armstrong deliver her first lecture?

January the 4th

When will Rey Chow deliver her second lecture?

January the 5th

1. _____

_____

2. _____

_____

3. _____

_____

K Based on the three situations in this unit, write three questions beginning with **What**, and answer them. The questions do not need to come directly from these situations.

Examples

What contributions has Professor Daming made?

In the field of medical quality management

What is the topic of the symposium to be held in Taiwan?

Current trends in medical quality management

1. _____

   _____

2. _____

   _____

3. _____

   _____

L Based on the three situations in this unit, write three questions beginning with **Why**, and answer them. The questions do not need to come directly from these situations.

Examples

Why is Jim thanking Mrs. Perez?

For her positive reply to the invitation of Dr. Kanbinsky as a guest speaker at the

PIDA technical seminar on current trends in laser technology

Why will Dr. Kanbinsky meet with PIDA employees on Jan. 31, 2005?

To discuss seminar topics

1. _____

   _____

2. _____

   _____

3. _____

   _____

M Write questions that match the answers provided.

1. _____

   _____

   Mr. Armstrong's contribution

2. _____

   _____

   To enjoy some of the natural and cultural wonders that the island offers

3. _____

   _____

   That Dr. Kanbinsky and Mrs. Kanbinsky stay for at least two days to experience
   traditional Asian culture firsthand

N Listening Comprehension II

Situation 4

1. Why will the seminar participants discuss effective management strategies?

   A. to achieve management goals

   B. to achieve marketing goals

   C. to achieve commercial goals

2. When will seminar participants attend the Taiwanese Film Festival?

   A. from 7 pm — 9 pm, January the 3rd to January the 9th

   B. from 9 am — noon, January the 3rd to January the 9th

   C. from 1:30 pm — 4:30 pm, January the 3rd to January the 9th

3. When will Nancy Armstrong deliver her speech?

   A. on the morning of January the 4th

   B. on the afternoon of January the 5th

   C. on the morning of January the 6th

4. When is the free activity scheduled?

   A. January the 9th

   B. January the 8th

   C. January the 7th

5. When will Kaja Silverman deliver his lecture?

   A. on the afternoon of January the 7th

   B. on the evening of January the 4th

   C. on the morning of January the 5th

Situation 5

1. What contributions has Professor Daming made?

   A. in the field of marketing management

   B. in the field of business management

C. in the field of medical quality management

2. When will Professor Daming deliver the opening address?

A. 08:30－09:00　B. 09:00－09:20　C. 09:20－10:20

3. When is the first roundtable discussion (Q&A) scheduled?

A. 4:40－4:50　B. 2:20－2:30　C. 10:20－10:30

4. When is the lecture on recent trends in Taiwanese medical quality control scheduled?

A. 3:50－4:40　B. 2:30－3:20　C. 10:50－11:50

5. When will refreshments be served in the afternoon?

A. 3:50－4:40　B. 3:30－3:50　C. 3:50－4:40

Situation 6

1. When is Dr. Kanbinsky scheduled to meet with PIDA employees and discuss seminar topics?

A. Feb. 1, 2005　B. Jan. 31, 2005　C. Feb. 2, 2005

2. When will Dr. Kanbinsky meet with PIDA president Dr. Shih to discuss future cooperative opportunities?

A. Feb. 5, 2005　B. Feb. 7, 2005　C. Feb. 8, 2005

3. When will Dr. Kanbinsky deliver a lecture on current trends in display technologies?

A. Feb. 1, 2005　B. Feb. 3, 2005　C. Feb. 4, 2005

4. When will Dr. Kanbinsky and Mrs. Kanbinsky return to Holland?

A. Feb. 6, 2005　B. Feb. 8, 2005　C. Feb. 9, 2005

5. Why does Jim strongly recommend that Dr. Kanbinsky and Mrs. Kanbinsky stay for at least two days after the seminar?

A. to deliver a lecture on LED - backlight sources for cellular phones

B. to experience traditional Asian culture firsthand

C. to deliver a lecture on TFT-LCD panel applications

O Reading Comprehension II
Pick the work or expression whose meaning is closest to the meaning of the underlined word or expression in the following passages.

Situation 4

1. Thank you for <u>agreeing</u> to serve as an invited speaker at the upcoming marketing seminar to be held at Yuanpei University of Science and Technology on March 9, 2005.

   A. dissenting   B. consenting   C. deviating

2. Thank you for agreeing to serve as an invited speaker at the <u>upcoming</u> marketing seminar to be held at Yuanpei University of Science and Technology on March 9, 2005.

   A. discontinued   B. approaching   C. belated

3. The seminar will <u>concentrate</u> on (a) effective management strategies to achieve marketing goals and (b) advanced product development strategies and the product life cycle.

   A. focus   B. divert   C. deflect

4. A brief <u>outline</u> of the seminar is as follows.

   A. obstruction   B. impediment   C. profile

5. The organizing committee will provide a roundtrip airfare (business class), hotel accommodation during your stay and a speech <u>honorarium</u> for each lecture.

   A. payment for airfare   B. payment for lecture   C. payment for insurance

6. Let me know if you have any questions regarding the above <u>itinerary</u>.

   A. hypothesis   B. speculation   C. agenda

Situation 5

1. Given your <u>celebrated</u> research and contributions in the field of medical quality management, we would like formally to invite you to participate as an Invited Speaker at a symposium to be held in Taiwan on current trends in medical quality management.

   A. flagrant   B. famed   C. stigmatized

2. Given your celebrated research and contributions in the field of medical quality management, we would like formally to invite you to participate as an Invited Speaker at a symposium to be held in Taiwan on current <u>trends</u> in medical quality management.

   A. retrospective   B. retroactive   C. orientations

3. A <u>suggested</u> schedule for the upcoming symposium is as follows.

   A. advised   B. commanded   C. demanded

4. A suggested schedule for the <u>upcoming</u> symposium is as follows.

   A. postponed   B. soon to come   C. delayed

5. A discussion is held on the <u>systematic</u> monitoring of medical quality systems

   A. routine   B. chaotic   C. irregular

6. A discussion is held on the systematic <u>monitoring</u> of medical quality systems

   A. shunning   B. buffing   C. scrutinizing

7. We will provide a roundtrip airfare and <u>accommodation</u> during your stay.

   A. transportation   B. lodging   C. insurance

8. I suggest you that stay in Taiwan following the end of the symposium to enjoy some of the natural and cultural <u>wonders</u> that the island offers.

   A. attractions   B. blemish   C. impairment

9. Once you have <u>confirmed</u> your trip, let us know your flight details so we can meet you at the airport.

   A. nullified   B. corroborated   C. confuted

10. Please send me your lecture title and related handouts by December 30th, 2004, so that we will have <u>ample</u> time for translation.

A. bountiful (correct answer)   B. hemmed in   C. confined

Situation 6

1. Thank you for your <u>positive</u> reply to our inviting Dr. Kanbinsky as a guest speaker at the PIDA technical seminar on current trends in laser technology.

A. glum   B. affirmative   C. averse

2. A <u>tentative</u> agenda for this upcoming trip is as follows.

A. completed   B. finalized   C. under consideration

3. A tentative <u>agenda</u> for this upcoming trip is as follows.

A. skill   B. competency   C. timetable

4. Meet with PIDA <u>employees</u> and discuss seminar topics.

A. board of directors   B. staff   C. chief executives

5. The schedule and topics can be <u>modified</u> if necessary.

A. altered   B. static   C. stationary

6. Any comments or suggestions regarding this proposal would be greatly <u>appreciated</u>.

A. criticized   B. denigrated   C. thought highly of

P Matching Exercise

1. Each sentence in the following is commonly used to arrange travel itineraries: acknowledging the upcoming visit 旅行安排信函. Each phrase on the left should be matched with one on the right in order to complete the sentence. Match a number on the left with a letter on the right.

1. Thank you for your response regarding Mr. Smith's	a. as an invited speaker at the upcoming seminar to be held at Yuanpei University of Science and Technology, November 22-30, 2004.
2. Thanks for your recent reply that Mr. Robbins has	b. a major highlight of the upcoming event.
3. Thank you for agreeing to serve	c. definitely benefit all of the attendees.
4. Your address to members of The Association of Radiology Technologists of the Republic of China will be	d. visit to our Taiwan branch office.
5. Your participation in the upcoming symposium will	e. at the PIDA technical seminar on current trends in laser technology.
6. Thanks for your positive reply to our invitation of Dr. Kanbinsky as a guest speaker	f. agreed to participate in our academic discussion on intellectual capital-related topics in Taiwan.

2. Arranging travel itineraries: listing details of the travel itinerary 旅行安排信函：行程細節列表

1. Meet with R&D staff in the Taiwan branch office	a. as arranged by the General Affairs Section of the Taiwan branch office.
2. Tour the northern coast of Taiwan	b. to the Ambassador Hotel in Hsinchu.
3. Deliver an introductory lecture	c. discussion on intellectual capital (2 to 3 hrs).
4. Discuss areas	d. below a tentative agenda of Mr. Robbins' visit:
5. Continue with discussion on areas of cooperation	e. time sightseeing Taipei.
6. Tour the campus of National Tsing Hua	f. and discuss Mr. Smith's schedule.
7. Spend free	g. academic activities in the future.
8. Discuss the possibilities for collaborative	h. on cyclotron and synchrotron.
9. A tentative agenda for Mr. Smith's	i. between our two organizations.
10. Meet Mr. Smith at Chiang-Kai Shek International Airport in transit	j. ten day visit is summarized below:
11. Chair a roundtable	k. of cooperation in developing innovative product technologies.
12. Tour cultural attractions and historical sites,	l. and National Chiao Tung Universities.
13. Please find	m. and experience the island's art of drinking tea.
14. Return to the United States	n. on China Airlines at 3:00 pm.

3. Arranging travel itineraries: welcoming suggestions about the proposed itinerary 旅行安排信函：對行程細節列表的建議

1. The above itinerary and consulting topics	a. regarding the aforementioned proposal would be highly appreciated.
2. Any comments or suggestions	b. if you feel any changes should be made.
3. Let us know if you have any suggestions regarding	c. send us Dr. Robbins' presentation topics and curriculum vitae as soon as possible.
4. The agenda and consulting topics can be changed,	d. the above schedule.
5. If you have any valuable suggestions regarding the above	e. are only tentative.
6. If the proposal is acceptable, please	f. if necessary.
7. We welcome your feedback	g. agenda and lecture topics, please do not hesitate to contact me.

Unit Six

Requesting Information

資訊請求信函

Vocabulary and related expressions 相關字詞

pioneering work 倡導工作
published articles 發行的文章
extensively used 被廣泛地使用
multi-criteria 多重標準
potential risks 潛在的風險
forecasting 預報
assumptions 假定
intently 專注地
mortality 失敗率
complications 複雜（化）
clinical errors 臨床的錯誤
scarce 缺乏的
pertinent data 有關的資料
impressed by 給……極深的印象
collaborative research activities
合作的研究活動

positive reply 肯定的回覆
designating 指定的
exposed to 暴露於……
elucidated 闡明
magnitude 重要
research interests 研究的興趣
expertise 專門技術
mutual interests 相互的興趣
pursuing collaborative activities 追求合作活動
practicum internship （大學的）實驗（習）課程
global reputation 全球性的名譽
an ideal environment 一個理想的環境
pursue my professional interests
追求我的專業興趣
particular points 獨特的論點
maintenance 保持

Unit Six

intellectual capital 智慧財產
intangible 無形的
evolving field 逐步形成領域
compatible with 可和……並立的
As you are well aware 如您所知
budget constraints 預算限制
perspective 洞察力

components 構成要素
infancy 未發達階段
future trends 未來的趨勢
perusing 仔細研究
coordinated 協調一致的
preliminary program schedule 初步的節目行程
program schedule 節目行程

Situation 1

Ashley Wu

interested in your research

Satty

Situation 2

Matt Fung

Nurse Staffing, Organizational Characteristics and Patient Outcome

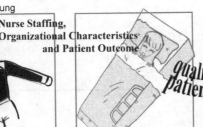

quality care patient safety

Situation 3

Mary Wang

interested

Intellectual Capital Measurement

loaning bank

On-line gaming company

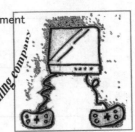

A Write down the key points of the situations on the preceding page, while the instructor reads aloud the script from the Answer Key.

Situation 1

_____

_____

_____

Situation 2

_____

_____

_____

Situation 3

_____

_____

_____

B Oral practice I

Based on the three situations in this unit, write three questions beginning with **What**, and answer them. The questions do not need to come directly from these situations.

Examples

What institute does Ashley belong to at Yuanpei University of Science and Technology?

The Institute of Business Management

What aspect of Dr. Satty's research is Ashley very interested in?

His research on correlation data

1. _____

_____

2. _____

_____

3. _____

_____

C Based on the three situations in this unit, write three questions beginning with **How**, and answer them. The questions do not need to come directly from these situations.

Examples

How did Matt listen to Ms. Beatrice's recent lecture?

Intently

How did Matt react to the issues that Ms. Beatric raised at the symposium held in Taiwan?

He was fascinated.

1. _____

   _____

2. _____

   _____

3. _____

   _____

D Based on the three situations in this unit, write three questions beginning with **Why**, and answer them. The questions do not need to come directly from these situations.

Examples

Why did Mary write to Professor Jones for further details on particular points?
Because she carefully read the article, "Intellectual Capital Measurement: Introducing and Comparing Various IC Measurements," which Professor Jones published in the conference proceedings

Why is there an urgency to measure the intellectual capital value of hi-tech firms?
As Taiwan's industrial infrastructure is being transformed into a hi-tech infrastructure, an increasing fraction of companies' capital is intellectual, and is intangible.

1. _____

_____

2. _____

_____

3. _____

_____

E Write questions that match the answers provided.

1. _____

   _____

   To achieve success

2. _____

   _____

   Any pertinent data from Taiwan as part of an exchange of information

3. _____

   _____

   Professor Jones's lecture last month at the Intellectual Capital Measurement Symposium in Taipei

F Listening Comprehension I

Situation 1

1. What area of Dr. Satty's research is Ashley interested in?

   A. decision theory　B. correlation data　C. the Analytic Network Process (ANP)

2. What has Dr. Satty conducted pioneering work on?

   A. forecasting of outcomes

   B. multi-criteria decision problems that are large-scale and multiparty-oriented

   C. decision theory

3. What area has AHP often been applied to?

   A. correlation data

   B. multi-criteria decision problems that are large-scale and multiparty-oriented

   C. the relationship between AHP and ANP

4. How many books has Dr. Satty written on decision theory, the Analytic Hierarchy Process (AHP) and the Analytic Network Process (ANP)?

   A. more than 10 books　B. 12 books　C. more than 12 books

5. What has AHP been extensively used in?

   A. decision making in multi-criteria decision problems

   B. decision making in business, industry and government

   C. decision making in the Analytic Network Process (ANP)

Situation 2

1. Where was the symposium held in which Matt listened intently to Ms. Beatrice's lecture?

   A. in the United States　B. in Taiwan　C. in Japan

2. What has led to the establishment of health care systems worldwide?

   A. efforts to ensure quality health care and patient safety

B. mortality/failure to rescue, length of stay (LOS), infection rates, pressure ulcers, falls, post-surgery complications, patient satisfaction, model of care and nursing considerations

C. regarding the adverse impact of nursing shortages on health care in the United States

3. Who is indispensable in significantly reducing the likelihood of clinical errors?

    A. hospital administrators   B. physicians   C. nurses

4. What are linked to higher mortality rates?

    A. nurse-patient ratios

    B. quality health care and patient safety

    C. mortality/failure to rescue, length of stay (LOS), infection rates, pressure ulcers, falls, post-surgery complications, patient satisfaction, model of care and nursing considerations

5. What threaten quality care and patient safety?

    A. shortages in physicians

    B. shortages in hospital administrators

    C. shortages in nursing personnel

Situation 3

1. When did Mary hear Professor Jones speak?

    A. in a lecture last year at the Intellectual Capital Measurement Symposium in Taipei

    B. in a lecture last month at the Intellectual Capital Measurement Symposium in Taipei

    C. in a lecture last month at the Intellectual Capital Valuation System Symposium in Taipei

2. Why has Mary's graduate school research focused on intellectual capital of on-line

gaming companies?

A. to adopt the perspective of a loaning bank institution in assessing the intellectual capital assets of an on-line gaming company

B. to measure intellectual capital

C. to identify its essential components

3. What can Mary offer to Professor Jones in his research?

A. an assessment of the intellectual capital assets of an on-line gaming company

B. pertinent data regarding Taiwanese companies

C. a summary of previous efforts to measure intellectual capital

4. Why does Mary hope to collaborate with Professor Jones in some way in the near future?

A. Professor Jones can briefly summarize future trends in intellectual capital.

B. Professor Jones can briefly introduce the intellectual capital valuation system in the United States.

C. He may find his area of research compatible with that of Mary's.

5. What is Mary requesting?

A. literature or materials related to measuring the intellectual capital value of hi-tech firms

B. pertinent data regarding Taiwanese companies

C. information on Taiwan's industrial infrastructure

G Reading Comprehension I
Pick the work or expression whose meaning is closest to the meaning of the underlined word or expression in the following passages.

Situation 1

1. Given your <u>pioneering</u> work on decision theory, the Analytic Hierarchy Process (AHP) and the Analytic Network Process (ANP), I have read many of your published articles and am well aware of your more than 12 books on these topics.

   A. prevailing   B. conventional   C. trailblazing

2. Given your pioneering work on decision theory, the Analytic Hierarchy Process (AHP) and the Analytic Network Process (ANP), I have read many of your published articles and am well <u>aware of</u> your more than 12 books on these topics.

   A. unacquainted with   B. cognizant of   C. unconscious of

3. As is well known, AHP has not only been <u>extensively</u> used in decision making in business, industry and government, but has also been often applied to multi-criteria decision problems that are large-scale and multiparty-oriented.

   A. voluminously   B. selectively   C. restrictively

4. ANP has played a <u>major</u> role in various decisions, involving benefits, costs, opportunities, potential risks and the forecasting of outcomes.

   A. secondary   B. predominant   C. subordinate

Situation 2

1. I listened <u>intently</u> to your recent lecture.

   A. listlessly   B. half-heartedly   C. alertly

2. I was <u>fascinated</u> with the issues you raised about mortality/failure to rescue, length of stay (LOS), infection rates, pressure ulcers, falls, post-surgery complications,

patient satisfaction, model of care and nursing considerations.

    A. allured by   B. detached from   C. lukewarm to

3. I was fascinated with the issues you raised about mortality/failure to rescue, length of stay (LOS), infection rates, pressure ulcers, falls, post-surgery complications, patient satisfaction, model of care and nursing <u>considerations</u>.

    A. mirages   B. illusions   C. deliberations

4. As you know, efforts to ensure quality health care and patient safety have led to the <u>establishment</u> of health care systems worldwide.

    A. eradication   B. formation   C. elimination

5. In such systems, while nurses are <u>indispensable</u> in significantly reducing the likelihood of clinical errors, shortages in nursing personnel threaten quality care and patient safety.

    A. expendable   B. superfluous   C. essential

6. In such systems, while nurses are indispensable in significantly reducing the <u>likelihood</u> of clinical errors, shortages in nursing personnel threaten quality care and patient safety.

    A. probability   B. implausibility   C. inconceivability

7. In such systems, while nurses are indispensable in significantly reducing the likelihood of clinical errors, <u>shortages</u> in nursing personnel threaten quality care and patient safety.

    A. plethora   B. glut   C. deficiencies

8. Although such data for Taiwanese hospitals are <u>scarce</u>, I am actively engaged in researching related topics.

    A. exorbitant   B. seldom   C. excessive

9. Could you pass on to me <u>pertinent</u> data regarding the adverse impact of nursing shortages on health care in the United States?

    A. relevant   B. inapplicable   C. extraneous

10. I would be <u>delighted</u> to send you any pertinent data from Taiwan as part of an exchange of information.

   A. melancholy   B. elated   C. disheartened

Situation 3

1. My Master's thesis is on <u>measuring</u> the intellectual capital of certain enterprises.

   A. hypothesizing   B. determining   C. speculating on

2. As Taiwan's industrial infrastructure is being <u>transformed</u> into a hi-tech infrastructure, an increasing fraction of companies' capital is intellectual, and is intangible.

   A. deposited   B. saved   C. converted

3. This fact explains the <u>urgency</u> to measure the intellectual capital value of hi-tech firms.

   A. immediacy   B. deferment   C. procrastination

4. This area of research is in its <u>infancy</u> in Taiwan and, hopefully my work will contribute to this evolving field.

   A. mature stage   B. preliminary stage   C. commercialization stage

5. This area of research is in its infancy in Taiwan and, hopefully my work will contribute to this <u>evolving</u> field.

   A. receding   B. recessive   C. emerging

6. My graduate school research <u>focuses on</u> intellectual capital of on-line gaming companies in an attempt to identify its essential components.

   A. concentrates on   B. deflects from   C. transgresses from

7. My graduate school research focuses on intellectual capital of on-line gaming companies in an attempt to identify its <u>essential</u> components.

   A. trivial   B. indispensable   C. immaterial

8. I am especially interested in adopting the <u>perspective</u> of a loaning bank institution

to assess the intellectual capital assets of an on-line gaming company and, then, to compare the intellectual capital of a bank with that of such a company.

A. outlook   B. mirage   C. illusion

9. Also, if you find my area of research <u>compatible with</u> that of yours, perhaps we could collaborate in some way in the near future.

A. out of place   B. conducive to   C. incongruous

H Common elements in writing a letter requesting information（資訊請求信函）include the following contents:
1. Explaining why contact was made to request information 解釋請求資訊的目的
2. Summarizing one's academic or professional experiences 說明學術專業經驗

In the space below, write a letter requesting information.

_____

_____

_____

_____

_____

_____

_____

_____

Unit six

Requesting Information
資訊請求信函

1. Explaining why contact was made to request information
   解釋請求資訊的目的

2. Summarizing one's academic or professional experiences
   說明學術專業經驗

Look at the following examples of letters requesting information.

Dear, Dr. Wu,

While speaking with your products manager Mr. Li over the phone regarding the purchase of your company's electronics equipment, he suggested that I directly contact you to obtain your company's latest products catalog. Does your company have a sales representative in Taiwan? If so, please ask him/her to contact me. We look forward to establishing ties with your supplier, anticipating that you will forward to us a brief introduction of your product line, range of services and technical support and price quotations. Once having received this information, we can hopefully begin purchasing relevant products and services. I look forward to your prompt reply.

Sincerely yours,

Dear Mr. Wang,

After I talked to Mr. Yang over the phone regarding your line of TFT- LCD products, he suggested that I contact you. Earlier this year, on March 20, we ordered one hundred of your company's color filters (CF No.5123).

Our company is currently involved in a project to develop slide systems that involves the use of TFT- LCD panels. This project is part of a government-sponsored collaborative effort we are participating in with U.P.O. Company, aimed at contributing to our country's information technology infrastructure.

Please provide us with the following documentation and samples:

Certified report that analyzes the effectiveness of your company's TFT- LCD panels;

Reference standard of TFT LCD panel;

Analytical profiles and test protocols of TFT- LCD panel;

Other pertinent information your company can release regarding this material;

Material Safety Data Sheet (M.S.D.S.);

Description of the manufacturing approach of the new type TFT- LCD panel;

Documented proof that your TFT-LCD panel displays the light and contains key components;

Poor light module main key material;

Description of the shelf with respect to color featuresto verify that the equipment is corrected and changed;

Information on solid immersion lens technology;

Information on chemical manufacturing programs that produce environmentally benign TFT -LCD panels;

Overview of the Common Sense Initiative Program; and

Information on other pertinent TFT-LCD programs.

Thanks in advance for your kind assistance.

Sincerely yours,

Dear Dr. Satty,

As a graduate student in the Institute of Business and Management at Yuanpei University of Science and Technology, I am highly interested in your research on correlation data. Given your pioneering work on the decision theory, Analytic Hierarchy Process (AHP) and the Analytic Network Process (ANP), I have read many of your published articles and am well aware of your more than twelve books on these topics. I particularly enjoyed your articles "Decision Making—The Analytic Hierarchy and Network Processes (AHP/ANP)", "Fundamentals of the Analytic Network Process: Dependence and Feedback in Decision-Making with a Single Network", "Theory of the Analytic Hierarchy and Analytic Network Process—Examples Part 2.2" and "Decision-making with the AHP: Why is the principal eigenvector necessary".

As is well known, AHP is not only extensively adopted in individual and group decision making by business, industry, and governmental officials, but also especially applicable to multicriteria decision problems that are large-scale and multiparty-oriented. ANP has played a major role in a variety of decisions involving benefits, costs, opportunities, potential risks and forecasting outcomes.

Given my interest in AHP and your expertise in the above areas, I am interested in the following topics:

1. AHP decision-making procedures adopted in business to achieve success;

2. Some of the assumptions you made when deriving the AHP model;

3. Mutual relations between AHP and ANP;

I would also appreciate it if you could send me the first article that you wrote on AHP.

Thanks in advance for your kind assistance.

Sincerely yours,

347

Dear Ms. Beatrice,

While listened intently to your recent lecture entitled, "Nurse Staffing, Organizational Characteristics and Patient Outcome" at a recent symposium held in Taiwan on March 24-26, 2004, I was fascinated with the topics you addressed involving mortality/failure to rescue, length of stay (LOS), infection rates, pressure ulcers, falls, post-surgery complications, patient satisfaction, model of care and nursing considerations. As you are well aware, efforts to ensure quality health care and patient safety have led to the establishment of health care systems worldwide. In such systems, while nurses play an indispensable role in significantly lower the likelihood of clinical errors, shortages in nursing personnel pose a threat to quality care and patient safety. For instance, low nurse-patient ratios are linked to higher mortality rates. Although such data for Taiwanese hospitals is scarce, I am actively engaged in researching related topics.

Could pass on to me pertinent data regarding the adverse impact of nursing shortages on health care in the United States? Likewise, I would send to you any pertinent data from Taiwan to facilitate our information exchange.

Thanks in advance for your careful consideration. I anxiously look forward to your favorable reply.

Sincerely yours,

Dr. Smith,

Quite some time has passed since we have been in contact with each other. We are looking forward to your lecture, especially given your widely recognized expertise in this field. Hopefully, this lecture will lead to a discussion among conference participants on how to initiate this area of research in our country. In addition to your lecture topic and handouts, do you have other relevant literature or materials that you could pass on to us prior to our conference so that we can fully realize the practical implications of your lecture for our local researchers and practitioners in this field?

The market demand for long-term care in Taiwan has increased given the increasing elderly population island wide. Please provide me with pertinent information on topics such as legislation, strategies, welfare policies and quality control. I would be more than happy to provide you with similar information on recent development in Taiwan in

this area. Thanks in advance for your kind assistance.
Sincerely yours,

Dear Professor Jam,

I immensely enjoyed your article in the January 2003 edition of *Journal of Business Research* on the glass ceiling barrier that many female CEOs face in traditional organizational structures, or what you refer to as an invisible barrier that they encounter that hurts their opportunities for promotion. As for literature in Taiwan on the glass ceiling that female CEOs face, most empirical studies are only in the beginning stages, with the focus mainly on public organizations such as schools and governmental institutions. I am curious as to whether the glass ceiling phenomenon for female CEOs can be found in other sectors. Therefore, I am eager to learn more about your current research direction. In particular, I would be most appreciative if you would send me pertinent literature or materials in response to the following questions:

1. As for the awareness of this glass ceiling phenomenon and level of satisfaction with one's work, what individual factors contribute to this relation?
2. Is any correlating data available regarding awareness of the glass ceiling phenomenon in the workplace for both the public and private sector?

Thanks in advance for your attention to my above concerns. I anxiously look forward to your reply.

Sincerely yours,

Dear Mr. Lin,

I regret that the price that you quoted us for your advertising marketing service is considerably higher than what is available in our allocated budget. Tight budget restrictions in our organizations make it impossible for us to offer more than what is currently available. In comparison with what other advertising companies have quoted us, your price quotation markedly exceeds theirs. Still, we are eager to seek your company for this service and hope that you would adjust this quotation given our current circumstances. Thanks in advance for your careful consideration.

Sincerely yours,

Dear Professor Jones,

I was quite impressed with your lecture last month at the Intellectual Capital Measurement Symposium in Taipei. Having carefully reading your recent article "Intellectual Capital Measurement: To introduce and compare a variety of IC measurement" that you published in the conference proceedings, I found it necessary to write you for further details on specific points that you brought up in the article.

As I am pursuing a Master's degree in the Institute of Business Management at Yuanpei University of Science and Technology, my master's thesis research focuses on measuring the intellectual capital of certain enterprises. As Taiwan's industrial infrastructure is transforming to a hi tech one, an increasing amount of a company's capital is intellectual, which is intangible. This explains the urgency to measure the intellectual capital value of hi tech firms. This area of research is in its infant stages in Taiwan and, hopefully, the results of my research will contribute to this evolving field of research. Having gone thoroughly read your article, I was wondering whether you would send me pertinent literature or materials of the following areas:

a brief introduction of intellectual capital;

a summary of previous efforts to measure intellectual capital;

a brief introduction of the intellectual capital valuation ststem in the United States;

a brief introduction of the financing mechanism in the United States;

a brief introduction of financing mechanisms in other countries; and

a brief summary of future trends in intellectual capital

My graduate school research is focusing mainly on intellectual capital of on-line gaming companies in an attempt to identify the essential components. I am especially interested in adopting the perspective of a loaning bank institution when assessing the intellectual capital assets of an on-line gaming company and, then, comparing the intellectual capital of a bank with that of an on-line gaming company.

I hope that you will be able to provide me with the above information. Also, if you find my area of research compatible with that of yours, perhaps we could collaborate in some way in the near future. I would be more than happy to provide you with pertinent data from the perspective of a Taiwanese company. Thanks in advance for your kind assistance. I look forward to our future cooperative efforts.

Sincerely yours,

Dear Mr. Brown,

We are finally in the position to undertake this CRM project.

The literature you sent me on September 9, 2004, concerning your customer value evaluation systems, is highly informative. Not only are we interested in mining the text information with content analysis method, but we are also interested in integrating the information to construct the data warehouse for the same analytical purposes. Which of your theories are appropriate for this application? What we have in mind is to assign a value compass to each customer. I was therefore wondering if it would be possible to choose a specifically text mining technology to indicate the most valuable customer so as to preventing the wrong decision for customer services?

Please let me know if you have any advice. I look forward to your response.

Sincerely yours,

Dear Mr. Smith,

Data accumulated over the past six months and a recent visit with management personnel of the retail store Simmons, whose brand is well known islandwide, revealed our company's decline in generated revenues from mattress products in the bedding sector. We are clearly losing our market niche, as evidenced by a 10% decline in our mattress sales in the summer of 2004 and a downward sales trend for the year in the third quarter with a slide of 12%. I consulted with the Marketing Director of Sogo Department Store to understand why our products are selling so poorly there, We conferred that our main competitor, Simmons, has been adopted a new advertising campaign that highlights the company's use of the most advanced nano-technology techniques in its products to enhance the quality of performance.

Thus, I recommend the following measures to solve the above problem. First, retail prices of mattresses should be reduced, a creative advertising campaign launched through integrated marketing communication (IMC) a trade show to highlight the advantages of our products over those of our competitors. Second, R&D should be initiated to create an innovative mattress that adopts nanotechnology, thus keeping up with market trends. Therefore, our branch office requires the headquarter's comments and suggestions on the above proposal, as well as pertinent information on the latest nano-technology-based manufacturing processes to produce mattresses.

I look forward to your instruction on the above matter.

Sincerely yours,

Dear Mr. Smith,

Thank you for sending us your latest company catalogue and product samples. Your product offerings are in line with our organizational needs. As a governmental subsidized, non-profit organization, we strive to promote health awareness among the general public by holding civic activities and promulgating governmental policy. Attracting the public to actively participate in such activities requires sending out fliers and other promotional materials. As participants may be ordinary men, women, children or the elderly, promotional materials must be general and appeal to all groups. The sample you provided, a packet containing medical-oriented information, contains many practical items for daily use. Given our budget constraints, I hope that you would re-evaluate your original price quotation. As we hope to purchase 1200 information packets, I hope that your re-evaluated price quotation would include packaging charges, transportation expenses and business tax. As our organization is a non-profit one and given the amount that we are purchasing, a discount would be most appreciated as well Given that a similar marketing agency quoted us a price of U.S.10 dollars per information packet, I hope that you will reflect upon our circumstances and adjust the quoted price accordingly. If, however, we are unable to reach an agreement on this case, I hope that we will be able to cooperate with each other next time.

Please do not hesitate to contact us if you have any suggestions regarding our above concerns. I look forward to your favorable reply.

Sincerely yours,

Dear Mr. Thompson,

Your recent presentation on the database system containing long term care-related information, as developed by your company, was most informative. As your demonstrated, the system is quite reliable and compatible with our organizational needs. In addition to our institution, several other universities have expressed to us their interest in incorporating your system into their daily operations and would like to acquire further information on purchasing, installation and customer service. This information will undoubtedly determine whether they purchase the database system from your corporation.

Previously, we cooperated with another consulting company in setting up and servicing another database system that integrates various educational indexes from different countries. However, their quoted fee was considerably lower than what you have stated. In light of our budget constraints, we would appreciate it if you would reconsider your original quotation. With regard to the price quotation, please include both set up and servicing of the system, as well as related training. A training session during April or May would be preferable for us, if you could fit this in your schedule.

As the procurement period for this fiscal year will end this month, we need your decision as soon as possible that we can reach a preliminary consensus. If everything works out well, we will arrange another formal discussion with your corporation next month for a demonstration. By the way, as we are a non-profit research institute, would that qualify us for a discount?

Thanks in advance for your thoughtful consideration. I look forward to hearing from you soon.

Sincerely yours,

Dear Ms. Chang,

This is a letter of inquiry from the Institute of Business Administration at Yuanpei University of Science and Technology (YUST) in Hsinchu, Taiwan. Could you provide us with information from your statistical database regarding medical organizations in your country in 2003? Specifically, I am interested in the number of outpatients and inpatients, visits to emergency services, operating tables, obstetric tables, consulting rooms, ambulances, sickrooms, patients who transfer to other hospitals, patients infected while in the hospital and overall mortality rate.

The Graduate Institute of Business Management actively engages in many National Science Council-sponsored research projects in collaboration with government and industry. These projects are wide ranging in scope and encompass many management-related disciplines. My current research project, which is a case study of a Taiwanese hospital, attempts to optimize the efficiency when assessing the practices of nonprofit organizations using the AHP/DEA model. This research heavily relies on data from your statistical database.

We recognize that the continued success of our efforts will hinge on our willingness to share and exchange information with other, similar organizations. Enclosed please find an introductory document that provides additional information regarding the Institute of Business Administration at YUST. I hope that you will be able to provide us with some of the above information. Thank you for your consideration. I look forward to our future cooperative efforts.

Sincerely yours,

Dear Ms. Jones,

This is a letter of inquiry from the ABC Company in Taiwan. Could you provide us with marketing strategy-related information regarding the cosmetics sector in your country? As a governmental, non-profit organization, ABC Company largely focuses on publishing a bi-monthly, cosmetics marketing magazine, facilitating the use of biotechnology domestically, disseminating skin absorptive and cosmetics-related marketing strategies and implementing the latest product technologies.

Continued success of our efforts hinges on our willingness to share and exchange information with other similar organizations such as yours Please find an introductory brochure of ABC Company. I hope that you would provide us with marketing strategy-related information regarding the cosmetics sector with respect to adopting the latest biotechnology methods and encouraging the use of skin absorptive cosmetics. Anticipating close cooperative ties between your two organizations in the future, I hope that this could take the form of technical visits, symposiums, technology consultation and other activities you deem feasible.

Thank you for your consideration. Again, I look forward to our future collaboration.

Sincerely yours,

Dear Mr. Cheng,

I came across an article in the July 2000 edition of *Infection and Immunty* regarding your use of transposon shuttle mutagenesis to establish a Helicobacter pylori mutation strain library. I am extremely interested in this technology and hope that you would give me the opportunity to exchange data with you on recent developments in the laboratory. Our laboratory focuses mainly on identifying *Helicobacter pylori* as an infectious agent responsible for peptic ulcer diseases. This line of research has completely transformed our understanding of the microbiology and pathology of the human stomach. In the laboratory, I am responsible primarily for technical support, information exchanges, and technology transfer opportunities.

I am especially interested in what materials you use in the laboratory, particularly for purposes of the gene library, relevant strains and unsual plasmids. As Helicobacter pylori is naturally transformable, we are interested in how it develops its resistance to metronidazole. We intend to explore the feasibility of treating the antibiotic resistant strains of Helocobacter pyloriunder low pH conditions. We hope to further understand why Helicobacter pylori acquires the antibiotic resistance gene by natural transformation in vitro. I would appreciate if you could share relevant data with us that would be mutually beneficial for both of our laboratory's efforts in this area of research.

Thank you for your kind attention. I look forward to hearing from you.

Sincerely yours,

Dear Dr. Kandinsky,

How have you been lately? I hope that your stay in Taiwan allowed you to experience the difference between Asian and European cultures. While recently perusing your association's website, I became intrigued with the area of exhibition management skills. As you are well aware, PIDA holds several widely attended exhibitions, including OPTO Taiwan (since 1980, over 700 exhibitors & 50,000 international visitors annually) and Computex (since, 1976, over 2,000 exhibitors & 300,000 visitors annually). I have recently been transferred to the exhibition department as chief operations manager.

While working for CMP Taiwan, I served as a coordinator of several exhibitions at PIDA, such as allocating exhibition booths, constructing the booths, forwarding materials, and making travel arrangements. However, I lack expertise on the management side, such as planning and budgeting. Hopefully, this training program will enable me to resolve some of our current problems, such as tightening budget constraints. The preliminary program schedule on the Internet includes a guide of technologies on exhibit, which is probably unnecessary from my perspectives since all of the participates are all senior professionals in this field. On the other hand, special events, i.e., selective brand image trade shows — brands invited only, could be highlighted in this program, as such events will be most beneficial to the participants.

Furthermore, could you please send me the detail program schedule, so that I can more thoroughly understand the event before it is held?

Thanks in advance for your kind assistance and I look forward to receiving your positive reply.

Sincerely yours,

Dear Ms Wiedmann,

We sent you a email, dated July 17, requesting the following information:

1. A list of European LED manufacturers, including the following:
    a. company names, addresses, telephone and fax numbers, and
    b. product lines and sales records for each product

2. Information on field emission display module (FEDM) and vacuum fluorescent display module (VFDM). As we are aware, WKK Corporation, Sun East Corporation, Oenline Inc, and Picute Company are global leaders in these fields. Some of them are already at advanced stages of manufacturing design.

3. Global sales and marketing statistics on European display and peripheral products

4. Future market trends in European display & peripheral products

We plan to introduce these advanced technologies from Europe by advertising them on our web site. Therefore, the 20,000 employees of PIDA could strive to create opportunities for technological exchanges andglobal cooperative agreements. If the response is favorable, we plan to hold further programs, such as presentations, seminars or exhibitions from interested companies. We urgently require the above information and appreciate your kind attention to this matter. Look forward to hearing

from you soon.
Sincerely yours,

Dear Professor Li,

In our conversation last December, I mentioned the possibility of arranging for you to deliver an intensive training course for our colleagues on GC MASS extraction and stripping apparatus for Chinese rhubarb in traditional Chinese medicine. As for your encouraging reply dated December 19, thank you for your valuable suggestions concerning the development of Chinese rhubarb in traditional Chinese medicine.

As you mentioned, GC MASS extraction and stripping apparatus are effective means of identifying the chemical components of Chinese rhubarb. I wholeheartedly agree that introducing GC MASS extraction and stripping apparatus for Chinese rhubarb in traditional Chinese medicine would shed light on how extraction properties are related in traditional Chinese medicine.

Identifying the components and suppressing the mechanisms of bacteria are obviously among the major topics to be explored in the extraction analysis of traditional Chinese medicine. Therefore, many of our future research activities will focus on the adhesion, chemical component analysis and suppression of interaction forces in bacteria. We are especially interested in adopting extraction treatments involving traditional Chinese medicine. Hopefully, this short training program will allow us to determine the systems to be adopted and research topics to be addressed. The following topics may be a helpful guide when determining the contents of this intensive training course:

1. Current developments and the application of GC mass in traditional Chinese medicine extraction research.
2. Applications of traditional Chinese medicine composition/structure/property.
3. Chinese rhubarb conformation/properties

The above topics are simply for your reference. Of course, you should feel free to expand any of these topics. Moreover, I hope that the training curriculum will include fundamental concepts, e.g., theory, foundation and structure of GC, and state-of-the-art GC technology.

I look forward to your response to some of the above concerns.
Sincerely yours,

Dear Dr. Joplin,

Allow me to introduce myself. I am a researcher in the Intensity Modulate Proton Therapy Technology Center (IMPTTC) of the Medical Center Laboratories at Loma Linda University. I am actively engaged in National Science Council-sponsored research in collaboration with the Industrial Technology Research Institute in Taiwan. We have received your publication *Oncology of Medical Technical Exchange Service* on a regular basis for quite some time.

As a governmental subsidized, non-profit organization, IMPTTC largely focuses on facilitating the treatment of tumor patients and preventing diffusion before metal lymph nodes. Please find enclosed an introductory brochure of IMPTTC that clarifies our organizational goals, missions and activities. Given that our goals closely resemble those of your organization, we would like to develop an information exchange relation with *Oncology of Medical Technical Exchange Service*. Such a relation would enable to freely exchange pertinent data on the latest developments in this field. Would you please send me introductory information as well as other relative publications that provide information on your planning, methodologies, results, achievements and future objectives? Thanks in advance for your assistance.

Sincerely yours,

Dear Dr. Chen,

By designating ABC as my primary interest area in ASME and having received the *ABC Newsletter* for quite some time, I realized that CGFM would be a resourceful group for my professional interest in oligomeric proanthocyanidins, which constitute a group of water-soluble polyphenolic tannins that are present in the female inflorescences (up to 5% dry wt) of the hop plant (Humulus lupulus). Humans are exposed to hop proanthocyanidins through consumption of beer. Previous studies have characterized proanthocyanidins from hops for their chemical structure and their in vitro biological activities. Chemically, these proanthocyanidins consist mainly of oligomeric catechins ranging from dimers to octamers, with minor amounts of catechin oligomers containing one or two gallocatechin units. Additionally, the chemical structures of four procyanidin dimers (B1, B2, B3, and B4) and one trimer, epicatechin-$(4\beta \rightarrow 8)$-catechin-$(4\alpha \rightarrow 8)$-catechin (TR), have been elucidated using mass spectrometry, NMR spectroscopy, and chemical degradation. When tested as a mixture, the hop oligomeric proanthocyanidins (PC) were found to be potent inhibitors of neuronal nitric oxide synthase (nNOS) activity. Among the oligomers tested, procyanidin B2 was the most inhibitory against nNOS activity. Procyanidin B3, catechin, and epicatechin were non-inhibitory against nNOS activity. PC and the individual oligomers were all strong inhibitors of 3-morpholinosydnonimine (SIN-1)-induced oxidation of LDL, with procyanidin B3 displaying the highest antioxidant activity at 0.1 μ g/mL. Moreover, the catechin trimer (TR) exhibited antioxidant activity more than 1 order of magnitude higher than that of α-tocopherol or ascorbic acid on a molar basis.

Given my above research interests and your expertise in this field, could you send me introductory information on your laboratory's current efforts in these areas? Based on our mutual interests, we are interested in pursuing collaborative activities with your research organization. I look forward to hearing from you.

Sincerely yours,

Dear Mr. Wang,

Thank you for your encouraging letter, in which you expressed high expectations for our technical cooperation. Your suggestions regarding the proposal were also most helpful. I have also thoroughly discussed this proposal with colleagues in my department. The medical instrumentation that your hospital uses closely resembles that used in ours. Could you write a proposal detailing the instrumentation we would need to purchase, the time frame for this cooperative agreement , the required personnel, their specific responsibilities,the type of patient control group required for this study, a specific list of medicines required (along with their specific dosages) and the anticipated results of this project? As both sides will be responsible for the research outcome, patients in the control groups should be equally distributed from both hospitals, thus ensuring objectivity of the entire research process. Moreover, could you include a checklist for all major administrative work required to implement the project smoothly.

Thanks in advance for your careful preparation, and I anxiously look forward to your reply.

Sincerely yours,

Dear Mr. Thompson,

Having located your company on the Internet last month, I found your line of products, services and technical support to closely match the needs of our current research direction. I am especially interested in the listed retail prices of anticancer drugs that your biotechnology company offers. I need three species of an anticancer drug for chemotherapy purposes. The product code numbers are attached below.

I am also interested in the cancer cells from other parts of the body, including the lungs, liver, brain, breast, stomach and cervix. The medicine dosage appears to produce different responses. If such cancer cells are available for purchase, please quote me their retail pricesas well.

Specifically, I need roughly 15 grams of each species for the chemotherapy anticancer drug. By the way, I was told that each variety of medicine influences different organs to varying extents during cancer cell research. If your company has the above cancer cells that I am interested in, please inform me of the varieties available and their retail prices. As our department belongs to a non-profit research institute, I was wondering whether this would qualify us for some kind of discount? Thanks in advance for your kind assistance.

Sincerely yours,

Dear Ms. Jones,

Thank you for your fax dated June 14, 2003 regarding the training program aimed at assembliing the PPS. Following a meeting among our colleagues to discuss your training program, we have reached the following conclusions, as summarized below.

We hope to enhance our technical expertise in handling PPS, particularly with respect to gene expression, assay function of proteins and related transformation mechanisms. Following the training program, we hope that your engineers could help us set up the PPS in Taiwan. As we prepare to assemble PPS, it would be appreciated if you could provide us with a more detailed introduction to your ACT Program before we reach a final decision. If not too much of an inconvenience, please offer a detailed list of the PPS components, such as those on the attached page.

Sincerely yours,

Dear Professor Coutrakon,

Thank you for you serving as invited speaker at a seminar held recently in the Institute of Medical Imagery at Yuanpei University of Science and Technology (YUST). Three of your lectures for staff of the Radiation Detection Laboratory were highly informative and directly related to our current research direction. Despite Taiwan's lack of clinical experience in proton therapy research, YUST plans to establish a proton spectra laboratory in order to further develop proton treatment methods for clinical applications. Thus, my academic advisor, Professor Hsu, would like me to receive clinical experience in proton therapy technology from the Proton Therapy Center at Loma Linda University, especially in the area of proton microdosimetry spectra. If you allow me to serve as a guest worker in your laboratory, I will send the detailed visiting itinerary shortly.

If given the opportunity, I would like exposure to the following topics:

1. Construction of the shielding of cyclotron to avoid neutron pollution and gamma ray scattering;
2. Operation of the negative ion cyclotron;
3. Blending and design of the shielding material with respect to the half-value layer of lead and concrete;
4. Operating rules of proton spectra analysis facility, with a particular focus on Spread out Bragg Peak (SOBP) analysis; and
5. Clinical information regarding curative doses of proton for different tumor types.

As for my accommodation during the guest stay, I would like to lease a single-room hotel, at range between US$ 50 to US$ 100 daily. Thank you for your generous assistance. I look forward to opportunity for our laboratories to cooperate with each other again.

Sincerely yours,

Dear Professor Smith,

I came across an article in the May 1997 issue of *Protein Science* regarding your purification of an interleukin-1 converting enzyme-related cysteine protease technology. I found it to be of great interest to my own research direction. Our laboratory is currently attempting to understand cysteine protease in cell apoptosis mechanisms, a self-destructive biochemical process in our cells.

As is well known, your research group is devoted to thoroughly investigating biopharmaceutical-related topics. In order for me to more clearly understand the focus of your research group and the technologies that you employ, could you send me information on how you adopt cysteine protease purification in your laboratory. We intend to explore the potential applications of protease in human diseases, particularly in trauma therapy, Your protein purified technologies appear to meet our particular needs.

Thank you for your kind attention. I look forward to hearing from you.

Sincerely yours,

Dear Dr. May,

I immensely enjoyed reading an article in the October 2004 issue of *Biochemistry* regarding your use of protein purification technology. As a non-profit research institute that serves the biotechnology industry in Taiwan, our organization is responsible mainly for research and development, as well as technology transfer to local industry.

Given our common research interests, I would like to understand what product technologies you are adopting in your laboratory. Could you please send me information about the status of technologies used in your laboratory to achieve protein expression and protein purification? Also, if possible, could you send us protein samples of purification, along with data on affinity chromatography? We intend to explore possible technology transfer opportunities, especially in protein expression and protein purification, for Taiwanese biotech sector. Moreover, your protein purification process seems most appropriate for our particular needs.

Thank you for your kind attention. I look forward to hearing from you.

Sincerely yours,

Dear Professor Smith,

I came across your intriguing article in the May 2004 issue of *Physical Review*

Letters regarding multi-electrode array biochips for use in electrophysiology. As a postgraduate student in the Bioimagery Laboratory in the Institute of Medical Imagery at Yuanpei University of Science and Technology in Taiwan, I am researching the synchronization of firing in ventricle cell of a grown rat. I would like to more clearly understand your devised MEA and related technological applications. Could you send me information mentioned in your article on the feasibility of applying MEA to cell culture in your field?

Thank you for your kind attention. I look forward to hearing from you.

Sincerely yours,

Dear Dr. Huang,

As a researcher in the Cell Culture Laboratory at Yuanpei University of Science and Technology (YUST) in Taiwan, I found the results from your recent article, "Effect of Green Tea Polyphenols on RAW 264.7" to be extremely helpful to my own research direction. I was wondering whether you could refer me to pertinent literature regarding how antioxidants affect the gut epithelia cell, or any other relevant publications that you would find helpful to my research?

The Cell Culture Laboratory at YUST focuses mainly on investigating cell cultures, antioxidant functions, spray drying, e.g. incubating cell lines and macrophage (RAW 264.7), to observe how antioxidants in green tea polyphenols affect RAW 264.7.

Thanks in advance for your assistance. I would also be interested in pursuing a collaborative relationship between our two laboratories that would allow us to share pertinent data based on our mutual scientific interests.

Sincerely yours,

Situation 4

Mary Li

difference cultures

booths, forwarding materials, and making travel arrangements

receiving your positive reply

Situation 5

Max Wang

ASME

Situation 6

Lucy Lin

LLUMC

Proton Radiation Treatment Center

laboratory

I Write down the key points of the situations on the preceding page, while the instructor reads aloud the script from the Answer Key.

Situation 4

_____

_____

_____

Situation 5

_____

_____

_____

Situation 6

_____

_____

_____

J Oral practice II

Based on the three situations in this unit, write three questions beginning with **When**, and answer them. The questions do not need to come directly from these situations.

Examples

When does Mary hope that Dr. Kandinsky experienced the difference between Asian and European cultures?

During his stay in Taiwan

When did Mary become intrigued with the area of exhibition management skills?

While recently perusing the association's website that Dr. Kandinsky belongs to

1. _____

_____

2. _____

_____

3. _____

_____

K Based on the three situations in this unit, write three questions beginning with **What**, and answer them. The questions do not need to come directly from these situations.

Examples

What did Max realize by designating ABC as his primary interest area in ASME? That CGFM could resourcefully support his professional interest in oligomeric proanthocyanidins

What are oligomeric proanthocyanidins?
Water-soluble polyphenolic tannins that are present in the female inflorescences (up to 5% dry wt) of the hop plant (Humulus lupulus)

1. _____

_____

2. _____

_____

3. _____

_____

L Based on the three situations in this unit, write three questions beginning with **Where**, and answer them. The questions do not need to come directly from these situations.

Examples

Where is Lucy conducting research as a graduate student?

At the Proton Radiation Treatment Center

Where did Lucy receive a Master's degree in Medical Imagery?

From Yuanpei University of Science and Technology

1. _____

_____

2. _____

_____

3. _____

_____

M Write questions that match the answers provided.

1. _____

_____

A guide to the exhibited technologies

2. _____

_____

Given Max's above research interests and Dr. Chen's expertise in this field

3. _____

_____

The Proton Radiation Treatment Center

N Listening Comprehension II

Situation 4

1. How did Mary become intrigued with exhibition management skills?

   A. by allocating exhibition booths, constructing the booths, forwarding materials, and making travel arrangements

   B. while recently perusing the website of Dr. Kandinsky's association

   C. by experiencing the difference between Asian and European cultures

2. When did Mary coordinate several exhibitions at PIDA?

   A. while studying a master's degree

   B. while attempting to solve problems, such as tightening budget constraints

   C. while working for CMP Taiwan

3. How many visitors does Computex have annually?

   A. 50,000   B. 300,000   C. 150,000

4. In what area does Mary lack expertise in management?

   A. exhibition management skills

   B. tightening budget constraints

   C. planning and budgeting

5. Why does Mary feel that the preliminary program schedule on the Internet that includes a guide to the exhibited technologies is unnecessary?

   A. since all of the participants are senior professionals in this field

   B. since she has recently been transferred to the Exhibition Department as Chief Operations Manager

   C. since such events will be of greatest benefit to the participants

Situation 5

1. What does Max have a professional interest in?

A. procyanidin B2

B. oligomeric proanthocyanidins

C. procyanidin dimmers

2. What have previous studies characterized?

A. proanthocyanidins from hops in terms of their chemical structure and their *in vitro* biological activities

B. the chemical structures of four procyanidin dimers (B1, B2, B3 and B4) and one trimer, epicatechin-(4β→8)-catechin-(4α→8)-catechin (TR)

C. catechin trimer (TR)

3. How did Max realize that CGFM could resourcefully support his professional interest in oligomeric proanthocyanidins?

A. the fact that catechin trimer (TR) exhibited antioxidant activity that was more than one order of magnitude greater than that of α-tocopherol or ascorbic acid on a molar basis

B. the hop oligomeric proanthocyanidins (PC) were found to be potent inhibitors of neuronal nitric oxide synthase (nNOS) activity

C. by designating ABC as his primary interest area in ASME and having received the *ABC Newsletter* for quite some time

4. What inhibited nNOS activity the most?

A. four procyanidin dimers (B1, B2, B3 and B4)

B. procyanidin B2

C. one trimer

5. What exhibited antioxidant activity that was more than one order of magnitude greater than that of α-tocopherol or ascorbic acid on a molar basis?

A. the catechin trimer (TR)

B. the hop oligomeric proanthocyanidins (PC)

C. water-soluble polyphenolic tannins

Situation 6

1. What is Lucy interested in assessing?

   A. the quality of the maintenance components available at Dr. Stevens' Center

   B. the quality of proton radiotherapy

   C. the quality of proton radiotherapy

2. Why is Lucy interested in the proton accelerator, the beam transport system, the gantry, the nozzle and the patient positioning system?

   A. LLUMC represents an ideal environment in which I could pursue my professional interests.

   B. The Proton Radiation Treatment Center is tentatively planning to establish a national high dose exposure measurement laboratory in Taiwan.

   C. LLUMC represents an ideal environment in which Lucy could pursue her professional interests.

3. Why does LLUMC represent an ideal environment in which Lucy could pursue her professional interests?

   A. owing to its global reputation

   B. owing to its careful consideration

   C. professional interests in proton radiotherapy

4. In what area is Lucy concerned with enhancing her technical knowledge of proton radiotherapy?

   A. efforts to form a radiation protection study group

   B. plans to establish a national high dose exposure measurement laboratory

   C. dose measurement and operator training, radiation shield design and instrument maintenance

5. What will Lucy's laboratory study once established?

   A. the proton accelerator, the beam transport system, the gantry, the nozzle and the patient positioning system

B. the effect of dose on relatively heavy particles, such as protons, their chemical characteristics, dose distribution, radiation protection, treatment quality assessment and biological effects

C. the feasibility of establishing a national high dose exposure measurement laboratory in Taiwan

O Reading Comprehension II
Pick the work or expression whose meaning is closest to the meaning of the underlined word or expression in the following passages.

Situation 4

1. I hope that your stay in Taiwan <u>allowed</u> you to experience the difference between Asian and European cultures.

   A. obstructed   B. permitted   C. prevented

2. I hope that your stay in Taiwan allowed you to experience the <u>difference</u> between Asian and European cultures.

   A. equivalence   B. congruity   C. contrast

3. While recently <u>perusing</u> your association's website, I became intrigued with the area of exhibition management skills.

   A. scanning   B. neglecting   C. ignoring

4. While recently perusing your association's website, I became <u>intrigued with</u> the area of exhibition management skills.

   A. neutral towards   B. detached from   C. aroused by

5. While working for CMP Taiwan, I <u>coordinated</u> several exhibitions at PIDA, allocating exhibition booths, constructing the booths, forwarding materials, and making travel arrangements.

   A. arranged   B. blurred   C. confounded

6. While working for CMP Taiwan, I coordinated several exhibitions at PIDA, <u>allocating</u> exhibition booths, constructing the booths, forwarding materials, and making travel arrangements.

   A. retracting   B. recanting   C. appropriating

7. While working for CMP Taiwan, I coordinated several exhibitions at PIDA,

allocating exhibition booths, <u>constructing</u> the booths, forwarding materials, and making travel arrangements.

A. erecting　B. exterminate　C. annihilate

8. However, I <u>lack</u> expertise on the management side, such as in planning and budgeting.

A. surpass in　B. fall short of　C. exceed in

9. Hopefully, this training program will enable me to solve some of our current problems, such as <u>tightening</u> budget constraints.

A. lax　B. constricting　C. unfettered

10. Hopefully, this training program will enable me to solve some of our current problems, such as tightening budget <u>constraints</u>.

A. accessibility　B. attainability　C. limitations

11. The <u>preliminary</u> program schedule on the Internet includes a guide to the exhibited technologies, which is unnecessary from my perspective since all of the participants are senior professionals in this field.

A. finalized　B. initial　C. completed

12. The preliminary program schedule on the Internet includes a guide to the exhibited technologies, which is unnecessary from my <u>perspective</u> since all of the participants are senior professionals in this field.

A. viewpoint　B. background　C. summary

13. However, special events, selected brand image trade shows 一to which particular brands are invited, could be <u>highlighted</u> in this program schedule, as such events will be of greatest benefit to the participants.

A. played down　B. de-emphasized　C. accentuated

Situation 5

1. By <u>designating</u> ABC as my primary interest area in ASME and having received

the *ABC Newsletter* for quite some time,

A. disregarding   B. signifying   C. overlooking

2. Additionally, the chemical structures of four procyanidin dimers (B1, B2, B3 and B4) and one trimer, epicatechin-(4$\beta \rightarrow$8)-catechin-(4$\alpha \rightarrow$8)-catechin (TR), were <u>elucidated</u> using mass spectrometry, NMR spectroscopy and chemical degradation.

A. baffled   B. blurred   C. clarified

3. Given my above research interests and your <u>expertise</u> in this field, could you send me introductory information on your laboratory's current efforts in these areas?

A. immaturity   B. adeptness   C. incompleteness

4. Given my above research interests and your expertise in this field, could you send me <u>introductory</u> information on your laboratory's current efforts in these areas?

A. summary   B. finalized   C. preliminary

5. Given my above research interests and your expertise in this field, could you send me introductory information on your laboratory's current <u>efforts</u> in these areas?

A. impossibilities   B. undertakings   C. inconclusiveness

Situation 6

1. I am a graduate student at the Proton Radiation Treatment Center, which <u>is similar to</u> Loma Linda University's Medical Center (LLUMC).

A. differentiates from   B. resembles   C. distinguishes from

2. I am interested in <u>assessing</u> the quality of proton radiotherapy.

A. refuting   B. disproving   C. appraising

3. Given its global <u>reputation</u>, LLUMC represents an ideal environment in which I could pursue my professional interests.

A. standing   B. infamy   C. stigma

4. The Proton Radiation Treatment Center is <u>tentatively</u> planning to establish a

national high dose exposure measurement laboratory in Taiwan.

A. definitely   B. temporarily   C. certainly

5. We hope to <u>form</u> a radiation protection study group.

A. establish   B. discard   C. expel

6. We hope to <u>enhance</u> our technical knowledge of proton radiotherapy, particularly of dose measurement and operator training, radiation shield design and instrument maintenance.

A. demote   B. debase   C. elevate

P Matching Exercise

1. Each sentence in the following is commonly used to request information: explaining why contact was made to request information 資訊請求信函：解釋請求資訊的目的. Each phrase on the left should be matched with one on the right in order to complete the sentence. Match a number on the left with a letter on the right.

1. While speaking with your products manager Mr. Li over the phone regarding the purchase of	a. to write you for further details on specific points that you brought up in the article.
2. After I talked to Mr. Yang over the phone regarding your line of TFT- LCD products,	b. many of your published articles and am well aware of your more than twelve books on these topics.
3. Thank you for sending us your latest company catalogue and product samples.	c. about your current research direction.
4. Given your pioneering work on the decision theory, Analytic Hierarchy Process (AHP) and the Analytic Network Process (ANP), I have read	d. by your company, was most informative.
5. Your recent presentation on the database system containing long term care-related information, as developed	e. he suggested that I contact you.
6. Having carefully reading your recent article published in the conference proceedings, I found it necessary	f. *Journal of Business Research* on the glass ceiling barrier that many female CEOs face in traditional organizational structures
7. I immensely enjoyed your article in the January 2003 edition of	g. your company's electronics equipment, he suggested that I directly contact you to obtain your company's latest products catalog.
8. I am eager to learn more	h. of Science and Technology, I am highly interested in your research on correlation data.
9. As a graduate student in the Institute of Business and Management at Yuanpei University	i. Your product offerings are in line with our organizational needs.
10. While listened intently to your recent lecture entitled,	j. "Nurse Staffing, Organizational Characteristics and Patient Outcome" at a recent symposium held in Taiwan on March 24-26, 2004, I was fascinated with the topics you addressed.

2. Requesting information: describing one's organizational need for information 資訊請求信函

1. Our company is currently involved in	a. as evidenced by a 10% decline in our mattress sales in the summer of 2004 and a downward sales trend for the year in the third quarter with a slide of 12%.
2. The project we are participating in	b. I am actively engaged in researching related topics.
3. Although such data for Taiwanese hospitals is scarce,	c. is part of a government-sponsored collaborative effort with U.P.O. Company, aimed at contributing to our country's information technology infrastructure.
4. We are interested not only in mining the text information with content analysis method,	d. expressed to us their interest in incorporating your system into their daily operations and would like to acquire further information on purchasing, installation and customer service.
5. In addition to our institution, several other universities have	e. a project to develop slide systems that involves the use of TFT- LCD panels.
6. We are clearly losing our market niche,	f. on the above proposal, as well as pertinent information on the latest nano-technology-based manufacturing processes to produce mattresses.
7. Our branch office requires the headquarter's comments and suggestions	g. data from your statistical database.
8. My current research heavily relies on	h. but also in integrating the information to construct the data warehouse for the same analytical purposes.

3. Requesting information: requesting information 資訊 請求信函

1. Does your company have a sales representative in Taiwan?	a. I was wondering whether you would send me pertinent literature or materials of the following areas:
2. Having gone thoroughly read your article,	b. on health care in the United States?
3. In light of our budget constraints,	c. us with some of the above detailed information.
4. I hope that you will be able to provide	d. documentation and samples:
5. Could you provide us with information from your statistical database	e. and your expertise in the above areas, I am interested in the following topics:
6. Could pass on to me pertinent data regarding the adverse impact of nursing shortages	f. If so, please ask him/her to contact me.
7. Please provide us with the following	g. with that of yours, perhaps we could collaborate in some way in the near future.
8. Given my interest in AHP	h. could send me the first article that you wrote on AHP.
9. I would also appreciate it if you	i. we would appreciate it if you would reconsider your original quotation.
10. Also, if you find my area of research compatible	j. regarding medical organizations in your country in 2003?

4. Requesting information: requesting information 資訊 請求信函

1. Likewise, I could send to you any pertinent	a. the perspective of a Taiwanese company.
2. Could you provide us with information from your statistical database	b. regarding medical organizations in your country in 2003?
3. In addition to your lecture topic and handouts,	c. forward to your instruction on the above matter.
4. I would also appreciate it if you	d. on topics such as legislation, strategies, welfare policies and quality control.
5. Please provide me with pertinent information	e. with that of yours, perhaps we could collaborate in some way in the near future.
6. Also, if you find my area of research compatible	f. data from Taiwan to facilitate our information exchange.
7. I would be more than happy to provide you with pertinent data from	g. could send me the first article that you wrote on AHP.
8. Given my interest in AHP	h. do you have other relevant literature or materials that you could pass on to us prior to our conference so that we can fully realize the practical implications of your lecture for our local researchers and practitioners in this field?
9. I look	i. we would appreciate it if you would reconsider your original quotation.
10. In light of our budget constraints,	j. and your expertise in the above areas, I am interested in the following topics:

Answer Key

解　答

A

Situation 1

Dear Dr. Smith,

Allow me to introduce myself. After graduating from Yuanpei University of Science and Technology (YUST) in 1991, I passed the Taiwanese governmental civil service examination in 1994, subsequently securing an administrative position in our country's National Health Insurance organization. While working, I continued to enhance my administrative skills by taking courses on management in the medical sector at Yangming University. My rich experience in hospital management has familiarized me with formulae for calculating hospital fees. I was transferred to a new post in the insurance revenue sector of the National Health Institute in 2003. My experiences of generating income in the medical sector, and those of monitoring remitted funds in the insurance revenue sector, have greatly matured me as an administrator. Taiwan's National Health Insurance scheme is currently faced with strained financial resources and societal and political pressures not to raise monthly health insurance premiums. Innovative approaches are definitely needed to resolve this dilemma.

Your country initiated one of the earliest health insurance systems worldwide, initiated by Chancellor Bismarck in 1883. Given the radical political, social and economic transformations that Germany went through during the First and Second World Wars, and the more recent reunification of Eastern and Western Germany, your country's health insurance system has withstood many challenges, making it a model worthy of closer examination. Many industrialized countries, including Japan, point to the success of your national health insurance scheme, and especially your adoption of a global budget. Expenditure targets for hospital inpatients are strictly adhered to, and inpatients may pay only 25% of the total cost. An expenditure cap has been established to reduce customer fees for outpatient services. Given your aggressive efforts to keep down overhead costs, the average German citizen in 1997 enjoyed an annual average of 11 outpatient services, which was markedly lower than the annual average of 16 in Taiwan. Specifically, we are concerned with how effectively to restrain increases in medical fees. I hope to visit your organization for three months this year as a visiting researcher to learn about the latest trends in this area. My organization will cover my expenses during the stay.

Please find attached my personal resume that describes my professional experiences in the above area. I look forward to hearing from you soon as to whether the cooperation I have described would be feasible. Thanks in advance for your kind assistance.

Sincerely yours,

Mary Lin

Situation 2

Dear Professor Jones,

Professor Lin Chin Tsai, President of Yuanpei University of Science and Technology, referred me to you. I am pursuing a Master's degree at the Institute of Business and Management at the university. My graduate school research has focused on Sociometric Science, with specialized training in Statistics and Gray Mathematical Theory. I am currently developing a movement disability morbidity model capable not only of accurately forecasting the population of disabled elderly in Taiwan, but also of overcoming the limitations of the conventional population projection model, which incorporates static disability morbidity.

The university would like me to receive advanced training that would not only familiarize me with the long-term health care system, but also expose me to population distribution research, including variations among long-term health care systems worldwide. Your laboratory, a leader in this field of research, could expose me to the latest trends in long-term health care from a global perspective. I hope therefore to join your laboratory for three months this year, preferably from March to

June, if convenient for you. I am most concerned with how such trends in long-term health care will affect Taiwan. The proposed format is that of a self-supported guest worker at your laboratory.

The attached resume will hopefully give you a better idea of my previous academic and professional experiences. A university colleague of mine (Mr. Jeffrey Wu, tel. (408)1234567) who is currently serving as an administrator in a non-profit healthcare organization near your laboratory, can provide you with further information on my background and the purpose of my visit.

I would greatly appreciate your comments regarding this proposal. Thank you for your assistance. I look forward to our future cooperation.

Sincerely yours,

Jason Wu

Situation 3

Dear Professor Wallace,

I hope to receive training at your hospital in the latest advances in infarct stroke technology. I am a second year graduate student at the Institute of Medical Imagery at Yuanpei University of Science and Technology (YUST), as well as a full-time radiological technologist at Shin-Kong Wu Ho-Su Memorial Hospital in Taipei. I received a Bachelor's degree in Radiology from Yuanpei University. In addition to my academic and professional activities, I often read supplemental literature to remain abreast of the latest technological trends. While planning to fulfill my graduate school requirements by June, 2005, I hope to continue in this field of research to integrate the theoretical knowledge acquired at graduate school with my clinical experience in the Radiotechnology Department.

Three associate professors at YUST supervised my graduate school research in magnetic resonance technology. I am currently involved in writing computer programs in the field of image quality and resolution, applying the latest technologies to enable physicians accurately to diagnose diseases in their early stages. I have already drawn up an outline of this project. I am firstly reviewing pertinent patient histories to obtain large volumes of relevant data, which are then analyzed. Pertinent research is then reviewed. The acute infarct of brain tumor patients is then studied. According to the results generated by my academic advisor's laboratory, less than six hours is required to perform the first diffusion-weighted image (DWI) examination of acute infract patients. DWI is then conducted on the first, third, fifth, seventh days, and then at one month intervals. The B value infarct region is then measured, and then the time changes in the B value curve are analyzed. The results of this study will help physicians to determine proper medication times and their therapeutic effects.

I hope to measure the order of severity of the infarct field in order to enable infarct stroke patients to receive subsequent optimal treatment. Writing an effective integral diffusion mode map requires taking advantage of the latest programs in which different maps appear in direct relation to different diseases. Using these programs, clinical physicians can precisely understand how a disease diffuses to the brain area, and increase the clinical effectiveness of evaluations of patients and curative outcomes. In this area, Taiwan currently lacks technology and qualified technological personnel. I hope eventually to collaborate with a local medical instrument manufacturer to develop relevant software programs. Your hospital provides comprehensive and challenging training of individuals who are committed to this area of research and development. In particular, it is distinguished in training highly skilled radiological technologists.

I will hopefully be able to determine the scope of application of infarct stroke technology in our hospital. The results are used to analyze the feasibility of adopting this technology. Our current research direction is to investigate differences among infarct stroke patients across races and gender. The proposed format, approved by the hospital ethics committee, is that of a self-supported guest worker at your laboratory.

For further information regarding my academic and professional expertise, please contact my academic advisor, Dr. Hong-Jue Liu. His contact information can be found in the accompanying resume. I would greatly appreciate your comments regarding this proposal. Thank for your kind assistance. I look forward to our future cooperation.

Sincerely yours,

Jack Wang

B

How did Mary secure an administrative position in Taiwan's National Health Insurance organization?

By passing the governmental civil service examination in 1994

How did Mary continue to enhance her administrative skills while working?

By taking courses on management in the medical sector at Yangming University.

How did Mary familiarize herself with formulae for calculating hospital fees?

By her rich experience in hospital management

How has Mary greatly matured me as an administrator?

Through her experiences of generating income in the medical sector, and those of monitoring remitted funds in the insurance revenue sector

How did Germany's health insurance system become a model worthy of closer examination?

Owing to the radical political, social and economic transformations that it went through during the First and Second World Wars, and the more recent reunification of Eastern and Western Germany

C

What is the movement disability morbidity model that Jason is developing capable of doing?

Accurately forecasting the population of disabled elderly in Taiwan and overcoming the limitations of the conventional population projection model

What has Jason's graduate school research focused on?

Sociometric Science, with specialized training in Statistics and Gray Mathematical Theory

What advanced training would Jason's university like for him to receive?

Training that would not only familiarize him with the long-term health care system, but also expose him to population distribution research, including variations among long-term health care systems worldwide

What exposure would Jason like to receive as a guest worker in the laboratory?

Exposure to the latest trends in long-term health care from a global perspective

What is Jason most concerned with?

How such trends in long-term health care will affect Taiwan

D

Why does Jack hope to receive training at a hospital in the latest advances in infarct stroke technology?

Because he is a a second year graduate student at the Institute of Medical Imagery at Yuanpei University of Science and Technology (YUST), as well as a full-time radiological technologist at Shin-Kong Wu Ho-Su Memorial Hospital in Taipei.

Why does Jack often read supplemental literature in addition to his academic and professional activities?
To remain abreast of the latest technological trends

Why does Jack hope to continue in this field of research?
To integrate the theoretical knowledge acquired at graduate school with his clinical experience in the Radiotechnology Department.

Why will physicians benefit from the results of Jack's study?
To determine proper medication times and their therapeutic effects.

Why does Jack hope to measure the order of severity of the infarct field?
In order to enable infarct stroke patients to receive subsequent optimal treatment

E
Where was Mary transferred to in 2003?
A new post in the insurance revenue sector of the National Health Institute

Who is currently serving as an administrator in a non-profit healthcare organization near Professor Jones's laboratory?
Mr. Jeffrey Wu

How many associate professors at YUST supervised Jack's graduate school research in magnetic resonance technology?
Three

F

Situation 1

1.C 2.C 3.B 4.A 5.B

Situation 2

1.C 2.B 3.A 4.C 5.B

Situation 3

1.B 2.A 3.B 4.C 5.A

G

Situation 1

1.B 2.A 3.A 4.C 5.B 6.C 7.A 8.B 9.B 10.B 11.A 12.B 13.C
14.A 15.B 16.C 17.B 18.A 19.C 20.B 21.A 22.A 23.C 24.B
25.B 26.A 27.B 28.B 29.C 30.A 31.B 32.A 33.A 34.B 35.A
36.B 37.C 38.A 39.C

Situation 2

1.B 2.A 3.C 4.A 5.B 6.C 7.B 8.C 9.A 10.C 11.A 12.C 13.A
14.B

Situation 3

1.C 2.B 3.A 4.A 5.C 6.B 7.B 8.C 9.B 10.C 11.A 12.C 13.B
14.C 15.A 16.C 17.A 18.B 19.A 20.C 21.B 22.A 23.A 24.C
25.B 26.C 27.B 28.A 29.A 30.A 31.C 32.A 33.C 34.B 35.A
36.C 37.A 38.C 39.B 40.A

I

Situation 4

Dear Professor Tung,

My academic advisor, Professor Hsu, suggested that I contact you to ask to work
in your laboratory at National Tsing Hua University as a visiting researcher. My

academic advisor and you lead the way in dosimetry and microdosimetry-related research in Taiwan. Having acquired four years of clinical experience as a radiographer at a regional hospital, I am currently pursuing a Master's degree in Medical Imagery at Yuanpei University of Science and Technology, where I am a member of the Radiation Detection Laboratory. As well as having a strong background in engineering mathematics, I enjoy researching dosimetry, atomic physics, radiation physics and radiation detection physics-related topics. Despite my lack of a pure science or engineering-related background, I am confident that my solid logical and statistical skills will prove invaluable to any research effort in which I am involved at your laboratory. Moreover, I consider myself diligent and able to grasp new concepts easily.

If given the opportunity to work in your laboratory, I will increase my understanding of the dosimetry-related principles that apply when proton beams are used in radiation therapy. Proton beam instrumentation has been used in radiation therapy for several years. According to Taiwan's Department of Health, only five facilities worldwide are equipped to conduct proton beam radiation therapy. Owing to Taiwanese governmental legislation on medical treatment, the Department of Health is drafting a resolution on whether to import proton beam instrumentation from abroad for radiation therapy. This is a particularly relevant issue given the planned opening of Hsinchu Biomedical Science Park in 2007.

As widely anticipated, proton beam radiation therapy has many promising applications in Taiwan, making dosimetry-related principles applicable by medical physicists in radiation therapy. The opportunity to serve as a visiting researcher in your laboratory will allow me more fully to explore the above topics and their clinical implications.

Please carefully consider my application. I look forward to your favorable response.

Sincerely yours,

Mary Li

Situation 5

Dear Professor Dong,

Given your laboratory's expertise in developing excellent software for medical instrumentation, I would like to receive technical training in your laboratory during my upcoming summer vacation. I wish to understand how Bioimage, Java and C++ programs can be more effectively implemented in clinical settings in Taiwan. My academic advisor recommended that working in your laboratory would help me to understand what potential technology transfer opportunities are possible in the local medical instrumentation sector.

Earlier this year, following my participation in three National Science Council-sponsored research projects as an undergraduate student at Tzu Chi College of Technology, I entered the Master's degree program at the Institute of Medical Imagery at Yuanpei University of Science and Technology. My graduate school research is on the synchronization of firing in a growing neural network. Specifically, our research group is developing an experimental system to observe quantitatively the formation of functional synapses between cerebral cortical neurons from a mouse. Our experimental results have so far elucidated the interesting phenomenon of synchronous firing, whose frequency increases as a function of the culture period. Our laboratory is developing a unique scanning laser confocal microscope to measure the firing fluorescence image.

However, continuing with this experimentation requires additional instrumentation and technological expertise, which I currently lack. I would therefore like to receive technical training for four months in your laboratory. Unlike ordinary technical training, this four month technical visit will hopefully initiate a long-term collaborative relationship between our two laboratories. During this period, I am keen to become more proficient in Bioimage technology and learn how effectively to operate related instruments.

I look forward to hearing your ideas regarding the above proposal.

Sincerely yours,

Jenny Lin

Situation 6

Dear Dr. Curtin,

The Radiation Therapy Department at National Taiwan University Hospital, where I have acquired more than two decades of clinical experience as a radiology technician, would like me to receive advanced training in cancer therapy as a visiting researcher in your Clinical Cancer Center. I have extensive professional experience, and am now pursuing a Master's degree in Medical Imagery at Yuanpei University of Science and Technology. Given the opportunity, I will perform advanced research at the NYU Clinical Cancer Center, which has highly skilled personnel and state-of-the-art equipment and facilities. It is globally recognized for its services that improve the lives of cancer patients. The NYU Clinical Cancer Center has distinguished itself by its quality of patient care, including privacy, safety and comfort.

In my graduate school courses on advanced imaging processing, I became aware of advanced imaging procedures and other diagnostic tests performed at the NYU Clinical Cancer Center to diagnose cancer. Working in your organization would give me a practical context for the concepts learned in class. Our research group has published three articles in *Gamma Journal* over the past three years. One of our articles addressed the preservation of hearing in nasal and pharyngeal cancer patients who had received post-irradiation treatment. Another article examined the role of magnetic resonance imaging in a herniated inter-vertebral disc, while the third one addressed the perfusion function of F-FDG in SPECT. My current research is on intensity-modulated radiation therapy.

As the NYU Clinical Cancer Center is widely regarded as having the best radiation therapy planning system for cancer treatment worldwide, I hope that my above research interests are in line with those of your research group. More specifically, I am interested in developing a radiation therapy planning system that would ensure optimal imaging for diagnosing and treating cancer. I am also interested in learning of new ways to offer patients not only physiological, but also spiritual encouragement. Thank you in advance for your careful consideration of this proposed stay as a visiting researcher in your laboratory. I look forward to our future cooperation.

Sincerely yours,

Matt Fung

J

What did Mary's academic advisor, Professor Hsu, suggested that she do?

Contact Professor Tung to ask to work in his laboratory at National Tsing Hua University as a visiting researcher

What clinical experience has Mary acquired?

Four years as a radiographer at a regional hospital

What does Mary enjoy researching?

Dosimetry, atomic physics, radiation physics and radiation detection physics-related topics

What does Mary believe will prove invaluable to any research effort in which she is involved at Professor's Tung's laboratory?

Her solid logical and statistical skills

What makes dosimetry-related principles applicable by medical physicists in radiation therapy?

The fact that proton beam radiation therapy has many promising applications in Taiwan

K

Why would Jenny like to receive technical training in Professor Dong's laboratory during her upcoming summer vacation?

Because of the laboratory's expertise in developing excellent software for medical instrumentation

Why did Jenny's academic advisor recommend her to work in Professor Dong's laboratory?

To understand what potential technology transfer opportunities are possible in the local medical instrumentation sector

Why is Jenny's research group developing an experimental system?

To observe quantitatively the formation of functional synapses between cerebral cortical neurons from a mouse

Why is Jenny's laboratory developing a unique scanning laser confocal microscope?

To measure the firing fluorescence image

Why would Jenny like to receive technical training for four months in Professor Dong's laboratory

To acquire further knowledge of additional instrumentation and technological expertise, which she currently lacks.

L

How much clinical experience has Matt acquired as a radiology technician?
More than two decades

How has the NYU Clinical Cancer Center distinguished itself?
By its quality of patient care, including privacy, safety and comfort.

How did Matt become aware of advanced imaging procedures and other diagnostic tests performed at the NYU Clinical Cancer Center to diagnose cancer?
In his graduate school courses on advanced imaging processing

How could Matt acquire a practical context for the concepts learned in class?
By working in Dr. Curtin's organization

How does Matt hope to ensure optimal imaging for diagnosing and treating cancer?
By developing a radiation therapy planning system

M

How will Mary increase her understanding of the dosimetry-related principles that apply when proton beams are used in radiation therapy?
By working in Professor Tung's laboratory

When did Jenny enter the Master's degree program at the Institute of Medical Imagery at Yuanpei University of Science and Technology?
Earlier this year

Which organization is widely regarded as having the best radiation therapy planning system for cancer treatment worldwide?

The NYU Clinical Cancer Center

N

Situation 4

1.C 2.A 3.B 4.A 5.C

Situation 5

1.B 2.C 3.B 4.A 5.A

Situation 6

1.B 2.B 3.A 4.C 5.B

O

Situation 4

1.B 2.A 3.A 4.C 5.B 6.A 7.B 8.C 9.A 10.C 11.A 12.B 13.B
14.C 15.B 16.A 17.B 18.B 19.A 20.C 21.B 22.A

Situation 5

1.A 2.C 3.B 4.C 5.A 6.C 7.B 8.C 9.A 10.C 11.A 12.C 13.A
14.B 15.C 16.A 17.C 18.B 19.C 20.A 21.C 22.A 23.C

Situation 6

1.C 2.A 3.C 4.B 5.C 6.A 7.C 8.B 9.C 10.B 11.C 12.A 13.B
14.C 15.B 16.A 17.C 18.A 19.A 20.B 21.A 22.A

P

Exercise 1

1.e 2.h 3.j 4.a 5.g 6.b 7.c 8.f 9.d 10.i

Exercise 2

1.g 2.j 3.a 4.i 5.b 6.h 7.c 8.e 9.d 10.f

Exercise 3

1.h 2.j 3.e 4.b 5.a 6.g 7.c 8.d 9.f 10.i

Exercise 4

1.h 2.j 3.a 4.i 5.b 6.g 7.f 8.c 9.d 10.e

Exercise 5

1.g 2.i 3.a 4.j 5.h 6.b 7.c 8.f 9.d 10.e

Exercise 6

1.h 2.d 3.a 4.j 5.b 6.e 7.f 8.c 9.g 10.i

Exercise 7

1.h 2.d 3.a 4.i 5.b 6.c 7.e 8.f 9.g 10.j

Exercise 8

1.g 2.i 3.b 4.a 5.h 6.d 7.j 8.c 9.e 10.f

Exercise 9

1.g 2.i 3.b 4.e 5.c 6.a 7.d 8.f 9.j 10.h

Exercise 10

1.g 2.i 3.a 4.j 5.d 6.h 7.e 8.f 9.b 10.c

Exercise 11

1.h 2.c 3.a 4.j 5.b 6.i 7.f 8.d 9.g 10.e

A

Situation 1

Dear Mr. Smith,

Thank you for your message sent via e-mail and dated December 31, 2004, inviting our Taiwanese branch office to exhibit its innovative bedding and pillow products in Cologne, Germany on May 2005. Before participating in the exhibition, I would like to propose an information exchange relationship between our two organizations regarding the sleeping needs of elderly individuals, hopefully leading to a technology transfer or joint venture opportunity in the near future.

The Taiwanese branch of this bedding company has increased its number of business units by pursuing an aggressive marketing strategy since 2000. It has more than 20 units across the island and has seen a dramatic increase in sales volume. The branch office tentatively plans to construct a new factory next year and broaden its organizational scope. Franchises are helped to outperform the competition, as evidenced by our development of several bedding and pillow types and emphasis on electrically heated bedding and customized pillows.

Taiwan's elderly population has grown rapidly in recent years, and the bedding market has generated considerable revenues. Given this trend, the R&D Division of the Taiwanese branch has committed significant resources to designing bedding customized for elderly individuals. The Intellectual Property Office of the Ministry of Economic Affairs has already granted the relevant patents. Given our headquarters' vast knowledge of consumer trends and technological developments in this area, we would like to exchange product information and manufacturing technology expertise with your R&D unit. Germany has distinguished itself in the latest technological developments in bedding comfort, the marketing of these products, and consumer relations in this niche.

To initiate this collaborative relationship, five colleagues from the Taiwan branch (including myself) would like to visit your R&D unit, this upcoming January, hopefully to meet with your departmental managers and research personnel. Let me know which dates would be the most convenient for such a visit. Prior to our visit, we would appreciate your forwarding to us any materials regarding your company's technological developments and marketing strategies in this area. I look forward to hearing your ideas or suggestions regarding this information exchange opportunity. Thank you in advance for your careful consideration. I look forward to this mutually beneficial, cooperative effort.

Sincerely yours,

Becky Ko

Situation 2

Dear Mr. Push,

As a member of the technical staff of the Nuclear Medicine Department at S.W.M Memorial Hospital, I am involved in various stages of the therapeutic treatment of acute stroke patients. Given your institution's state-of-the-art technology and advanced expertise in neurology, I would like to propose a technological information exchange between our two hospital departments on the subject of treating patients with brain ischemia and acute brain stroke. Medical research in Taiwan heavily emphasizes stroke-related factors leading to mortality.

We are anxious to develop long-lasting cooperative relationships with an institution such as yours. Neurological departments in Taiwan admit weekly nearly 100 stroke patients for clinical treatment. Our hospital has spent considerable resources to reduce the risk of stroke and solve problems that involve blood flow in the brain. As growth in the medical technology sector appears to be unlimited, the neurological department of our hospital is committed to overcoming stroke-related illnesses and reducing the incidence rate of strokes in Taiwan. Progress in this area depends on the ability of medical institutions to share and exchange relevant experiences ─ and we look forward to an opportunity to do the same with you.

Reading the January 2003 issue of *Nuclear Medicine Journal*, I learned how your laboratory has reduced semihemisphere bleeding using coregisteration technology. Your ability to differentiate the infarction area in irreversibly damaged tissue is a respectable achievement. HMPAO SPECT can be used to determine the extent to which tracer uptake reduction can accurately predict neurological recovery and various programming languages can be used to write software to identify abnormal sites in the infarct area. I hope that our staff will have the opportunity to exchange data and experiences in the field of brain stroke patients. Given our hospital's advanced PET technological capacity to reduce the incidence of strokes, such collaboration would be mutually beneficial, allowing both of our organizations to improve continuously expertise in medical diagnosis.

We look forward to hearing your ideas or suggestions regarding this technological information exchange, covering your work in voxel-based correlations in stroke patients and our research on advanced ischemic damaged tissue. If you agree, I would like to arrange a 14-day technical visit to your department this upcoming October as the first step of our cooperation. Please let me know if you would like to discuss any areas of common knowledge.

Sincerely yours,

Sam Long

Situation 3

Dear Mr. Haas,

Thank you for your letter dated Nov 10, 2003, which included your article, "Isolation and characterization of functions of genes essential for DNA transformation in *Helicobacter pylori*". In response to your invitation, I would like to visit your organization to exchange technological information regarding gene expression, the assay function of proteins and related transformation mechanisms.

As a graduate student at the Institute of Biotechnology Research at Yuanpei

University of Science and Technology in Hsinchu, Taiwan, I am collaborating with my professor in a National Science Council-sponsored research project, to generate a mutant library from a clinical isolate of *Helicobacter pylori*. The results from our laboratory on *Helicobacter pylori*, have demonstrated that some gene mutants induce dramatic natural transformation. Our recent findings have been published in a monthly JBC magazine. The article attempted to characterize genes and their role in the natural transformation of *Helicobacter pylori*. The experimental results obtained in this project have already greatly helped Taiwan's development of attenuated vaccine strains of *Helicobacter pylori*.

Individuals of all ages can get ulcers. The incidence rates of women and men are nearly identical. Over 25 million Americans suffer from an ulcer during their lifetimes. Fortunately, most ulcers are caused by an infection with *Helicobacter pylori*, opening the possibility of prevention through the development of an effective and safe vaccine. Our research is focused mainly on identifying associated proteins. The results will be helpful in producing an antiserum, preparing membranes and purifying proteins from inclusion bodies. Your recognized expertise in this area would greatly benefit our own research efforts. I hope that through a technological information exchange, we will be able to identify areas of mutual interest, possibly leading to a technology transfer or joint venture.

I look forward to your response to some of the above points concerning this information exchange opportunity. Visiting your laboratory for two weeks to exchange ideas of mutual interest would appear to be a good first step. Let me know which dates would be the most convenient for you. Thank you in advance for your careful consideration. I hope that this information exchange opportunity will open doors to future collaboration between our two organizations.

Sincerely yours,

Amy Huang

B

How has the Taiwanese branch of this bedding company increased its number of business units?

By pursuing an aggressive marketing strategy since 2000

How has the R&D Division of the Taiwanese branch responded to the rapid growth of Taiwan's elderly population?

By committing significant resources to designing bedding customized for elderly individuals

How has the Taiwanese branch office helped franchises to outperform the competition?

By developing several bedding and pillow types and emphasizing electrically heated bedding and customized pillows

How would headquarters like to exchange product information and manufacturing technology expertise with the German R&D unit?

Through its vast knowledge of consumer trends and technological developments in this area

How would Becky like the German R&D unit to prepare for the upcoming visit?

By forwarding any materials regarding the company's technological developments and marketing strategies in this area

C

What position does Sam hold at S.W.M. Memorial Hospital?

A member of the technical staff of the Nuclear Medicine Department

What does Sam's work involve?

various stages of the therapeutic treatment of acute stroke patients

What has S.W.M. Memorial Hospital spent considerable resources in doing?

Reducing the risk of stroke and solving problems that involve blood flow in the brain.

What is the neurological department of S.W.M. Memorial Hospital committed to doing?

Overcoming stroke-related illnesses and reducing the incidence rate of strokes in Taiwan

What does S.W.M. Memorial Hospital advanced PET technological capacity enable it to do?

Reduce the incidence of strokes

D

Why would Amy like to visit Mr. Haas's organization?

To exchange technological information regarding gene expression, the assay function of proteins and related transformation mechanisms

Why is Amy collaborating with her professor in a National Science Council-sponsored research project?

To generate a mutant library from a clinical isolate of Helicobacter pylori.

Why would Amy like to visit Dr. Haas's laboratory for two weeks?

To exchange ideas of mutual interest

Why is Amy optimistic about this information exchange opportunity?

She hopes that it will open doors to future collaboration between their two organizations

Why are ulcers a common threat?

Because individuals of all ages can get them

E

What does the branch office tentatively plan to construct?

A new factory next year

How many stroke patients are admitted to neurological departments for clinical treatment weekly?

Nearly 100

What will the results of Amy's research be helpful in doing?

Producing an antiserum, preparing membranes and purifying proteins from inclusion bodies

F

Situation 1

1.C   2.C   3.B   4.A   5.B

Situation 2

1.B   2.C   3.B   4.A   5.C

Situation 3

1.C   2.B   3.C   4.B   5.A

G

Situation 1

1.B　2.C　3.B　4.C　5.A　6.A　7.C　8.C　9.B　10.B　11.A　12.A　13.C
14.A　15.A　16.B　17.C　18.B　19.A　20.C　21.C　22.B　23.A　24.A
25.B　26.A　27.B　28.A　29.A　30.C　31.B　32.B　33.C　34.B

Situation 2

1.A　2.C　3.B　4.C　5.C　6.A　7.C　8.C　9.B　10.C　11.A　12.B　13.A
14.C　15.C　16.C　17.A　18.C　19.A　20.B　21.A　22.C　23.B　24.B
25.C

Situation 3

1.B　2.C　3.A　4.C　5.B　6.B　7.B　8.A　9.C　10.C　11.A　12.C　13.C
14.B　15.A　16.C　17.B　18.C　19.B　20.A

I

Situation 4

Dear Mr. Wang,

Thank you for your message sent via e-mail and dated November 8, 2004 inviting the branch office in Taiwan to exhibit our innovative TFT-LCD products in New York this upcoming March. Before our participation at this exhibition, I would like to propose an information exchange between our two organizations regarding the material development of TFT-LCD products, hopefully leading to a technology transfer in the near future.

As TFT-LCD technology advances, our branch office strives to offer a line of quality products that satisfy consumer demand, both locally and abroad. Such innovation contributes to the maturation of Taiwan's recently emerging electronics sector, accelerating technological efforts that boost international competitiveness. The Taiwanese branch of this TFT-LCD company has increased its number of business units to ten by pursuing an aggressive marketing strategy since 1995, increasing revenues. The branch office tentatively plans to construct a new production facility next year and to broaden its organizational scope.

The range of TFT-LCD products manufactured in Taiwan has grown rapidly in recent years; such products have generated considerable profits. The Taiwanese branch has committed significant resources to designing TFT-LCD products, and the Intellectual Property Office of the Ministry of Economic Affairs has granted several patents. To continue this progress, we would like to exchange product-related information and manufacturing technology expertise with your R&D unit, possibly leading to a joint venture once ties are established.

To initiate this collaborative relationship, ten colleagues from the Taiwanese branch would like to visit your R&D unit next year, hopefully meeting with your departmental managers and research personnel. Let me know which dates would be the most convenient for such a visit. Taiwan's TFT-LCD manufacturers focus on producing small and medium-sized panels. Establishing long-term collaborative ties with renowned manufacturers such as yours reflects our resolve to maintain innovation in the production of TFT-LCD in Taiwan.

I look forward to hearing your suggestions regarding this information exchange opportunity. Thank you in advance for your careful consideration. I firmly believe that such a cooperative relationship would mutually benefit both of our organizations.

Sincerely yours,

Jason Wu

Situation 5

Dear Mr. Smith,

Thank you for your letter dated December 18, 2004, containing the publication *Advanced Medical Knowledge*. In response, I'd like to propose an information exchange between our two organizations, on the integration of digital image processing, biochemistry and medical technologies for extracting Chinese herbal medicine from natural substances.

As a graduate student at the Institute of Biotechnology at Yuanpei University of Science and Technology (YUST) in Hsinchu, Taiwan, I am currently involved in a project on Chinese herbal medicine extracts. The project is a joint collaboration between our research institute and the Institute of Nuclear Science at National Tsing Hua University, and focuses on generating data regarding Chinese herbal medicine extracts. Our important work includes publishing a bimonthly magazine that describes the extraction and dissemination of Chinese herbal medicine compounds for commercialization. The experimental results generated in this project have already greatly helped efforts to identify Chinese herbal medicine compounds.

The potential integration of digital image processing, biochemistry and medical technology could contribute to Taiwan's rapid economic growth, fueled by the development of many innovative technologies. Chinese and Taiwanese have extensively used Chinese herbal medicine for centuries. Given advances in laboratory facilities, instrumentation and available technologies, educational institutions in Taiwan now employ highly qualified technical personnel to conduct advanced research on Chinese herbal medicine-related topics.

Many such projects currently focus on the feasibility of integrating digital image processing with biochemical assessment, molecular biology technologies and the extraction of Chinese herbal medicine from natural substances. We recognize that ensuring the continued success of our efforts in Taiwan depends on the open sharing and exchange of experiences with other similar organizations. Please find enclosed an introductory brochure about the Institute of Biotechnology at YUST, which will provide further details on our mission, methods and current research.

I look forward to hearing your ideas or suggestions regarding this information exchange opportunity. I would also like to arrange for a 15-day technical visit to your organization this upcoming January, as the first step of our cooperation. If at all possible, please notify me as to which dates are most convenient for you. A tentative visiting schedule would also be appreciated. Thank you in advance for your careful consideration.

Sincerely yours,

Sally Lin

Situation 6

Dear Dr. Curtin,

Given our concern over upgrading the quality of universal medical and teaching facilities worldwide, our organization, National Taiwan University Hospital (NTUH), would like to apply for membership in your society. Having gained more than two decades of clinical experience in radiation therapy, NTUH is the first medical institute and teaching hospital in Asia. I believe that such an opportunity would be mutually beneficial to both of our organizations.

While focusing on teaching, research and service, NTUH has acquired the best medical personnel and technologists in Asia. Pedagogical activities advance not only medical knowledge, but also the quality of health care. While aspiring to become a leading medical and teaching hospital worldwide, we hope to participate in the activities of other medical and teaching hospital organizations. As well as providing medical services, we strive to improve medical techniques and medical research. For instance, the hospital's Clinical Cancer Center has recently implemented a therapeutic planning system for cervical cancer, which is the most common cancer among women worldwide. Using this novel system, we can more efficiently locate the target organ and use lower dosages of radiation for normal tissues.

Continuing with the success of our organization by further upgrading our medical and teaching capabilities depends on our ability to be involved with in wide-reaching organizations such as yours, with a view to improving medical practice in Asia. Joining your organization would allow us openly to exchange experiences with other medical and teaching hospitals worldwide.

Sincerely yours,

Max Bai

J

What does Jason's branch office strives to offer?

A line of quality products that satisfy consumer demand, both locally and abroad

What has the Taiwanese branch of this TFT-LCD company increased?

Its number of business units to ten

What does the branch office tentatively plan to do?

Construct a new production facility next year and to broaden its organizational scope

What has the Taiwanese branch committed significant resources to doing?

Designing TFT-LCD products

What do Taiwan's TFT-LCD manufacturers focus on?

Producing small and medium-sized panels

K

Why is Sally's research institute and the Institute of Nuclear Science at National
Tsing Hua University jointly collaborating on a project?

To generate data regarding Chinese herbal medicine extracts.

Why have the experimental results generated in this project been beneficial?

They have greatly helped efforts to identify Chinese herbal medicine compounds.

Why could the potential integration of digital image processing, biochemistry and medical technology contribute to Taiwan's rapid economic growth?
It is fueled by the development of many innovative technologies.

Why do educational institutions in Taiwan now employ highly qualified technical personnel?
To conduct advanced research on Chinese herbal medicine-related topics.

Why is Sally including an introductory brochure about the Institute of Biotechnology at YUST?
To provide further details on her laboratory's mission, methods and current research

L

How is National Taiwan University Hospital concerned over upgrading the quality of universal medical and teaching facilities worldwide?
Owing to its intention to apply for membership in Dr. Curtin's society.

How is National Taiwan University Hospital qualified for membership in Dr. Curtin's society?
By its more than two decades of clinical experience in radiation therapy

How has National Taiwan University Hospital acquired the best medical personnel and technologists in Asia?
By focusing on teaching, research and service

How do pedagogical activities advance?
Not only medical knowledge, but also the quality of health care

How has National Taiwan University Hospital been able to more efficiently locate the target organ and use lower dosages of radiation for normal tissues?

By implementing a therapeutic planning system for cervical cancer

M

Why would ten colleagues from the Taiwanese branch like to visit Mr. Wang's R&D unit next year?

To initiate this collaborative relationship

Where is Sally a graduate student?

At the Institute of Biotechnology at Yuanpei University of Science and Technology (YUST) in Hsinchu, Taiwan

Which organization is aspiring to become a leading medical and teaching hospital worldwide?

Max's hospital

N

Situation 4

1.C   2.B   3.A   4.C   5.B

Situation 5

1.B   2.C   3.B   4.A   5.B

Situation 6

1.C   2.A   3.B   4.A   5.C

O

Situation 4

1.B   2.A   3.C   4.B   5.A   6.C   7.A   8.C   9.C   10.B   11.A   12.A   13.C

14.A 15.A 16.C 17.B 18.A 19.C 20.B 21.A 22.C 23.A 24.B

25.A 26.B 27.A 28.C 29.A 30.B 31.C 32.A

Situation 5

1.B 2.C 3.B 4.B 5.A 6.C 7.B 8.C 9.B 10.A 11.B 12.A 13.C

14.A 15.C 16.C 17.A 18.C 19.A 20.C 21.B 22.A 23.A 24.A

Situation 6

1.B 2.C 3.C 4.A 5.C 6.B 7.A 8.C 9.B 10.A 11.A

P

Exercise 1

1.g 2.d 3.a 4.h 5.c 6.e 7.i 8.f 9.b

Exercise 2

1.g 2.i 3.b 4.a 5.c 6.d 7.e 8.f 9.h

Exercise 3

1.f 2.i 3.a 4.h 5.b 6.c 7.d 8.e 9.g

Exercise 4

1.g 2.a 3.i 4.b 5.c 6.j 7.e 8.d 9.f 10.h

Exercise 5

1.i 2.c 3.j 4.a 5.g 6.d 7.b 8.e 9.f 10.h

Exercise 6

1.d 2.g 3.b 4.a 5.c 6.h 7.e 8.f

Exercise 7

1.g 2.a 3.e 4.c 5.b 6.d 7.f

Exercise 8

1.f 2.c 3.a 4.b 5.g 6.e 7.d

Exercise 9

1.e 2.a 3.j 4.c 5.b 6.h 7.d 8.f 9.g 10.i

Exercise 10

1.d　2.g　3.f　4.j　5.a　6.i　7.b　8.c　9.h　10.e

Exercise 11

1.f　2.h　3.a　4.i　5.b　6.j　7.c　8.g　9.e　10.d

Answer Key
Making Technical Visits Overseas
科技訪問信函

A

Situation 1

Dear Mr. Push,

I belong to the Department of Nuclear Medicine at Kaohsiung Medical College. Your research group has expended considerable effort in treating stroke patients using state-of-the-art instrumentation to solve brain ischemia-related problems. Although I strongly desire to undergo extensive training from your medical group on the latest technological developments in this area, arranging the required large block of time is impossible given my hectic schedule at work. However, I would like to arrange for a five-day technical visit with the Head of your Nuclear Medicine Department, Dr. Smith, and his recently formed research group, to learn of the latest medical technologies available to combat brain ischemia. I am especially interested in learning about your successful treatments that have reduced the likelihood of strokes. I am very impressed with the medical software program developed by your research group, which has been successful adopted at UCLA. At graduate school, I attempted to elucidate the actual mechanism that operates during ischemia. The ability to integrate the advances of your medical research program with unique aspects of image fusion would significantly reduce the incidence of strokes at our hospital.

A five-day technical visit to your institution would provide me with useful information on the latest computer software that could greatly reduce examination time. Specialists in the field of nuclear medicine are well aware that ensuring continuous advances in computer software programs to alleviate brain ischemia depends on aggressive efforts such as those that are currently being made by your research group, to reduce the incidence of failure during brain operations.

If such a visit is acceptable to you, please let me which dates are convenient. A suggested itinerary would also be most appreciated, including time for discussion, and a tour of research facilities and accommodation. Of course, all expenses incurred during the visit will be covered by my organization. I look forward to your favorable reply.

Sincerely yours,

Larry Wang

Situation 2

Dear Mr. Wang,

I hope that you received my letter dated May 30, 2004 in which I invited you to accompany representatives of the Taiwan branch office of DISPLAY Corporation to Korea, to explore potential product development opportunities. I hope that you will be present for the signing of this memorandum of understanding (MOU) that would allow our two companies to engage in technical cooperation.

Our R&D Department strives to develop state-of-the-art technologies by continually upgrading our technological capabilities and innovation in product design. Our employees are highly motivated, as evidenced by our recent development of several TFT-LCD products. Our turning point in corporate growth arose from our ability to remain abreast of the latest technologies that leaders in the field adopted to ensure continued growth, research and development of products, and product innovation. Notable examples include 10.4-inch TFT-LCD products, as well as 2.45W and 3.5W-inch products for digital cameras, pocket TVs and TV cameras. While 5W, 6.4W, 6.5W, 7W, 8W and 10W inch offerings are for DVD, automobile navigation, portable TV, entertainment products and digital TV cameras, the 6.4W and 10.4W inch offerings are for industrial products.

The signing of this MOU at the Korean headquarters of DISPLAY Corporation would allow our Taiwan branch to participate in a technology transfer to help develop some of the above product technologies. Given our lack of expertise in developing TFT-LCD materials, this cooperative agreement will ultimately increase our brand awareness and market share. Again, your presence at this signing would be meaningful to both of our organizations given your expertise in this area.

We will provide roundtrip airfare and accommodation during your stay in Korea. Please let us know of a convenient time for the signing of this agreement. This trip will hopefully strengthen the collaborative ties between our organizations. Your prompt reply regarding the details of this upcoming visit would be most appreciated.

Sincerely yours,

Mary Lu

Situation 3

Dear Mr. Smith,

Thank you for allowing us to visit your laboratory on December 28th. As I mentioned in earlier correspondence, as a researcher at the Bioimage Laboratories at Yuanpei University of Science and Technology in Taiwan, I am concerned with upgrading the precision of bioimaging instruments, which Taiwan severely lacks. As a global leader in the development of medical instrumentation, your laboratory definitely has much to offer our country as we attempt to increase our research capacity in this area.

Allow me to brief you on our ongoing projects. We are currently engaged in the synchronization firing of neural networks and their aggregation in the dictyostelium system. These nonlinear complex systems have a large degree of freedom in which cooperative effects play a significant role. Often exhibiting unusual and physically interesting phenomena, these nonlinear complex systems are extensively adopted in materials science and exploited in particular technologies used in industrial applications. Hopefully, the opportunity to visit your laboratory and more thoroughly understand our organizational needs will lead to a technology transfer and/or a cooperative venture in the near future.

Having recently received training in how to use advanced computer software to operate the confocal scanning microscope and thus more thoroughly understand nerve cells, I am most impressed with your laboratory's development of computer software compatible with Linux and IDL. State-of-the-art design program applications could automate a part of the experimental procedure, saving us considerable laboratory resources. We are especially interested in discussing this issue with you, and especially current technologies used to study transgenic animals.

I am confident that the upcoming visit to your laboratory will pave the way for a further exchange of data on the aforementioned program developments. We are intent on establishing a long-term collaborative relationship with your laboratory. I look forward to meeting you in December.

Sincerely yours,

Jim Lin

B

What department at Kaohsiung Medical College does Larry belong to?

The Department of Nuclear Medicine

What has Mr. Push's research group expended considerable effort in doing?

Treating stroke patients using state-of-the-art instrumentation to solve brain ischemia-related problems

What does Larry hope to achieve in a five-day technical visit with the Head of Mr. Push's Nuclear Medicine Department, Dr. Smith, and his recently formed research group?

To learn of the latest medical technologies available to combat brain ischemia.

What has been successful adopted at UCLA?

The medical software program developed by your research group

What are specialists in the field of nuclear medicine are well aware of?

That ensuring continuous advances in computer software programs to alleviate brain ischemia depends on aggressive efforts such as those that are currently being made by Mr. Push's research group

C

Why did Mary invite Mr. Wang to accompany representatives of the Taiwan branch office of DISPLAY Corporation to Korea?

To explore potential product development opportunities

Why is the signing of this memorandum of understanding (MOU) important?

It will allow the two companies to engage in technical cooperation.

Why does Mary's R&D Department continuously upgrade its technological capabilities and innovation in product design?

To develop state-of-the-art technologies

Why does Mary believe that the employees in her R&D Department are highly motivated?

Owing to their recent development of several TFT-LCD products

Why is Mary optimistic about the signing of this MOU at the Korean headquarters of DISPLAY Corporation?

It will allow the Taiwan branch to participate in a technology transfer to help develop some of the above product technologies.

D

How does Mr. Smith's laboratory have much to offer Taiwan as it attempts to increase its research capacity in this area?

As a global leader in the development of medical instrumentation

How are these nonlinear complex systems extensively adopted?

In materials science and exploited in particular technologies used in industrial applications

How does Jim believe the opportunity to visit Mr. Smith's laboratory will be beneficial?

It will lead to a technology transfer and/or a cooperative venture in the near future.

How has Jim learned to operate the confocal scanning microscope and thus more thoroughly understand nerve cells?

By recently receiving training in how to use advanced computer software

How can Jim's laboratory save considerable resources?

State-of-the-art design program applications that can automate a part of the experimental procedure

E

How could the incidence of strokes at Larry's hospital's be significantly reduced?

By integrating the advances of your medical research program with unique aspects of image fusion

How was Mary's company able to achieve corporate growth?

Owing to its ability to remain abreast of the latest technologies that leaders in the field adopted to ensure continued growth, research and development of products, and product innovation

What is Jim's laboratory currently engaged in?

The synchronization firing of neural networks and their aggregation in the dictyostelium system

F

Situation 1

1.B   2.A   3.C   4.A   5.B

Situation 2

1.C   2.C   3.B   4.A   5.C

Situation 3

1.C   2.A   3.B   4.C

G

Situation 1

1.B   2.A   3.C   4.B   5.A   6.C   7.B   8.C   9.B   10.A   11.B   12.A   13.C
14.B   15.A   16.C   17.C   18.A   19.B   20.A   21.B   22.B   23.C   24.A
25.A

Situation 2

1.B   2.B   3.C   4.A   5.C   6.B   7.A   8.C   9.B   10.B   11.A   12.C   13.A
14.C   15.A   16.C   17.B   18.B   19.A

Situation 3

1.A   2.B   3.C   4.A   5.B   6.A   7.C   8.B   9.A   10.B   11.C   12.A   13.C
14.B

I

Situation 4

Dear Mr. Wilson,

I apologize for the delay in responding to your fax. In addition to preparing for our hospital's tenth anniversary, I have been assigned the task of procuring advanced MRI instrumentation for our hospital. In particular, I am evaluating the feasibility of using the 1.5 Tesla MRI in performing as many patient examinations daily as possible. During such examinations, determining the pulse sequences for various diseases is a priority. Importantly, integrating the MRI and PACS systems depends strongly on the communication gateway. Given the various MRI system designs from manufacturers such as Philips, Siemens and GE, I must determine which design concept most effectively meets our hospital's needs.

GE has arranged for me to travel to the United States next month and consult with its research group on our clinical needs. As I understand, your hospital uses the MRI and PACS systems manufactured by GE; the PACS system in your hospital is the same as that in our hospital. Therefore, on the final two days of my trip, I would like to visit your hospital and learn of your clinical experience of using this instrumentation. I have two specific concerns. First, with respect to the patient's work-list generated by the PACS server, I am interested in how to connect the broker to the MRI system through the hospital's Intranet. Second, with respect to GE's MRI system in which varying pulse sequences are developed (including multi-IR pulse sequence and DW imaging), I hope to learn of the correct parameter settings and the optimal coil.

I hope that this trip will strengthen the cooperative ties between our hospitals. I am open to any suggestions you may have regarding the itinerary or any materials you would like me to prepare prior to my visit.

Sincerely yours,

Karen Su

Situation 5

Dear Dr. Curtin,

Thank you for allowing us to observe firsthand some of the latest research at the

New York Clinical Cancer Center during our upcoming visit. We also greatly appreciated your agreeing to meet us at the Seasons Hotel at 10:00 on December 20th, where we hope to clarify our concerns regarding research in this area and potential areas of collaboration between our two organizations.

The New York Clinical Cancer (N.Y.C.C) Center is globally renowned for its therapeutic treatment of cancer, especially in the field of radiation therapy. As treatment planning for all forms of cancer has advanced, the N.Y.C.C Center has perfected a therapeutic strategy for breast cancer, cervical cancer and head and neck cancer. In Taiwan, head and neck cancer is the second most prevalent cancer. Unfortunately, irradiation treatment for head and neck cancer may damage normal tissues and cause loss of hearing, highlighting the necessity for precise treatment planning. NYCC Center has a reputation built on the fact that its cancer patients have the highest survival rate, and receive nurturing care following irradiation treatment. Such care is essential to elevating the quality of living for those patients. Hopefully, our upcoming visit will allow us to exchange relevant experiences of not only handling the side effects of treatment, but also providing better nurturing care to patients.

As is well known, a medical technician stands at the forefront of safeguarding a patient's health and well-being. A hospital offers a diverse array of services and support staff to effectively address the emotional, physical and societal challenges that patients might encounter while they receive cancer therapy. Besides providing state-of-the-art medical care, medical technicians actively encourage patients who are undergoing therapeutic treatment in a highly supportive environment to ensure the most productive outcome.

We hope that this upcoming visit will open doors for future cooperation between our two hospitals.

Sincerely yours,

Mark Wang

Situation 6

Dear Mr. Slater,

Thank you for your fax dated April 12, 2004. We greatly appreciate the help of Mr. David in arranging our visiting schedule.

Unfortunately, a slight change has been made in our visiting schedule, which will hopefully not inconvenience you. Our colleagues have decided to push back the tour to ensure they have sufficient time to obtain American visas. Therefore, I was wondering whether May 14-16 would be acceptable to you? If so, Dr. Jones can book his flight to arrive in the United States on May the 14th. Accordingly, could you please provide an itinerary that would allow our colleagues to receive their visas?

I would like to pose the following questions before our discussion on May 14, to give you plenty of time to prepare your responses:

1. What treatment planning software program does your Proton Treatment Center use to reduce errors in treatment plan data, especially when tumors are in an irregular area?

2. How does your Medical Center laboratory develop or implement a forecasting animal model based on a treatment database?

3. Taiwan will be establishing a proton treatment center in the near future. Specifically, Taiwan needs more long-term health care facilities, providing different services. What standard services does your Proton Treatment Center offer to classify long-term health care facilities in different countries?

If you could provide the travel party with an itinerary, I would like to make a hotel reservation for three single rooms (for two nights) from May 14 to May 16, 2005, and another single room (for one night) from May 15 to May 16, 2005. My colleagues and I will arrive at 9 p.m. on May 14, and will be registered under the names of Mr. Ting, Mrs. Lin, Mr. Lin (May 14 to May 16) and Ms. Chi (May 15 to May 16). We would appreciate your assistance in arranging hotel accommodations. I look forward to meeting you on May 14.

Sincerely yours,

Mary Lin

J

Why did Karen delay in responding to Mr. Wilson's fax?

In addition to preparing for her hospital's tenth anniversary, she has been assigned the task of procuring advanced MRI instrumentation for her hospital.

Why is Karen interested in the patient's work-list generated by the PACS server? To learn how to connect the broker to the MRI system through the hospital's Intranet

Why has GE arranged for Karen to travel to the United States next month?

To consult with its research group on her hospital's clinical needs

Why is Karen evaluating the feasibility of using the 1.5 Tesla MRI?

To perform as many patient examinations daily as possible

Why does Karen hope to learn of the correct parameter settings and the optimal coil?

To understand GE's MRI system in which varying pulse sequences are developed (including multi-IR pulse sequence and DW imaging)

K

What is the New York Clinical Cancer (N.Y.C.C) Center globally renowned for?

Its therapeutic treatment of cancer, especially in the field of radiation therapy

What concerns does Mark hope to clarify?

Concerns over research in this area and potential areas of collaboration between the two organizations

What has the N.Y.C.C Center perfected a therapeutic strategy for?

Breast cancer, cervical cancer and head and neck cancer

What is the second most prevalent cancer in Taiwan?

Head and neck cancer

What has NYCC Center built a reputation on?

The fact that its cancer patients have the highest survival rate, and receive nurturing

care following irradiation treatment

L

How can Mr. Slater help Mary's colleagues to receive their visas?

By providing an itinerary for their visit

How will Mary's colleagues have sufficient time to obtain American visas?

By pushing back the tour

How can Taiwan provide different services?

By establishing more long-term health care facilities

How does Mary want to prepare for her discussion Mr. Slater on May 14?

By posing the following questions

How does Mr. Slater's Proton Treatment Center attempt to reduce errors in treatment

plan data, especially when tumors are in an irregular area?

By using treatment planning software program

M

When is determining the pulse sequences for various diseases a priority?

During such examinations

Where is head and neck cancer the second most prevalent cancer?

In Taiwan

What was Mary wondering?

Whether May 14-16 would be acceptable to Mr. Slater?

N

Situation 4

1.C   2.A   3.B   4.B   5.A

Situation 5

1.A   2.C   3.B   4.C   5.A

Situation 6

1.B   2.A   3.C   4.A   5.B

O

Situation 4

1.B   2.C   3.A   4.B   5.C   6.C   7.C   8.B   9.C   10.A   11.B

Situation 5

1.B   2.C   3.B   4.C   5.A   6.C   7.A   8.B   9.C   10.B   11.C   12.A   13.C
14.A   15.C   16.B   17.B   18.C   19.A

Situation 6

1.B   2.C   3.B   4.C   5.A   6.C   7.A   8.C   9.B   10.A

P

Exercise 1

1.h 2.d 3.a 4.j 5.c 6.b 7.i 8.g 9.e 10.f

Exercise 2

1.d 2.a 3.f 4.g 5.c 6.b 7.e

Exercise 3

1.h 2.e 3.b 4.j 5.a 6.g 7.c 8.d 9.f 10.i

Exercise 4

1.b 2.e 3.a 4.d 5.c

Exercise 5

1.d 2.a 3.f 4.c 5.b 6.g 7.e

Exercise 6

1.g 2.c 3.i 4.b 5.h 6.k 7.d 8.l 9.a 10.e 11.f 12.j

Exercise 7

1.f 2.a 3.h 4.b 5.j 6.g 7.i 8.e 9.d 10.c

Exercise 8

1.e 2.g 3.a 4.c 5.f 6.b 7.d

A

Situation 1

Dear Mr. Smith,

Our hospital constantly strives to promote its long-term care facilities and services, and offers medical treatment to meet the demands of the growing elderly population. They require urgent medical treatment daily, with efficient follow-up services, including discharge planning, respiratory care, nursing facilities and home care as part of a visiting nursing program. Despite our aspirations, our hospital is lacking in many of the above areas, explaining the lack of confidence among patients and their relatives in the quality of medical care offered by Taiwanese hospitals. Given your organization's extensive experience in implementing long-term care programs, we hope that you could recommend a consultant who could instruct our hospital staff on the following topics.

1. How do governmental authorities in your country implement long-term care national policies?

2. How do practitioners assess the various levels of long-term care services provided to the nation's elderly?

3. What measures can be adopted to control the quality of long term care services?

4. How is national health insurance integrated into the provision of long term care services?

We will provide roundtrip airfare and accommodations during the consultancy period. I advise that the consultant stay here for an additional week or so to enjoy some of the sights that Taiwan has to offer. Once final arrangements are made, please advise us of the consultant's flight details so that we can meet him/her at the airport. Please ask your consultant to send us his/her lecture titles and handouts before January 10, 2005 so that we will have sufficient time to make copies and appropriate arrangements. I also need his/her curriculum vitae, including, NAME, DATE OF BIRTH, PLACE OF BIRTH, NATIONALITY, MARITAL STATUS,

ACADEMIC QUALIFICATIONS, PROFESSIONAL EXPERIENCE, SCIENTIFIC ACHIEVEMENTS, CURRENT SCIENTIFIC ACTIVITIES, OTHER SCIENCE-RELATED ACTIVITIES AND SELECTED PUBLICATIONS.

Each lecture will last two hours, and the consultant will be reimbursed with a speech honorarium. The consultancy period will hopefully begin before February 2005. We welcome any suggestions or comments that you might have regarding the above proposal.

Sincerely yours,

Suzy Chen

Situation 2

Dear Dr. Lin,

In light of your renowned research and contributions in the field of treatment planning systems, we would like to formally invite you to serve as an Invited Speaker at the upcoming Radiotherapy Oncology Conference. We hope your lecture will include a discussion of the current developmental trends in radiotherapy and radiation protection. This conference is to be held at the International Conference Hall at National Taiwan University in Taipei, Taiwan, on April 23, 2004.

The following is a tentative schedule for your visit:

April 23, 2004: Arrival in Taiwan at Chiang Kai Shek International, and transit to hotel accommodation

April 24, 2004: Tour of Proton Therapy Cancer Center

Lecture on a special topic in radiotherapy and radiation protection: 2 to 3 hrs

April 25, 2004: Discussion of how to assess current developments in proton therapy

April 26, 2004: Discussion of how to improve the quality of proton therapy

April 27, 2004: Discussion of the role of radiation protection in proton therapy

April 28, 2004: Sightseeing of Taipei's cultural attractions, as arranged by the faculty and the staff at National Taiwan University

April 28, 2004: Return to the United States

Any comments or suggestions regarding the above itinerary or topics of discussion would be most appreciated. If you find the above itinerary acceptable, please send your lecture topics to Dr. Ting, before February 28, 2004. We will then have sufficient time to make copies and appropriate arrangements. I also need your curriculum vitae, including name, date of birth, nationality, academic qualifications, professional experiences, scientific achievements, current scientific activities, other science-related activities and selected publications.

Please pay in advance for your roundtrip airfare and other incidental expenses, and hold onto those receipts for reimbursement prior to your departure from Taiwan. According to our government's tax system, a technical service fee is subject to a 20% tax levy. You must make a copy of the receipt and the counterfoil for us to reimburse you for transportation.

Please do not hesitate to let me know if you have any concerns and suggestions.

Your contribution to this conference would definitely benefit all of the participants.

Sincerely yours,

Marvin Lu

Situation 3

Dear Dr. Jones,

We are pleased to hear that you will be returning to Taiwan next month to lecture on recent advances in diagnosing severe ischemia. The incidence of brain strokes among the younger population has increased in Taiwan. Many medical technologies have emerged, aimed at resolving salvageable tissue and irreversible damage. Let me briefly describe the severity of strokes among the younger aged population. The younger population dominates the country's economic activities, so increases in ischemia or severe brain strokes strain economic resources. Additionally, the island's national defense heavily relies on its youth: all males perform nearly two years of compulsory military service. Moreover, diagnosing cardiac-vessel-cerebral disease requires expensive medical instrumentation, with related medical insurance coverage that is too expensive for most young people.

In light of your renowned research on the role of SPECT and PET scan in nuclear medicine and pharmaceutical-based nuclear medicine, we would like to invite you to serve as an Invited Speaker at National Taiwan University, which is to be held on December 15, 2004. Your lecture will hopefully cover recent trends in SPECT and PET-CT technologies. Your presence at this event would indeed be an honor for us. We will provide a roundtrip airfare ticket and accommodation during your stay in Taiwan. I hope that you can allot extra time to see some of the cultural wonders of Taiwan. Please advise us of your flight number so that we can meet you at Chiang Kai Shek International Airport in Taoyuan. Please also send us your lecture title and outline, along with references, so that we will have sufficient time to make copies. I look forward to hearing from you soon.

Sincerely yours,

Christi Fung

B

What does Suzy's hospital constantly strive to do?

Promote its long-term care facilities and services

What does the growing elderly population require?

Urgent medical treatment daily, with efficient follow-up services, including discharge planning, respiratory care, nursing facilities and home care as part of a visiting nursing program

What do many patients and their relatives lack?

Confidence in the quality of medical care offered by Taiwanese hospitals

What will Suzy's organization provide the consultant?

Roundtrip airfare and accommodations during the consultancy period

What does Mr. Smith's organization have extensive experience in?

Implementing long-term care programs

C

Why does Marvin want to formally to invite Dr. Lin to serve as an Invited Speaker at the upcoming Radiotherapy Oncology Conference?

In light of his renowned research and contributions in the field of treatment planning systems

Why is a discussion to be held on April 25, 2004?

On how to assess current developments in proton therapy

Why is a discussion to be held on April 27, 2004?

On the role of radiation protection in proton therapy

Why should Dr. Lin's lecture topics be sent to Dr. Ting before February 28, 2004? To allow sufficient time to make copies and appropriate arrangements.

Why must Dr. Lin make a copy of the receipt and the counterfoil?

To be reimbursed for transportation

D

Which part of the population in Taiwan has the incidence of brain strokes increased?
The younger population

Which technologies have emerged, aimed at resolving salvageable tissue and irreversible damage?
Medical ones

Which age group dominates the country's economic activities?
The younger population

Which part of the population performs nearly two years of compulsory military service?
All males

Which topic does Christi hope that Dr. Jones's lecture will cover?
Recent trends in SPECT and PET-CT technologies

E

How long will each lecture last?
Two hours

What does Marvin hope that Dr. Lin's lecture will include?
A discussion of the current developmental trends in radiotherapy and radiation protection

Why would Christi like to invite Dr. Jones to serve as an Invited Speaker at National Taiwan University?

In light of his renowned research on the role of SPECT and PET scan in nuclear medicine and pharmaceutical-based nuclear medicine

F

Situation 1

1.C   2.A   3.A   4.C   5.B

Situation 2

1.B   2.A   3.C   4.B   5.A

Situation 3

1.B   2.A   3.B   4.C   5.A

G

Situation 1

1.C   2.A   3.B   4.A   5.C   6.B   7.A   8.C   9.B   10.A   11.C   12.B

Situation 2

1.C   2.B   3.C   4.A   5.C   6.B   7.A   8.B

Situation 3

1.B   2.C   3.B   4.C   5.A   6.B   7.C   8.B   9.A   10.C   11.A

I

Situation 4

Dear Dr. Chang,

Quite some time has passed since you visited our laboratories in June of 2004. I hope that all is going well at your institute. With regard to the scientific and non-scientific collaboration between China and Taiwan, R.O.C., as outlined in our signing of a memorandum of understanding (MOU) between our two organizations on research into traditional Chinese medicine-related topics, the time seems right for the Yuanpei University of Science and Technology Research Institute and National

Tsing Hua University to begin collaborative activities. As I mentioned in our earlier conversation, we could begin by exchanging scientific experts. I would thus like to propose the following.

Please recommend one scientific expert to serve as a short-term consultant at Yuanpei University of Science and Technology. Naturally, we would like someone whose expertise is highly relevant to the following subjects.

1. Proficiency in the latest technologies related to traditional Chinese medicine.
2. Solid background in designing and integrating approaches to facilitating commercial applications of traditional Chinese medicine.

This expert must also be fluent in English and Chinese (and hopefully have a fundamental grasp of the Taiwanese dialect). We hope that he/she will be able to lecture on the following topics during his or her roughly two-week stay at our laboratory.

1. Recent advances in research on Chinese herbal medicine at Yuanpei University of Science and Technology (2 hours)
2. Technological advances in traditional Chinese pharmacology (3 hours)
3. Introduction to chemical components in Chinese herbal medicine (3 hours)
4. GC mass machine-related applications in Chinese herbal medicine

We will offer a round-trip airfare from China to Taipei, and accommodation in Taiwan during the consultancy period. An honorarium will also be provided for the seminars. If you have such a person available or if you have any comments regarding this proposal, please let us know at your earliest convenience.

Sincerely yours,

Marty Wang

Situation 5

Dear Dr. Lin,

Quite some time has passed since you visited our laboratories in December 2004.

I hope you can come to our laboratories again. Once the schedule has been finalized, I will reserve a hotel room for you. The average price of a single room in Hsinchu ranges from US$ 100 to US$ 150.

If you decide to come, please purchase your roundtrip ticket (business class) in advance and save the receipt for reimbursement. I should also mention that Taiwan's government levies a technical service fee tax of 20%.

During your stay, we hope to consult with you on enzyme-linked immunosobent assay (ELISA), with particular focus on the following areas;

   a. how to produce the cortisol antibody;

   b. how to produce the HRP;

   c. how to ameliorate a defect in enzyme-linked immunosobent assay (ELISA);

   d. a brief review of the status of your current research;

   e. explanation of developmental trends in the biotech sector and related manufacturing, and

   f. descriptions of your previous research collaborations with the biotech sector.

For your participation in this event, we will offer round-trip airfare from New York to Taipei, as well as accommodation in Taiwan during the consultancy period. An honorarium for the seminars will also be given.

If you have any comments regarding the above proposal or topics to be added for discussion, please let us know at your earliest convenience.

Sincerely yours,

Christine Huang

Situation 6

Dear Professor Lin,

   Given your eminence in the field of marketing, we would like formally invite you to participate as an Invited Speaker at the upcoming Internet Marketing Symposium to be held at Yuanpei University of Science and Technology (Taiwan) on February

10, 2005. We hope that your lecture will cover recent trends and developments in Internet-based advertising and marketing strategies.

As February is normally a busy month as everyone prepares for Chinese New Year, I would suggest rescheduling the symposium to March 22nd. I advise you to extend your visit until March 26 to give you time to tour some of Taiwan's areas of natural beauty.

The organizing committee will provide a roundtrip airfare ticket, hotel accommodation and a speech honorarium for your lecture. Please let us know as soon as possible whether you will be able to accept our invitation and if this change in dates is acceptable to you. If so, please send us your lecture title and related handouts before December 31, 2004. I will be in touch with you shortly regarding further details of the symposium and travel arrangements. Your contribution to the symposium would definitely benefit all of the participants.

I anxiously look forward to your favorable reply.

Sincerely yours,

John Su

J

How long has it been since Dr. Chang visited Marty's laboratories?

Quite some time

How was the scientific and non-scientific collaboration between China and Taiwan, R.O.C. initiated?

In the signing of a memorandum of understanding (MOU) between the two organizations

How should the two organization begin their collaborative activities?

By exchanging scientific experts

How could the scientific expert's solid background in designing and integrating approaches benefit Yuanpei University of Science and Technology?
By facilitating commercial applications of traditional Chinese medicine

How will Yuanpei University of Science and Technology compensate the scientific expert for the consultancy period?
A round-trip airfare from China to Taipei, and accommodation in Taiwan

K

What will Christine do once the schedule has been finalized?
She will reserve a hotel room for Dr. Lin.

What is the range for the average price of a single hotel room in Hsinchu?
From US$ 100 to US$ 150

For what amount does Taiwan's government levy a technical service fee tax?
20%

What does Christine's laboratory want to consult with Dr. Lin on?
Enzyme-linked immunosobent assay (ELISA)

What will Christine's laboratory offer Dr. Lin for participation in this event?
Round-trip airfare from New York to Taipei, as well as accommodation in Taiwan during the consultancy period

L

Why does John want to invite Professor Lin to participate as an Invited Speaker at the upcoming Internet Marketing Symposium?

Because of his eminence in the field of marketing

Why is February normally a busy month?
Everyone is preparing for Chinese New Year.

Why does John advise Professor Lin to extend his visit until March 26?
To give him time to tour some of Taiwan's areas of natural beauty

Why will John be in touch with Professor Lin shortly?
Regarding further details of the symposium and travel arrangements

Why does John suggest rescheduling the symposium to March 22nd?
Because February is normally a busy month as everyone prepares for Chinese New Year

M

What must the scientific expert be proficient in?
The latest technologies related to traditional Chinese medicine

How long has it been since Dr. Lin visited Christine's laboratories?
Quite some time

What will the organizing committee provide Professor Lin with?
Roundtrip airfare, hotel accommodation and a speech honorarium for his lecture

N

Situation 4

1.C　2.B　3.A　4.C　5.B

Situation 5

1.A 2.C 3.B 4.A 5.C

Situation 6

1.B 2.C 3.A 4.C 5.B

O

Situation 4

1.B 2.A 3.C 4.C 5.B 6.A 7.B 8.A

Situation 5

1.B 2.A 3.C 4.C 5.A 6.C 7.A

Situation 6

1.C 2.C 3.A 4.C 5.B 6.C 7.B 8.A

P

Exercise 1

1.f 2.h 3.a 4.b 5.c 6.i 7.e 8.d 9.g

Exercise 2

1.f 2.a 3.i 4.c 5.k 6.h 7.d 8.g 9.e 10.b 11.j

Exercise 3

1.g 2.j 3.a 4.d 5.h 6.b 7.k 8.c 9.e 10.i 11.f 12.l

Exercise 4

1.h 2.d 3.j 4.a 5.g 6.i 7.e 8.b 9.c 10.f

Exercise 5

1.e 2.h 3.b 4.c 5.a 6.i 7.g 8.f 9.d

Exercise 6

1.c　2.e　3.b　4.a　5.d

Answer Key
Arranging Travel Itineraries
旅行安排信函

A

Situation 1

Dear Professor Coutrakon,

Thank you for agreeing to participate as an invited speaker at the upcoming seminar to be held in the Institute of Medical Imagery at Yuanpei University of Science and Technology (YUST) on December 22-31, 2004. As eminent scholars in dosimetry-related research, my academic advisor Professor Hsu, Professor Tung and you, will be the keynote speakers for this event. The seminar will focus on three topics; (a) comparison of microdosimetry spectra and biological efficacy during proton beam treatment; (b) developmental trends in proton therapy, heavily charged particles therapy, fast neutron therapy and boron neutron capture therapy, and (c) clinical experiences of the Proton Therapy Center at Loma Linda University.

A tentative schedule of your visit follows.

Dec. 22, 2004 (Wed): Arrive in Taiwan and meet Mr. Chang at Chiang Kai Shek International Airport for transit to Hsinchu.

Dec. 23, 2004 (Thu): Tour the Institute of Medical Imagery at YUST.

Dec. 24, 2004 (Fri): Tour the Institute of Nuclear Science at National Tsing Hua University.

Dec. 25, 2004 (Sat): Attend the seminar at the International Conference Hall at YUST. Deliver an introductory lecture on cyclotrons and synchrotrons.

Dec. 26, 2004 (Sun): Spend free time visiting cultural attractions in Taipei.

Dec. 27, 2004 (Mon): Attend a seminar in the Radiation Detection Laboratory at YUST. Deliver a lecture on the current status of proton therapy research.

Dec. 28, 2004 (Tue): Attend a seminar at the Radiation Detection Laboratory at YUST. Deliver a lecture on a clinical case that involves proton therapy.

Dec. 29, 2004 (Wed): Attend a seminar in the Radiation Detection Laboratory at YUST. Discuss collaborative opportunities in dosimetry-related research between the Proton Therapy Center at Loma Linda University and the Institute of Medical Imagery at YUST.

Dec. 30, 2004 (Thu): Spend free time sightseeing at Hsinchu Science-based Industrial Park.

Dec. 31, 2004 (Fri): Return to the United States.

If you have any suggestions regarding the above schedule and lecture topics, please do not hesitate to contact me. The average price of a single room hotel room in Hsinchu is from US$200 to US$250 daily. Keep your receipts so that we can reimburse you prior to your departure from Taiwan. I look forward to meeting you.

Sincerely yours,

Connie Li

Situation 2

Dear Mr. Curtin,

Thank you for accepting our invitation to come to Taiwan for consultation on our latest research efforts. I was most impressed with the lecture you delivered during The Annual Meeting of Radiology Therapy in 1998. Your address to members of The Association of Radiology Technologists of the Republic of China will be a major highlight of the upcoming event. I am responsible for arranging the details of your visit.

The following is a tentative schedule for your upcoming visit to Taiwan.

1/10: Arrive at the Chiang Kai Shek International Airport in Taoyuan for transit to the Hyatt Hotel in Taipei.

1/11: Meet with Dr. Chen and myself at 10:00 am in the hotel lobby.

1/12: Deliver the keynote speech at the Annual Meeting of The Association of

Radiology Technologists of the Republic of China.

1/13: Tour the northern coast of Taiwan and enjoy some traditional Chinese tea.

1/14: Lecture the staff and researchers at the Institute of Medical Imagery at Yuanpei University of Science and Technology on recent advances in IMRT for breast cancer and head and neck cancer.

1/15: Return to the United States on China Airlines at 3:00 pm.

We are interested in your recent research on the latest advances in IMRT for breast cancer as well as head and neck cancer. We also hope that we will have sufficient time to discuss advanced cancer therapeutic treatments. In particular, we will raise the following questions during our meeting.

1. Could you share your experiences of diagnosing and treating cancer at Stanford University?

2. In what ways do the latest advances in IMRT represent improvements over other therapeutic planning systems?

3. What are the clinical implications for implementing the latest advances in IMRT when treating breast and head and neck cancer?

I hope that the above questions will give you a clearer idea of our intention to improve medical services at our hospital and implement a state-of-the-art therapeutic planning system.

Sincerely yours,

Donald Wang

Situation 3

Dear Dr. Kawasaki,

Recognizing your distinguished contributions in the field of IMRT, we would like to formally invite you to participate as an Invited Speaker at the upcoming meeting of the Chinese Association of Radiological Technologists. We hope that your lecture will include a discussion of the latest developments in radiation treatment used in

IMRT. We will provide a roundtrip airfare and accommodation during your stay. I suggest you to stay here for one week to enjoy some of the sights that Taiwan has to offer. Please advise us of your flight number so that we can meet you at the airport.

Thank you for your faxed response regarding cooperation between our two organizations. We generally agree with your proposal. However, I would suggest that you visit in February 2005 because we are usually quite busy during the month of January in preparation for Chinese New Year. A tentative agenda for Dr. Brown's visit is as follows.

Feb. 6, 2005 (Sun): Arrive in Taiwan at Chiang Kai International Airport and meet colleagues for transit to hotel

Feb. 7, 2005 (Mon): Meet with CART staff members and discuss Dr. Kawasaki's schedule.

Feb. 8, 2005 (Tue): Consult with staff of Radiation Treatment Laboratory on reciprocity-related topics.

Feb. 9, 2005 (Wed): Lecture on quality control for IMRT.

Feb. 10, 2005 (Thu) to Feb. 11, 2005 (Fri): Enjoy a tour of cultural and historical sites in Taiwan, arranged by staff members.

Feb. 12, 2005 (Sat): Discuss potential collaborative activities of our two organizations in the area of radiation treatment.

Feb. 13, 2005 (Sun): Return to Japan

The above itinerary and consultation topics are only tentative. We welcome your feedback if you feel any changes should be made. Any comments or suggestions regarding the aforementioned proposal would be greatly appreciated. If the proposal is acceptable, please send us your presentation topics and curriculum vitae as soon as possible.

Sincerely yours,

Jessamine Su

B

What has Professor Coutrakon agreed to participate as?
An invited speaker at the upcoming seminar to be held in the Institute of Medical Imagery at Yuanpei University of Science and Technology (YUST)

What area is Professor Coutrakon an eminent scholar in?
Dosimetry-related research

What has Connie prepared?
A tentative schedule Professor Coutrakon's visit

What institute will Professor Coutrakon tour at National Tsing Hua University?
The Institute of Nuclear Science

What will Professor Coutrakon spend his free time doing in Taipei?
Visiting cultural attractions

C

Why is Dr. Curtin invited to come to Taiwan?
For consultation

Why is Donald writing Dr. Curtin?
He is responsible for arranging the details of his visit.

Why is Mr. Curtin's recent research on the latest advances in IMRT important?
For breast cancer as well as head and neck cancer

Why does Donald hope to have sufficient time with Mr. Curtin?

To discuss advanced cancer therapeutic treatments

Why was Donald impressed with Mr. Curtin?
Because of the lecture he delivered during The Annual Meeting of Radiology Therapy in 1998

D

How has Dr. Kawasaki contributed to radiological technologists?
In the field of IMRT

How would Jessamine like Dr. Kawasaki to participate at the upcoming meeting of the Chinese Association of Radiological Technologists?
As an Invited Speaker

How will the organizing committee compensate Dr. Kawasaki for participating at the upcoming meeting?
It will provide a roundtrip airfare and accommodation during your stay.

How does Jessamine suggest that Dr. Kawasaki enjoy some of the sights that Taiwan has to offer?
By staying here for one week

How could the two organizations potentially collaborate?
In the area of radiation treatment

E

Who is Connie's academic advisor?
Professor Hsu

What will be a major highlight of the upcoming event?

Mr. Curtin's address to members of The Association of Radiology Technologists of the Republic of China

What are only tentative?

The above itinerary and consultation topics

F

Situation 1

1.B 2.C 3.B 4.A 5.C

Situation 2

1.B 2.C 3.A 4.B 5.A

Situation 3

1.B 2.C 3.A 4.C 5.B

G

Situation 1

1.C 2.A 3.C 4.C 5.B 6.A 7.B

Situation 2

1.B 2.A 3.A 4.C 5.B 6.B 7.C

Situation 3

1.B 2.C 3.A 4.A 5.C 6.A 7.C 8.A

I

Situation 4

Dear Mr. Armstrong,

Thank you for agreeing to serve as an invited speaker at the upcoming marketing seminar to be held at Yuanpei University of Science and Technology on March 9,

2005. The seminar will concentrate on (a) effective management strategies to achieve marketing goals and (b) advanced product development strategies and the product life cycle. A brief outline of the seminar is as follows.

Agenda

Date	Morning 9 am — noon	Afternoon 1:30 pm — 4:30 pm	Evening 7 pm — 9 pm
January the 3rd (Monday)	Overseas and local scholars arrive for registration		Taiwanese Film Festival
January the 4th (Tuesday)	First lecture: Rey Chow	First lecture: Nancy Armstrong	Taiwanese Film Festival
January the 5th (Wednesday)	Second lecture: Rey Chow	Rey Chow responds to questions: chaired by Shi Pi-fang and Wu Chen-zu	Taiwanese Film Festival
January the 6th (Thursday)	Third lecture: Nancy Armstrong speech	Nancy Armstrong responds to questions: chaired by Shi Pi-fang and Wu Chen-zu	Taiwanese Film Festival
January the 7th (Friday)	First lecture: Meaghan Morris	First lecture: Kaja Silverman	Taiwanese Film Festival
January the 8th (Saturday)	Free activity		Taiwanese Film Festival
January the 9th (Sunday)	Conclusion and Adjournment		Taiwanese Film Festival

The organizing committee will provide a roundtrip airfare (business class), hotel accommodation during your stay and a speech honorarium for each lecture. Let me know if you have any questions regarding the above itinerary. Thank you again for your participation in this event. Your contribution will definitely benefit all of the participants.

Sincerely yours,

Shane Huang

Situation 5

Dear Professor Daming,

Given your celebrated research and contributions in the field of medical quality management, we would like formally to invite you to participate as an Invited Speaker at a symposium to be held in Taiwan on current trends in medical quality management. The symposium will be held in the International Conference Hall of the Municipal WanFang Hospital in Taipei on January the 15th, 2005. A suggested schedule for the upcoming symposium is as follows.

Time	
08:30—09:00	Registration
09:00—09:20	Professor Daming delivers the opening address.
09:20—10:20	A discussion is held on the systematic monitoring of medical quality systems
10:20—10:30	Roundtable discussion (Q&A)
10:30—10:50	Refreshments
10:50—11:50	Lecture on the role of medicine and disease in providing quality care
11:50—12:00	Roundtable discussion (Q & A)
12:00—1:30	Lunch
1:30—2:20	Lecture on a system for monitoring health insurance premiums
2:20—2:30	Roundtable discussion (Q & A)
2:30—3:20	Lecture on medical quality control and patient security
3:20—3:30	Roundtable discussion (Q & A)
3:30—3:50	Refreshments
3:50—4:40	Lecture on recent trends in Taiwanese medical quality control
4:40—4:50	Final roundtable discussion (Q & A)
4:50	Adjournment

We will provide a roundtrip airfare and accommodation during your stay. I suggest you to stay in Taiwan following the end of the symposium to enjoy some of the natural and cultural wonders that the island offers. Once you have confirmed your trip, let us know your flight details so we can meet you at the airport.

Please send me your lecture title and related handouts by December 30th, 2004, so that we will have ample time for translation. Also, please send us your curriculum vitae, including your name, date of birth, nationality, marital status, academic qualifications, professional experiences, scientific achievements and selected publications.

I look forward to seeing you.

Sincerely yours,

Jeannie Lin

Situation 6

Dear Mrs. Perez,

　Thank you for your positive reply to our inviting Dr. Kanbinsky as a guest speaker at the PIDA technical seminar on current trends in laser technology. A tentative agenda for this upcoming trip is as follows.

Jan. 30, 2005 (Sun):	Dr. Kanbinsky and Mrs. Kanbinsky arrive at Chiang-Kai Shek International Airport (Flight details: CX461, 21:00)
Jan. 31, 2005 (Mon):	Meet with PIDA employees and discuss seminar topics
Feb. 1, 2005 (Tue):	Deliver lecture on current trends in display technologies
Feb. 2, 2005 (Wed):	Deliver morning lecture on difficulties with, and solutions to problems of producing blue light Deliver afternoon lecture on laboratory achievement
Feb. 3, 2005 (Thu):	Deliver morning lecture on TFT-LCD panel applications Deliver afternoon lecture on a special topic
Feb. 4, 2005 (Fri):	Deliver morning lecture on LED - backlight sources for cellular phones Participate in afternoon panel discussion
Feb. 5, 2005 (Sat.):	Sightseeing (arranged by PIDA staff members)
Feb. 6, 2005 (Sun):	Sightseeing (arranged by PIDA staff members)
Feb. 7, 2005 (Mon):	Visit PIDA at Ming Chuan E. Rd., Taipei,
Feb. 8, 2005 (Tue):	Meet with PIDA president Dr. Shih on future cooperative opportunities
Feb. 9, 2005 (Wed):	Dr. Kanbinsky and Mrs. Kanbinsky return to Holland

(CX759, 12:00)

The schedule and topics can be modified if necessary. Any comments or suggestions regarding this proposal would be greatly appreciated. If the proposal is acceptable, please send us the content of your presentation and your curriculum vitae.

Sincerely yours,

Jim Wu

P.S.: Options for the entertainment program: Feb. 8 will be Chinese New Year, so we strongly recommend that Dr. Kanbinsky and Mrs. Kanbinsky stay for at least two days to experience traditional Asian culture firsthand.

J

When will Nancy Armstrong deliver her first lecture?

January the 4th

When will Rey Chow deliver her second lecture?

January the 5th

When will overseas and local scholars arrive for registration?

January the 3rd

When will Meaghan Morris deliver her first lecture?

January the 7th

When will the participants attend the Taiwanese Film Festival?

Each evening, from 7 pm — 9 pm

K

What contributions has Professor Daming made?

In the field of medical quality management

What is the topic of the symposium to be held in Taiwan?

Current trends in medical quality management

What time will the first roundtable discussion be held?

10:20－10:30

What time will lunch be held?

12:00－1:30

What will the organizing committee provide Professor Daming with during his stay?

Roundtrip airfare and accommodation

L

Why is Jim thanking Mrs. Perez?

For her positive reply to the invitation of Dr. Kanbinsky as a guest speaker at the PIDA technical seminar on current trends in laser technology

Why will Dr. Kanbinsky meet with PIDA employees on Jan. 31, 2005?

To discuss seminar topics

Why will Dr. Kanbinsky deliver a lecture on Feb. 1, 2005?

To discuss current trends in display technologies

Why will Dr. Kanbinsky deliver a morning lecture on Feb. 4, 2005?

To discuss LED - backlight sources for cellular phones

Why will Dr. Kanbinsky meet with PIDA president Dr. Shih on Feb. 8, 2005?

To discuss future cooperative opportunities

M

What will definitely benefit all of the participants?

Mr. Armstrong's contribution

Why does Jenny suggest that Professor Daming stay in Taiwan following the end of the symposium?

To enjoy some of the natural and cultural wonders that the island offers

What does Jim strongly recommend?

That Dr. Kanbinsky and Mrs. Kanbinsky stay for at least two days to experience traditional Asian culture firsthand

N

Situation 4

1.B   2.A   3.C   4.B   5.A

Situation 5

1.C   2.B   3.C   4.A   5.B

Situation 6

1.B   2.C   3.A   4.C   5.B

O

Situation 4

1.B   2.B   3.A   4.C   5.B   6.C

Situation 5

1.B　2.C　3.A　4.B　5.A　6.C　7.B　8.A　9.B　10.A

Situation 6

1.B　2.C　3.C　4.B　5.A　6.C

P

Exercise 1

1.d　2.f　3.a　4.b　5.c　6.e

Exercise 2

1.f　2.m　3.h　4.k　5.i　6.l　7.e　8.g　9.j　10.b　11.c　12.a　13.d　14.n

Exercise 3

1.e　2.a　3.d　4.f　5.g　6.c　7.b

Answer Key
Requesting Information
資訊請求信函

A

Situation 1

Dear Dr. Saaty,

As a graduate student at the Institute of Business Management at Yuanpei University of Science and Technology, I am very interested in your research on correlation data. Given your pioneering work on decision theory, the Analytic Hierarchy Process (AHP) and the Analytic Network Process (ANP), I have read many of your published articles and am well aware of your more than 12 books on these topics. I particularly enjoyed your articles, "Decision Making—The Analytic Hierarchy and Network Processes (AHP/ANP)", "Fundamentals of the Analytic Network Process: Dependence and Feedback in Decision-Making with a Single Network", "Theory of the Analytic Hierarchy and Analytic Network Process—Examples Part 2.2" and "Decision-making with the AHP: Why is the Principal Eigenvector Necessary?".

As is well known, AHP has not only been extensively used in decision making in business, industry and government, but has also been often applied to multi-criteria decision problems that are large-scale and multiparty-oriented. ANP has played a major role in various decisions, involving benefits, costs, opportunities, potential risks and the forecasting of outcomes.

I am interested in the following.

1. AHP decision-making procedures adopted in business to achieve success;

2. Some of the assumptions you made when deriving the AHP model;

3. The relationship between AHP and ANP.

I would also appreciate your sending me the first article that you wrote on AHP.

Thank you in advance for your kind assistance.

Sincerely yours,

Ashley Wu

Situation 2

Dear Ms. Beatrice,

I listened intently to your recent lecture entitled, "Nurse Staffing, Organizational Characteristics and Patient Outcome" at the symposium held in Taiwan on March 24-26, 2004. I was fascinated with the issues you raised about mortality/failure to rescue, length of stay (LOS), infection rates, pressure ulcers, falls, post-surgery complications, patient satisfaction, model of care and nursing considerations. As you know, efforts to ensure quality health care and patient safety have led to the establishment of health care systems worldwide. In such systems, while nurses are indispensable in significantly reducing the likelihood of clinical errors, shortages in nursing personnel threaten quality care and patient safety. For instance, low nurse-patient ratios are linked to higher mortality rates. Although such data for Taiwanese hospitals are scarce, I am actively engaged in researching related topics.

Could you pass on to me pertinent data regarding the adverse impact of nursing shortages on health care in the United States? I would be delighted to send you any pertinent data from Taiwan as part of an exchange of information.

Thank you in advance for your careful consideration. I look forward to your favorable reply.

Sincerely yours,

Matt Fung

Situation 3

Dear Professor Jones,

I was very impressed by your lecture last month at the Intellectual Capital Measurement Symposium in Taipei. Having carefully read the article, " Intellectual Capital Measurement: Introducing and Comparing Various IC Measurements" , which you published in the conference proceedings, I was motivated to write to you for further details on particular points.

I am pursuing a Master's degree in the Institute of Business Management at Yuanpei University of Science and Technology. My Master's thesis is on measuring the intellectual capital of certain enterprises. As Taiwan's industrial infrastructure is being transformed into a hi-tech infrastructure, an increasing fraction of companies' capital is intellectual, and is intangible. This fact explains the urgency to measure the intellectual capital value of hi-tech firms. This area of research is in its infancy in Taiwan and, hopefully, my work will contribute to this evolving field. I was wondering whether you could send me literature or materials in the following areas.

A brief introduction to intellectual capital;

A summary of previous efforts to measure intellectual capital;

A brief introduction of the intellectual capital valuation system in the United States;

A brief introduction to the financing mechanism adopted in the United States;

A brief introduction to financing mechanisms in other countries;

A brief summary of future trends in intellectual capital.

My graduate school research focuses on intellectual capital of on-line gaming companies in an attempt to identify its essential components. I am especially interested in adopting the perspective of a loaning bank institution to assess the intellectual capital assets of an on-line gaming company and, then, to compare the intellectual capital of a bank with that of such a company.

I hope that you will be able to provide the above information. Also, if you find my area of research compatible with that of yours, perhaps we could collaborate in some way in the near future. I would be more than happy to provide you with pertinent data regarding Taiwanese companies. Thank you in advance for your kind assistance. I look forward to our future cooperative efforts.

Sincerely yours,

Mary Wang

B

What institute does Ashley belong to at Yuanpei University of Science and Technology?

The Institute of Business Management

What aspect of Dr. Saaty's research is Ashley very interested in?

His research on correlation data

What areas has Dr. Saaty conducted pioneering work on?

Decision theory, the Analytic Hierarchy Process (AHP) and the Analytic Network Process (ANP)

What is Ashley well aware of?

Dr. Satty's more than 12 books on decision theory, the Analytic Hierarchy Process (AHP) and the Analytic Network Process (ANP)

What has AHP played a major role in?

Various decisions, involving benefits, costs, opportunities, potential risks and the forecasting of outcomes

C

How did Matt listen to Ms. Beatrice's recent lecture?

Intently

How did Matt react to the issues that Ms. Beatric raised at the symposium held in Taiwan?

He was fascinated.

How are quality care and patient safety threatened?

By shortages in nursing personnel

How can the likelihood of clinical errors be significantly reduced?

Through the indispensable role of nurses

How can Matt participate in an exchange of information with Ms. Beatrice?

By sending send any pertinent data from Taiwan

D

Why was Mary motivated to write to Professor Jones for further details on particular points?

Because she carefully read the article, "Intellectual Capital Measurement: Introducing and Comparing Various IC Measurements," which Professor Jones published in the conference proceedings

Why is there an urgency to measure the intellectual capital value of hi-tech firms?

As Taiwan's industrial infrastructure is being transformed into a hi-tech infrastructure, an increasing fraction of companies' capital is intellectual, and is intangible.

Why is Mary contacting Professor Jones?

She was wondering whether he could send her literature or materials in the following areas.

Why is Mary's graduate school research focusing on intellectual capital of on-line gaming companies?

In an attempt to identify its essential components

Why is Mary especially interested in adopting the perspective of a loaning bank institution?

To assess the intellectual capital assets of an on-line gaming company and, then, to compare the intellectual capital of a bank with that of such a company

E

Why are AHP decision-making procedures adopted in business?

To achieve success

What would Matt be delighted to send to Ms. Beatrice?

Any pertinent data from Taiwan as part of an exchange of information

What was Mary very impressed by?

Professor Jones's lecture last month at the Intellectual Capital Measurement Symposium in Taipei

F

Situation 1

1.B   2.C   3.B   4.C   5.B

Situation 2

1.B   2.A   3.C   4.A   5.C

Situation 3

1.B   2.C   3.B   4.C   5.A

G

Situation 1

1.C   2.B   3.A   4.B

Situation 2

1.C   2.A   3.C   4.B   5.C   6.A   7.C   8.B   9.A   10.B

Situation 3

1.B   2.C   3.A   4.B   5.C   6.A   7.B   8.A   9.B

|

Situation 4

Dear Dr. Kandinsky,

How have you been lately? I hope that your stay in Taiwan allowed you to experience the difference between Asian and European cultures. While recently perusing your association's website, I became intrigued with the area of exhibition management skills. As you are well aware, PIDA holds several widely attended exhibitions, including OPTO Taiwan (since 1980, with over 700 exhibitors and 50,000 international visitors annually) and Computex (since 1976, with over 2,000 exhibitors and 300,000 visitors annually). I have recently been transferred to the Exhibition Department as Chief Operations Manager.

While working for CMP Taiwan, I coordinated several exhibitions at PIDA, allocating exhibition booths, constructing the booths, forwarding materials, and making travel arrangements. However, I lack expertise on the management side, such as in planning and budgeting. Hopefully, this training program will enable me to solve some of our current problems, such as tightening budget constraints.

The preliminary program schedule on the Internet includes a guide to the exhibited technologies, which is unnecessary from my perspective since all of the participants are senior professionals in this field. However, special events could be highlighted in this program schedule, as such events will be of greatest benefit to the participants. Could you please send me a detailed program schedule, so that I can more completely understand the event before it is held?

Thank you in advance for your kind assistance and I look forward to receiving your positive reply.

Sincerely yours,

Mary Li

Situation 5

Dear Dr. Chen,

By designating ABC as my primary interest area in ASME and having received the *ABC Newsletter* for quite some time, I realize that CGFM could resourcefully support my professional interest in oligomeric proanthocyanidins, which are water-soluble polyphenolic tannins that are present in the female inflorescences (up to 5% dry wt) of the hop plant (Humulus lupulus). Humans are exposed to hop proanthocyanidins through their consumption of beer. Previous studies have characterized proanthocyanidins from hops in terms of their chemical structure and their *in vitro* biological activities. Chemically, these proanthocyanidins consist mainly of oligomeric catechins, ranging from dimers to octamers, with minor amounts of catechin oligomers that contain one or two gallocatechin units. Additionally, the chemical structures of four procyanidin dimers (B1, B2, B3 and B4) and one trimer, epicatechin-($4\beta \rightarrow 8$)-catechin-($4\alpha \rightarrow 8$)-catechin (TR), were elucidated using mass spectrometry, NMR spectroscopy and chemical degradation. When tested as a mixture, the hop oligomeric proanthocyanidins (PC) were found to be potent inhibitors of neuronal nitric oxide synthase (nNOS) activity. Among the oligomers tested, procyanidin B2 was the most inhibitory of nNOS activity. Procyanidin B3, catechin and epicatechin were non-inhibitory against nNOS activity. PC and the individual oligomers were all strong inhibitors of 3-morpholinosydnonimine (SIN-1)-induced oxidation of LDL, with procyanidin B3 displaying the highest antioxidant activity at 0.1 μg/mL. Moreover, the catechin trimer (TR) exhibited antioxidant activity that was more than one order of magnitude greater than that of α-tocopherol or ascorbic acid on a molar basis.

Given my above research interests and your expertise in this field, could you send me introductory information on your laboratory's current efforts in these areas? Based on our mutual interests, we are interested in pursuing collaborative activities with your research organization. I look forward to hearing from you.

Sincerely yours,

Max Wang

Situation 6

Dear Dr. Stevens,

Allow me to introduce myself. I am a graduate student at the Proton Radiation Treatment Center, which is similar to Loma Linda University's Medical Center (LLUMC). I have received a Master's degree in Medical Imagery from Yuanpei University of Science and Technology and, during that period, served in a seven-month practicum internship at Chang Gung Memorial Hospital in Linkou of central Taiwan. I am interested in assessing the quality of proton radiotherapy. Given its global reputation, LLUMC represents an ideal environment in which I could pursue my professional interests. The Proton Radiation Treatment Center is tentatively planning to establish a national high dose exposure measurement laboratory in Taiwan. I am interested in the proton accelerator, the beam transport system, the gantry, the nozzle and the patient positioning system.

Once established, this laboratory will study the effect of dose on relatively heavy particles, such as protons, their chemical characteristics, dose distribution, radiation protection, treatment quality assessment and biological effects. Could you send me information on how to conduct such work? We are also interested in pursuing collaborative research activities with your Center. Having discussed the contents of your proton radiotherapy training course with my colleagues, we have reached the following conclusions.

1. We hope to form a radiation protection study group.

2. We hope to enhance our technical knowledge of proton radiotherapy, particularly of dose measurement and operator training, radiation shield design and instrument maintenance.

If convenient, would you please send a detailed list of the maintenance components available at your Center, such as those on the attached page? I would greatly appreciate your comments and suggestions regarding the above proposal. Thank you in advance for your careful consideration. I look forward to our future cooperation.

Sincerely yours,

Lucy Lin

J

When does Mary hope that Dr. Kandinsky experienced the difference between Asian and European cultures?

During his stay in Taiwan

When did Mary become intrigued with the area of exhibition management skills?

While recently perusing the association's website that Dr. Kandinsky belongs to

When was Mary transferred to the Exhibition Department as Chief Operations Manager?

Recently

When did Mary coordinate several exhibitions at PIDA, allocating exhibition booths, constructing the booths, forwarding materials, and making travel arrangements?

While working for CMP Taiwan

When does PIDA hold several widely attended exhibitions?

Annually

K

What did Max realize by designating ABC as his primary interest area in ASME?
That CGFM could resourcefully support his professional interest in oligomeric proanthocyanidins

What are oligomeric proanthocyanidins?
Water-soluble polyphenolic tannins that are present in the female inflorescences (up to 5% dry wt) of the hop plant (Humulus lupulus)

What are humans exposed to?
Hop proanthocyanidins through their consumption of beer

What was the most inhibitory of nNOS activity?
Procyanidin B2
Listening Comprehension

What is Max interested in?
Pursuing collaborative activities with Dr. Chen's research organization

L

Where is Lucy conducting research as a graduate student?
At the Proton Radiation Treatment Center

Where did Lucy receive a Master's degree in Medical Imagery
From Yuanpei University of Science and Technology

Where did Lucy serve in a seven-month practicum internship?

At Chang Gung Memorial Hospital in Linkou of central Taiwan

Where is an ideal environment in which Lucy could pursue her professional interests?

LLUMC

Where will the effect of dose on relatively heavy particles be studied?

A national high dose exposure measurement laboratory in Taiwan

M

What does the preliminary program schedule on the Internet include?

A guide to the exhibited technologies

Why should Dr. Chen send Max introductory information on his laboratory's current efforts in these areas?

Given Max's above research interests and Dr. Chen's expertise in this field

What is similar to Loma Linda University's Medical Center?

The Proton Radiation Treatment Center

N

Situation 4

1.B   2.C   3.B   4.C   5.A

Situation 5

1.B   2.A   3.C   4.B   5.A

Situation 6

1.C   2.B   3.A   4.C   5.B

O

Situation 4

1.B   2.C   3.A   4.C   5.A   6.C   7.A   8.B   9.B   10.C   11.B   12.A   13.C

Situation 5

1.B   2.C   3.B   4.C   5.B

Situation 6

1.B   2.C   3.A   4.B   5.A   6.C

P

Exercise 1

1.g   2.e   3.i   4.b   5.d   6.a   7.f   8.c   9.h   10.j

Exercise 2

1.e   2.c   3.b   4.h   5.d   6.a   7.f   8.h

Exercise 3

1.f   2.a   3.i   4.c   5.j   6.b   7.d   8.e   9.h   10.g

Exercise 4

1.f   2.b   3.h   4.g   5.d   6.e   7.a   8.j   9.c   10.i

About the Author

Born on his father's birthday, Ted Knoy received a Bachelor of Arts in History at Franklin College of Indiana (Franklin, Indiana) and a Master's degree in Public Administration at American International College (Springfield, Massachusetts). He is currently a Ph.D. student in Education at the University of East Anglia (Norwich, England). Having conducted research and independent study in New Zealand, Ukraine, Scotland, South Africa, India, Nicaragua and Switzerland, he has lived in Taiwan since 1989 where he has been a permanent resident since 2000.

Having taught technical writing in the graduate school programs of National Chiao Tung University (Institute of Information Management, Institute of Communications Engineering and, currently, in the College of Management) and National Tsing Hua University (Computer Science, Life Science, Electrical Engineering, Power Mechanical Engineering, Chemistry and Chemical Engineering Departments) since 1989, Ted also teaches in the Institute of Business Management at Yuan Pei University of Science and Technology. He is also the English editor of several technical and medical journals and publications in Taiwan.

Ted is the author of *The Chinese Technical Writers' Series*, which includes An English Style Approach for Chinese Technical Writers, English Oral Presentations for Chinese Technical Writers, A Correspondence Manual for Chinese Technical Writers, An Editing Workbook for Chinese Technical Writers and Advanced Copyediting Practice for Chinese Technical Writers. He is also the author of *The Chinese Professional Writers' Series*, which includes Writing Effective Study Plans, Writing Effective Work Proposals, Writing Effective Employment Application Statements, Writing Effective Career Statements and Effectively Communicating

471

Online.

Ted created and coordinates the Chinese On-line Writing Lab (OWL) at http://www.cc.nctu.edu.tw/~tedknoy, as well as the Online Writing Lab (OWL) at Yuanpei University of Science and Technology at www.owl.yust.edu.tw.

Acknowledgments

Thanks to the following individuals for contributing to this book:

元培科學技術學院　經營管理研究所

許碧芳（所長）　王貞穎　李仁智　陳彥谷　胡惠眞　陳碧俞　王連慶　蔡玟純　高青莉　賴妹惠　李雅玎　戴碧美　楊明雄　陳皇助　林宏隆　鍾玠融　李昭蓉　許美菁　葉伯彥　林羿君

元培科學技術學院　影像醫學研究所

王愛義（所長）　周美榮　顏映君　林孟聰　張雅玲　彭薇莉　張明偉　李玉綸　聶伊辛　黃勝賢　張格瑜　龔慧敏　林永健　呂忠祐　李仁忠　王國偉　李政翰　黃國明　蔡明輝　杜俊元　丁健益　方詩涵　余宗銘　劉力瑛　郭明杰

元培科學技術學院　生物技術研究所

陳媛孃（所長）　范齡文　彭姵華　鄭啓軒　許凱文　李昇憲　陳雪君　鄭凱暹　尤鼎元　陳玉梅　鄭美玲　郭軒中　朱芳儀　周佩穎　吳佳眞

Thanks also to Wang Chen-Yin for illustrating this book and Wang Lien Ching for providing technical support. Graduate students at Yuanpei University of Science and Technology in the Institute of Business Management, the Institute of Biotechnology and the Institute of Medical Imagery are also appreciated. My technical writing students in the Department of Computer Science and Institute of Life Science at National Tsing Hua University, as well as the College of Management at National Chiao Tung University are also appreciated. Thanks also to Seamus Harris and Russell Greenwood for reviewing this workbook.

精通科技論文（報告）寫作之捷徑
An English Style Approach for Chinese Technical Writers （修訂版）

作者：柯泰德（Ted Knoy）

內容簡介
使用直接而流利的英文會話
讓您所寫的英文科技論文很容易被了解
提供不同形式的句型供您參考利用
比較中英句子結構之異同
利用介系詞片語將二個句子連接在一起

萬其超／李國鼎科技發展基金會秘書長

本書是多年實務經驗和專注力之結晶，因此是一本坊間少見而極具實用
價值的書。

陳文華／國立清華大學工學院院長

中國人使用英文寫作時，語法上常會犯錯，本書提供了很好的實例示
範，對於科技論文寫作有相當參考價值。

徐　章／工業技術研究院量測中心主任

這是一個讓初學英文寫作的人，能夠先由不犯寫作的錯誤開始再根據書
中的步驟逐步學習提升寫作能力的好工具，此書的內容及解說方式使讀
者也可以無師自通，藉由自修的方式學習進步，但是更重要的是它雖然
是一本好書，當您學會了書中的許多技巧，如果您還想要更進步，那麼
基本原則還是要常常練習，才能發揮書的精髓。

Kathleen Ford, English Editor, Proceedings(Life Science Divison),

National Science Council

The Chinese Technical Writers Series is valuable for anyone involved with
creating scientific documentation.

※若有任何英文文件修改問題，請直接與柯泰德先生聯絡：（03）5724895

特　　價　新台幣300元
劃　　撥　19419482 清蔚科技股份有限公司
線上訂購　四方書網 www.4Book.com.tw
發 行 所　華香園出版社

作好英語會議簡報
English Oral Presentations for Chinese Technical Writers

作者：柯泰德（Ted Kony）

內容簡介

本書共分十二個單元，涵括產品開發、組織、部門、科技、及產業的介紹、科技背景、公司訪問、研究能力及論文之發表等，每一單元提供不同型態的科技口頭簡報範例，以進行英文口頭簡報的寫作及表達練習，是一本非常實用的著作。

李鍾熙／工業技術研究院化學工業研究所所長

一個成功的科技簡報，就是使演講流暢，用簡單直接的方法、清楚表達內容。本書提供一個創新的方法（途徑），給組織每一成員做為借鏡，得以自行準備口頭簡報。利用本書這套有系統的方法加以練習，將必然使您信心備增，簡報更加順利成功。

薛敬和／IUPAC台北國際高分子研討會執行長
國立清華大學教授

本書以個案方式介紹各英文會議簡報之執行方式，深入簡出，為邁入實用狀況的最佳參考書籍。

沙晉康／清華大學化學研究所所長
第十五屆國際雜環化學會議主席

本書介紹英文簡報的格式，值得國人參考。今天在學術或工商界與外國接觸來往均日益增多，我們應加強表達的技巧，尤其是英文的簡報應具有很高的專業水準。本書做為一個很好的範例。

張俊彥／國立交通大學電機資訊學院教授兼院長

針對中國學生協助他們寫好英文的國際論文參加國際會議如何以英語演講、內容切中要害特別推薦。

※若有任何英文文件修改問題，請直接與柯泰德先生聯絡：（03）5724895

特　　價　新台幣250元
劃　　撥　19419482 清蔚科技股份有限公司
線上訂購　四方書網 www.4Book.com.tw
發 行 所　工業技術研究院

英文信函參考手冊
A Correspondence Manual for Chinese Technical Writers

作者：柯泰德（Ted Knoy）

內容簡介

本書期望成為從事專業管理與科技之中國人，在國際場合上溝通交流時之參考指導書籍。本書所提供的書信範例（附磁碟片），可為您撰述信件時的參考範本。更實際的是，本書如同一「寫作計畫小組」，能因應特定場合（狀況）撰寫出所需要的信函。

李國鼎 / 總統府資政

我國科技人員在國際場合溝通表達之機會急遽增加，希望大家都來重視英文說寫之能力。

羅明哲 / 國立中興大學教務長

一份表達精準且適切的英文信函，在國際間的往來交流上，重要性不亞於研究成果的報告發表。本書介紹各類英文技術信函的特徵及寫作指引，所附範例中肯實用，為優良的學習及參考書籍。

廖俊臣 / 國立清華大學理學院院長

本書提供許多有關工業技術合作、技術轉移、工業資訊、人員訓練及互訪等接洽信函的例句和範例，頗為實用，極具參考價值。

于樹偉 / 工業安全衛生技術發展中心主任

國際間往來日益頻繁，以英文有效地溝通交流，是現今從事科技研究人員所需具備的重要技能。本書在寫作風格、文法結構與取材等方面，提供極佳的寫作參考與指引，所列舉的範例，皆經過作者細心的修訂與潤飾，必能切合讀者的實際需要。

※若有任何英文文件修改問題，請直接與柯泰德先生聯絡： (03) 5724895

特　　價	新台幣250元	
劃　　撥	19419482 清蔚科技股份有限公司	
線上訂購	四方書網 www.4Book.com.tw	
發 行 所	工業技術研究院	

科技英文編修訓練手冊
An Editing Workbook for Chinese Technical Writers

作者：柯泰德（Ted Knoy）

內容簡介

要把科技英文寫的精確並不是件容易的事情。通常在投寄文稿發表前，作者都要前前後後修改草稿，在這樣繁複過程中甚至最後可能請專業的文件編修人士代勞雕琢使全文更為清楚明確。

本書由科技論文的寫作型式、方法型式、內容結構及內容品質著手，並以習題方式使學生透過反覆練習熟能生巧，能確實提昇科技英文之寫作及編修能力。

劉炯明／國立清華大學校長

「科技英文寫作」是一項非常重要的技巧。本書針對台灣科技研究人員在英文寫作發表這方面的訓練，書中以實用性練習對症下藥，期望科技英文寫作者熟能生巧，實在是一個很有用的教材。

彭旭明／國立台灣大學副校長

本書為科技英文寫作系列之四；以練習題為主，由反覆練習中提昇寫作反編輯能力。適合理、工、醫、農的學生及研究人員使用，特為推薦。

許千樹／國立交通大學研究發展處研發長

處於今日高科技時代，國人用到科技英文寫作之機會甚多，如何能以精練的手法寫出一篇好的科技論文，極為重要。本書針對國人寫作之缺點提供了各種清楚的編修範例，實用性高，極具參考價值。

陳文村／國立清華大學電機資訊學院院長

處在我國日益國際化、資訊化的社會裡，英文書寫是必備的能力，本書提供很多極具參考價值的範例。柯泰德先生在清大任教科技英文寫作多年，深受學生喜愛，本人樂於推薦此書。

※若有任何英文文件修改問題，請直接與柯泰德先生聯絡：（03）5724895

特　　價　　新台幣350元
劃　　撥　　19419482 清蔚科技股份有限公司
線上訂購　　四方書網 www.4Book.com.tw
發 行 所　　清蔚科技股份有限公司

科技英文編修訓練手冊【進階篇】
Advanced Copyediting Practice for Chinese Technical Writers

作者：柯泰德（Ted Knoy）

內容簡介

本書延續科技英文寫作系列之四「科技英文編修訓練手冊」之寫作指導原則，更進一步把重點放在如何讓作者想表達的意思更明顯，即明白寫作。把文章中曖昧不清全部去除，使閱讀您文章的讀者很容易的理解您作品的精髓。

本手冊同時國立清華大學資訊工程學系非同步遠距教學科技英文寫作課程指導範本。

張俊彥 / 國立交通大學校長暨中研院院士

對於國內理工學生及從事科技研究之人士而言，可說是一本相當有用的書籍，特向讀者推薦。

蔡仁堅 / 前新竹市長

科技不分國界，隨著進入公元兩千年的資訊時代，使用國際語言撰寫學術報告已是時勢所趨；今欣見柯泰德先生致力於編撰此著作，並彙集了許多實例詳加解說，相信對於科技英文的撰寫有著莫大的裨益，特予以推薦。

史欽泰 / 工研院院長

本書即以實用範例，針對國人寫作的缺點提供簡單、明白的寫作原則，非常適合科技研發人員使用。

張智星 / 國立清華大學資訊工程學系副教授、計算中心組長

本書是特別針對系上所開科技英文寫作非同步遠距教學而設計，範圍內容豐富，所列練習也非常實用，學生可以配合課程來使用，在時間上更有彈性的針對自己情況來練習，很有助益。

劉世東 / 長庚大學醫學院微生物免疫科主任

書中的例子及習題對閱讀者會有很大的助益。這是一本研究生必讀的書，也是一般研究者重要的參考書。

※若有任何英文文件修改問題，請直接與柯泰德先生聯絡：（03）5724895

特　　價　新台幣450元
劃　　撥　19419482 清蔚科技股份有限公司
線上訂購　四方書網 www.4Book.com.tw
發 行 所　清蔚科技股份有限公司

有效撰寫英文讀書計畫
Writing Effective Study Plans

作者：柯泰德（Ted Knoy）

內容簡介

本書指導準備出國進修的學生撰寫精簡切要的英文讀書計畫，內容包括：表達學習的領域及興趣、展現所具備之專業領域知識、敘述學歷背景及成就等。本書的每個單元皆提供視覺化的具體情境及相關寫作訓練，讓讀者進行實際的訊息運用練習。此外，書中的編修訓練並可加強「精確寫作」及「明白寫作」的技巧。本書適用於個人自修以及團體授課，能確實引導讀者寫出精簡而有效的英文讀書計畫。

本手冊同時為國立清華大學資訊工程學系非同步遠距教學科技英文寫作課程指導範本。

于樹偉／工業技術研究院主任

　　《有效撰寫讀書計畫》一書主旨在提供國人精深學習前的準備，包括：讀書計畫及推薦信函的建構、完成。藉由本書中視覺化訊息的互動及練習，國人可以更明確的掌握全篇的意涵，及更完整的表達心中的意念。這也是本書異於坊間同類書籍只著重在片斷記憶，不求理解最大之處。

王　玫／工業研究技術院、化學工業研究所組長

　　《有效撰寫讀書計畫》主要是針對想要進階學習的讀者，由基本的自我學習經驗描述延伸至未來目標的設定，更進一步強調推薦信函的撰寫，藉由圖片式訊息互動，讓讀者主動聯想及運用寫作知識及技巧，避免一味的記憶零星的範例；如此一來，讀者可以更清楚表明個別的特質及快速掌握重點。

※若有任何英文文件修改問題，請直接與柯泰德先生聯絡：（03）5724895

特　　價　新台幣450元
劃　　撥　19419482 清蔚科技股份有限公司
線上訂購　四方書網 www.4Book.com.tw
發 行 所　清蔚科技股份有限公司

有效撰寫英文工作提案
Writing Effective Work Proposals

作者：柯泰德（Ted Knoy）

內容簡介

許多國人都是在工作方案完成時才開始撰寫相關英文提案，他們視撰寫提案為行政工作的一環，只是消極記錄已完成的事項，而不是積極的規劃掌控未來及現在正進行的工作。如果國人可以在撰寫英文提案時，事先仔細明辨工作計畫提案的背景及目標，不僅可以確保寫作進度、寫作結構的完整性，更可兼顧提案相關讀者的興趣強調。本書中詳細的步驟可指導工作提案寫作者達成此一目標。 書中的每個單元呈現三個視覺化的情境，提供國人英文工作提案寫作實質訊息，而相關附加的寫作練習讓讀者做實際的訊息運用。此外，本書也非常適合在課堂上使用，教師可以先描述單元情境而讓學生藉由書中練習循序完成具有良好架構的工作提案。書中內容包括：1.工作提案計畫（第一部分）：背景 2.工作提案計畫（第二部分）：行動 3.問題描述 4.假設描述 5.摘要撰寫（第一部分）： 簡介背景、目標及方法 6.摘要撰寫（第二部分）： 歸納希望的結果及其對特定領域的貢獻 7.綜合上述寫成精確工作提案。

唐傳義／國立清華大學資訊工程學系主任

本書重點放在如何在工作計畫一開始時便可以用英文來規劃整個工作提案，由工作提案的背景、行動、方法及預期的結果漸次教導國人如何寫出具有良好結構的英文工作提案。如此用英文明確界定工作提案的程序及工作目標更可以確保英文工作提案及工作計畫的即時完成。對工作效率而言也有助益。

在國人積極加入WTO之後的調整期，優良的英文工作提案寫作能力絕對是一項競爭力快速加分的工具。

※若有任何英文文件修改問題，請直接與柯泰德先生聯絡： （03）5724895

特 價 新台幣450元
劃 撥 19735365 葉忠賢
線上訂購 www.ycrc.com.tw
發 行 所 揚智文化事業股份有限公司

有效撰寫求職英文自傳
Writing Effective Employment Application Statements

作者：柯泰德（Ted Knoy）

內容簡介

本書主要教導讀者如何建構良好的求職英文自傳。書中內容包括：1.表達工作相關興趣；2.興趣相關產業描寫；3.描述所參與方案裡專業興趣的表現；4.描述學歷背景及已獲成就；5.介紹研究及工作經驗；6.描述與求職相關的課外活動；7.綜合上述寫成精確求職英文自傳。

有效的求職英文自傳不僅必須能讓求職者在企業主限定的字數內精確的描述自身的背景資訊及先前成就，更關鍵性的因素是有效的求職英文自傳更能讓企業主快速明瞭求職者如何應用相關知識技能或其特殊領導特質來貢獻企業主。

書中的每個單元呈現三個視覺化的情境，提供國人求職英文自傳寫作實質訊息，而相關附加的寫作練習讓讀者做實際的訊息運用。此外，本書也非常適合在課堂上使用，教師可以先描述單元情境而讓學生藉由書中練習循序完成具有良好架構的求職英文自傳。

黎漢林／國立交通大學管理學院院長

我國加入WTO後，國際化的腳步日益加快；而企業人員之英文寫作能力更形重要。它不僅可促進國際合作夥伴間的溝通，同時也增加了國際客戶的信任。因此國際企業在求才時無不特別注意其員工的英文表達能力。

柯泰德先生著作《有效撰寫求職英文自傳》即希望幫助求職者能以英文有系統的介紹其能力、經驗與抱負。這本書是柯先生有關英文寫作的第八本專書，柯先生教學與編書十分專注，我相信這本書對求職者是甚佳的參考書籍。

※若有任何英文文件修改問題，請直接與柯泰德先生聯絡：（03）5724895

特　　價　新台幣450元
劃　　撥　19735365 葉忠賢
線上訂購　www.ycrc.com.tw
發 行 所　揚智文化事業股份有限公司

有效撰寫英文職涯經歷
Writing Effective Career Statements

作者：柯泰德（Ted Knoy）

內容簡介

本書主要教導讀者如何建構良好的英文職涯經歷。書中內容包括：1.表達工作相關興趣；2.興趣相關產業描寫；3.描述所參與方案裡專業興趣的表現；4.描述學歷背景及已獲成就；5.介紹研究及工作經驗；6.描述與求職相關的課外活動；7.綜合上述寫成英文職涯經歷。

有效的職涯經歷描述不僅能讓再度就業者在企業主限定的字數內精準的描述自身的背景資訊及先前工作經驗及成就，更關鍵性的，有效的職涯經歷能讓企業主快速明瞭求職者如何應用相關知識技能及先前的就業經驗結合來貢獻企業主。

書中的每個單元呈現六個視覺化的情境，經由以全民英語檢定為標準而設計的口說訓練、聽力、閱讀及寫作四種不同功能來強化英文能力。此外，本書也非常適合在課堂上使用，教師可以先描述單元情境而讓學生藉由書中練習循序在短期內完成。

林進財 / 元培科學技術學院校長

近年來，台灣無不時時刻刻地努力提高國際競爭力，不論政府或企業界求才皆以英文表達能力為主要考量之一。唯有員工具備優秀的英文能力，才足以把本身的能力、工作經驗與國際競爭舞台接軌。

柯泰德先生著作《有效撰寫英文職涯經歷》，即希望幫助已有工作經驗的求職者能以英文有效地介紹其能力、工作經驗與成就。此書是柯先生有關英文寫作的第九本專書，相信對再度求職者是進入職場絕佳的工具書。

※若有任何英文文件修改問題，請直接與柯泰德先生聯絡：（03）5724895

特　　　價　新台幣480元
劃　　　撥　19735365 葉忠賢
線上訂購　www.ycrc.com.tw
發 行 所　揚智文化事業股份有限公司

The Chinese
Online Writing Lab
【 柯泰德線上英文論文編修訓練服務 】
http://www.cc.nctu.edu.tw/~tedknoy

您有科技英文寫作上的困擾嗎？

您的文章在投稿時常被國外論文審核人員批評文法很爛嗎？以至於被退稿嗎？

您對論文段落的時式使用上常混淆不清嗎？

您在寫作論文時同一個動詞或名詞常常重複使用嗎？

您的這些煩惱現在均可透過柯泰德網路線上科技英文論文編修
服務來替您加以解決。本服務項目分別含括如下：

1. 英文論文編輯與修改
2. 科技英文寫作開課訓練服務
3. 線上寫作家教
4. 免費寫作格式建議服務，及網頁問題討論區解答
5. 線上遠距教學（互動練習）

另外，為能廣為服務中國人士對論文寫作上之缺點，柯泰德亦
同時著作下列參考書籍可供有志人士為寫作上之參考。

＜1.精通科技論文（報告）寫作之捷徑
＜2.做好英文會議簡報
＜3.英文信函參考手冊
＜4.科技英文編修訓練手冊
＜5.科技英文編修訓練手冊（進階篇）
＜6.有效撰寫英文讀書計畫

上部分亦可由柯泰德先生的首頁中下載得到。

如果您對本服務有興趣的話，可參考柯泰德先生的首頁標示。

柯泰德網路線上科技英文論文編修服務

地址：新竹市大學路50號8樓之三
TEL:03-5724895
FAX:03-5724938
網址：http://www.cc.nctu.edu.tw/~tedknoy
E-mail:tedaknoy@ms11.hinet.net

國家圖書館出版品預行編目資料

有效撰寫專業英文電子郵件 ＝ Effectively
communicating online/柯泰德（Ted Knoy）
著；王貞穎插圖. -- 初版. -- 臺北市：揚智
文化，2006[民 95]
　　面；　公分. --（應用英文寫作系列；5）

ISBN　957-818-770-X（平裝）

1. 英國語言 - 應用文　2. 電子郵件

805.179　　　　　　　　　　　　94025770

有效撰寫專業英文電子郵件　應用英文寫作系列05

著　　者／柯泰德 (Ted Knoy)
出 版 者／揚智文化事業股份有限公司
發 行 人／葉忠賢
總 編 輯／林新倫
執行編輯／吳曉芳
登 記 證／局版北市業字第 1117 號
地　　址／台北市新生南路三段 88 號 5 樓之 6
電　　話／（02）23660309
傳　　眞／（02）23660310
郵政劃撥／19735365　戶名：葉忠賢
印　　刷／上海印刷廠股份有限公司
法律顧問／北辰著作權事務所　蕭雄淋律師
初版一刷／2006 年 2 月
ＩＳＢＮ／957-818-770-X
定　　價／新台幣 520 元
E-mail／service@ycrc.com.tw
網　　址／http://www.ycrc.com.tw